FOREVER WILD

USA TODAY BESTSELLING AUTHOR

REBECCA JENSHAK

Rebecca Jenshak
www.rebeccajenshak.com
Cover Design by Books and Moods
Editing by Rebecca at Fairest Reviews Editing Services
Proofreading by Sarah at All Encompassing Books

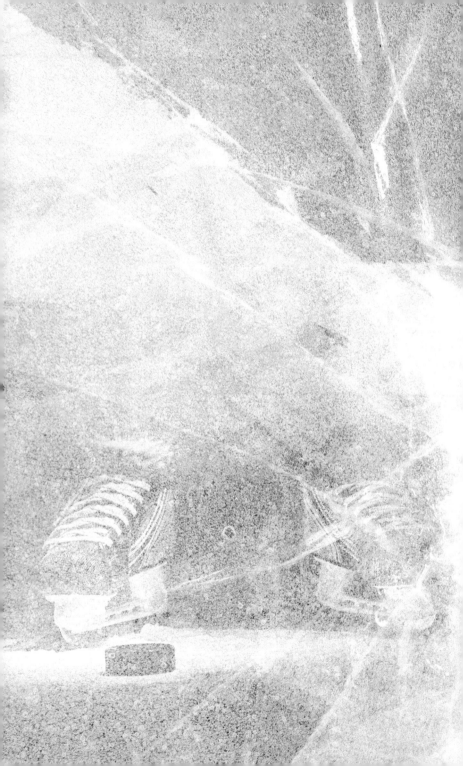

PROLOGUE

Jack

FOUR WEEKS EARLIER

Snow falls on the windshield in big, thick flakes. I round the final curve of the winding road and slow in front of the darkened house.

"Thanks for the ride. I'm sorry you had to drive so far out of your way." Nick unbuckles as I pull to a stop.

Ignoring the aches and pains from the game, I shift forward in my seat and wave off his appreciation. "It was no problem."

He shoots a crooked smile at me as he opens the passenger door. Light floods down into the interior of my car, making the skepticism in his expression more present. "I owe you. I should have known that old truck wasn't going to make it through another Minnesota winter."

"You don't owe me anything. I told you a dozen times, I don't mind." I truly don't. It's all part of the job. I'd do anything for him or any other guy on my team. I make their lives easier and that lets them focus on showing up every day to play their best hockey.

"Now you can listen to your music without judgment." He shakes his head at me before getting out of the vehicle.

"I don't care what you say, that song just hits," I say in defense of the Sabrina Carpenter song on my playlist.

He laughs, shaking his head, as he gets his bag from the back seat. While he does that, I glance around at the soundless, forested area. Even the snow seems to fall quieter out here as if not to intrude on the stillness of nature. There isn't another house in sight for miles. "It's awfully quiet out here."

"Just how I like it," Nick says as he stands next to the car, snowflakes falling onto his black beanie and coat.

I've always liked having community, friends, teammates, even neighbors, but I can see the appeal of this too. A man has to have a certain level of peace within himself to enjoy this sort of tranquility, and I guess I've never had that. Still, I can appreciate it.

The porch light turns on and we both glance toward it. An older man stands with Nick's little boy just inside the glass door. Aidan has a mess of dark hair the same color as his father's and a stuffed bear, tan with a blue bowtie, clutched in one hand.

Nick's grin widens at the sight of his son and he spares me only a short glance as he says, "Thanks again for the ride."

"Any time."

He shuts the door and hurries up to the front of his house to pull his son into his arms. The little boy wraps himself around Nick's neck as he's carried into the house and then the door shuts, blocking out their happy reunion.

I let out a long breath as the exhaustion of the past week finally seeps in. Three road games in six days. I'm glad to be home, even if the weather is doing its best to keep me away a little longer.

Pulling back onto the road, I turn up the music.

"This song really is a bop," I say quietly to myself as Sabrina's voice fills the cab.

The snow blankets the narrow road and my headlights cut through the darkness. I make my way back slowly, stretching my neck side to side and rolling my shoulders back to ease the tension. I took a couple of hard hits in tonight's game and I feel about ten years older than my thirty-two years.

At the end of the season, the aches and pains always feel worse, but come summer I'll be missing it like usual.

As I'm taking a corner, I feel the tires of my G-Wagon slide on a slick spot. My SUV usually does okay in the snow, but the roads were already icy before this snowfall started.

Despite how badly I want to be home, take a hot shower, and climb into bed with ice packs strapped to my body, I force myself to slow down. Nick lives in the middle of nowhere, so everyone else should have already made it home. Still, I press a button on the steering wheel and send a group text to the guys to make sure no one else had any problems.

The messages back come in quickly. Thumbs up, "All good, Captain," and a variety of other replies, indicating my teammates managed in the snowy weather conditions.

Most of the team either grew up in areas with snow or moved to one for hockey, but every year we have one or two guys coming from Southern California or Florida that are surprised by the amount of snow that gets dumped on us during the winter season.

Or spring in this case. It's April but it seems winter wasn't quite done with us.

With everyone else taken care of, I run through everything I need to do while making my way carefully over the dark, icy roads. It's late in the season and playoffs begin in less than two weeks. Which means there are no days off. We'll have tomorrow free from scrimmage, but there are still a million other things to do. Keeping everyone healthy is imperative, and part of that is skating even when we're tired. Keep the body loose, stay in routine.

This year feels special. Words I've thought a dozen times recently but haven't spoken out loud. I've played on a lot of great teams that haven't won the last game of the season. I know that it takes a mixture of talent and luck, but I still can't shake the feeling that this group has that spark of magic. We can do it. I know we can. Our team is talented and full of heart. We just have to stay focused. I plan to make that as easy as possible for everyone.

I'm lost in thought as the main road finally comes back into view. I roll my neck and shoulders again. First thing tomorrow I need to get in with the team therapist so I'm ready to go come Wednesday. We get two days to prepare for our next game. Just enough time to patch up any injuries, rest, and plan for our opponent.

While breathing a sigh of relief that I'm one road closer to home, movement catches my attention off to the left side just beyond the tree line. Tensing reactively, my grip tightens on the steering wheel but that's all I manage to do before the buck sprints in front of my vehicle.

Shit.

I slam on the brakes and cut the wheel to the right. Things I know aren't ideal in these conditions, but neither is crashing into the big animal darting inches from my front fender.

The deer manages to escape unscathed, but my relief is short-lived as the back end of my SUV spins around and I slide quickly toward the tree-lined landscape beyond the paved road. I try helplessly to slow down and veer back on course, but it's no use. My SUV heads straight for the rough forest area, soaring like it's on skates. Panic surges through me as I fight for control.

"No," I plead to no one and anyone. The only answer is the sound of my tires bumping across the rocky terrain as they finally find purchase and then the slam of the front of my vehicle against a tree. White hot pain splinters through me as the crash echoes in the quiet forest.

Then, silence.

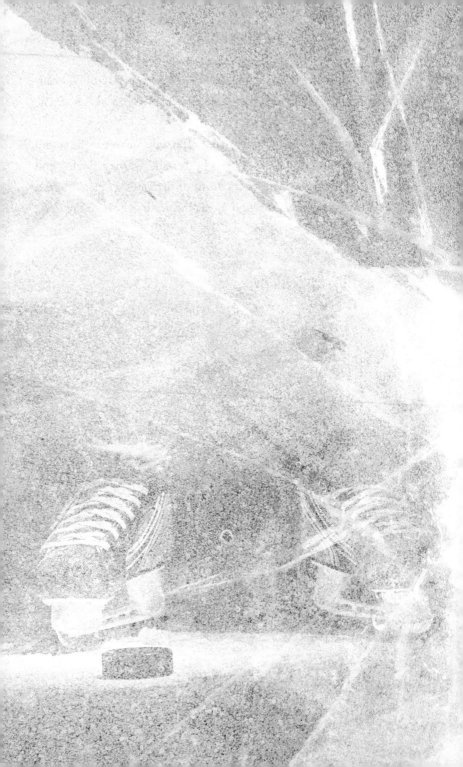

CHAPTER ONE

Everly

STOP TALKING IF YOU WANT TO SURVIVE

"I'm going to miss you so much," I say to my favorite person in the world in a sweet tone I reserve only for her.

Charlotte smiles up at me from where she lies on her changing table and bats at the loose strands of hair hanging in my face. One tiny hand gets a death grip on my blonde locks and I laugh even as I wince and unclench her fist to free (most) of my hair.

I pick her up, then lift her above my head like she's flying. Her grin widens and my heart feels like it might burst. She has my brother's smile and Piper's dark hair and blue eyes. She's a shy baby with strangers or people she doesn't trust, but she's such a lovebug with those she does.

Pulling her down against my hip, I breathe her in. She smells like lavender and baby powder. I love the feel of her little body nuzzled up to me.

"I think she's going to miss you too." Piper leans in and kisses

Charlotte's soft cheek. She looks at her daughter with so much love and adoration that it makes my chest hurt. Her love for Charlotte is so big. It's the kind of pure maternal affection that most people take for granted. But not me. "We all will. Are you sure you don't want to come with us?"

"No." I shake my head, not even having to think about it. "But maybe you could just leave her here with me." I sit on the pink chair in the nursery with Charlotte while Piper continues packing for their upcoming vacation.

I want to soak up all my niece's little laughs and kisses before they leave. Hockey season is over, and my brother and his teammates are all taking some much-needed time off. Tyler and Piper are headed east. They rented a place on the beach where Charlotte can play in the sand and dip her toes into the ocean. It does sound nice, but with college just ending and real life hovering on the horizon, my ideal summer is staying here, sleeping in, lounging by the pool, and pretending that nothing has changed.

"I think you'd be ready for a break after a day or two. She's cute until she wakes you up at two in the morning."

That does sound exhausting. "I don't know how you do it."

"She has me." Tyler walks into the nursery and shoots his wife a wink before settling his gaze on me and Charlotte. "How are all my favorite girls?"

"We're great," I say reverting back to baby talk. I don't know what it is about a tiny little human that makes us all coo and talk weird, but I am not immune to it. Especially when it makes Charlotte smile at me like I'm the coolest person alive. As she should.

"Stressed." Piper adds another outfit to the suitcase. "I'm running out of room. Do you have another bag?"

Tyler's brows rise as he takes in the very large, very full bag on the floor. "You know there's a washer and dryer at the beach house, right? You don't have to bring every scrap of clothing she owns."

I clear my throat and give Ty our secret sibling look, which isn't really that secret. Wide eyes, shake of the head. It's a clear "stop talking if you want to survive" look that we've perfected over the years.

He trails off and then flashes Piper a smile. "I'll go see if I can find another bag."

"Thank you." Piper's shoulders sag in relief. Ty brushes his lips over hers before disappearing out of the door he entered only seconds ago.

When he's gone she glances at me. "And thank you."

"No problem," I say with a laugh. "My niece wants to be the best-dressed baby on all the beaches."

Piper takes a break from packing and sits on the floor next to the suitcase. "So, what about you? You're really just going to hang around here all summer?"

"I'm sure I'll take a few weekend trips here and there, but with the long list of things everyone left me to check on, I think I'll stay pretty busy."

Nearly all the Wildcat guys leave in the off-season. Some go back to wherever they're from, others travel. And while they're gone, they need someone to check in on their houses, get the mail, water plants, and one guy even asked me to check in on his elderly neighbor once a week. It's not the most glamorous job, being their house sitter/errand runner, but it saves me from getting a real job for a few more months. Plus, most of them have pools that they've agreed I can use.

"When do you have to be in Briar Lake for the internship?" she asks, a big smile pulling her pink lips apart to flash her straight, white teeth.

Nerves swirl around in my stomach and settle into a tight ball. "The last week of July."

"Your brother is so proud. So am I." She continues beaming at me. I can feel her pride stretching across the room. In a lot of ways, she's responsible for me graduating high school and college. She was a student teacher my senior year when I came to live with Ty. She believed in me when few people did. Without her and Ty, I don't know where I'd be.

My brother took me in after everyone else had given up trying to get through to me, and Piper treated me like a little sister, even before she and my brother were together. I owe so much to them both. The words of gratitude get stuck in my throat. With their happiness for all I've accomplished comes expectations and hope. Sometimes I feel like I'm one wrong move from letting them down.

Piper continues smiling at me like she can see all my hopes and dreams floating above my head. "The houses there are so gorgeous and you're going to get to decorate them. It's a dream job. You're so perfect for it."

Each word makes me a little more anxious, but it is a great opportunity, and I did work hard for it. In six weeks, I'll be heading two hours north for an interior design internship with one of the most prestigious design companies in Minnesota. They work on everything from boutique hotels to million-dollar lake homes. It *is* a dream job, really, and the woman I'll be working with is basically my idol. She was named one of the "Top 30 under 30" in the state. She has a waitlist of clients a year out hoping to work with her.

If I impress her during my internship, she might offer me a permanent job. Though she's not known for taking on a lot of full-time staff. But even a recommendation from her would be incredible for my career.

"I'm not sure how much hands-on work I'll be doing. I will probably spend most of my time running errands for her, pulling samples, ordering things, and helping move furniture and artwork."

"At first, but you're so talented. I have no doubt that you'll be one of their most requested designers in no time."

I chuckle softly. I love her confidence in me, even if it does make me nauseous. "Fingers crossed!"

Tyler returns with a big duffel bag that looks like it could fit a body. "This is all I could find," he says.

"Thank you." She takes it from him, then eyes the overflowing suitcase in front of her. "But I think you were right. The more clothes we take, the more laundry I'll end up doing."

Smiling, she hands it back to him. Charlotte flails her arms around in my lap, making a sound that's awfully close to a giggle as she watches her parents.

"*We* will do. I told you, I can help more this summer. Laundry included."

He leans down and kisses her. Instead of the quick, chaste kiss I was expecting, he lingers, taking her mouth in a way that has me looking away and covering Charlotte's eyes. And this is another reason why I'm not going on vacation with them. I think it's sweet that they're still so in love, but watching my brother constantly make out with his wife is not the summer of my dreams.

"Ev," Ty says my name, alerting me that they've finally stopped kissing.

I glance over at him. "Hmmm?"

"Are you sure you don't want to fly out one weekend? Fourth of

July maybe?"

It's at least the third time he's asked in the past week.

"I'm not sure if you're worried I can't function on my own or if you're just going to miss me so much you're panicking."

An easy smile spreads across his face. "Both, I think."

"I'll be fine. And I already promised Grace that I'd do something with her for the Fourth."

All my friends are graduating and moving away or starting jobs this summer. Maybe it should make me more eager to do the same, but instead it makes me want to appreciate a few more weeks of the lax life even more.

Sweet Charlotte starts crying in my arms. I swear the sound breaks my heart every time.

"What's wrong?" I ask, bouncing her gently in my lap.

"It's time for her nap." Tyler comes over and steals her from me, but not before I take one more whiff of her lavender and baby powder scent. This summer will be the longest I've gone without seeing her. "Then we can grab lunch or something if you want."

"It's okay," I say, standing. "I need to go to Ash and Bridget's house to bring in their mail, stop by Declan and Jade's to water the plants, and then Leo and Scarlett's house to double-check they turned off all the lights."

Ty grins. "Is that all?"

"For today."

"All right." After he places Charlotte down in her crib, he moves toward me with his arms outstretched. I let him wrap me up in his embrace like I'm still his baby sister and he's the only person in the world that can keep me safe. No matter how old I get, he still fills me with the same sense of security. "If you change your mind or decide you miss me too much, just say the word and I'll have you on the next flight out."

"Go. Enjoy your vacation. Don't worry about me or your house. I'll take good care of it. Especially the pool. And I promise not to throw any parties with more than fifty to a hundred people."

"No parties." He laughs like I'm joking, then his expression goes serious. "And no boys."

Piper and I both roll our eyes at him.

After I leave my brother's house, I head to Ash and Bridget's place. It feels beyond weird pulling into the abandoned driveway. He and several of the other guys live in the same neighborhood, but with all of them gone it's eerily quiet.

I check the mail and then as I'm letting myself in, I get a call from Bridget.

"Are you watching me on your door cam?" I ask.

"No," she says the word slowly. "Are you at the house?"

"I just walked in." I set the pile of envelopes on the kitchen counter. "Your junk mail is safe and sound."

"Oh, thank goodness," she says with a small laugh. "But that's not why I called."

"What's up?" I ask, noting the hint of concern in her voice.

"Have you seen any of the guys?"

"I just left Ty's place."

"Anyone else?"

She's acting strange, but I go with it.

"Before he left on vacation yesterday, Leo stopped by to give me the key to his mailbox."

A beat of silence hangs between us as I turn and lean against the counter.

"What about Jack?"

"No." I walk toward the living room window that looks out toward the hockey team captain's house. All I can make out from here is his driveway. A red van is parked behind his SUV. "Why would I see him?"

"I got a call from a nurse friend of mine. She does scheduling for the home aide service he's using and she wanted to see if I was available for a *difficult* client."

I snort. "Nobody is less surprised than me to learn he's not sunshine and rainbows after his surgery."

A twinge of sympathy fills me as I think about him laid up. His car accident a month ago brought a devastating end to the season for him and the team.

"That's not all. I texted Scarlett and she said none of the guys have seen him since the surgery and he's barely responding to texts or calls."

I'm not really that shocked. Jack is great at being there for other people, but he tends to shut everyone out when he's dealing with things or in a bad mood—which is often.

"What are you going to do?" I ask because I know she's trying to figure out how to help him. When Bridget sees someone hurting, she's incapable of standing by.

"Nothing. I offered to stay and help before we left, but he wouldn't hear it. He didn't want to ruin my and Ash's vacation plans."

"Sounds like Jack."

"I should have stuck around a little longer. At least until he was back on his feet."

I hear the regret in her voice, but she's being too hard on herself.

"You offered and he said no. We both know that when he makes up his mind, there's no changing it."

"Yeah," she says, but her tone tells me she still isn't sure she did the right thing. Bridget has a good heart. She's much nicer than me, which is probably why we're friends. Every nice girl needs a mean friend. It's just facts.

"Maybe I should come home."

"Don't do that," I say. She would do it because she's just that caring, but it isn't her fault that Jack is being *difficult*. "There has to be someone else that can take care of him who also won't let him be a big jerk just because he's in pain."

"I think most of the nurses are afraid of him. The others probably want to sleep with him."

He does seem to have that sort of effect on people.

"Do you want me to go check on him?" I offer because I know it's what she'd do if our roles were reversed, then silently pray she says no. Jack and I butt heads on the best of days.

"Would you?" Her tone is tentative like she isn't sure that's a good idea, but she doesn't have a better one.

That makes two of us.

Dammit. I did not have *deal with Jack* on my to-do list today or I would have started the day with some yoga or Zen music. I let out a quiet, resolved breath. "Yeah, of course. I'll stop by, tell him to stop being a pain in the ass, and you can keep enjoying your vacation. Are you and Ash having fun?"

I hear her fiancé's muffled voice on the other end, something that sounds a lot like kissing, and then her giggle.

"I'll take that as a yes," I say. "I'll text you after I see Jack."

"Thank you, Ev," she says, then adds, "Be nice."

"I'll make no such promise."

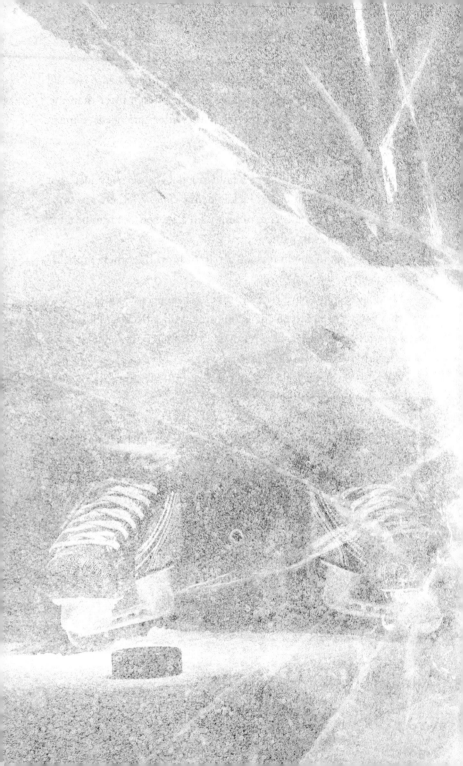

CHAPTER TWO

Jack

RUNNING ON COFFEE AND FURY

"What are you doing?" Sandra, the nurse sent to check on me today, glares at me as I stand after her assessment of my knee (it's still fucked) and start toward the kitchen with my phone in one hand. "Where is your cane?"

"I think I left it in the bedroom." I carefully hobble the short distance, using furniture and the wall to help keep me upright.

"I still need to run a few more vitals and then help you through some exercises. The doctor asked me to bring a walker. It's out in my van. We could take a short walk down the sidewalk. It's a beautiful day out." Her voice brightens and she smiles at me. Why the fuck is she smiling at me? That's the worst idea I've ever heard. Maybe she's kidding.

Pushing to a stand, she says, "I'll go grab it while you take a short break."

It's bad enough that I'm holed up in my house in this condition.

There's no way I'm going outside for the whole world to see me like this. I shake my head, "Thank you for stopping by, but I don't need anything else. I'll do the therapy on my own."

Her smile falls into a disapproving scowl. "That isn't how this works. I have orders from the doctor."

"And my orders are that you're no longer needed."

With a huff, she heads off in the direction of my room, presumably to get my cane and beat me with it.

My attention falls to the phone clutched in my hand. I stop once I'm in the kitchen and read the news alert that popped up while she was examining my surgery incisions.

> *Florida Wins Cup!*
> *Last night Florida defeated Colorado in game four, winning the series in a blowout 8-0 and adding their name to the Cup. For many fans it was a lackluster end to the hockey season.*
> *The heavily favored Wildcats lost captain Jack Wyld after a severe car accident last month. Without the center and six-year captain, the Wildcats fell to Colorado in the semi-finals.*

My grip on the phone tightens until it slips from my hand, clattering onto the counter. It's just one of many articles that have been written about how my fuck up derailed my team's season, but each one cuts deep.

Before I can reach for my phone, it starts ringing. I want to ignore it. Actually, what I want to do is throw it out the goddamn window, but when Nick's name flashes on the screen, I know I have to answer. If I don't, he'll show up here. And more people invading my space is the only thing I can think of that would make this day worse.

I take a few steadying breaths before I accept the call.

"Hey, man, what's up?" I force a cheeriness into my tone as I squeeze my eyes shut and bring my other hand up to rub at the throbbing headache pulsing in the middle of my forehead. Only, when I spot the black cast on my left arm, it just makes me more irritated.

"I was calling to ask you the same thing," Nick says. The sounds of the rink in the background. Skates gliding over the ice and the slap of a stick.

I drop my bad arm back to my side. "All good here."

"I'm heading out this afternoon, but I thought if you were up for it, Aidan and I could drop by and bring you some lunch before we hit the road."

"Wish I could, but I have physical therapy."

"We can just do a drop off then, if you want."

"No, no. I'm good. My, uh, nurse is cooking something now." I glance around the kitchen at the takeout boxes lining the countertop. Sandra and the other nurses do not cook but sometimes they answer the door to get my delivery, if I ask nicely. Which admittedly is challenging in my current state.

"Of course. I should have known." He chuckles softly. "I was offering greasy burgers and fries and here you're enjoying home-cooked meals."

My stomach grumbles. I don't remember the last time I ate, though the evidence that I did is all around me. I feel like I'm running on coffee and fury alone.

"You're going back to Kansas City for the entire summer?" I ask, steering the conversation away from me and the lies that are starting to stack up like noodle containers.

"Yes, but don't worry. I'm going to use the time off wisely, Captain."

Off-season conditioning is the furthest thing from my mind. The old me would have cared about that, and buried deep beyond my own selfish rage-filled feelings I know I still do. The team means everything to me. "Good. I'm glad to hear it."

Someone shoots a puck and it bangs off the goal post. The sound is so familiar, but it's been weeks since I've heard it. What I would give to be out there. I think this is the longest I've been away since I started playing hockey as a kid. I miss it, but I haven't been able to bring myself to swing by yet. I know what I'll see. Pity from everyone and questions, *so many questions.*

How are you doing? When will you be back? Will you ever be back in the same way? Is everything you worked for over just like that? Why did you swerve off the fucking road and destroy everything?

If they weren't asking the questions, they'd be thinking them all the same. Just like me.

So it's better on my own. I'm not exactly mobile anyway. My left arm is broken and in a hard cast and my knee is fucked. The accident, combined with years of getting busted up on the ice, meant I needed a complete replacement. They were finally able to do surgery last week, but recovery is slow. I'm looking at a month, maybe longer, before I can do any meaningful activity.

My knee takes that particular moment to twinge with pain. I lean onto the counter and breathe through it until the discomfort abates.

Nick's voice cuts through the haze as I grit my teeth. "All right. I know you're busy, so I won't keep you. Take care of yourself."

"Yeah, you too. Enjoy your time in Kansas City." As I end the call, I carefully turn around and blow out a slow breath. Sandra is standing eight feet away with one hand propped on her hip and both brows lifted in surprise. My cane is in her other hand and I'm a little frightened. I'm not quick enough in my current state to dodge it if she decides to throw it at me.

"You don't want me to do my job, but you expect me to cook for you?!" Her glare intensifies, daring me to ask her to do something besides check on my well-being and provide medical care.

"Of course not. I didn't mean—"

"I am too old for this bullshit," she mutters under her breath as she heads for her bag, shouldering it like she's leaving. I should be more apologetic, but I'm just glad she's going.

"Thanks for coming by," I say.

She's still talking to herself, swearing and mumbling as she goes. All I feel is relief as I hear the door open.

She's the fourth nurse they've sent me since I left the hospital last week, and they all leave in a similar fashion. I don't need someone to dote on me. It's unnecessary. My agent, James, coordinated my rehabilitation schedule. I didn't fight it because I was still out of it on pain meds. But someone coming to check in on me every day and reminding me that I'm basically helpless? No thanks.

I can manage just fine on my own.

CHAPTER THREE

Everly

YOUR WINNING PERSONALITY

J ack lives in the biggest house I've ever seen. Since Tyler became a big, hotshot professional hockey player, I have seen a lot of oversized, elaborate houses, but this one still takes my breath away. The circle drive is paved with intricate stonework and surrounded by lush landscaping. The house itself is brick, two-story, and stretches out so far in either direction that you could easily assume the inhabitant refers to them as "wings."

I park my car at the end of the large circle drive and walk up. Sprinklers are going along the grassy area next to the house. I can't avoid them as I step closer, and they spray my feet, soaking my flip flops.

A woman appears as I get closer to the van. From her profile, she looks like the sweet grandma everyone wants. Gray hair swept up in a bun, black scrubs, and a Minnie Mouse purse slung over one shoulder. The back door is open, and she stops and pulls out a walker, muttering under her breath. She stops, walker raised, when she spots me. The look on her face makes her look a lot less sweet.

"Hi," I say tentatively.

The anger on her face slowly melts away and she raises one brow as she takes in my outfit. I did not plan to stop over in a crop top, cut off shorts, and flip flops, but I wasn't going home to change first just to check in on Jack.

"He says he doesn't need *my* help. Maybe you will have better luck looking like that."

I don't know what she thinks I'm going to accomplish, but I could walk in there naked and Jack would still be the same stubborn jerk.

She sets the walker down in front of me, shuts the van door, and marches around the front. There's a window decal on the back with Minnie Mouse and the name Sandra underneath.

I'm still frozen in place as she starts up the engine and pulls away, leaving me in her dust.

An uneasy, foreboding feeling settles over me.

What the hell did he do to sweet Sandra?

I take the walker with me as I approach the house. It's a heavy, wooden double-door with no windows to look in, but it's cracked open a tiny bit. Like maybe Sandra slammed it but it bounced open. I ring the doorbell and then knock. I tap my foot impatiently while I wait. Leaning closer, I put my ear up to the crack. The faint sound of music, or maybe the TV, indicates he's in there.

Pushing it open, I step in. Concern immediately replaces my hesitation at walking in unannounced. What is that smell? I hold my arm over my nose as I continue. It smells like spoiled food or dirty feet. Maybe a combination of the two. And when I see the kitchen, I know why. Empty brown bags and containers of half-eaten food are spread out along the counter.

I set the walker down next to me and pick up a large McDonalds cup with what I think was a strawberry shake. The smell nearly knocks me over. What in the ever-loving hell is going on around here?

"What are you doing here?" The gruff voice sends tingles down my spine.

I drop the cup and then spin around to face him, completely unprepared for the sight that greets me. Jack has the kind of universal good looks that can't be denied. He towers over most people at six foot three. His dark hair and square jaw give him a rugged edge, but he has a polish to him that reads more white-collar than blue. He's a professional hockey player so he has the broad shoulders, muscular, thick thighs thing going for him as well. Plus, he just has this arrogant, bossy, I don't give a fuck attitude that makes people do what he says. People that aren't *me*, that is.

But right now, I'm looking at a completely different guy.

His usual neat and put-together appearance is gone and in its place is a surly looking man in baggy shorts, a stained T-shirt, uncombed hair that's a touch too long and hangs in his eyes, and an unruly beard that is so far beyond the usual playoff beard some of the guys sport this time of year. If I had run into him anywhere else, I'm not even sure I would have recognized him.

"And why is there a fucking walker in my house?" he asks, snapping me out of my shock.

"Nice to see you too." My smile is saccharine sweet. "Your nurse gave it to me before she peeled out of your driveway, flipping the finger in your general direction. Now I think I know why. What the hell is going on, and why are you holed up in here looking like an injured bear that raided a campsite?"

He makes a harrumph noise that reminds me of a child, then steps forward using a cane as he avoids putting too much weight on his left leg.

Dammit. He's injured and I'm yelling at him. I swear he just provokes this kind of reaction from me.

"Why are you here, Ev?"

"Should you be standing?" I ask, letting my gaze drop to the bandage on his knee.

His jaw tightens and he doesn't move.

Okay, I see we're not going to chitchat. "I'm here to check in on you. Bridget is worried."

"Why?"

"Maybe because you're scaring off sweet old nurses."

"As you can see, I'm fine. Make sure you lock the door on your way out." He gingerly plops himself down on the couch in front of the TV. He's watching the Food Network and a woman smiles at the camera as she plates a steak next to steamed vegetables. This is officially the weirdest day of my life.

"Where is your chef?" I pick up a food wrapper and toss it into an empty brown takeout bag. "And your housekeeper?"

"I gave everyone some time off while I recover. I don't want people in my space right now." He gives me a pointed stare.

"Glaring at me isn't going to get me to leave faster."

"What will?" he asks coolly, then runs his fingers through his messy hair.

I walk into the living room and stand between him and the TV. "Maybe I just want to hang out and soak up some of your winning personality."

Dammit, I keep letting him provoke me. I need to channel my

inner Bridget.

Be nice. Be more like Bridget.

"Don't you have better things to do?" His gaze finally treks over my outfit and my very short jean shorts. "A backyard barbecue to attend, maybe."

"I was going to lie out by a pool and relax, so yes." I cross my arms over my chest. "But I'm glad I stopped by. This is so much more fun."

His mouth falls into an unimpressed straight line at my sarcasm.

"I'm all out of fun right now so go ahead and scamper off." He lifts a hand and shoos me away.

God, he's infuriating.

"I would love nothing more than that, but I'm not leaving here until I can report back to Bridget that you're okay. She's worried."

"All I need is for you to get the hell out of here. And take that walker with you."

"What am I supposed to do with it?"

"Back over it for all I care."

I can feel my last nerve fraying, but I count slowly in my head and reach for the sympathy that I walked in here with. "Are you doing all right? Seriously?"

He sighs in a way that makes his broad chest lift and fall dramatically, then shifts uncomfortably on the couch. His knee is propped up on the ottoman in front of him. An ice pack is abandoned on the floor in front of it. I lean forward and retrieve it.

"It's warm." I turn over the ice pack in my hand. "Do you want me to grab another?"

"I've got it." With quite a bit of effort, he stands again and hobbles toward the kitchen.

"Are you really so stubborn you won't even let someone grab you an ice pack?"

"I don't need any help." He swaps out the hot ice pack for a cold one, but as he's closing the freezer, it drops in front of him.

He glances down at where it lies on the floor. So do I. I start to step forward and he growls, halting me.

"Did you just growl at me?" I do my best to hide the smile slowly pulling at the corner of my lips. I know he's in pain and that recovery is probably frustrating, but he's being ridiculous. It would be so much easier for him if he stopped pushing people out the door.

Shifting his weight over to his good leg, Jack grimaces as he bends slightly at the waist. I once saw this man take a stick to the eye. Blood poured down his face from a deep gash just under his eyebrow. He calmly skated off and returned a few minutes later with a bandage, ready to get back out there.

So I know that if he's struggling, the pain is real and it's beyond what most other people could manage.

"Do you maybe need me to—"

"Just go, alright?" His tone is gruff and tight. He closes his eyes and then points his gaze to the floor. "I don't have the energy to fight with you today and I just want to be left the hell alone."

My face heats at the verbal scolding. I've known Jack since I was barely eighteen, a total mess, and mad at the world. He's never pulled any punches with me. While everyone else walked on eggshells around me, he wasn't afraid to speak his mind even if it hurt my feelings. It made me feel less meek in a time when I desperately needed it.

But I'm not that girl anymore. If he wants to grump around here all alone and not accept anyone's help, then that's on him.

"Happily." I move toward him and pick up the cold ice pack. Heat and frustration radiate off him and his jaw clenches. There are dark circles under his eyes and that beard is really not doing him any favors. Still, he's a handsome guy. I can't deny it. Too bad he's a big ole jerk.

With a look of pure annoyance, he reaches forward to take the ice pack from me. His fingertips drag over my palm, replacing the cool feel with his warmth.

And then I turn on my heel and head out to leave him to brood in his castle. Alone.

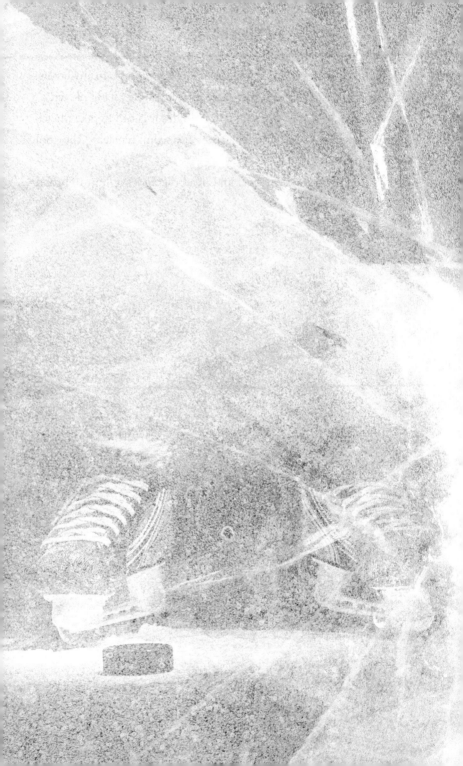

CHAPTER FOUR

Jack

WOAH, BUDDY

'm on the exercise bike in my gym when the doorbell rings. Ignoring it, I keep going. I was in great shape before the accident and now I'm struggling to cycle for more than five minutes without feeling like my body is going to give out. I hate it so much it fuels me to push harder.

Sweat drips from my face as I lean over the bike, holding on with one hand, and pedal faster. I left my air pods in my bedroom and didn't want to hobble across the house for them, but now the only sound is my ragged breathing, which reminds me that I have a long way to go before training camp in September.

A knock on the front door is barely audible over the sound of me sucking in air. My hackles go up immediately. I've come to really fucking hate that sound lately.

I don't stop pedaling. The nurse already came by today. Another new one. She barely spoke as she quickly checked on me, removed the last bandage, and asked me how I was doing.

I answered in a grunt and she fled like a scared rabbit soon after, when it was clear I wasn't going to let her take me for a walk around the block either. What the fuck is their obsession with leisurely afternoon walks in the neighborhood?

The knocking turns to banging. For all of two seconds I reconsider answering it or at least going to see who it is, but then it stops. Good.

I'm focusing back on my workout, pumping my legs, and trying to ignore the weakness of my left leg. The doctor said to be patient, but he doesn't have a career depending on his ability to skate like hell and knock people against the boards.

The season ended because of my fuck up. Not just my season, but the team's too. They were depending on me, and I had to sit by and watch, completely helpless, while they struggled to shift players around to fill my absence.

A sound pulls me from my focus—something that sounds an awful lot like the front door closing.

What the hell?

I stop pedaling and listen closely. Quick footsteps click on the hardwood floors. There is definitely someone in my house. Few people would just let themselves in. Maybe my agent James came back early from vacation?

I'm staring toward the door, waiting for the intruder to announce themselves, when a woman with long, tan legs in cut-off shorts and a red and white striped tube top appears in the doorway.

"Oh, good. You're alive," Everly says in a tone that suggests maybe she's not all that happy I haven't reached an untimely demise.

"Was that really a question?" I arch one brow, feeling another trickle of sweat slide down into my eye. It burns, but it's a welcome feeling to distract from the pain in my knee.

"Seeing as how you aren't answering the door or your phone, it was among the possibilities."

"Couldn't be that I'm just busy."

Ignoring me, she holds up a white bag. "I brought lunch."

"I'm not hungry." I go back to biking while she lowers the food sack and glowers at me. "And why are *you* bringing me food? I'm not helpless."

"Wow, Everly, that was so nice. Thank you," she says in a sugary-sweet tone as she mocks me. Her blonde hair is pulled up today in a ponytail that swings from side-to-side as she speaks. "I was in the neighborhood. I'm looking after Leo, Declan, and Ash's houses while they're gone. I thought you might like something to eat that wasn't fried in vegetable oil."

She disappears out of view. Now in addition to being interrupted, I feel like a jerk. I try to get back to my workout, but I can hear her moving around in my house. What is she doing?!

I like Everly more than I like the average person, but at this moment I can't remember why.

I continue to stew as I watch the miles on my bike increase. Eventually, I must get into a frustration-fueled haze because when I stop, I can't hear her anymore. Good. Maybe she left.

I ignore the twinge of guilt for running her off. She doesn't want to be around me right now. Can't she see that I need space to recover on my own? If she's smart, she'll stay the hell away from me and enjoy her last summer of carefree fun.

Everly just finished college and has an internship waiting for her at the end of the summer. Her brother Tyler can't stop talking about it. He's so proud of his younger sister. And for all the hell she caused him when she was younger, I guess I understand why.

In the kitchen I eye the white bag, then peek inside. My stomach growls at the sight of a salad. I might have had one too many cheeseburgers in the past week if my body is now craving lettuce.

I'm about to pull out the container when movement catches my eye. Everly's steps come up short when she spots me. She's changed into a swimsuit—some tiny black thing that barely covers her. My mouth goes dry and heat courses through me.

Woah, buddy. Eyes up. Moving my gaze to her face and reminding myself that she's my teammate's little sister doesn't seem to help. It's been more than a month since I've seen a woman naked and suddenly, I am thinking that's one day too many.

It isn't like I didn't already know she's a beautiful woman. Ev is gorgeous. She has a heart-shaped face, pouty lips, and these big, expressive hazel eyes. She's average height, but still feels tiny next to me. Her legs are long and toned and if I had ever looked at her boobs—which I definitely haven't—I'd know they are nice and perky.

Sometime over the past year I looked at her and realized all this. *Objectively,* she's stunning.

But hooking up with a teammate's sister is completely off-limits. Hell, I wouldn't even sleep with someone's cousin. It's too messy. My loyalty is to my teammates and besides, I'm not that hard up for attention.

Except lately I've been screening every text or call, including those wanting to help make me feel better with a quick fuck. Let me tell you how much I want some chick looking to score with Jack Wyld, hockey captain, to see me in this condition. Hell, I'm not even sure I could give them the good, hard dicking they'd be expecting. If my workout today was any indication, I'd be huffing and puffing and asking them to watch out for my bad leg while trying not to accidentally bang them in the head with the cast on my arm. No fucking thanks.

She arches a brow, reminding me that I'm still staring at her.

"Thank you for the food."

Surprise plays over her features. "Wow. He speaks without growling at me."

Her taunt, of course, makes me want to growl at her. My leg is tired though, so instead I pull out a chair and take a seat. Everly watches me so closely my skin feels tight.

"How are you doing?" she asks, a touch brighter and without the snark.

"Here to check in and report back to Bridget?"

"No." She comes closer, stopping a foot away where I can smell the coconut-scented sunscreen on her skin. "I told Bridget I was staying out of it from now on."

That would explain why Ash texted me five times already today.

"I don't need anyone to check in on me. I'm—"

"Fine?" she asks, a smirk on her sexy mouth. "Don't need anyone's help? Want to be left alone?"

Yes, to all those things.

"I don't want them worrying about me. We only get a few months off the entire year. The other nine months are a grind of nonstop hard work and time away from families and loved ones. They deserve this time to relax and unwind."

"That's stupid. They care about you. They're your *friends*. Of course, they're going to worry."

She digs into the bag and pulls out two containers, then hands me one. She walks through my kitchen and directly to the silverware drawer. Grabbing two forks, she brings them over and sets one in front of me. The familiarity she has with my house speaks some truth to her words. They are my friends. And by extension, she is too. I'm not ready to invite everyone over and make small talk, but I can have lunch with Everly. One lunch, then maybe she'll be satisfied that I don't need her either.

Except…

"Did you clean in here?"

Her cheeks take on the slightest hint of pink. "I threw out the moldy shake, yes."

"I would have gotten around to it."

She says nothing, which is almost more aggravating than her sass.

We eat in silence. I devour mine, really. Breakfast this morning was toast and a protein shake. I need to get some groceries. I could also tell my chef that I changed my mind and need some meals prepared and ready to go, but he was so excited about having the summer off that taking that back now feels shitty. *What the hell did I think I was going to eat?* I haven't cooked for myself in years and suddenly taking up the hobby when I can barely move around without breaking a sweat, seems like the worst possible idea.

"I made cookies too," she says, abandoning her salad to walk over to a big, beach bag looking duffel next to the back door. She leans over and I'm once again averting my eyes from the way the black material stretches over her chest, gaping in the middle. Not that it helps. I need a cold shower and a few minutes to myself.

Everly returns, that sweet scent following her. Somewhere between being annoyed that she was here and trying not to ogle her, I didn't consider why she was in a swimsuit to begin with.

She drops a container of cookies in front of me. Sugar cookies. Coincidence that it's my favorite? Probably not. A slow trickle of unease works its way down my spine.

"Why are you here, Everly?"

"I told you, I was in the neighborhood."

"Uh-huh." I point to her tits. This time I don't even bother not looking. "Did you walk around Declan's house in that?"

She looks down at herself.

"It was underneath my other clothes," she says slowly like she's trying to understand.

"*Why* are you here?"

Her face takes on a slight blush. "You have that great pool and you won't even know I'm here."

Impossible.

"I don't want your pity lunch or your bribery cookies." I push the container toward her.

"Oh my god." She rolls her eyes, and her lips curve up into a smile. "Stop being so dramatic."

"I told you, I don't need anyone's help."

"Really?" she asks. Both hands go to her hips. It'd be less distracting if she weren't mostly naked. "Because you look like shit and this place is a mess."

I motion with both hands toward my leg.

"I know. I know." She throws up her hands. And she says I'm the dramatic one? She lets out a long breath. "I don't mean to keep yelling at you, but god, you're frustrating."

"Right back at ya." I take the cookies back and retrieve two from the container. I deserve them for this conversation alone.

Her voice is softer when she speaks this time. "You need help whether you like it or not. And I need access to the best pool in the city."

I huff a short laugh.

"It's just lunch. For all the things you've done for me over the years, I'd say we are many *many* lunches away from us being even."

I bite into a cookie as I think about it. I don't want her here, but she's stubborn and hard-headed, and this was the best lunch I've had in weeks.

"Fine. You can use the pool."

She squeals and jumps around, reminding me that she's ten years younger than me. It doesn't help that I feel about fifty years old right now.

"Just for today," I add.

Her head nods quickly and she smiles at me happily before stuffing another forkful of salad into her mouth.

"No reporting back to Bridget or anyone else," I say pointedly.

She continues to nod away. Why do I feel like I'm going to regret this?

"And I'm taking the rest of these." I grab the cookies, stand, and start my slow hobble to the couch.

CHAPTER FIVE

Everly

NOT DEAD

The sun is shining bright and high in the sky, and my smile widens as I turn my face up toward it. We don't get a lot of hot weather in Minnesota, but there's just something about lying by the pool, occasionally dipping my toes in the water or taking a swim, that makes summertime feel right.

For all Jack's complaining and acting like he was annoyed that I'm here, he turned on the outdoor speakers for me and pop music plays just loud enough that it feels like the soundtrack to this perfect day.

All the outdoor furniture is covered in a fine layer of dust, indicating he hasn't been out here in a while. The pool is clean, though. I guess he didn't run off the pool boy like all the rest of his staff.

My mom calls as I'm contemplating either turning over in my lounge chair or slathering on another layer of sunscreen. I love the sun, but I do not want to look like I do.

I hesitate before answering it, but guilt wins out.

"Hi, Mom."

"Hello! Hello!" She sounds chipper and happy. I never know what mood I'm going to get her in, but I sigh in relief that today is a good mood day. "What are you up to? I haven't heard from you in a while."

"Sorry, I've been busy. I'm taking care of Tyler's place while he's gone, and some of the other Wildcat players." Was there time to call her? Yes, of course. Was I afraid she'd somehow unintentionally make me feel like shit? Also, yes. It's a gift, really. She can say the most hurtful things in the most innocuous way.

"It's okay. I remember what it was like to be your age," she says with a fondness that makes me want to cling to this summer even harder. "When do you leave for your internship?"

"I start on August first." I stare out at the clear water as my stomach flutters with nerves.

"You don't sound very excited," she comments. I hate that she can still pick up on things. That feels like a gift that should be reserved for more present parents. But she seems to know me, even if she's not always been the most attentive mom.

"No, I am," I insist, pushing out the uneasiness I feel every time I think about the job. "It's a really great opportunity."

"But?"

Sighing quietly, I wonder if I should just keep it to myself. I don't want her to hold it over my head later if I fail. *You weren't excited enough. You can't accomplish anything with that attitude. You didn't give it your all.* Or whatever other words of wisdom she'll find to make me feel worse. I think she generally means well, but she has adopted some toxic positivity over the past year that can really pile on an already shitty situation.

"I don't know," I say finally. "I was thinking I could stay in school.

46

Maybe get a master's degree or something."

Silence hangs on the line. Holding the phone between my shoulder and ear, I free my hands to pick at my chipped, blue nail polish.

"A master's degree?" She repeats it back after an uncomfortable amount of time has passed. Her tone would suggest I told her I was going to sail around the world in a rowboat. "Honey, you barely managed to finish high school."

She lets out a small laugh that makes my entire body flush with shame. A shame rooted in truth. It's no secret that I barely eked by in high school, but having it thrown in my face still feels awful.

"That was different. I enjoyed college and my grades were good." Better than good. I managed to get straight As the last two years. If it weren't for an asshole psychology professor who loved to design tests to trick his students, I would have escaped without anything lower than a B. That C will haunt me until the day I die.

"You were an art major." The underlying blow of her comment that indicates how little brains she thinks it takes to get an art degree and of my intellect, goes unsaid.

"It was just something I was thinking," I say dismissively. I knew better than to bring it up. It's been on my mind a lot and all my friends are busy. Grace took a job and started work right after graduation, so did most of my other college friends. Bridget and everyone else I know are taking the off-season to vacation and spend time with family. Tyler and Piper would always drop everything for me, but they're so excited about it that I can almost see the hurt it would cause them if I mentioned being uncertain. They have done so much for me and I don't want them to think I'm ungrateful.

"It's normal to be nervous about taking the next step. This

internship will be great. You'll see."

"You're right." I close my eyes and picture myself designing spaces, picking out furniture and art, making houses feel like an extension of the people that live there. I can see it so clearly and it fills me with some of the sparks of anticipation that have been missing these past weeks since I found out I was selected for the internship.

"Of course, I am. You have such a great eye." The praise mixed with the playful smugness of her voice makes everything she said earlier hurt a little less. "So, what else is new?"

We talk for a few more minutes before she claims she has to go so she can help dad find something to eat.

Immediately after, I call Bridget.

"Hellooo!" Her voice makes a real smile tug at both corners of my mouth.

"Hello to you." I stand and stretch. Sitting for so long in that lounge chair has my butt numb. "How's vacation?"

I walk barefoot around the pool. The ground is warm, and a breeze blows my hair lightly.

"Good. We just got back from a farmer's market and we're going to take a little picnic out on the boat."

My nose scrunches up. I can picture it. Bridget's curly blonde hair blowing in the wind and Ash nearly crashing the boat as he stares at her. The man is obsessed with her. "You two are adorable."

"I can feel you making a face at me, but I am choosing to take the compliment."

Light laughter escapes and, god, I miss her. I have no idea how I'll survive living in another city all the time. She's been gone for two days and I'm almost ready to pack up and invade their cozy couple vacation.

"You should. It sounds perfect."

"How are things there?" she asks. "Are you at Tyler's, lying by the pool?"

"Close." I sit at the edge of the pool. The water is a little cool as I dip in my toes. Staring at my matching blue toenails, I kick my legs slowly. "I'm at Jack's house."

"You're at Jack's?!" Her voice pitches higher and from her tone I'd bet her eyes are bugging out of her head.

"Yes. Why do you sound so shocked? I'm checking in on him, just like you wanted."

"Aside from the fact you two usually can't be in the same room together without annoying the shit out of each other?"

"We're not in the same room. I'm outside. He's inside. I'm too far away to see him glaring at me, and he's out of throwing distance. Safety first."

Her rich laughter makes my smile grow. When it trails off, she asks, "How is he?"

An image of him flashes through my mind. His dark hair, too long and hanging in his eyes, the unruly beard, his strong body bruised and bandaged, and the haunted look in his eyes. He seems a little lost, which is honestly unnerving.

But if I tell Bridget that, she and Ash will be packing up and heading back here. And I know how much Jack doesn't want that.

I understand not wanting people around to witness you at your most vulnerable. I think he's being unnecessarily obstinate by not letting *anyone* in, but I still get it.

"Grumpier than normal, but he seems okay." The lie slips out easily. Maybe I should tell someone. If the team returns weeks from now and finds out that I knew he was in bad shape and said nothing, they would be furious with me.

The thing is, it's hard for me to imagine Jack not being okay. Even seeing him like this I know he'll bounce back. He's Jack Wyld. Formidable. Bigger than life. Invincible.

"Is he doing his physio?"

"I'm not sure," I say. "He isn't exactly chatty."

Even on the best days, he's always been quieter. Not shy or reserved, just careful. Every word out of his mouth feels purposeful. Sometimes that purpose is that he's a jerk.

"But he was on the bike when I got here," I add.

"Oh good. That must mean the doctor cleared him to start some light exercise."

"What kind of stuff would he be doing for physical therapy?" I doubt scowling is part of the plan, but if it were, he'd be crushing it.

"Usually, it's a lot of flexion and extension stretches to get full motion back. I'm sure his doctors are coming over to work with him."

I am not so sure based on the way he ran off his nurse yesterday. Then again, I know Jack will want to be back in top form as soon as possible.

Ash's muffled voice pauses our conversation and then Bridget says, "I gotta go."

"Okay." A stab of melancholy slices through me. I'm so happy that she's happy, but selfishly I wish I could talk to her for another hour. "Text me later and tell Ash to keep his eyes on the water."

She laughs at my odd request. "Will do. Bye, babe."

"Bye." I hang up, then hold my phone in my hands and tip my head up toward the sky. Sometime while I was on the phone, dark clouds rolled in, and the breeze is cool.

So much for my perfect pool day.

By the time I gather up my stuff and head inside, light rain has begun to fall. The cool air from the air conditioning makes goosebumps rise on my skin. The TV is going in the living room, but from this spot I can't see if Jack is in there or not.

I pull on my shorts and shirt and slide my feet into my flip flops.

"I'm gonna go," I yell, then wait for his reply.

Nothing.

With my bag over one shoulder, I walk through the house to the living room. Jack is in the same spot on the massive couch where he sat yesterday. His left leg is propped up and the container of cookies sits next to his foot.

"It's starting to rain, so I'm heading out," I say as I get closer, then realize his eyes are closed.

Asleep? Dead? I chuckle a little to myself. Of course he isn't dead.

Except, oh my god, what if something happened? Maybe he took too much pain medicine or choked on one of the cookies. I creep forward. He's so still I can't tell.

I shimmy between the couch and the ottoman on his right side, careful not to accidentally bump his left leg, then lean in.

I search for signs of life, but my gaze gets stuck on his mouth. If you can look past the beard, and it's hard, he has a great mouth. Full lips set against a square jaw.

His scent wraps around me. It's faint, a hint of citrus mixed with something else. I want to move even closer and keep trying to place it, but then I hear it. His quiet breath comes in a steady rhythm.

"What are you doing?" His voice is thick from sleep.

I squeak and jump back. My calves hit the ottoman, and I fall back. Somehow, he catches me with one hand, guiding me so I don't land on his bad leg or the cookies.

He's not dead. Good. Because I might be soon. I place a hand over my racing heart.

"I was making sure you were breathing." I glance over at his foot. "I didn't jostle your leg too much, did I?"

He shakes his head. His fingers are still on the curve of my waist and the warmth of his touch is welcome against my cool skin. Heat pools in my stomach. There's something very sensual about a man placing his hand at your waist. His big, rough hand against soft skin. To no one's surprise, Jack's caress has that perfect touch of tender protectiveness.

A crack of thunder makes me jolt again, this time out of his hold. I ignore the way my skin tingles. I need to get a freaking grip or maybe partake in an orgasm or two.

I make a mental note to swipe right on someone later tonight and get to my feet. "Thanks for letting me use the pool today."

"Thanks for lunch."

"Same time tomorrow?" I ask in a joking tone, then smile. "You do have the best pool in the neighborhood."

He really, really does. It's a travesty that it's going to go unused all summer. Or maybe not. Maybe Jack and his new beard are going to enjoy it once he gets the cast off his arm. All alone. Just like he wants.

"Goodbye, Ev."

"So that's a maybe?" I head toward the front door.

He doesn't respond.

CHAPTER SIX

Jack

I HOPE YOU CHOKE ON THEM

"You look like hell," James says. "Do you need me to contact a barber?" My agent scrutinizes me through the screen. If he were sitting across from me, he'd have already made the call, but instead he's sitting on a beach somewhere in Hawaii.

"No, I'll go by next week." Maybe.

"What did the doctor say this morning?"

I'm not surprised that he's keeping tabs on my schedule, even from three-thousand miles away. "Arm cast comes off next week and he gave me some new physical therapy exercises. I told you, everything is going fine here."

"I'm glad it's fine for you. Meanwhile I'm developing an ulcer." He picks up a drink with a pink umbrella in it and his mouth turns down at the corners. "I am not a vacation person. Sitting around, drinking, and watching the water. How many hours can one guy be expected to do that before he cracks?"

The first real smile in days pulls at my lips. "Where's your husband?"

James sighs. "Yoga on the beach with some other tourists. Are you sure you don't need me to come back sooner?"

"Go join him," I say sternly. "That's the only thing I need from you."

He doesn't look happy about it, but he nods. "Okay."

"Have fun."

"Oh, before I forget," James interjects before I can end the call. "I sent over a dozen or more emails since last week. Sponsorships, events, a new lease agreement..." He trails off.

"I saw them," I admit. Sort of. I turned off email notifications on my phone after the first few I didn't want to deal with.

"Good, good." He chuckles softly. "Now how about responding to them before the summer is over?"

"On my list."

When we hang up, I feel a little lighter. James has that effect. He's the best agent in the game. He's been with me since the beginning, both of us just starting out. Now I'm the highest paid hockey player in the league, and he owns an entire company with dozens of sports agents under him.

My light mood doesn't last too long. I open my email, intending to go through them, but when I see how many have piled up, I break out in a cool sweat. I scan the list. Sponsors inviting me to attend events or reaching out with potential dates to shoot commercials, as stipulated in my contracts. Charities I regularly donate to or visit, such as the local children's hospital, asking me back. And so many more things, all that require me to reply and none that I want to let down.

I set the computer aside and go to the kitchen, but there's nothing to cook and I'm not that hungry anyway.

I think I'm tired of being cooped up. I can't drive, or maybe shouldn't is the better word, but some fresh air might be needed. Donning a pair of shorts and a T-shirt, I head out to the backyard. The first step outside, I inhale deeply. Damn. I didn't realize how badly I needed this. Maybe I should have taken Sandra up on the walk around the neighborhood with the walker. Nah, absolutely not.

Scanning the yard, I do a double take when I spot the pink circle floatie in the middle of my pool. Or rather the woman on it.

Surprise shoots through me, but, actually, it's not that shocking. With Everly, you always expect the unexpected.

As if she can feel my stare, her head snaps around and our gazes lock. She's wearing a pair of sunglasses, but her dark brows lift beneath them.

By the time I make it to the edge of the pool, Everly has lifted the dark shades and paddled closer.

"Do I even want to know how you got in here?"

"I climbed over the fence." She tips her head in the general direction.

My gaze drifts over to the fence that surrounds my house. It's six feet tall, and Ev...she's not short, but that couldn't have been easy.

"I didn't want to bother you again, but this pool deserves to be used."

"Oh good. You didn't want to bother me. This is way less intrusive."

She rolls her gorgeous hazel eyes. Today they're lined with black that extends out past the corners of her eyes. "Fine. Fine. I should get out of the sun anyway."

Her comment makes me wonder how long she's been out here.

Everly slides off the pink floatie, tosses it over the side out of the pool, and then pulls herself up. Water cascades down her body, from the ends of her blonde hair, over smooth curves and long legs. Today's bikini is red. Appropriate since I should absolutely *stop* looking at her.

"How's the knee?" she asks casually, leaning her head to one side and squeezing water from her hair.

"Better."

"How much longer do you have to wear the cast?" Her chin juts toward my left arm.

"It comes off next week." I fidget in place as she fires questions at me. I wasn't prepared to see her and my defenses slowly rise back up, turning me back into the grumpy asshole I've become this past month.

"What kind of physical therapy are you—"

"You can't just show up uninvited, scale my fence, and act like my pool is your personal getaway."

Her eyes widen like a hurt puppy at my gruff tone and scolding words, but then slowly a fire lights up behind those hazel irises and everything in her body language stiffens.

"So sorry I invaded your fortress." She stomps over to a lounge chair and grabs her towel and beach bag. Her march back has the same haughtiness, but she stops in front of me and pulls something from the bag.

"Here." She shoves a plastic container at me. "I made you more cookies. I hope you choke on them."

She circles wide around me and heads for the back door.

"Not gonna jump the fence again?"

She lifts one arm over her head and flips me off as she keeps going, disappearing into my house.

I blow out a long breath. The girl makes my blood pressure rise. Getting fresh air seems pointless now.

As I'm stepping into the house, my phone rings. I'm half expecting it to be Everly calling to yell at me some more. And when I see who it is, I wish it were.

Bracing myself, I set Ev's cookies on the kitchen island, then accept the call and bring it to my ear. "Hey, Dad."

It is not my dad who replies. "Jackie boy. It's John."

"Coach." My brows pull together as I recognize my old hockey coach's voice. "Everything okay?"

It's a stupid question. Things are never okay when he or my dad calls.

"Your dad is here. A new bartender overserved him and we're having a hard time getting him to leave. I hate to call you, I know you're dealing with a lot right now, but I really don't want to have to call the police."

Fuck.

"Don't call them. I'm on my way," I say, searching for my keys and finding them on the front entryway table.

"I'll do my best to keep him calm and happy until then."

"Thanks." I hang up and shove my phone in my pocket. It isn't until I walk outside to get in my SUV that I remember I can't/shouldn't drive.

Dammit. I could call an Uber but by the time it gets here, I could already be halfway to my dad.

My eyes lift from my vehicle to the car behind it. *Everly.*

She's changed, or rather pulled on a short, white dress over the wet bikini. She tosses her bag in the back and then glares at me.

"I'm leaving. Geez. You don't need to follow me and shoo me off your property."

"I need you to drive me somewhere."

She just stares at me, squinting slightly like she's not sure she heard me right.

I unlock my SUV and open the door for her. I haven't even driven it yet. My last one was totaled. James went with me to pick this one up and bring it home. It still has that new car smell.

Everly doesn't move. Instead, she continues to look at me skeptically.

"Please? It's not far, but I shouldn't drive yet."

She opens the driver's side door of her car. "Maybe you can finally take that walker out for a spin."

Fuck. I hate needing people and right now I need Everly to do this for me.

"You can use the pool again tomorrow. No scaling the fence necessary."

She doesn't look as tempted by my offer as I hoped.

"Tomorrow and the day after."

No reply.

"Any time you want!"

Her expression shifts, gaze narrowing and lips turning down at the corners.

"Please?" It's a last-ditch attempt and I've already accepted that I'm going to have to call for a ride when she grabs her purse and heads for me.

Relief sweeps through me.

"Thank you," I say as she climbs behind the wheel of my G-Wagon.

I don't wait for her reply. I hustle as much as I can around to the other side. Everly adjusts the mirrors and the seat while I struggle to get myself up into the passenger seat.

"Where am I going?" she asks as she pulls through my circle drive and onto the road.

"Take a right out of the neighborhood."

I'm grateful that she doesn't pepper me with more questions. The beginning of a headache is starting behind my eyes. We drive in silence, except for the prompts I give her at each turn. When we reach Brettwood, the small town my dad lives in, anxious energy starts to thrum through me, making it hard to sit still. Luckily, it's not that big of a town and I'm instructing Everly to pull up to the curb of Perry's Pool Hall a few moments later.

"Stay here. I'll be right back," I say.

The old bar smells like stale cigarettes. It's been years since smoking was banned inside this place, but the scent still hangs thick in the air. Country music plays from a jukebox. The pool tables are empty, as are the few tables set up in front of the windows looking out toward the street.

A handful of people sit at the small wooden bar, but I head toward the only one slumped over, too drunk to hold his head up at two o'clock in the afternoon.

His dark hair is streaked with white. The greasy strands are slicked back and hang down onto the back collar of a dingy white button-up shirt. His face is buried into one arm but what I can see of his skin has that reddish flush that would be a telltale sign that he was drunk if that weren't already obvious.

"Jackie boy." My gaze lifts to the man behind the bar. He's almost more familiar to me than my father. Gray hair, same old mustache he's been sporting since the nineties, and his usual attire of pocket T-shirt and khakis. It's hard to believe of the two, Coach John is older than my dad.

"Hey, Coach."

"Good to see you." His eyes crinkle with a smile, but then his expression falls into one more appropriate for the situation. "I'm sorry about this."

"Not your fault."

His nod isn't all that convincing, but he pivots asking, "How are you?"

"Been better," I admit. Certainly didn't plan on leaving the house in this condition today.

"Thank you for calling me." It's preferable to bailing my dad out of jail again. He isn't on a first-name basis with the booking officers or anything, but once is enough to earn a place on the "never again" list.

"You'll be okay." His words temporarily heal that nagging seed of doubt since the accident, but I don't have time to dwell right now. "You didn't drive here, did you?"

"No. I got a ride from a friend." I tip my head toward my dad. "What's he owe you?"

My old hockey coach shakes me off. "He's all settled."

"Bullshit."

"It's on me for overserving him." Coach owns Perry's but hasn't worked here in years. His presence is purely to keep my dad out of more trouble because someone else didn't know that Lance Wyld is the town drunk. My gaze cuts quickly to the younger guy working behind the bar. I hate that my dad is a cautionary tale. *Don't serve the old man or he'll get belligerent and refuse to leave.*

I take out my wallet and stuff all the cash I have into the tip jar. "Thank you."

"Need some help getting him out?" Coach asks, but it's more of a statement than a question.

Fuck. How the hell am I going to carry him home like I've done a million times before? Like I'll have to do a million more.

Swallowing down my frustration and loathing, I nod.

As Coach comes around the bar to help me, I rest a hand on my dad's shoulder. It's hard to believe this frail man in front of me was once the most promising and talented hockey player in the state. I used to dream of having his height, his broad shoulders, and his slapshot. If I'd known then what I know now, I might have dreamed of more practical things, like a father that doesn't drink himself into a stupor regularly.

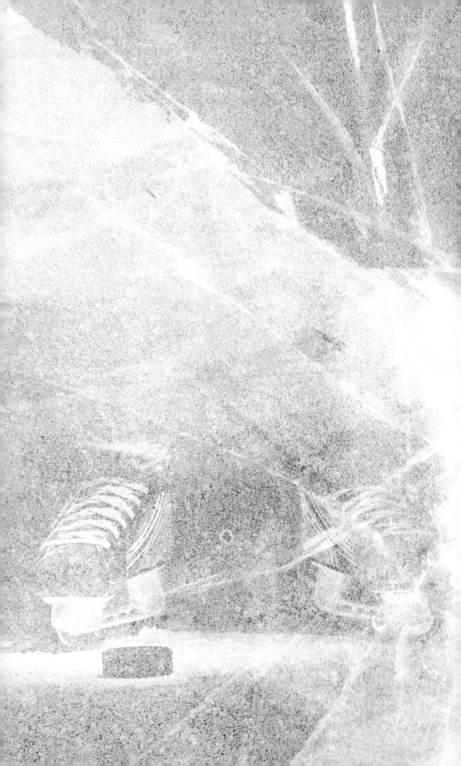

CHAPTER SEVEN

Everly

JACKIE BOY

I n all the wildest places I could have imagined Jack asking me to drive him, this shitty bar in some rundown town wouldn't have even been in my top one thousand.

An old, faded sign hangs above the front door. *Perry's* could be any dive bar in any small town, but the fact Jack is in there makes it feel even more rundown. Even with the beard that makes him look like a reclusive, wilderness man named Barnaby, there's no way he doesn't stick out.

I tap my thumb against the smooth leather steering wheel of his very expensive SUV. No one is around so it isn't like I think I'm going to get jumped, but I do feel incredibly out of place.

What could he possibly be doing in there?

No matter how hard I stare at the door, he doesn't appear. My patience and curiosity eventually get the best of me.

I get out of the vehicle, lock it behind me, and head inside. Once I step into the small bar, I have to stop and let my eyes adjust to the dark lighting. Every head in the place turns in my direction, but it's Jack's gaze that makes the hair on the back of my neck rise.

He does not look happy to see me. I smile at the bartender and other patrons, then walk to the far side of the bar to him.

Jack steps toward me. His eyes are dark and his jaw is set tight. He's always a little bit of an asshole, but right now he looks like a lethal and brutal star hockey player about to smash someone into the boards. That someone being me. My skin tingles, oblivious to the danger he radiates.

"I told you to stay in the car." His voice is low, but the words are still harsh. "God, do you ever just listen?"

I suck in a sharp breath. The question stings more than I'd care to admit. It isn't the first time I've been called insubordinate. Or stupid.

"Do you ever stop being an asshole?" I fire back. You know what? He can do whatever he wants in here. I'm going back outside, waiting five more minutes, and then calling an Uber. I don't care if he has to drive himself home with one arm and one leg. That's his problem.

I turn to go, but Jack's hand reaches out, circling my wrist and keeping me from fleeing. His eyes close and when he opens them, the intensity there swirls with some other emotion, desperation, I think. "Will you help me get him out to the car?"

"Who?" I ask. I'm embarrassed to admit that I didn't notice the two men standing behind him.

Both are older, in their fifties or sixties maybe. One of them is looking at me. A surprised smile plays over his face, making his mustache pull up over thin lips. The grin he aims at me has me wondering if he just heard me call Jack an asshole.

I'd like to be sorry, but he was acting like an asshole.

The other man's head hangs down. He's on his feet, but not of his own accord. Drunk in the afternoon. I have been there.

Jack moves to the drunk guy's other side.

"Let me," I say when I realize what's happening. Does he really think he's in any shape to help anyone else walk? He couldn't even drive here.

A waft of alcohol and body odor take my breath away as I wrap the drunk man's limp, left arm around my shoulders. He lifts his head to look at me, and the hairs stand up on the back of my neck. Those dark eyes are so familiar. Not as harsh as the ones I know, but the same.

I smile wobbly at him.

"Who are you?" he asks.

"Everly. Who are you?"

"Nice to meet you, pretty girl." His eyes close and the words are slightly slurred. I don't get his name, but then again, he might not know it right now.

Jack walks ahead of us through the bar, then holds the door open for us. I squint at the bright sun, reacclimating the way I had to do when I came in.

It's only when I'm helping get this very drunk man into the back of Jack's SUV that the full weight of the situation hits me.

We just picked up who I am quite confident is Jack's dad from some random bar and are taking him...well, that part I don't know.

I hurry around to the driver's seat and get in. Jack and the other guy take their time, talking on the sidewalk. The older gentleman lays a hand on Jack's shoulder. It's such an endearing, supportive gesture. I don't think I've ever seen anyone treat Jack that way. He's always the one reassuring others.

Jack glances back at the vehicle and I avert my gaze. His dad is snoring in the back.

When he finally opens the passenger door, Jack climbs in and then says nothing.

We sit in a heavy silence until I can't bear it any longer.

"Where to?"

He sighs, then rests his head against the headrest. He rubs absently at the top of his left knee. I wonder if he tweaked it or maybe it just hurts from sitting with his feet dangling down instead of elevated.

"Follow Coach." Without opening his eyes, he points in front of us.

I hadn't noticed the other man, but he's pulled up beside me in a black truck with the windows down. I roll mine down so he can see me past the tinted windows and give him a thumbs-up.

I am not good at keeping my mouth shut, which often gets me into trouble. But I can't just drive along and not ask some very basic questions. I open my mouth, but Jack cuts me off first.

"Later." His tone is weary. He meets my stare, and his expression is so pleading that I find myself nodding.

When the black truck pulls to a stop in front of a big, brick house with pristine landscaping, I figure there can't be any more surprises today. I know drunks don't necessarily live in run-down shacks and all that, but this place is so nice.

"You're home, Dad." Jack's voice is loud but curt.

I already knew it, but it still shocks me. His *dad*.

Coach is already parked and coming to help get the other man inside. Not just some other guy. Jack's father. I didn't even know Jack had a father. I mean, of course, he has a father, but he never talks about his family. I thought he was born in the arena with hockey skates on his feet.

The same way we got him out of the bar, we take him into the house. The TV in the living room is on, but otherwise the place is quiet and still.

Coach and I deposit Jack's dad on the couch. I let out a long breath. His dad is thin, but he's tall and limp, which makes him heavy.

Jack is taking in the place, the beer bottles and the dirty plates scattered on the coffee table.

"I got it from here," Jack says, giving me a quick side-eye. Am I dismissed? Is that what's happening?

I hate being ordered around and he hates people not listening to him. Every instinct in me wants to rebel. Not just with him, with everyone. However, I can see the way he's fighting for control right now. I know this isn't the first time this has happened. Probably not even the tenth. His dad is just another person that Jack takes care of. Meanwhile, he won't let anyone take care of him.

"Okay," I relent. "I'll be outside."

As I close the door behind me, I decide I don't want to get back in the SUV, so I sit on the front step. It's a nice neighborhood. A mix of houses, new and old, but all maintained well.

Minutes pass by before the front door opens again. Coach steps out and takes a seat next to me.

"Everything okay in there?" I ask. I don't know this man, but I feel like we're trauma buddies or something.

"Yeah. He'll be okay. Thanks for your help." He holds a big hand out to me. "I'm John."

I guess I should have known his name wasn't really Coach, but this whole situation has my brain not firing on all cylinders. John must read my confusion because he says, "I was Jackie's hockey coach when he was a kid."

"Ah. Makes sense," I say. "Everly. I'm a friend."

I'm not sure Jack would call me his friend but explaining the intricacies of how we know each other and how I'm the only one that was nearby and available at the exact time he needed me feels like overkill.

"Well, Everly, it's nice to meet you. Jackie boy won't be long. He's just taking a few moments alone with his dad, probably scolding him. Not like it'll do any good." The last part is a quiet mutter more to himself than me.

"Does this kind of thing happen a lot?" I ask.

"Too often." He nods his head, looking out toward the street.

We sit in silence until Jack finally emerges. He pauses, looking between us. John places both hands on his thighs and stands.

"I best be getting back to the bar."

"Thank you," Jack says to him.

"Don't owe me any thanks. Sorry you had to drive all the way down here." His gaze cuts to me. "Though I'm glad I got to meet this one. He never brings anyone around for me to meet."

"I wonder why." Jack runs a hand through his hair, but a small smile creeps into his expression. It's gone almost as quickly as it appears. "I'll see you in a couple of weeks, Coach."

"Looking forward to it. Take care of that knee."

Coach gives us his back as he heads off to his truck. I slowly get to my feet.

"All good?" I ask, then wince inwardly. Of course he isn't all good. "I mean, are you ready?"

"You can take my SUV back. I'm going to stay the night, and I'll grab a ride home tomorrow."

"Oh."

"I just need to grab my phone." I'm still processing when he starts for his SUV. His limping is more pronounced, and his brow is creased with pain or frustration, probably both. He opens the passenger door, retrieves his phone, and heads back.

"Look, I know you're going to hate this idea, but I think I should stay too. I can help."

He opens his mouth with what is sure to be a protest, but I've had enough of his bullshit.

"Let me fucking help you."

His brows rise in surprise. "Thank you for today, Ev, but this isn't your mess to clean up."

"And it's yours?"

His clenched jaw is my answer.

"I'm not going back without you."

He mutters something. The only word I catch is stubborn. Like he's one to talk.

I march past him into the house, but because I'm not a jerk, I hold the door open for him. Now that I've made the decision to stay, I'm second-guessing myself. I don't know what to do in this scenario. I've dealt with plenty of drunk girlfriends, getting them home and putting them to bed with a glass of water and Advil. I doubt that's the play here.

"How can I help?" I ask.

"He's sleeping it off. He'll be fine." Jack walks into the living room and I follow.

He blows out a breath that puffs out his cheeks as he looks around the mess. He reaches for a couple of empty bottles.

"I got this," I say, falling in beside him and taking the bottles from him. "You should sit and elevate your leg."

He must be in a lot of pain because he listens. Gingerly dropping down in a chair opposite the couch where his dad is snoring, he says, "You don't need to clean up. I can do it later."

"I don't mind." I'm holding as many bottles as I can in both hands. I turn to the opening of the living room. "Which way is the kitchen?"

"Take a right, end of the hall."

When I find it, I set the bottles on the counter and then sigh as I look around. The kitchen is also a mess. I get to work cleaning. It's nice to turn off my brain and accomplish something. I don't love to clean under normal circumstances, but a good stress clean always makes me feel better.

It actually isn't as bad as I thought originally. The bottles and cans go in the recycling. I put a few empty cups and dishes into the dishwasher and start it and then wipe down the counters.

As I'm finishing up, I go to the fridge. There's a newspaper clipping hanging from a magnet. The paper is yellowed and curls at the edges around a young Jack. He's wearing a Wildcat jersey and hat. The headline reads: Number 1 Draft Pick, Jack Wyld, Signs with Wildcats.

I smile at the angsty teen version of Jack staring back at me. I mean honestly, he hasn't changed that much. His baby face is now chiseled and currently covered by a lot of unruly facial hair, but he has those same intense eyes and serious expression.

Movement catches my eye and I turn as Jack steps into the kitchen. He walks toward me, opening the freezer and grabbing a bag of frozen peas.

"Are you okay?" I glance at his knee indicating I mean physically. I know better than to touch on his emotional state. I wouldn't be okay either.

"It hurts."

My brows rise in shock. "Wow. I can't believe you just admitted that."

He glares but there's no real malice behind it.

"So…"

"Thank you for today. I'm sorry I was an asshole. My dad…" He trails off and that muscle in his cheek jumps again. "Thank you, Ev."

"You're welcome."

We stare at each other. The strain on his face reminds me that he's in pain.

"You should probably elevate your knee."

"Yeah." He lifts the peas.

"Is there a shower in this giant house?" I ask. I smell like chlorine and sunscreen and am still in my suit underneath the dress.

His gaze travels over me from head to feet and back again slowly. "Yeah. Upstairs. Second door on the left."

Still neither of us moves. I have so many questions that I don't know where to start. It strikes me that I've known Jack for four years, have spent a lot of time with or around him, and yet I don't really know him. I wonder if anyone does.

CHAPTER EIGHT

Jack

GIRL TALK

I settle into a chair in the living room. Dad's gentle snores have increased to a rumble that nearly drowns out the television. Not that I'm really paying attention.

My attention is tuned to the sounds upstairs: the water running, the soft footsteps, the opening of a door. I hate that she's here. Hate that she saw my dad like this. I'm not embarrassed of him, but it's just not something I share. I remember that well enough from being a kid. When your dad is the town drunk, people give you these pitying looks and everything you do is measured against him.

Right after I was drafted to the league, I ran into a teacher from middle school and she couldn't stop telling me how proud she was of me, how great it was that I had made something of myself despite my circumstances.

My circumstances never held me back. If anything, they were the fuel pushing me to be anyone but him.

I'm deep in my thoughts and still craning my head to listen for any movement upstairs when Dad's hoarse voice says, "Jackson."

His blue irises are dimmed by his glassy and bloodshot eyes. He's taking stock of the situation: lying on the couch, me sitting with him, the clean room. Hell, maybe he doesn't even remember that he made a mess of the place before he headed to Perry's.

"Dad," I say keeping all emotion out of my tone. Once upon a time, I might have been sad or angry but now I'm just resigned that this is who he is. No matter what I say or do, no matter how much money I make or success I have, he's a variable I can't control. If he were anyone else, I would have cut him from my life.

"I'm guessing by the look of disgust on your face that this visit isn't a happy one."

Christ, he doesn't even remember us picking him up from the bar. I shouldn't be surprised. Just another Saturday afternoon bender.

"Coach called. You were giving his new bartender a hard time after he cut you off."

A spark of recollection flashes in his face, some of his color returning, and the light in his eyes returns too. As he processes through the memory, his expression turns remorseful. "I met up with some of the guys to watch the game. You know Bruce is always buying rounds for everyone. I might have gone a little too hard."

Yeah, let's blame Bruce and not the entire case of beer that he likely drank before he left the house. I hold in the thoughts. His friends are drunks, just like him. Though they all somehow manage to get home without passing out or driving under the influence. Wishing he could be a more responsible drunk is among the many wishes I've cast over the years.

Dad sits up with a groan. He looks like shit. He needs a shave and a haircut, definitely a shower.

"I'm sorry Coach called you. He shouldn't have done that. I know how busy you are. You don't have time to be driving up and taking care of me. Let me make you a cup of coffee for your trouble." He stands, wobbling on his feet.

I get to my feet instinctively and move toward him, catching him when he sways. My knee protests with a twinge of pain that makes stars dance before my eyes.

"Oops. I think my leg is still asleep. I better sit down again for a minute, then I'll get the coffee."

I situate him and adjust his weight so my left leg isn't taking the bulk of the pressure. "I don't need any goddamn coffee, Dad."

The outburst silences him and then I curse myself. Yelling at him in this condition isn't going to help anything. If it would, then he would have been cured twenty years ago. And it never makes me feel better anyway.

Softening my tone, I say, "You should rest."

"I'll do that after you leave. I haven't seen you in too long." His eyelashes flutter closed. "I missed my boy."

"I'm not going anywhere. We can talk later."

"All right." Eyes opening, he reaches over and pats me on the shoulder. "Maybe just a little rest. I have steaks in the freezer. Will you stay for dinner?"

"Yeah, of course."

I convince him to go to bed instead of sleeping on the couch. He's a little steadier on his feet, but it takes some effort for me to get him to the master bedroom. I give silent thanks, once again, that it's on the lower level. It wasn't a selling point I considered when I bought the house for him, but there's no way I could get him upstairs right now.

On the walls are pictures of me growing up. I doubt he remembers much of my childhood, but he has the photos up like a proud parent anyway.

Once I've put him to bed, I close his bedroom door and then lean against it. Letting out a long breath, I grimace through the ache of my knee. Dammit. The last thing I need is to tweak it less than two weeks into recovery.

Movement catches the corner of my eye. In all the commotion with my dad, I'd stopped listening to her moving around upstairs, but here Ev stands, freshly showered and in one of my old hockey T-shirts.

Something stirs inside my chest at the way the fabric hangs off her shoulder and grazes her upper thigh. Her long, wet hair has soaked the right side of her shirt, and like the asshole I am, I notice that she's not wearing a bra.

"Enjoy rifling through my clothes?" I ask with bite in my tone. It has nothing to do with her taking my shirt and everything to do with my reaction to this whole fucking day. I don't know what I would have done if she hadn't been here. I'm glad and I'm mad and it's confusing.

"My dress smells like sunscreen and stale beer, but if you would prefer to see me in my bikini then all you have to do is ask. Should I go change into it? Maybe lather myself in suntan oil for you too?" The challenge in her voice makes me smile. Only on the inside, of course. I'm not sure what would be worse at this point: her strutting around in a bikini or what she's wearing now. I'm starting to think it doesn't matter what she has on. Everly is gorgeous and I can't deny my attraction to her.

Acting on it is a whole different story.

I clear my throat before answering her question. "I don't care what you wear."

The tension between us teeters precociously. Her hazel eyes narrow in on me but if she can tell that I'm full of shit, she doesn't say.

"How's your knee? Did the peas help?"

"Fine." I take a step to prove it to her.

"Liar." She smiles like she's happy to have caught me exaggerating the truth, but then sympathy splashes across her features. "What can I do?"

"I'll be fine. I've just been on my feet more than I should."

"Okay." She straightens. "You sit. I am going to find us something to eat. I'm starving."

"Order whatever you want. It's on me."

"Does this town do delivery?"

Fuck. No, of course not. Nothing good anyway. "There's a pizza place that does for sure."

"I don't mind cooking." She takes off toward the kitchen.

I follow behind her instead of going to the living room.

"Sit," she commands when she sees that I've trailed after her.

I take a seat at the oval table just outside of the kitchen. Unopened mail and vitamin bottles sit in the center, as well as a worn paperback.

Before I'm fully situated, Everly is already approaching me with a fresh bag of frozen vegetables.

"Thanks," I mutter quietly.

She laughs. "Why does it always sound like it pains you so much when you say thank you. Did your parents not teach you any manners?"

"As you can see, the parental lessons I got were a little less constructive."

Her sassy smile slips. Shit. I didn't mean to make her feel bad. I know she was joking and I turned it into a personal attack. Having her here has me all out of whack. My dad is not someone I introduce to people. They either pity me, which sucks, or they want to help somehow and there's nothing anyone can do. Trust me. I've tried it all.

"I think there are steaks in the freezer."

With a nod, she moves back to the fridge. She finds them and sets the package on the island.

"Those are going to take awhile to thaw out."

Fuck, can nothing go right today?

"You know what, I got this." She whirls around, opening cabinets and drawers to find whatever she needs.

"Pizza is still an option," I say.

"This will be better."

I'm intrigued but I don't ask. Instead, I pick up the envelopes on the table. I started paying Dad's bills years ago so there aren't any surprises here, mostly junk.

The book is dog-eared about fifty pages in. When I was a kid, Dad was a big reader. He always carried a paperback with him: to my games, to doctor appointments, anywhere he might have a moment to sit and read. It's been years since I thought about that. Though to be fair, it's been years since I've seen him with a book lying around.

"Do you like to read?" Everly asks.

I set the book down. "No, not really. You?"

"I'm obsessed with thrillers." Her face lights up. She has a big block of cheese in one hand and grates it into a bowl. It's a shock to see either of those gadgets being used in Dad's kitchen. Grilled steaks or burgers and takeout make up ninety-five percent of the meals that grace this kitchen.

"I'm reading this one right now about a woman who is a nanny for this really rich family. The wife is crazy and the husband totally has the hots for her. I think it's going to be one of those snapped situations where the wife goes all scorned woman and kills everyone."

I snort a laugh at the premise.

"Don't laugh. With all the women you've left heartbroken, you could be one scorned woman away from a thriller plotline."

She's talking about my demise, but all it reminds me is that I haven't fucked anyone in a while.

"Relax, I was kidding."

When I clear the thoughts of sex (mostly) from my brain, I look over at her. Everly has one dark brow lifted and a smirk on her face.

"What are you making over there?" I ask, changing the subject for the sake of my sanity, and stand.

My knee is already feeling better, but I sit at the island on one of the stools and prop my leg up on the empty one beside it.

She waits until I'm situated before answering. "Macaroni and cheese."

A laugh slips from my lips. "Seriously."

"Don't knock it until you've tried it."

"I haven't had mac and cheese in years."

"I have it at least once a week."

"Of course you do."

"Is that a knock on my age or my eating habits?" she asks, going back to grating the cheese. The movement makes her boobs jiggle, and I am going to hell for noticing.

"Both. Let me do that." I motion for the grater. "I'm just sitting here. I can be useful."

Reluctantly, she hands me the block of cheese and grater and then pushes the bowl toward me. After she's found a pot, filled it with water and set it on the stove to boil, she comes back to stand on the other side of the island from me.

"What about you? Break any hearts lately?" I ask when my mind keeps circling sex. As far as I know she isn't dating anyone, but it isn't like she typically shares that kind of stuff with me.

She snorts with an eye roll. "Are we going to make girl talk now?"

I grit my teeth, but I'm distracted from the job at hand and grate my finger on the last hunk of cheese.

"Fuck." I pull back and instinctively place my pointer finger in my mouth to relieve the sting.

The tangy metallic taste of blood hits my tongue.

Everly laughs. Not loudly, but clearly she's amused by my pain.

"I think that's enough cheese," she says. She takes the bowl and weapon away from me.

When she returns to stand across from me, she pulls herself up and sits on the counter, feet dangling off the side and my T-shirt riding high on her thighs.

"I had big plans for a summer fling before I went off to my internship in August, but that is not working out very well so far."

"Why not?" I ask, unable to help myself. I know guys have to be throwing themselves at her.

"You say that like there's a plethora of attractive, fun, single guys out there."

"Isn't there?"

"How many of your friends are single?"

Huh. I would have said most of them, but that's not true anymore. Leo, Declan, Ash, Ty, Maverick...nearly all my closest teammates have settled down.

"Galaxy," I say, then add, "Mikey." Our goalie.

"Two guys and both hockey players."

"What's wrong with hockey players?"

Amusement dances over her features. "Nothing. It's just that you all still treat me like Ty's annoying little sister."

"That's because you are."

She reaches over and grabs a handful of my hair, then tugs it.

"What the hell?" I ask, then laugh before I can think better of it. "And you wonder why we treat you like an annoying little sister."

"Wow, was that a laugh? I didn't know you were capable of that noise," she taunts, then says. "You should do it more often. It sounds nice."

I'm still stuck on those words when she adds, "That reminds me I need to cancel my date tonight."

Everly hops off the counter. When she does, the shirt rides up and she flashes the red bikini bottoms. Thank fuck she's not going commando. Although just that small peek of her ass has me needing a cold shower.

She grins as she taps away on her phone. Everly walks back toward me, but instead of sitting on the island like before, she leans forward on her elbows. The pose makes her blonde hair fall over her shoulders and puts her face closer to mine. She has a sprinkling of light freckles across the bridge of her nose and her cheeks are a slight pink from the sun.

"Who is he?" I ask.

She doesn't look at me as she responds, "Just some guy."

Plucking the phone out of her grasp, I bring it closer to look at their back and forth.

"Give that back," she protests.

"His name is Will?" I ask. That is the least of my concerns though as I read through a few of their messages.

She comes around to take her phone back. I hold her at bay with my injured arm. Look at that, the cast is finally good for something.

Their messages aren't all that exciting. The dude is eager to meet up with her and disappointed she's canceled tonight. Everly is playing it more casual, but her texts indicate she was looking forward to it too.

"Jack!" She lifts up on her toes and reaches over me. The position puts her boobs right in my face and I'm distracted long enough that she's able to snatch her phone back.

"Rude." She marches back around with her phone.

"Where'd you and Will meet?"

"Online."

"Seriously?"

"Uhh…yeah."

"Let me see his profile."

"No."

"Come on."

"You're just going to make fun of him."

"Only if there's something to make fun of." I'm definitely going to make fun of him.

She doesn't look like she's going to budge.

"Fine. Tell me something about him then. What's *Will* like?"

"Stop saying his name like that." Mild amusement laces her tone as she moves to the stove and puts the noodles in the boiling water to cook.

When she's done, she leans against the counter next to the stove and crosses her arms over her stomach.

I'm silent, waiting for her to tell me about her date. Is this really what my life has come to? I'm at my dad's house asking my teammate's little sister about her love life, which is sadly more interesting than my own.

"I just swiped right on him two days ago, so I don't know much. I was going to get to know him more on our date tonight."

A date that isn't happening because of me. I should probably feel bad, but I don't.

"That guy was not looking to get to know you. At least not in the way you mean."

Her face lights up with mischief. "Bold of you to assume I didn't want to get to know him the same way."

I can't tell if she's kidding. Warmth spreads in my gut as I stare at her smug expression. She knows she's shocked me and she likes it.

"Still time to drive back and meet up with him."

Her mask slips ever so slightly. She might want to play it off like I'm keeping her here, but I'm not. She chose to stay here tonight, and she wouldn't have if she really wanted to be fucking Will.

Not that any of that gives me the right to be an asshole. I can't seem to stop myself lately. And Everly doesn't deserve that. This is why I've spent all summer alone. No one should be subjected to me in this state.

Standing, I'm glad that my knee seems to be feeling better so I can walk away from this conversation and leave her in peace.

"You can have the guest room upstairs. Second door on the right. Across from mine," I add since she seems to have found that one just fine.

"You don't want dinner?"

"I'm not hungry."

CHAPTER NINE

Everly

FORTRESS OF SADNESS

I sleep like shit. It's not the weird house, but the fact that Jack is sleeping across the hall. What a strange day yesterday was.

At a little after five, I give up and decide I might as well do something. After pulling on a pair of sweatpants I found in Jack's room last night, I quietly open the door. His bedroom door is closed, so I tiptoe down the stairs. The TV is on and there's a blanket and pillow like someone slept on the couch, but no one is in sight.

I come up short in the kitchen. The man in front of me looks more like Jack than I realized yesterday. With his eyes clear and coloring back in his face, it's like looking at Jack in thirty years.

"Hi," I say when he looks up from over his coffee mug. There's no recollection in his expression, which tells me he probably doesn't remember much of yesterday. "I'm Everly. A friend of Jack's."

"Well, this is a treat. I can't remember the last time Jackson brought a girl home." He slowly lowers the mug.

Jackson? That's fun. I file that information away for later.

"We're just friends," I clarify. "My brother is one of his teammates." And because I can't seem to stop justifying why I'm here, I add, "Jack was letting me use the pool at his house yesterday and asked me to give him a ride."

"Friendly, accommodating…are you sure you're talking about my Jackson?" A tiny quirk of a smile lifts one side of his mouth.

I didn't even realize how tense I was around him until a laugh bubbles up in my chest. Moving farther into the kitchen with him, I nod. "He has his moments."

"That he does." He lifts his mug again. "You want some coffee?"

"Yeah. That'd be great."

He starts to stand, wobbling a bit as he does. I wave him off. "I can get it."

I cross over to the coffee pot as he settles back in his chair.

"Mugs are in the cabinet to the right. Half and half is in the door of the fridge and sugar is on the table."

Finding it, I pull down a Wildcat Hockey mug that looks well-loved with a chipped handle and a scratch over the logo. Once I have my drink, I take it to the table and sit across from him.

I'm staring, unabashedly. His expression is softer than his son's, friendlier but also warmer.

"It's a little unnerving how much you two look alike," I say.

"Don't let him hear you say that. He's spent a lot of his life doing everything he can to not be like his old man."

Before I can question him about that, though I have no idea what I'd even ask, he lobs one at me. "What do you do, Everly?"

"I just graduated college, so nothing yet."

"Congratulations. That's impressive."

It kind of is. Weird how I hadn't really thought about it until now. Maybe because everyone was so relieved that I even went to college, I forgot how big of a deal it is that I did it.

"Thank you. I have an internship at the end of the summer, but for now I'm house-sitting and annoying your son into letting me use his pool."

His body shakes with laughter, but the noise is too quiet to hear. "Something tells me he doesn't really mind that much."

I am not so sure about that, but I just smile and drink my hot coffee.

I've nearly forgotten about all the events that led us here when Jack senior reaches for a bottle on the table I hadn't noticed. He uncaps it and trickles some of the dark liquor into the mug.

When he notices me staring, he offers it to me. "Want some?"

I shake my head. "No thanks."

We drink in silence. I have no clue what to say now and he seems to sense my hesitation. Jack's dad is a drunk. It explains some things and confuses others. More than anything though, I feel a deep sense of empathy for both of them.

Nobody wants to drink hard liquor before sunrise and nobody wants to be the person responsible for them either. I wonder about Jack's mom, but don't ask. Maybe I can find out from Tyler or Ash. Though something tells me they won't know any more than I do.

Out the window I can see the sun is starting to rise. Jack senior picks up the worn paperback on the table.

"Do you like to read?" he asks.

"I do." Nodding, I tell him about my love of thrillers, and he surprises me by having read a few of my favorites.

"Ever read this one?" He turns his book around for me to see.

"No. I'm not big on books set in the legal world. It goes over my head."

"Not this one," he promises. He sets his copy of *The Pelican Brief* down in front of me. "Take it. I've read it a dozen times at least."

"No, I couldn't." It looks well-loved by the faded cover and bent edges.

"I insist."

"Thanks." I run a hand over the cover, more touched by the gesture than some of the nice gifts I've received in my life.

"Time to go." Jack's voice startles me. The air in the room is sucked out by his broody presence. He looks even grumpier than he had last night.

"Morning," I say cheerily, not moving.

"No need to hurry off. I could make some breakfast," his dad says.

"Everly needs to get back for work and I have physical therapy."

I doubt any of the guys would mind if I didn't check on their house one day under these circumstances, but I get to my feet and take one last long sip of the coffee, hoping it will fuel me for the drive back with Mister Grumpy Pants, then pour the rest into the sink and drop the mug into the dishwasher.

"Thank you for coming," Jack senior says. "It was good to see you, Son."

I sneak a peek at Jack. He nods slightly, jaw still clenched.

"Thanks for the book. I'm going to send you one of my favorites when I get back." I pick it up and smile at the older man. "It was nice to meet you."

"The pleasure was all mine." He tips his head.

I leave the kitchen to give them time to say goodbye. By the time I've grabbed all my things, Jack is waiting for me by the front door.

We walk out to his G-Wagon in silence. He's limping less this morning so that's good. Not that it seems to have helped his temperament any.

He plugs his phone in and pulls up directions without my asking and then stares out the window as I drive back.

I'm tired and about to ask if we can pull over for coffee when his phone rings over the speakers. I glance at the screen out of habit, then smile when I see James' name.

Jack's agent is a fun time. Basically the opposite of Jack in all ways, but I've seen him in business mode and he protects Jack like, well, it's his job.

Jack sighs as he reaches over and hits the screen to accept the call.

"Hey," he says by way of greeting.

"Oh good. You answered this time."

I snort quietly and steal a glance at the man sitting in the passenger seat.

"I was dealing with my dad."

"Oh." James' tone changes. "Everything okay?"

"Yeah. I'm headed home now. What's up?"

"You aren't driving, are you?"

"No." Jack looks over at me. "Everly drove me."

"Hi, James!" I chirp.

"Hey," he replies brightly. "How are you?"

"I'm good."

He slips back into business mode. "Jack, the director of the children's hospital called again this morning. I cancelled everything else through June, but I wasn't sure what you wanted to do about that one. They have you on the schedule but weren't sure if they should expect you."

"When is it?"

"Today. They're expecting you in two hours."

Jack is quiet like he's mulling it over, and James adds, "If you want me to send over some signed jerseys and let them know you're still on the mend and we'll reschedule at a later date, just say the word."

"Fuck," he mutters so quietly that I doubt James hears him. Jack rubs two fingers back and forth across his forehead. His mouth opens, lips curling and jaw moving side to side before he answers. "Yeah. Tell her I'm sorry and –"

"He'll be there," I blurt out.

Both men go quiet, then Jack says, "One sec, James."

He hits the mute button and lifts one brow.

"I'm sorry, but children in the hospital do not want a signed jersey. They want *you*."

"I can't even drive."

"I'll take you."

"Ev." His head tilts to the side and his expression is pained. I don't know if it's because he doesn't want to go or if he doesn't want me to go with him.

"Listen. I know that you are going through a lot right now, but friend to friend, I think getting out could be good for you."

"We're friends now?" He cocks a brow.

"Depends on the day," I say teasing him.

He still doesn't look convinced, so I say as nicely as possible, "Your house is a fortress of sadness. You can't keep hiding away. And kids are fun and genuine, and they don't care that you're not in peak form."

He smiles again, small at first, but it grows and the full weight of it aimed at me lights me up inside.

Jack hits the button on the screen. "I'll be there."

There's a beat of silence then James says, "Great. I'll let her know."

"That's all I'm committing to for the summer," Jack says. "No other events."

"Got it. If you're only doing one, this is the one I would suggest too."

Jack makes a noise that might be his agreement or maybe him already regretting letting me talk him into it.

I shift in my seat. If I got him into this, then the least I can do is make sure it'll be as easy as possible for him. "Make sure they know that he'll need to sit because of his knee and that he might need to cut the visit short if it's too much too soon." I watch Jack's expression carefully as I speak.

"Yeah, of course," James says. "Anything else?"

Jack stares back at me in a way that makes my stomach dip.

Smiling, I say, "I'd tell you to warn them of his attitude, but that isn't a new quirk so I'm sure they're aware."

James' laugh plays over the speakers and Jack rolls his eyes.

"That's all," Jack says. "Thanks, James."

He hangs up and the SUV falls silent.

"Soo…" I say to break the ice. "Want some coffee first?"

CHAPTER TEN

Everly

PERFECTLY AGREEABLE

I feel a little awkward as I walk beside Jack down the wing of the pediatric unit at the hospital. I know a couple of the nurses through Bridget, but Jack is walking at a clip, even with his bad leg, and I have to hustle to keep up with him.

"You don't have to come with me," he says as we follow behind Gina, the woman leading us to the conference room at the end of the hallway where she promised lots of children are eagerly waiting to meet him.

"Hospitals scare me," I say, sticking close. "I saw one too many *Grey's Anatomy* episodes as a kid."

His lips quirk with amusement. "I didn't think you were scared of anything."

Despite my reservations, once Jack steps into the room of kids, *a lot of them*, all of which are *very* excited to see him, I go a little soft inside.

One little girl runs over and tackles him around the legs, then stares up at him in wonder. She barely comes to his knees and has to tilt her head way back to look at his face.

She looks at him the same way most grown women do, but it's way cuter when she does it.

I watch Jack for any signs of discomfort, but thankfully the girl is latched on to his right side and he doesn't seem distressed at all. In fact, he looks…sweet.

Well, as sweet as Jack ever looks. But his jaw is unclenched and the glare he often sends my way is nowhere in sight.

"I'm so sorry." A woman, maybe the girl's mom, walks over and encourages the little one to step away. And, yep, there's that same look her daughter had.

Gina motions to a chair that they've placed in one corner of the room. Jack starts for it, and I step to Gina. "Can he also get a second chair to prop up his leg and maybe an ice pack."

She looks apologetic, like she should have foreseen all these things. "Absolutely. Give me two minutes."

"It's okay," Jack says as he gets situated in the chair. "That's not necessary."

Gina looks between us with an uncertain expression.

I start to protest, but then the man smiles. It makes my stomach flip. I know this was my idea, but I'm a little surprised it's working so well. He's a completely different guy than he was two hours ago.

"I'll be fine like this for an hour," Jack says.

"You're sure?" Gina asks. I have no doubt that she'd grab him ten chairs and a hundred ice packs if that's what he requested.

"Yeah." Jack nods and she hurries off, calling for the children's attention.

While she introduces Jack, he looks at me.

He tips his head to a free chair. "Take a load off, Ev. You look stressed."

"That's because *you* stress me out."

"I'm perfectly agreeable right now."

"Yeah, exactly. It's scaring me more than being in this hospital."

Then he laughs. Truly terrifying.

From my chair in the corner, I watch for the next hour as a dozen kids and some parents wait for their turn with Jack. He's gracious and personable. He signs jerseys and sticks and tons of other sports memorabilia items. All with an appreciative smile and a friendliness that makes the kids' faces light up.

He has a certain presence about him. He's a big guy, which I'm sure the kids find incredible on its own. But then he also has this celebrity look about him. It's a quiet confidence on top of his handsome face that's borderline too perfect. Even with the unkept beard and too long hair. He has a look that can't be completely dimmed no matter how he dresses or takes care of himself.

When the last kid is ushered out of the room, Gina reappears by his side.

"Thank you," she says with a sincerity in her tone that I know isn't fake. "I can't tell you how much it means to them when you stop by. It's always the highlight around here. You're good to us and we appreciate it more than I can say."

I'm not surprised to hear that Jack comes here often and that he's always the highlight, but I guess it's a good reminder that beneath his tough, broody exterior he's a really good guy. Sometimes I forget that amidst all our bickering.

"Happy to do it." Still smiling, he gets to his feet. Jack stands taller, like the weight of the world is no longer weighing down his shoulders. And he's still not glaring anywhere. Not even at me.

I'm officially weirded out.

"I'll be in touch to lock you down for another visit," Gina says with a final goodbye.

Jack and I start our trek back to the car.

"How's your knee?" I ask.

"A little stiff."

I spot a wheelchair against the wall. "Want a ride?"

"I don't think one is big enough." He smirks.

He's right. It's definitely made for someone smaller than him, which is basically ninety-nine percent of the population.

I step closer to him. "Wrap an arm around my shoulders and let me have some of your weight."

"No."

"Why not?"

"I'm fine. I can walk by myself."

With a huge eye roll, I move to him. "You can but you don't have to, *Jackson*."

He definitely glares at me and I fight a smile.

I wrap one arm around his waist and nuzzle carefully against his side. He has little choice but to drape his cast along my shoulders. Though it doesn't feel like he's letting me take much of his weight.

He grumbles and that uneasiness I was feeling from his happy attitude dissipates. It's good to be back on normal footing with him.

Once we settle into place with me helping him, a new kind of awareness hits me. The smell of him, burnt oranges and cinnamon and something else – something rich and lush, is like a drug. So are the hard ridges of muscle in his back and stomach. I'm not sure we've ever been this close, and I wish I could say that I am completely unaffected.

"Anywhere else you need to go?" I ask.

"Nope." He removes his arm as we approach his vehicle. "You can drop me off and then you'll be finally free of me."

Something about that isn't as freeing or as comforting as I imagined.

We ride in silence back to his house. I come to a stop behind my car and run my hand along the steering wheel, enjoying the soft, warm leather. I love my car, but I'm going to miss driving this one.

"Thank you," he says softly as I shut off the engine.

"You're welcome."

We sit in the quiet car, neither of us moving.

"I'm sorry I've been such a dick to you. The accident and my dad…" He trails off, some of that moodiness returning as he runs a hand through his hair. "I'm sorry."

"It's fine."

"No, it's not fine." His voice takes a hard edge. "People shouldn't treat you like shit. Least of all me."

I have no idea what to say to that. He's right, though. It's not fine. But I've given Jack plenty of reasons over the years to be a jerk and I know he's going through a lot. And it's not like I haven't given it right back to him.

"Okay, well, how about a clean slate then?"

He snorts a quiet laugh. "Seriously?"

"I can admit that I have enjoyed riling you up a time or two."

"A time or *two*?"

"Fine. It's basically a hobby at this point."

The smile Jack aims at me makes warmth spread through my chest.

"I should go," I say finally.

"Should I expect to find you in my backyard later?"

"I don't know. Is that an invitation?"

"Since when do you need an invitation?" He cocks a brow and a little of that bear I like to poke resurfaces.

Despite leaving things on good-ish terms, I don't see Jack for several days. When I do my daily check-ins at his teammates' houses, I look down the street for signs of life. Unknown vehicles, lights on, but I don't see or hear him.

On Wednesday afternoon we hit a rare ninety degrees and I finally cave.

I knock on the door instead of bulldozing in the front door (or over the fence). I don't really expect him to answer, but when he does, all thoughts fly right out the window.

Gone is the wild beard. The cast too. There's no sign of the cane either. Or maybe his shirtless appearance just won't let me see it because goddamn is the man a sight to behold in all his bulging bicep and ripped ab glory.

"Ev?" Jack's voice breaks me out of my haze.

Wow, is that drool there on the corner of my mouth?

"Hi!" My cheery tone is borderline screechy. "You got the cast off."

"Yeah." He holds out his left arm and twists it while he stares down at it. The movement makes the muscles in his bicep and forearm pop.

"And Barnaby is gone?"

"Who?"

"I named your beard," I admit with a sheepish smile.

"Right." He runs a hand along his smooth jaw all seductively. Okay, maybe not intentionally but goddamn.

Jack stands there like he's waiting for me to say more. When I don't, he asks, "Here for the pool?"

"It's a gorgeous day." I finally snap out of it. Not looking at his bare chest helps. Except, were his eyes always that blue?

He steps back to let me inside.

"How's physical therapy coming? Scare off any more nurses?"

Jack aims a playful glare at me that makes things feel more normal. "Not today."

"Well, it's only noon."

He lets out a short huff and follows me through the house to the kitchen. Then surprises me when he comes to the backyard.

I'm shooting him a confused look when he motions with his head toward the right side of the patio where he has a whole workout setup. Yoga mat, bands, a medicine ball. And a young guy in black athletic shorts and a red shirt, biceps popping but somehow not quite as nice as Jack's.

"I was just getting ready to work out," he says as if I weren't able to piece that together myself.

"Oh." Well, now I feel ridiculous.

He must read it on me because Jack says, "The pool is all yours."

"It's okay. I can leave. I didn't realize you had people over."

"Hey, I'm Brian." He walks over and extends a hand.

"Everly."

He looks about my age, maybe a smidge older. He has blond hair and one of those big smiles that guys with too much confidence like to flash in dimly lit bars just before closing. "You must be Jack's girlfriend."

"No," I say quickly. So quickly that Jack lets out a small snort.

"I'm just a friend," I clarify.

"Oh." He keeps that megawatt smile aimed at me as his gaze drops to my bare legs then back up to my face. I'm not sure I've ever been so blatantly ogled before. At least not in the light of day.

"We should get started," Jack says gruffly, giving me his back. I guess our truce is over. Big, grumpy bear.

"Nice to meet you, Brian."

"You, too." His smile slides into a more professional expression.

Rock music plays over the outdoor speakers as I walk over to the same lounge chair I claim each visit. I bet Jack would hate it that I have been here enough times to have one that is "mine."

By the time I've spread out my towel and begun to dig in my bag for sunscreen, Jack and Brian have begun working out.

I try not to watch. Try and fail. There's a lot of lunging and grunting and muscles popping. Look, I know that my brother's teammates are all in great shape, but most of the time when they're working out, they're covered in lots of padding and clothing. It's a whole other experience seeing Jack shirtless with sweat glistening on his hard, toned body.

It almost makes me wish he still had that unruly beard. Anything to take away from how fucking good he looks.

I distract myself by pulling out my phone. Someone in Human Resources at the design firm sent over an email with employment forms and a ton of information. I read over it, stomach swirling with that anxious feeling I can't seem to shake any time I think about the next step in my life.

I was always the kid who couldn't wait to be an adult and out in the world on my own, and now...now I kind of wish I still had a couple more years to figure things out.

I love interior design. Art is the one thing I always seemed to be good at. What started as drawing and painting turned into restoring old furniture and picking out the perfect combination of pieces to make a room functional and beautiful. I still like to draw and paint too, but I never aspired to do those things for a living.

Actually, if I'm completely honest, I never really wanted to be an interior designer either. I sort of fell into it while taking art classes. At some point, I was forced to pick a major and I couldn't think of anything else I'd rather do. That's still true.

When my nerves can't take it anymore, I close out of my email and open up my messages. And yes, I do steal another glance at Jack. His usual frown is in place. Except now it's more of a determined scowl. My body tingles. Jesus, I really need to have sex. I cannot be fantasizing about Jack. We're more likely to kill each other than fuck.

Oh god. Just the word has me feeling feral. What the hell is wrong with me?

ME

Help!

In true Bridget form, she calls five seconds later.

"Hello," I answer, smiling already.

"How many times do I have to tell you, I am not helping you hide a body," she says with a firm tone, then laughs. "Kidding. Tell me where to go and what to bring. Shovel? Duct tape?"

"Umm…condoms?"

"Ooh. I see. So it's a serious cry for help." Her soft laughter returns.

"Beyond serious. I'm having strange reactions to men I would never consider otherwise."

"You mean Will? I thought you said he seemed nice."

"No." I shake my head. "We haven't met up yet. *Other* people."

"It sounds like that's the answer to your problem then. You need a real date."

"Yeah," I say, but not loving the idea. "Maybe."

"Wait. Who are you having strange reactions to? Anyone I know?"

I bite my lip as I glance at Jack again. His dark hair hangs down over his forehead and into his eyes. It's longer than I've ever seen it and my fingers itch to push it back out of his face.

"No," I lie. "This morning I hit a pothole and the car bumping along had me squeezing my thighs together."

Ash's laughter joins with Bridget's.

"Sorry," she says when she can control herself. "I had you on speaker. I'm taking you off. One sec."

"It's fine. Hi, Ash."

"Hey, Little Sharpie."

"Any words of advice? You used to date around. Ever hit a dry spell?"

"It was all a dry spell before Bridget," he says.

I can practically see her rolling her eyes, but Ash is so gone for her, I don't even question if he's being serious. The moment he laid eyes on her, that was it.

"Hang in there, Ev," he says. "You'll find someone great."

"I don't want someone great. I want great sex." I've always been able to separate sex from relationships, and I prided myself on being independent and not needing to be part of a couple to be happy. I believe that big, all-consuming love is out there. I mean, of course, I do. So many of my friends are madly in love, there's no way I could deny it's possible. But I haven't sought it out. Everyone always says college is for having fun and finding yourself, and I took those words to heart. I always assumed I'd find love about the same time I started contributing to retirement.

Ash's deep chuckle continues. "I'm afraid I can't help you there. Though I am great at it. Has Bridget told you? She has, right?" He goes quiet and then asks her, "You tell your friends how great I am at making you come, right?"

I stifle a laugh as they playfully banter about what she does and doesn't tell her friends, then I can hear them kissing before Bridget says, "Okay. I'm going into the other room. Let's talk this out."

There are so many things I love about Bridget, but her sincerity and the seriousness in which she takes my cry for help makes me adore her that much more.

For the next few minutes, she lays out options like the world depends on my getting laid. She has some good suggestions, most obviously finally going out with Will or more practically, spending the rest of the day in bed with my vibrator.

But while she troubleshoots the problem, I'm only half-paying attention. Because the guy across the yard—the one I definitely should not be ogling—has other ideas in my head. Ones that are absolutely out of the question. Outlandish fantasies. Completely impractical.

But goddamn I watch anyway.

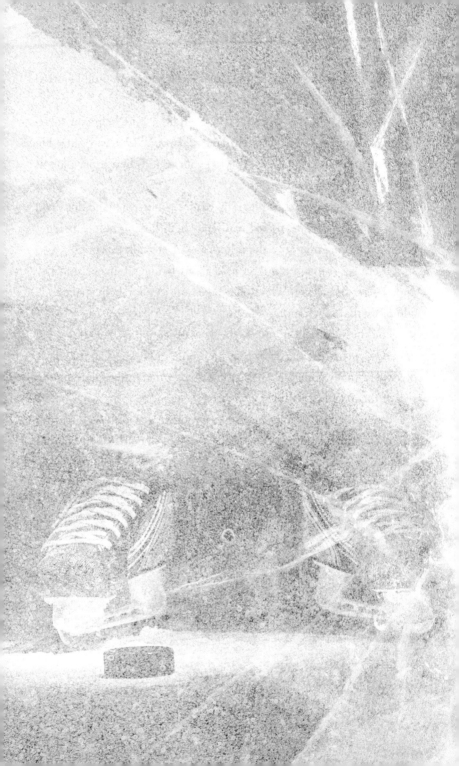

CHAPTER ELEVEN

Jack

SHE'S NOT HOT

"**S**he's hot," Brian says as we're finishing up our workout.

"Who?" I ask like I don't know. Like he hasn't been checking her out at every opportunity. I know because I was trying very hard not to do the same.

I don't like him looking at her and I especially don't like him calling her hot. She's not hot, she's…Everly.

Brian motions with his head toward where the girl in question is stepping out of the pool. Today's bikini is white and cuts up high on her hip bones. She's adjusting the sides, inching them up higher and exposing a tan line that makes me imagine where else she has them.

Not that I care. Because she's Everly. Off-limits for so many reasons. Not that my dick seems to have gotten the memo.

"Is she single?" Brian must be oblivious to the anger radiating off me. If he could read my thoughts, he'd know I'm imagining about a dozen different ways to dismember him. I'm not usually prone to violence off the ice, but my heart is pumping as my fingers curl into fists like I'm preparing to go at it with a member of the opposing team. It's Brian. He's the other team. I don't want him or anyone else near her and I'm ready to throw down. It's a startling realization that has me inhaling and forcing myself to chill the fuck out.

"As far as I know." I make it a point not to look at her, but Brian has no such self-control.

"How do you know her?"

"Are we done here?" I ask him. My tone borders on rude but considering he's checking out a girl while on the job, I don't feel too bad.

"Yeah, yeah." He manages to tear his gaze away from Everly and regain some of his professionalism. "Great workout, man. Same time tomorrow?"

I'd like to tell him to fuck right off, but he came highly recommended by the team doctor. He's young, but already making a name for himself with other professional athletes. So, I ignore my better instincts and say, "See you then."

While Brian packs up his bands and other miscellaneous workout gear, I head inside. I need a shower but settle for a clean shirt until I'm alone. Jerking off while I have company feels inhospitable and that's exactly what I plan to do. Me and some soapy water. It's sadly becoming a routine.

After I grab a Gatorade from the fridge, I head back out. Brian has moved from the patio where we were working out to a lounge chair next to Everly.

Annoyance prickles down my spine. He leans forward, talking and laughing. And she smiles back like she's just as thrilled.

As I approach them, Everly shifts her attention from Brian to me.

Her smile falters and then she inches back slowly.

"What's going on?" I ask.

"I was just telling Everly about a new restaurant that opened. It has a great patio and the best sushi in the city." He turns to her. "We should go sometime. I'd love to take you. Here, let me give you my number."

Before she can agree or object, I cut in. "I think it's time for you to go, Brian."

"Oh." He pulls his phone back and glances from me to Ev and then back. "Yeah, sure."

He stands and pockets his phone.

"Maybe I'll see you tomorrow," he says to her.

"I'm not paying you to ask out my house guests."

A flush creeps into his cheeks. "Of course not. Sorry, Jack."

He murmurs a *nice to meet you* and *goodbye* to Everly, and then I walk him back into the house to make sure he doesn't take another detour and ask out my house plants.

As I open the door for him, I say, "Don't bother coming back tomorrow."

He opens his mouth to protest, but then thinks better of it. "I'm sorry it didn't work out. Give me a call if you change your mind."

I let out a sigh of relief that he's gone, but it's short-lived when I get back outside and see Everly packing up as well.

"You don't have to go," I say.

"You don't seem like you're in a very good mood for company."

"He asked you out," I say as if that explains it.

"Yeah. So?" Her arms cross over her chest, pushing up her tits unintentionally. Or fuck, maybe it's intentional. If so, she's doing a fantastic job of pushing me toward the breaking point.

"It was unprofessional and rude."

"I get the unprofessional part, but how exactly was it rude?"

"You're my guest and he could have made you uncomfortable."

She stares at me, disbelieving.

"Or fuck, maybe not. You can probably still catch him if you want to grab some sushi and listen to him talk about himself. Knock yourself out."

She's quiet as she studies me for so long I want to squirm under her scrutiny. No one makes me squirm. I go up against the fastest, biggest, meanest guys in the league. Yet, something about Everly's gaze has my pulse kicking up a notch.

"As if you are going to let me go out with him," she says with amusement lacing her tone.

"I don't care who you go out with." Lies.

"Right." She laughs this time, and her pouty mouth pulls into a grin that sees right through me. "I get it. Ty isn't here so you have to go all big brother on me."

Wait. What? Did she just refer to me as her brother?

"It's fine," she says in a way that sounds like maybe it isn't fine at all. "Knowing my track record, things would end weird, and then I'd have to worry about seeing him any time I want to come over and use your pool."

Not anymore since he's never coming back. I stay quiet as she slides her sunglasses onto the top of her head.

"Well, thanks for letting me hang by the pool today," she says. "I guess I'll see you around."

Does that mean she's coming back tomorrow? It's been a few days since she invaded my space, and it isn't that I missed her because that would be weird. I just want to know when she'll be here. I like having a plan.

The uncertainty has me doing something I would never do. Not with her, anyway.

I clear my throat and say, "If you don't have plans, we could grab dinner."

The surprise plays over her face like a slideshow. Mouth agape, eyes wide, cheeks flushed.

When she recovers, she asks, "Dinner with *you*?"

"Do you see anyone else here?" I ask dryly.

I'm already regretting asking. It was a dumb idea. I should go inside, shower, and call someone else to come over. I'm healed enough that fucking someone into next week is no longer a concern.

"All right. Sure."

I hesitate. I'm not at all confident I heard her right. She's never this agreeable.

"What do you want to eat?" she asks.

There's a sudden rush of lust and anticipation thrumming through me. It's too late to rescind the offer. But I don't really want to either. And it's just Everly. We're friends. Nothing more.

Nothing more.

"I don't care," I say. "You pick. I'm gonna grab a shower quick."

"This is better than sushi." Ev grins before taking another bite. Each time she does, her eyes close and she hums as she chews.

I'm going to need another shower.

With all the food places to pick from, Ev chose pizza from a little shop she claims "has the nicest people that work there."

A strange way to choose dinner for sure, but we order delivery, and the pizza ends up being great. It's so good that it reminds me I need to get back on a better eating routine.

After I finish eating, I start to stand to take my plate to the kitchen, but Everly jumps up from where she's seated in front of my chair. Yes, she's sitting on the floor like a child whose parents relegated her there with orders not to get grease on the furniture.

And no, I didn't say that to her. I just shoved a bunch of napkins at her just in case.

"I got these," she says, taking my plate from me.

"I'm perfectly capable of walking to the kitchen," I grumble as she bounces along to throw away our trash and put the dishes in the sink.

"I know." She rolls her eyes. "But you should be resting more. Bridget said that was really important for your recovery."

My brows inch higher on my face. "Talking about me with your friends?"

Her cheeks are stained a light pink, but her response is all sass. "More like ranting to them about you."

A small laugh rumbles in my chest. "Now that I believe."

With a hand on the freezer door, she asks, "Need ice?"

"Yeah."

She grabs an ice pack and comes to the living room. She drops the cold pack in my lap, narrowly missing my balls.

"Thanks," I say dryly.

"Sorry. Gotta work on those reflexes." She reclaims her spot on the floor in front of me. The vision of her at my feet does weird things to me. I'm starting to think there aren't enough showers to erase my dirty thoughts of her.

"What happened with Will?" I ask. Mostly because I'm curious and a little because I need to remind myself that this isn't happening.

Not now. Not ever.

"We went out last night." Her tone is casual, but she struggles to meet my gaze. Interesting.

"Was it everything you hoped?"

Maybe if she tells me how great he was, it'll stop the thoughts swirling around in my head. Thoughts of her but not of him.

"No," she admits. Then her hazel eyes flick to me. "You were right."

I don't remember what I said about him, but it pleases me to hear her say it anyway.

"I'm sorry."

"No, you're not." She laughs.

"No, I'm not." But for different reasons than she thinks.

"It doesn't matter."

"Because you're leaving at the end of the summer?"

"That and other reasons." She sits taller. "What about you?"

"What about me?" I ask carefully, unsure what to make of the question. Does she mean...no, she can't mean that.

"I've not seen a single woman traipsing in or out of your house." She gets a contemplative look on her face then. "Actually, I don't think I've seen you with anyone in a while. Dry spell?"

"I'm not exactly in any shape to date right now."

"I wasn't talking about dating." She laughs again, but there's a tightening in my groin that makes it hard to reciprocate.

I need to change the conversation.

"Briar Lake is a cool town. You'll like it there."

Whatever expression I expected to get out of her by bringing up her internship, the one she flashes me isn't it.

"Yeah," she says finally. "That's what everyone tells me."

"You haven't been?"

"No, I have. A couple of times with Grace. Her parents have a place there, but we mostly stayed at their house or were out on the lake. I haven't really seen the town."

"You will," I say. "It's got a certain charm I think you'll like."

"Yeah, I'm sure I will."

CHAPTER TWELVE

Everly

PLEASE DON'T

The next few days pass in a similar fashion. I show up at Jack's after I've finished doing my house-sitting duties. He works out and I lie by the pool and try not to get caught staring at him.

I know that he sees me as Ty's little sister, but in some ways that just makes me feel safer in my crush. There's no way he would ever reciprocate so what's the harm in checking him out?

Jack finishes up his workout and walks over to where I'm sitting on my lounge chair. He uncaps a bottle of water, takes a long drink nearly emptying the bottle, and then splashes the rest on me.

The cold water startles me as much as his playful behavior. One side of his mouth pulls up in a boyish grin.

"That feels nice. It might be time to get in and cool off again."

"It is hot out today," he says as he stares toward the pool.

"Do you ever get in?" I ask.

"It's been a while," he replies.

"I bet swimming would be good for your knee."

"Did you get that from your pal Bridget?"

I never should have admitted that I talked with her about him.

"No," I reply. "It's just common sense."

"Oh, you have that, huh?"

"According to my mother, no."

His brows pull together. "I was kidding. You're smart. You know that you are."

I roll my eyes but have to swallow the lump in my throat. Do I know that?

"Does your mom really think that?" Jack asks.

Instead of answering, I get up and step quickly toward the pool, then jump and do a perfect cannon ball.

When I come up, he's standing at the edge looking down at me. A cannon ball isn't the sexiest way to get into a pool, but I don't have to care what Jack thinks because he doesn't look at me like that.

"Are you coming in or what?" I use my hands to splash water up at him.

Undeterred, he moves to sit and then slides into the water. When he treads water in front of me, it feels intimate in a way I can't describe. Our legs and chests are close and silently we stare at each other with two feet of distance separating us. My heart rate picks up as I watch a water droplet slide down his temple to his jaw.

"I really want to dunk you right now," I say. "But I'm afraid I'll hurt you."

His mouth pulls into a disbelieving smirk. "As if you could hurt me, Little Sharpie."

The nickname is like a bucket of ice water over my head. He never calls me that. Ash, Declan, Leo, and some of the other guys have been using that endearment for me since I was eighteen, but Jack never has. I can't explain why it hurts.

It's not that I think his reasoning for doing it now has any real significance, but it still catches me off guard. I guess it's just a reminder that to him, and all the other guys, I'll always just be Tyler's little sister.

Jack dips his head back into the water and gets his hair wet. When he flings it back, the long strands hang in his eyes. He runs a hand through it to slick it back out of his face.

He misses one strand and I move forward, without thinking, to push it back.

He stiffens under my touch for a second before his cool mask slips back into place. "Thanks."

"You should let me cut your hair," I say.

He arches one brow.

"What? I'm good at cutting hair."

"Uh huh. I'll bet."

"I am. I used to—"

My words are cut off when he moves into my space and pushes my head under the surface of the pool.

My mouth is still open, and I take in a big gulp of water. I'm coughing so I can't yell at him, but I retaliate by moving forward to attack him back. But he's ready for me. His hands wrap around my wrists to keep me from getting to him.

"I can't believe you dunked me," I say as I squirm and work to free my hands from his tight grip.

He's strong and I'm no match for him. We wrestle and splash. I'm squealing and laughing, and he's got one of his rare smiles splashed across his face.

Our legs bump under the water and I go still, afraid I'm going to bump his bad knee. He doesn't seem nearly as concerned about his own well-being as he continues holding me hostage. He's basically all that's keeping me from drowning since I'm no longer treading water.

"You're going to regret that, old man."

"Old man?" He barks out a laugh.

"I'm taking it easy on you."

"Please don't," he says. The playfulness in his expression morphs and before my eyes he turns back into the serious, stoic guy I'm used to. His dark blue eyes swirl with some undecipherable emotion. His grip loosens and because I'm not kicking my legs, I start to sink.

He grabs a hold of me again, this time his hands go to my rib cage just under the band of my suit top. His long fingers slide around me and his palms flatten. My self-preservation has kicked back in and our legs tangle again as I tread water.

The top of my thigh wedges between his legs and rubs against his crotch. It happens so fast. A slight brush against his dick. His *hard* dick. I think? I'm not usually confused by this kind of thing, but the contact is there and then gone so quickly that I'm not certain. Maybe he's just really big.

My face flames hot, but curiosity gets the better of me. Mom always said it was the reason I got into so much trouble. Curiosity didn't kill the cat, but it was the reason she barely passed high school, or something like that.

His hands still hold me up and I reach forward to grab on to his shoulders. My breasts brush against his chest and I fit into the spot between his legs, once again making contact with his crotch.

I inhale sharply when I confirm my suspicion. His dick is hard.

He reads it on my face, my surprise, but he doesn't back away or play like he's embarrassed. So I do the only thing I can think of. I dunk him under the water.

The next day, I show up at Jack's at the same time. He works out on the patio and I lie by the pool. He has a laptop set up on an outdoor coffee table and every once in a while, he scowls at the screen.

I can't seem to find the usual Zen of the sunshine today so I get up and walk over to him. He's lying on a mat on his side, a band around his thighs. He lifts the top leg and then lowers. When I plop down in a chair next to his laptop, he glances over as if just seeing me.

Only after he finishes the exercise does he ask, "Need something?"

"No. Just bored."

A notification sounds on his laptop. He glares at it.

"Yikes. What'd it do to you?"

"Nothing," he grumbles. "My email is out of control."

It dings again and I'm a little worried he's going to toss it into the pool.

"It can't be that bad."

"Bad enough that James is threatening to come back early if I don't start replying to some."

"Doesn't someone do that for you?"

"James responds to the things he can, but I've always handled my own schedule. I don't want someone signing me up for events or making those calls for me."

I fight a smile. Of course he doesn't want to relinquish control. He is always the boss of everything. I like that about him, even if it is one of the reasons we butt heads so often. Jack has built an amazing career and he's hands-on with every detail. Not only that but while juggling a career and businesses on the side, he still manages to be someone his teammates, friends, and family can depend on to always be there. It's impressive.

"What?" he asks, obviously reading something on my expression despite me trying to hide my amusement.

"Nothing." I peek at the screen as another notification comes in. His email is up and my eyes widen when I see there are over nine hundred unread emails. Okay, so it can be that bad.

"Are you serious?"

He nods. "Unfortunately."

I take the laptop and set it on the top of my legs. I realize only after the fact that this could be a huge invasion of privacy, but I'm already scanning the subject lines. Requests for interviews, invitations to parties, clubs, and one even has the word "Ball" in it. He's being invited to a freaking masquerade ball, and the most exciting thing on my summer calendar is a night out at our favorite club with some friends from school. How different our lives are.

"How long have you been avoiding your inbox?" I glance up at him over the top of the screen.

His jaw flexes instead of him answering. Since his accident if I had to guess.

He takes the laptop from me.

"I'll get to them," he says. Then quieter, "Eventually."

Like clockwork, another notification comes in. I stand and move around to confirm it's another email.

"Congratulations. You hit one thousand," I say.

This one's from James and it's marked Urgent. I smirk at the subject line. **If you don't answer them, I will.**

I like James and I especially like that Jack, who currently has a resigned look on his face, listens to him. He doesn't let anyone boss him around, but James isn't anyone.

"Like I don't have other shit to do." He sighs.

I sit next to him and watch as he opens the first email, replies 'No' and then deletes the original message.

"Oh, dear god. This is painful."

"They want an RSVP and I'm giving them one," he says brusquely.

"That sounded like a nice event and it's rude to reply with one word. You didn't even thank them."

"Right now, I don't feel very thankful."

I study him carefully. Jack is one of the biggest names in all of hockey. People throw his name around with the greats. But it's not just about hockey. He transcends the sport. He has endorsements and is friends with people all throughout the entertainment industry. He's dated models and actresses who regularly show up on the covers of magazines.

Ty said once he didn't know how Jack did it. That if it was him, he'd go out of his mind trying to juggle it all and still give hockey his everything. I didn't understand it then, but I'm starting to now.

He's a big fucking deal and the downside is that the pressure never stops. He's getting it from literally all sides. The Jack I saw last week who wanted to hide away and be left alone, I understand him a little better now.

"I got this." I take his computer from him.

"I'm not letting you anywhere near my schedule. You'd have me at more events than even James wants."

"I won't touch your precious schedule without your agreement. I'll read the details to you and you give me an answer," I say. Then add, "I'll reply however you want but with more appreciation than you're currently capable of."

He still doesn't look convinced for some reason.

"You can read them before I hit send."

With some reluctance, he agrees, and I settle into a chair, legs crossed with the computer resting in my lap.

"Do you have a schedule somewhere I can check dates against?"

He leans over the laptop. The movement puts his face so close to mine. I study the hard lines of his jaw, his straight nose, and the bow of his lips. He really is handsome. I'm still staring when his gaze flicks to mine. "There."

My stare doesn't move from his face. "Thanks."

With more self-control than I seem to possess, he looks away. Thank god I have a date tomorrow night. If the best way to get over an ex is to get under someone new, then it can't be that much of a stretch to assume the best way to stop fantasizing about my brother's teammate is to sleep with a guy I met online.

For the next hour, I go through Jack's inbox. He declines all interviews, says no to every bar/restaurant/new business grand opening. The only thing he doesn't fight me on is scheduling another visit to the children's hospital. He likes kids. Who would have guessed?

"What about the masquerade ball?" I ask for the second time. The first time I asked, he quickly said no, but I decided to wait and try again.

"Pass."

"Come on," I whine. "Who passes on a ball. Women will be dressed all sexy with masks, there will be lots of food and booze…"

I can see I'm not convincing him.

"James must think it's a good idea if he sent it over."

"James thinks I should go to everything."

"Not true. On one of the emails he forwarded he said if you were looking for something that night, he'd find something better."

One side of his mouth quirks up.

"Pretend you're James and I'll be you."

His brows lift in amusement and possibly annoyance.

"Yo, James, I got this invite to a ball. Balls are dumb. I don't want to go." I stop and wait for him to play along.

"I don't sound like that. When have you ever heard me say 'yo'?"

"Just go with it." I motion with my hand to encourage him. "What would James say to try to convince you."

His chest rises and falls with a heavy sigh. "He'd say that it's a good opportunity to talk with the people at Nike again. He wants to lock them into a contract before I retire."

The last part lands like a hammer, sucking the air from my lungs. "You're going to retire?"

I have absolutely no ability to hold in my reaction. I can't picture Jack not playing hockey, not being the Wildcats captain. What would he do? God, what would the team do without him?

"No, but I can't play forever. If the accident taught me anything, it's that I'm not invincible and I'm not getting any younger."

"You are kind of old." I scrunch up my nose. The truth is he's just gotten better looking the longer I've known him. It really isn't fair that men get hotter with age and meanwhile my friends are already performing a morning and nighttime skin and body routine to delay aging.

"I turn thirty-three next month. If I'm lucky, I have another seven or eight years."

He's planning almost a decade in advance, and I can barely manage to work out what I want to do on a daily basis. The age difference between us has never felt bigger.

"Seems like you should go to the ball then."

"What is it with you and this ball?" He's stretching on the ground in front of me. One hand rests protectively over his left knee. He's been getting around better on it, but every once in a while, I see him rubbing his thigh or extending it like he's testing the feel of it.

"I don't know. It sounds fun."

"Fine, I'll go."

I start to smile at his agreement, but then he adds, "*If* you come with me."

"Me?" I shake my head to say absolutely not but then stop myself. I mean, when else am I going to ever be invited to an event like this?

"Deal."

His smirk remains. I will deal with the repercussions of my agreement later. I'm pretty sure I'll have to buy a gown and a mask and…later. I will deal with it all later.

"James will be so happy," I say, then send the RSVP for Jack plus date (OMG, date?! Another thing I push off until later to deal with).

"Staying for dinner?" he asks when I close the laptop. I did not manage to get through all his unread emails, but I made a dent.

"No, I need to run some errands tonight."

He cocks a brow.

"I have a date tomorrow and I need something new to wear." Plus, I have a waxing appointment.

He nods his head slowly.

"Who's the guy?" he asks, going back to working out.

"Another online hopeful. His name is Thor. That has to be a good sign, right?"

"Sounds made-up. Are you sure he's real and not some psycho catfishing and preying on young women?"

"He's real."

"How can you be so sure?"

I bite on the corner of my lip before admitting, "I looked him up on social media."

"That could be fake too."

"Oh no, I went deep. I found his parents and his sister. There was even a yearbook photo of him. Thor is short for Thorson. Also, I can handle myself."

I stand to leave but then find I don't really want to go. I've gotten used to spending time with him. And while he's still not super chatty or warm, I enjoy his company.

"Are you going to work out all night?"

"Maybe," he says.

"Don't forget, rest is just as important for recovery." I beam at him.

"Another tidbit from Bridget?" he guesses.

"You know it. She's the best."

He grunts his acknowledgment.

"Speaking of nurses and the like, I haven't seen anyone around lately."

"I was cleared to drive so I can go to the office to meet with my doctor now."

"What about physical therapy? Is Brian still coming to the house?"

He hesitates for just long enough to make me suspicious when he says, "No. I'm doing PT on my own now."

"What happened to Brian?"

"I asked him not to come back."

"You ran off another person? Why?"

"He was hitting on you. I didn't like it. It was unprofessional."

Okay, yes, but firing him seems extreme.

"And you can do everything you need on your own?" I ask.

"I'm a big boy, Ev."

"You didn't answer the question."

"I wouldn't put my recovery in jeopardy like that. Not anymore. I need to be back on the ice and I need to be stronger than ever." The conviction in his tone sends a chill down my spine.

I can feel the determination radiating off him. He would do anything for the better of the team, and the best thing for the team is him being back in top form.

"Brian is the best, right?"

"Not happening."

"What if I don't come over when he's here? He can't hit on anyone if you're alone."

"No way. I'm not shoving you out the door for him."

"It wouldn't be like that."

"Uh-uh." He digs in hard with his conviction.

"You want to be back stronger than ever and he's the best. It seems like a no-brainer to me." I stand to leave.

"Are you coming back tomorrow?"

"Are you going to call Brian?"

His jaw flexes. "I'll see if he can come in the mornings."

"Perfect. It's usually lunchtime before I make it over anyway."

It doesn't escape my notice that just over a week ago he was yelling at me for trespassing on his property and acting like he didn't want me around. Now, he's moving his schedule around for me. I don't know what to make of it. But I think I like it.

"Then I guess I'll see you tomorrow." I point to his laptop. "Don't touch your inbox. I will deal with the rest of the emails tomorrow."

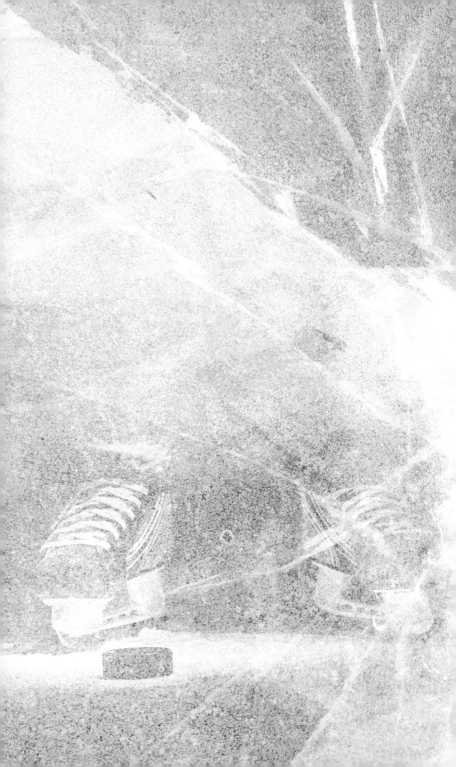

CHAPTER THIRTEEN

Jack

DARK AND MOODY

"How many businesses do you own?" Everly asks.

She's sitting on the workout mat next to me with the laptop open while I stretch.

"I don't know. A few."

"I can't believe you own Midnight." She narrows her gaze on me. "Though it does have a very *you* vibe."

"What does that mean?" I ask. I can't tell if she's giving me a compliment or an insult.

Midnight is a night club I bought a couple of years ago. I'm a silent partner with James' husband. He looks after the day to day, but I helped with the vision and getting it all up and running.

"It's all dark and moody." Her lips curve up into a smug smile as she basically tells me *I'm* dark and moody.

Lately, she wouldn't be wrong.

"It's the best club in the area. Everything is always clean and nice.

Most places you don't want to sit on the furniture for fear of catching something, but Midnight doesn't feel that way."

"If you knew the number of people that security has thrown out for nudity or groping, you might feel differently."

She scrunches up her nose adorably. "Okay, I think we're caught up on all the important emails. There are a few more personal ones I left for you."

One brow inches higher. "Personal?"

Her face takes on a slight blush that doesn't register until I take the laptop from her. It only takes a couple of seconds to find the ones she means. Meredith, an ex I dated a couple of years ago, has sent two. One right after the accident and another last week.

I click on the first one.

Hey Jack,

I'm so sorry to hear about the accident. Thinking of you.

X,

Meredith

And then the second.

How's recovery coming? I would love to grab a drink sometime and catch up.

I hand the laptop back without replying.

"You can delete those."

She doesn't say anything as she settles back in with the computer in her lap, but I see the questions in her eyes.

"What? You think I should reply and politely say 'no thanks?'" I ask, arching one brow.

"I didn't say anything."

"Your face is saying a lot."

The judgment is replaced with a coy smile. She sets the laptop aside and stretches her legs out. "I didn't know you were still talking to Meredith. I always liked her. She was nice."

I grunt a response.

"I know that the way things ended wasn't ideal, but she did help get Bridget's asshole ex fired so she and Ash could stay here so it's hard not to like her."

Meredith is a sports reporter. She covers baseball, not hockey, but when Ash was having issues with one of our assistant GMs, who just so happened to be Bridget's ex, I might have let some dirt on the guy slip to ensure it got out there, but it was Nick who supplied the firsthand knowledge of the creep that got him fired.

Some people assume I broke up with her for sharing that information, but that's not the reason. I just didn't see it going anywhere. Over the past few years, I've watched my teammates and friends settle down, one after the other. It's hard to see how happy they all are and not compare my situation. Meredith and I weren't going anywhere. Not long-term.

Though, since then, no one has really fit that label any better so maybe it wasn't really her at all.

"Meredith and I ended things on friendly-enough terms."

"But you don't want to *catch up*?" Everly asks with so much innuendo in her gorgeous hazel eyes that I want to roll mine.

"Busy."

She snorts. "That's the worst blow-off excuse."

"Which is why I said to just delete."

I finish stretching and stand to start my workout. Brian and I got in some good work this morning, but since my knee is starting to feel better, I want to push it a little more every day. Not too much that I cause a setback, but enough that I feel like I've done absolutely everything in my power to be back at one hundred percent come September.

Everly hovers nearby watching me.

"What?" I ask because clearly there's something she wants from me or she wouldn't be hanging around. Actually, she's barely been in the pool the last two days.

"I was just thinking I should start working out again." She looks longingly at the equipment scattered around. I have a gym inside but the fresh air has been good for me.

"You're welcome to use anything you want, whenever you want."

I pick up a ten-pound medicine ball and toss it to her. She catches it with an "oof."

"I didn't mean now," she says.

"What else are you doing?"

She shifts the weight of the ball from hand to hand.

"Sit down." I motion with my head in front of her and hold my hands out. She tosses the ball back to me and I do a sit-up then toss it to her. She does the same, struggling just a little at first like it is indeed the first time she's worked out in some time.

We finish one exercise and start another. She follows along, watching me and mimicking whatever I do.

She has a grit and determination that I admire and I don't take it easy on her.

"Okay, I give," she says eventually. My knee is starting to protest as well.

She's lying on her back, legs and arms spread out wide, as she stares up at the patio ceiling and catches her breath.

"You'll cramp up," I say as I step over her and reach down to take her hands and pull her up. She's dead weight at first but eventually gets to her feet with a pout.

"I think I'm good for another six months or so."

"Day one is always the hardest." I'm still holding her hands and a little too aware of how soft her skin is and how good she looks covered in sweat.

I drop her hands. "I'm gonna shower. Will you be here when I get out or do you have to get to your date?"

"Oh no, that got rescheduled until tomorrow."

"Thor already fucking it up," I say.

"He has to work late. It came up last minute…" She trails off. "Anyway, it worked out because Grace is free and we're going to hang out this afternoon. I haven't seen her much since she started her new job."

"Where'd she end up?" I ask.

"She took a marketing job for a coffee chain." Everly shrugs. "She seems to like it so far."

"What are you two going to do?"

"Probably hang out at the pool at her dad's house."

"Why don't you just invite her here?" I ask and motion toward the pool.

Everly's brows lift and then pull together. "Umm…I don't know. You'd be okay with that?"

"I don't mind." Which is surprising. Why the hell am I offering up my house and pool? I should go in and rest up, maybe call Meredith to catch up. Which absolutely means hook up.

"Okay. Thanks, Jack." She gives me a grateful smile and then skips off to get her phone from her bag.

I head inside, down a glass of water, and then stare out the window over the sink. Everly has the phone to her ear and she's pacing around the side of the pool, smiling as she talks.

"What the fuck are you doing?" I ask myself. I let my head fall back with a groan.

I give up watching her like some sort of creep and head to my bedroom. After stripping down, I shower, but I'm too annoyed with myself to do anything. I glance down at my dick, getting hard as soon as the water hits. It's become a Pavlovian response at this point. Fucking pathetic.

Grace shows up not long after I'm out of the shower, dressed, and heating up my post-workout meal. I hide inside while the two of them swim and lie by the pool.

I'm watching TV and eating chicken and rice when the back door opens.

Everly walks inside. Her skin is golden against her black suit. Her hair is pulled up in a high ponytail and she's smiling so big that I find my own lips curving up in response.

"You don't have to hide in here," she says as she walks into my kitchen and gets a glass of water. "Pizza will be here in five."

"It's fine." I pause the TV. I'm watching game film from last season. She comes over and sits on the arm of the couch.

"You're watching yourself on TV?" she asks with a hint of amusement, but then she reaches over and hits the play button. "I remember this game. You scored a goal off an assist from Ty."

My brows shoot up in surprise, but Ev's too busy staring at the screen, watching the play she mentioned unfold. She probably only remembers it because of her brother, but I still like it.

We watch in silence as Ty and I celebrate and then the game starts back up. Everly finally looks over at me. "You should come outside. I got enough pizza to share. It's better than whatever you have going on here." She looks down at my bowl with a look of pity.

I don't mind eating healthy. Food is fuel during the season and the more consistent I am with it, the better I feel and the harder I can push.

"No more junk food for me. The season will be here before you know it."

"Is fun not allowed either?" she asks, stands, and then takes my free hand. "Let's go."

CHAPTER FOURTEEN

Everly

HE'S JACK

Jack looks mildly uncomfortable for the first fifteen minutes I force him to hang out with me and Grace. When she asks about Thor, he excuses himself.

"What is going on with you two?" Grace asks as soon as he steps inside. Her eyes are wide and spark with excitement.

"Nothing."

She cocks her head to the side.

"We've gotten closer this summer." I didn't tell her about Jack's dad because that felt too invasive, but I wish I had so she wouldn't keep looking at me like this is something more.

"He's being nice to you. He's not nice to anyone."

"That's not true."

She rolls her eyes. "Okay, nice is the wrong word. He's nice to everyone but with you…he's different. And he was definitely checking you out."

My skin tingles and butterflies swarm in my stomach. I'm not usually one to play things off. If I can tell a guy is into me, I'll say it. And even though Grace makes some very good points, I'm just not sure.

"Are you into him?" she asks.

"He's Jack," I say as if that could explain it all. It should. I've never considered him like that, but is he hot and do I enjoy spending time with him? Yes. So much. Interacting with Jack before this summer always felt like I was part of the job. Like Jack needed to make sure I didn't do anything that caused trouble for my brother, which I resented, obviously. But things have changed. I don't feel like a potential problem anymore. I'm helping him and it feels good.

"Tell me about the new job." I turn the conversation to her and while she shoots me a knowing look—yes, I am avoiding talking about Jack—she goes with it.

For thirty minutes she tells me everything about her office, her coworkers, and how she spends her days. She's happy and enjoying it. Not for the first time this summer I wonder about my own future career plans. I still need to fill out my internship paperwork. The date to leave is inching closer and I wish I was as excited as everyone else seems to be. I love my life here and I'm nervous about uprooting my whole existence for a job.

Too soon, it's time for Grace to leave. It was a nice afternoon. When I decided to stay here this summer, I knew everyone would be gone or busy, but I didn't realize how much I'd miss them all.

When I walk Grace out through the house, Jack is in the kitchen.

"Thanks for letting me hang, Jack," Grace says as she waves to him.

He tips his head to her. "Anytime."

When she's gone, I move back into the kitchen with him. In my purse, I dig around until I find what I'm looking for.

"I brought my good scissors." I hold them up for him to see.

"O-kay." He eyes them and me carefully.

"I want to cut your hair."

"No."

"I watched a few more tutorials last night just in case. I got this."

"Did you also get a cosmetology license?"

I know that it's irrational because I, in fact, do not have any sort of training and very little practice, but it still stings that he's so adamant I can't do it. All the whispers that I'm not good enough or smart enough play through my head and feel like a kick to the stomach.

My head drops and then he sighs.

"Fine," he relents. "Just a trim. Nothing my regular barber can't un-fuck."

I kick those negative thoughts away and pull out a chair for him to sit. "It'll be easiest if you wet your hair."

With a sigh, he disappears, returning a couple minutes later with his hair freshly washed.

"I don't have one of those fancy capes to keep the hair off your clothes," I say as I get in position behind the chair.

He walks over to me, giving me his back before he pulls his T-shirt up over his head and tosses it out of the way.

The way his back muscles ripple with the movement makes my mouth go dry. I manage to squeak out, "Oh, right. That'll work."

At least it's his back and not his front. I shouldn't be trusted with sharp objects while his abs are on display. That would be a recipe for a trip to the emergency room.

He sits down and the smell of his shampoo mixed with the

proximity of him makes me more nervous.

"Everything okay?" he asks, making me realize too many seconds have passed with me staring at his broad shoulders and back.

"Yep," I say quickly. Totally fine. I run my fingers through his hair. A huge mistake. It's thick and soft and my body is having a strange reaction.

Okay, not strange. I'm turned the hell on.

I clear my throat and shake lust-filled thoughts from my head. I am a grown-ass woman and this is my brother's teammate, not some random guy. I am going to keep it together and then I'm going to go out with Thor. Nice, sweet Thor whose family looks like one of those families that go on vacations together and have dinners together every Sunday.

That reminds me, I want to ask Ty about family dinners once every couple of weeks when the season starts up again. I'll come back on some weekends, and I want to make the most of my time here. His schedule has gotten chaotic since Charlotte came along, and I don't ever want us to lose the closeness we've regained over the past five years.

"You have nice hair," I say once I've gotten ahold of myself.

He grunts his acknowledgment, and I tug the strands.

"Ow," he protests.

"The polite thing is to say thank you."

"Thanks," he mutters.

I start to snip the ends in a meticulous and slow fashion. He's quiet as I work and his body relaxes. His head too. It feels like an intimate moment, seeing him like this.

When I move to one side, I can see his eyes are closed. Long dark lashes fan out over his face and his lips are parted. He's really beautiful like this. His features are angular and perfect. He has a small scar just above the bow of his upper lip. It's faded into a white line that cuts through the slight stubble growing.

I cut another section and the hair falls onto his jaw. Reaching out with the hand not holding the scissors, I brush it off. His eyes open and lock onto me.

The softness in his face morphs back into the hard-ass hockey player I know, and I suck in a breath, pulse picking up speed.

Something passes between us. A heat and tension that I know I'm not making up in my head. He looks at me like he wants me the same way I want him. Except I know that can't be true. He's Jack Wyld. He can have anyone he wants.

He reaches up and circles my wrist, but I let my fingers rest on his jaw a moment longer. My thumb slowly rubs along the hard, scratchy skin, exploring.

"Ev." His voice is a gruff warning that I don't heed.

"How'd you get this scar?" I ask as I drag my thumb up and across it. He's still holding me by the wrist, but he doesn't pull my hand away.

"Playing hockey."

One side of my mouth quirks up. "I should have guessed."

My gaze drops to his chest and lower, scanning for more marks. "I bet young Jackson got into all sorts of trouble. Any other scars?"

His grip around my wrist tightens when I try to drop my hand.

"Not ones that would be appropriate to show you."

Well, that has my attention. My brows rise in question.

"Where?" I pull my hand away, and for a second I think he's going to show me, but then he shakes his head.

"I have a scar on my hip." I angle my body and then pull down the band of my shorts to show him the scar I got when I was a kid. "I was climbing in the kitchen and fell."

His eyes sear into my skin and then he looks away. He's seen me in far less the past few weeks, so it isn't like I'm flashing him my tits. Though...

"Am I done?" he asks.

"Yeah, I think so."

"Great. I'm going to shower." He stands abruptly. I don't know what's going on between us, but I want to find out. He doesn't seem to share that desire.

He stops just before entering his bedroom and turns. "Thanks for the haircut."

"You're welcome."

My pulse is still racing as I sweep up the hair and toss it in the trashcan. I still haven't heard the water turn on so I head toward his room. I need to know what the hell is going on between us. If I'm imagining it, then I'll chalk it up to needing sex. And if I'm not...I'm not sure what I'll do yet.

"Jack," I call as I enter his bedroom. The door is open. I've never stepped into the space before, but it's as neat and tidy as I expected. The bed is large and rests against one wall. A white comforter is tossed back on one side, showing gray sheets and matching pillowcases.

The shower turns on and I move to the cracked door, hoping to catch him before he gets in, but I don't look in obviously. I'm not looking to get an unexpected eyeful.

I open my mouth to call out to him again, but then I hear him say my name.

It's too quiet for him to be yelling out for help and something stops me from walking in. Instead, I keep listening.

He grunts and lets out a low hum in his throat. My skin warms and my pussy clenches because I know exactly what's happening in there. He's...oh my god. And he's saying *my* name.

CHAPTER FIFTEEN

Jack

BANG IT OUT

The next day when Ev comes over something's different. It's cloudy and the wind is blowing in a cool breeze. She sits in the same spot as usual, on one side of the workout area, as she goes through my inbox.

Everly reads off the details and waits for my reply. But instead of offering up her usual thoughts on my decisions, she says nothing. I just turned down an appearance request at a popular drag show in two weeks (love the show, but the time conflicted with James getting back into town and I know he'll have a million things to go over). Not a peep out of Everly.

"Newburg High School sent information for a silent auction. They're looking for items again this year and they thank you for your contribution last year."

"Screw the kids this year," I say.

She doesn't even crack a smile.

"Okay, no to—"

"Oh my god. I was kidding. What's up with you?"

She looks up and blinks several times like she's coming out of a haze, then stares back at the screen as she mumbles, "Nothing."

"Something." I stop what I'm doing. Instinctively, I go to run my hand through my hair but it's shorter and already slicked back. She did a good job. It was torturous having her hands on me. I don't know what the fuck is happening with me lately but I need to get a grip.

I was so keyed up I almost gave in and called Meredith. Thank god I didn't. That is not a road I want to go down again. Not even just for sex. There are far less complicated options. Not that I've called any of them either. I'm trying very hard not to think about why that is.

"We're friends, right?" she asks.

I swallow. "Sure."

"And friends sometimes do each other favors."

I'm not sure where she's going with this, but I nod. "Yeah, of course."

"I need to have sex."

My brows shoot right off my face and a strangled sound escapes from my lips.

For the first time today, she looks at me like her usual self.

"I'm serious."

"How am I going to help with that?"

She arches a brow, and all the blood from my face drains south as I realize her intent.

"No," I say adamantly.

"Why not?" She stands and walks over to me. Fuck she's gorgeous all fired up and confident like right now. I love it when she's wholly herself, no holding back. But there's no fucking way.

"So many reasons."

Tension stretches out like a rubber band and I'm not sticking around to watch it snap. I have to forcibly keep myself from moving closer. There's no reason to invade her space because this isn't happening. Can't happen. Won't happen. She doesn't know what she's asking for.

Turning, I head into the house.

"Okay, but hear me out." She follows me, leans against the counter as I go around to get a glass of cold water. Heat courses through me.

"No."

"I know you're attracted to me."

My lips part to deny it, but she doesn't let me.

"And I'm attracted to you. Besides, I'm leaving in a few weeks. It doesn't have to be a big thing."

"I think you know that's a lie."

"We're adults. We can handle this maturely."

Says the woman who scaled my fence a week ago.

"You're beautiful, Ev, but this can't happen."

Her hazel eyes spark with frustration and maybe a bit of embarrassment. "Why not?"

"You're Ty's sister and we're friends, nothing more. I don't want to complicate things."

Her gaze narrows. "Are you for real right now?"

I shrug one shoulder. I'm afraid to make any other movements for fear she'll see right through me. Instead, she turns on her heel, returning a minute later with all her stuff, bag slung over her shoulder.

"Come on, don't go. We can still hang out." Although now I'm definitely thinking about sleeping with her so it might be a painful afternoon.

"I don't want to hang out, I want to bang it out," she mutters quietly.

I nearly laugh at her words and how seriously she says them, but my groin tightens.

"Are you afraid I'm going to get all clingy? Because you're hot but honestly half the time I want to punch you in the face, so I don't think that'll be a problem."

"No, that isn't it. I told you. I don't see you like that. I'm sorry." Lies. Lies. All fucking lies.

Her gaze narrows and she glares at me so hard I want to squirm. Me? The guy who stares down the biggest, baddest guys in the league.

"You should go out with that guy you were talking to online." I barely get the words out before I clamp my mouth shut and grind down on my molars.

"You want me to go bang it out with someone else?"

I say nothing, and the silence hangs between us for so long I can hear the tick of the air conditioning as the fan shuts off.

Everly looks away first. She digs into her purse and pulls out her phone, presses some buttons, and puts it to her ear. I don't know who she's calling, but I already know I'm in trouble.

"Hey, Thor. It's Ev." Her voice is bubbly and sweet, and she giggles at something he says.

I tell myself I don't care but jealousy sweeps through me so strongly I'm moving to her to take the damn phone away. Possibly smash it.

She spins away from me. Every instinct in my body says to toss her over my shoulder and claim her, but that's fucking ridiculous. She's not mine.

"I know I said I was busy tonight, but my schedule freed up." Her head tilts back to stare at me. She's playing me, testing my sanity, and seeing if I'll stop her. And I'm having a hard time not falling for it hook, line, and sinker.

She spins back to face me with a smile stretched across her face. "Perfect. How about seven o'clock?"

She nods. "I can't wait."

After she hangs up, she bats her lashes innocently at me. "I'm sorry, what was it you wanted to say to me?"

"Don't play this game."

"What game?" she asks way too sweetly.

"You and I aren't a good idea but that doesn't mean you should go out with some guy just to try and piss me off."

"You literally just told me to go out with him. And why would you be pissed? You're not interested. Right?" She takes a step closer.

I can smell her coconut-scented sunscreen and her fruity shampoo.

My nostrils flare and my fingers itch to touch her, but I am nothing if not controlled.

I don't answer, but my silence is enough to have her stepping away.

"Great, then I guess I'll see you tomorrow."

CHAPTER SIXTEEN

Everly

THE RIGHT GUY

This may be the best first date I've ever been on.

Thor is everything I thought or hoped he would be. He's cute. He's smart and funny. Attentive.

He is that perfect combination of flirty yet respectful. I caught him checking out my cleavage, but he also spends a significant time on my eyes and he told me I looked nice.

We decided to meet up for drinks instead of dinner. It's my standard first date itinerary to make sure I like a guy before committing to two hours of awkward conversation while eating at lightning speed to hurry things along.

"I'm having a great time," he says, smiling at me. He has this golden retriever energy that is so likable and endearing.

"Me too."

"Do you want to grab dinner?" he asks as the bartender is setting our second drink in front of us.

I hesitate for only a beat. "Yeah, yeah, that would be great."

He takes the initiative and goes to the hostess up front to ask for a table. A few minutes later we're being escorted to a small table in the back of the restaurant and menus are put in front of us. And all of a sudden, the date feels a lot more serious than it did two minutes ago. Thor is great and he seems to be into this, into me. And I'm, well, I'm still thinking about the annoying hockey player I left earlier today.

I don't understand what his deal is. Jack's, not Thor's.

He's into me. Whether he'll admit it or not, I know that he is. The question is why wouldn't he admit it? He is a gold star member of casual relationships. It isn't like I asked him out on a date. And sure, I get that sleeping with a teammate's sister is probably off-limits in his mind, but I'm not just Ty's sister. I thought we'd moved past that over the last couple of weeks.

"So, where were we?" Thor asks, shaking me out of my Jack thoughts.

"Oh. Right." I blink away the haze and think. "I was telling you about my brother. He's great."

"Older or younger?"

"Four years older, but we're close."

A pleased smile lifts both corners of his lips. "I love that. I'm close with my siblings too."

I'm relieved he didn't ask more about Tyler. I never tell a guy on the first date that my brother plays for the Wildcats. Having different last names makes it hard for people to guess. All the guys are local heroes and get recognized easily within fifty miles of the arena, but as long as I'm not walking next to Tyler, people don't usually put it together.

I'm so proud of Ty, but all my life I've sat through dates and parties where people asked about him like I wasn't the one sitting in front of them. For at least our first date, I'd like Thor to be more interested in me than my brother.

"Brothers or sisters?" I ask. I already know he has one of each from the cyber sleuthing I did, but I'm not about to admit that.

"Older sister and a younger broth..." His words trail off as his gaze, which had been pinned on my face, lifts and his eyes widen. "HOLY SHIT. Jack Wyld."

My eyebrows crease. Did he just figure out somehow that my brother is a hockey player?

"No. I mean, yes, he's a Wildcat, but my brother is—"

Thor interrupts me. "Jack Wyld is *here*." He gives me this big, goofy grin like we're in on some secret together.

What the actual fuck?

"Holy shit." He looks away from me again. The hairs on the back of my neck stand up as I turn slowly in the direction of the front of the restaurant.

I already know it's going to be him. I can feel it in the fluttering of my stomach and the way my skin vibrates when he's nearby, but I'm still not prepared for laying eyes on him.

It's the first time I've seen him dressed in anything but athletic wear all summer, and goddamn I forgot how hot he is. A white T-shirt stretches across his chest. His jeans are casual but fit in a way that show off his fit and toned body. His dark hair, freshly cut by me, is styled in his signature slicked-back look. It really isn't fair that he's so fucking hot.

Jack is talking to the hostess. His lips are curved in a smile that doesn't meet his eyes. His gaze lifts and locks on me. I suck in a breath at the sight of him. He doesn't tear his eyes away as he continues talking to the woman. She nods and then he starts toward us.

Thor is talking, saying something about how much of a fan he is and how excited he is to see him. I barely hear any of it because Jack is headed straight for us.

I already knew it was too much of a coincidence for him to be here for any other reason, but my pulse still races with every step that brings him closer.

He comes to a stop next to our table and his stare burns into me. I can feel the way he notices my hair, my makeup, even the way I'm dressed. I put a lot of effort into my appearance tonight. Thirty seconds ago, I would have said it was for Thor's benefit. But the way Jack looks at me, I wonder if deep down I was waiting for this exact moment. His dark eyes finally flick up to meet mine.

"Oh my god, Jack Wyld!" Thor's excitement breaks the moment. "I am such a huge fan."

Almost lazily, Jack's gaze slides over to him. "Thanks."

"I'm Thor." My date stands and extends a hand. If he has any clue what's going on, I can't tell.

A muscle in Jack's cheek flexes as he shakes Thor's hand and he says, "Can we have a minute?"

"That's not necessary," I interject. I already know Thor will do anything Jack asks of him. With his big, kind eyes, he looks from me to Jack. I have to give Thor some credit because he doesn't leave.

"Fine," Jack relents. "Then, do you mind if I join you?"

"Yeah, of course." Thor looks around frantically. "Here. Take my chair. I'll get another."

I want to roll my eyes, but instead sigh and lift one elbow onto the table.

"Thanks, Thor." A smug smile pulls at his lips as Jack drags the chair over to the side of the table and takes a seat.

"What are you doing here?" I ask him.

His happy little façade slips and the serious and intense gaze that is far more familiar appears. "You know what I'm doing here."

"Do I?" I bat my lashes innocently.

Thor returns with the chair. As he takes a seat, he stares between us like he's trying to figure out what the hell is going on. That makes two of us.

"How do you two know each other?" Thor asks.

"We're *friends*." I enunciate the last word very clearly and that muscle in Jack's cheek jumps again.

"That's awesome." Thor's smile falters slightly. "That was a tough end to last season, but you look great and I heard you were going to be back ready to go by camp."

The discomfort that immediately takes hold of Jack makes a rush of sympathy temporarily erase my annoyance at him for ambushing my date.

Before Jack can reply, I say, "Excuse me. I'm going to grab another drink at the bar."

Both of them eye the not yet empty glass in front of me so I swallow it in one gulp, then proceed across the restaurant to the bar.

I haven't even ordered yet when Jack joins me.

I glare at him, not that it has any effect on him.

"Your date looks like he's five seconds from running."

"Don't act like you care."

"You and I can't happen."

"You came all the way here tonight, ruined my date, just to tell me you aren't interested? How sweet. You really know how to make a girl feel special." I step closer to him and his throat works with a swallow.

"Dammit, Ev. You know I'm right."

I break his gaze to glance over at the table. Thor is flagging down the server in a clear signal for the check. "Perfect. Now you've ruined my dinner too."

Jack's voice softens. "If he scares that easily, then he's not the right guy for you."

"I don't care about the *right* guy," I whisper-shout.

"Yes, you do. Deep down you do."

I don't know if he's just trying to tell me Thor isn't the right guy or if he's insinuating that he isn't either. Knowing Jack, both. Everything he says is a puzzle.

"You're not interested anyway so it doesn't concern you," I snap. "Why are you here, Jack?"

His jaw clenches as he stares at me without answering.

"Jack Wyld!" Another fan calls out to him, and I take the opportunity to flee back to the table.

Thor gives me an apologetic smile, still so nice even as he's about to end our date early.

"It seems like you two have some things to discuss so I went ahead and paid our check."

"No, we're all good," I say. "Sorry about all that. Do you want to go somewhere else and grab another drink? I'm not really hungry anyway."

"Uhh…" He glances at the bar and then back. "You seem like a cool girl, Everly. How about you call me in a few days if you're still interested."

My temper flares, but not at him, so I nod. "Yeah. I'll do that."

I head outside but don't call a ride yet. When Jack exits, he looks around for me and his features relax the instant he spots me. Then harden again as if he can't quite decide if he's relieved or angry. That makes two of us.

I turn toward him. "You don't get to tell me who or what I want. I'm not the teenage kid you used to protect. I'm a grown-ass woman."

"I know."

"Do you? Because it's a real asshole move showing up here and ruining my night after you already ruined my afternoon."

"That's not why I came here."

"Really? Because so far nothing you say or do makes any sense."

People in the parking lot are starting to stare. Not that I care, but he obviously does.

"Let's talk on the way home," he says.

"I'm not getting in the car with you."

"Yes, you are."

I arch a brow in defiance. I don't even know why anymore. He just makes me so angry. Who the hell does he think he is, showing up here and ruining my date and then bossing me around?

"You can walk or we can test out how strong my knee is and I'll carry you."

"You wouldn't dare," I seethe.

"Wouldn't I?"

He would, and god, why is that so hot?

"Whatever. You owe me a ride anyway." I take off toward his SUV at a quick pace. He unlocks it before I get there.

"You look nice," he says when we're seated with the engine running. Cool air blasts through the vents.

"Are you sure you can notice things like that? What with your total and complete disinterest in me and all."

"I never said I wasn't interested. I said we weren't happening."

"You said you didn't see me like that." The words still pain me. I'm a goddamn catch.

"You and I getting involved is a bad idea."

"Why? Afraid I'll get attached?" This time I do roll my eyes. "I told you, that won't happen."

He drives away from the restaurant without answering me. Not that I really expected him to.

There's a comfort in being with Jack, even when I'm fighting with him, but I don't let myself relax. I want to hold on to this anger.

"Can you drop me off at Mike's?" The local college bar is one of my favorites. I need to let off some steam. Possibly throw darts while imagining the board is Jack's big head.

"No." He keeps going, finally pulling up in front of my house. Mine for only a little while longer. Ty owns it and I've been renting from him.

It's a light-yellow three-bedroom within walking distance to campus. I'll be sad to leave it, but right now I am not ready to go inside.

"Thanks for the ride." My fingers grab hold of the door handle.

"Wait." His tone is sharp, and I hate the way my body reacts before my brain has time to kick in.

"What?" I look over at him.

The struggle on his face pushes me out of the vehicle. I don't need him to give me some pity speech or list all the reasons why he isn't interested in me. I have more pride than that.

I shut the passenger door and take off down the sidewalk in the direction of Mike's, but Jack is circling behind the SUV and cuts me off.

"God dammit, Everly. I'm not afraid of you getting attached."

He hovers over me. Even in my heels, he's a good head taller than me. His stare surveys my face, settling on my lips and then dragging up to my eyes. "I'm afraid I will."

I'm still deciphering his meaning when he steps to me, lifts his left hand to the side of my neck, and kisses me.

Shock makes my other senses slow to respond, but a tingle starts at my lips and works its way through my body.

He's afraid of getting attached to me?! It's too bizarre to comprehend, but my stomach bottoms out and a giddy sensation spreads through me.

Why haven't we been doing this every day, all day?

His lips work mine over, as demanding and controlling as I expected. Look at that, I found the one situation in which I don't want to fight back. Nope, I'm as compliant as I've ever been.

His thumb drags along the side of my neck and his teeth scrape against my lower lip as he tugs it before diving in again. He captures the needy groan that escapes my mouth and hums in appreciation.

He walks us backward until my shoulder blades ram into the side of his G-Wagon. I'm trapped between it and his body. Both of his hands now hold the sides of my neck, the tips of his fingers tangle in my hair.

I grip the front of his T-shirt and arch into him. The way our bodies line up feels so perfect. I'm seconds from rubbing up against him, when he pulls back.

His lips are wet and slightly swollen, and his chest heaves in time with mine.

"Do you want to come inside?" I ask, still hazy.

Instead of answering, Jack lowers his shoulder and picks me up.

"What are you doing?"

"Testing out the knee." His gravelly voice vibrates through me and an ache shoots straight to my core.

"Jack." I laugh. "I can walk."

But he's already taking the steps up the porch. He sets me down in front of the door. I punch in the code to unlock it and then push the door open.

I step inside but Jack doesn't move.

"Are you coming?" I ask.

He shakes his head. The heat in his gaze still burns through me. "Now you don't have to go to Mike's, looking for someone to kiss you."

"What if I was looking for more than kissing?"

One side of his mouth lifts. "If you think someone can fuck you better than I just kissed you, be my guest."

So fucking confident. Also, he's probably right.

"That's it?"

Reaching forward, he pulls the door closed between us.

"I can't believe you just did that," I yell at him through the door.

"Night, Ev."

A few seconds pass before his footsteps sound on the porch, heading back to his vehicle. I turn and rest my back against the wooden door and then laugh. "You win this round."

CHAPTER SEVENTEEN

Jack

WHATEVER YOU SAY, CAP

Hell is Everly in a bikini smiling at me like she wants me to kiss her again.

She hasn't said anything about the kiss all afternoon, but the way that she looks at me tells me she's thinking about it as much as I am.

She's already gone through my email, but she sits with her legs outstretched watching me while I finish my workout.

"Stop looking at me like that," I warn, cocking a brow.

She's the one in a skimpy suit, but she's looking at me like she can see my dick growing harder through my shorts.

"Like what?" she asks innocently.

She wants me to say it. She wants to know how I see her and watch me squirm as I wrangle with the fact I kissed her last night.

I should have done more. I should have fucked that look right off her face last night.

Because now that I've had some time and distance, I'm not going to let her push me into acting again.

She uncrosses her ankles, drawing my attention back to her long, tan legs. "I'm gonna swim. Are you coming in after you're done here?" Her eyes drop to my bare chest as she unabashedly checks me out.

"I can't. I have to go to the arena."

"Oh."

I want to kiss the disappointed look off her face. My head is conflicted. No, that's not true. My head is clear on what to do, but other parts of me are not on board. Nothing has changed. She's still too young for me, still my teammate's sister, and still completely off-limits.

"Maybe you could pick me up later though? I need to drop the SUV off to have some maintenance done."

"Maybe." She gets to her feet and then walks closer.

Don't look at her tits, man. Don't do it. I do not have time for a cold shower today.

"Or I can grab an Uber if you're going to be busy swimming in my pool."

"What time?" she asks with a small laugh. "I have plans later."

"It shouldn't take more than a couple hours."

I want to know what those plans are and if they include Thor, but asking would be admitting that I don't want her to go out with him or anyone else. Although that's probably clear after I crashed her date last night. I'm not sorry. Not even a little bit.

"If I pick you up later, will you kiss me again?"

"Ev." Her name comes out strangled and gruff. She's killing me and I am going to hell.

"Fine, fine. I see we're not talking about it still."

"Talking won't change anything."

She shrugs one shoulder. "By my memory of last night, I wouldn't want to change anything."

Yep, definitely trying to kill me.

When I get to the arena, it all hits me again. The accident. My career hanging delicately in the balance. All that I have to lose.

I love this place. It will be hard enough to walk away at the end of my career, but doing it years earlier than expected, would be excruciating.

I check in with Coach Miller, give him the update from the doctors, which he already knows because there is little that happens with his team or players that he doesn't know—except that time Leo was sleeping with his daughter—that was one sticky situation.

I'm feeling good, lighter than I have in months as I head to the locker room. I come up short when I find someone else already there pulling on his skates.

"What are you doing here?" I ask Nick as I walk across the green-carpeted floor. "I thought you were spending the summer in Kansas City."

"I was until my dad decided I needed a real vacation and sent me packing."

I arch a brow in question.

"Something about beaches and girls in bikinis." He runs a hand through his hair and then waves that same hand around to emphasize his next words. "Pina coladas and all that bullshit."

"And you ended up back here?" The beach sounds nice. So do girls in bikinis. One girl in particular.

"I don't do fun and sun," he says like the words pain him. "I don't know what my dad was thinking."

"He was probably thinking you could use a break from being a single dad."

"I don't need a break from Aidan."

"I don't mean it like that, but you do a lot for him all on your own while also managing our chaotic schedule. Taking a few days to recharge doesn't make you selfish or a bad dad. A break can be good."

He eyes me skeptically. "When did you become an expert of being a parent? Something you want to tell me."

"Fuck no. The only action I've seen recently is with my hand. And I'm an expert on everything." I take a seat next to him in my stall. It feels good to be here. The familiarity of it all.

"How's the rehab going?" he asks.

"Slower than I'd like, but I'm getting there."

"Are you hitting the ice today?"

"No, I just came to see Coach. The doctor wants me to give my knee a few more weeks before skating."

"It's gotta be killing you. What have you been doing all summer?" He finishes lacing his skates and stands.

"Nah," I say then bob my head. "A little, but I've been busy. Therapy, doctors' appointments, hanging by the pool." My lips pull into a smile.

"What's *that* look?" Nick asks.

"No look. I'm just enjoying the summer."

"Mhmm." He lifts both brows and aims a knowing smirk my way. "Who's the girl?"

A flare of panic blooms and bursts like ice water over my head. Nick stares expectantly, waiting for me to tell him about the newest girl that I'm seeing. I've never been big on sharing about my personal life so when I shake my head and say, "It's not like that," he just grins at me.

"Whatever you say, Cap."

CHAPTER EIGHTEEN

Everly

THERE'S NOTHING SMALL ABOUT IT, SWEETHEART

'm lying on a floatie in the middle of the pool talking on my phone. Jack's been gone for a little over an hour, but I keep glancing over at his workout area like I expect him to be there.

"Oh my gosh! I can't believe it! I so, silently, called this." Bridget squeals loud enough that I pull the phone away from my ear slightly.

Her response is exactly why I called her. She always knows when to be excited and when to be protective. Right now, I just want someone to live in the excitement with me. All the very real, very responsible reasons that this might be a bad idea are far from my mind. Which is exactly where I want to keep them.

"So, are you dating? Where'd you leave things?" she asks.

"We haven't talked about it."

"Oh my gosh!" she shrieks again. "What is Ty going to say?"

My stomach drops.

"I'm not going to tell him. There's nothing to tell anyway. We kissed. Once."

"Yeah, while he backed you up against his vehicle."

The memory makes goosebumps dot my arms, even with the sun warming my skin.

Ash's voice is in the distance. His sisters are visiting so I'm not worried about him listening in, but that does remind me.

"You can't say anything either. Not even to Ash."

"Ev! There's no way I can keep this from him." She's whispering now but her voice is no less screechy. "He'll know just by looking at my face."

"Well stop whatever your face is doing before he notices."

She laughs softly. "How was it?"

"Life-changing."

I'm rewarded with another loud squeal.

I temper my excitement and remind her, and maybe myself, "It was just a kiss."

Just a kiss that I plan to reenact with my clothes off.

I'm about to go inside and get changed out of my swimsuit when Jack calls.

"Hi," I answer, feeling a little shy.

"Hey. I'm done at the arena. Can you pick me up?"

"I'm not sure. What will you do for me?"

A gruff laugh tickles my ear, and I fight a giddy smile.

"Is using my pool every day not enough of a bargaining chip?"

"Hmm." I bring one finger to my chin, like he can see me. "I'm not sure. But you know what would definitely convince me?"

"What's that?" His tone is laced with humor as he entertains me.

"A dick pic."

A real, loud burst of laughter comes out of him. I can picture the wide smile on his face, the flash of teeth, and the twinkle in his dark eyes. Serious, stoic Jack makes my pulse race but happy and smiling Jack is my kryptonite.

"Just a small sneak peek."

"There's nothing small about it, sweetheart."

Sweetheart. My insides get all mushy at the endearment.

"That's what they all say."

He grunts. I've never asked a guy for a picture of his dick before, but I like that he doesn't sound very happy about the prospect. "I guess I'm walking then."

"Oh, fine. I suppose we can work something out." I stop taunting him. "Back parking lot?"

"Yeah. I have an extra key card in the Lamborghini. Check the console."

I'm familiar with where the players park for practices and games. There's a private lot around the back that can only be accessed with a key card.

"Okay. I'll be there in a few minutes."

"Take your time. You don't need to rush."

I'm a teenager again with how I don't want to hang up the phone, but I also need to get out the door.

"Okay. Maybe I'll just lie in the pool a little longer then."

His tone is all tempting tease when he says, "You are infuriating. You know that?"

"I do. Thank you." The anticipation of seeing him finally moves me into action. "Okay. Hanging up now. See you in fifteen."

After I end the call, I slip on a pair of jean shorts and my sandals.

In the garage, I flip on the light and then sigh in appreciation.

I'm not big on cars. I like ones that are pretty and fast but specific brands and all that don't mean a lot to me. Much to Tyler's dismay. My brother is a huge fan of cars, especially old Mustangs that he restores.

However, the car I'm staring at is an exception. The black paint job glistens under the lights. Jack's Lamborghini is sex on wheels. My heart rate ticks faster with each step closer. He doesn't drive it as much as he used to, mostly I see him in the Mercedes. A new version of the same one he had before, right down to the paint color. Black. Always black.

For a man that likes expensive vehicles, his variety is lacking.

I open the driver's door. It still smells and looks new, even on the inside. I don't see the key card, so I sit behind the wheel. The leather hugs my body and I can't resist running my hands over the wheel.

I find the card with the car key in the center console just like he said. God, if Jack could see me now. I take out my phone to snap a selfie to send him. But before I hit send, I get another idea.

A much better idea.

CHAPTER NINETEEN

Jack

STILL WANT TO LOAN ME YOUR CAR?

"Thanks for today," I say to Nick as we walk down the hall toward the parking lot together. Since I can't skate yet, he cut his on-ice training early and we kicked around a soccer ball like a lot of the guys do before games. I haven't participated in that type of pre-game ritual in years. That's mostly the younger guys, letting off steam and getting warmed up.

My before-game routine has shifted over the years, focusing less on myself and more on making sure the team is good to go. But it was nice messing around with Nick and catching up. I wasn't even worrying about him; I was just having fun.

After we did a little stretching, I slipped back into captain mode to try to convince him to go on the beach vacation his dad recommended. I don't think he was persuaded any more by me than he was from his dad's words, but I tried.

I don't know what it's like to be a dad, let alone a single father, but I know that the hockey season is long and tiring, and if a week of lying on the beach will help him unwind, I'm all for it. When he gets back here at the end of the summer, I want him to be relaxed and ready to grind.

We push out the back door of the arena. I glance around for Everly, but she's not here yet. Aside from Coach's truck, the only other car is Nick's rental. He hits the unlock on his key fob and the lights flash.

"A minivan?" I chuckle as I stare at the silver monstrosity.

"It's all they had."

"Shit. I'd demand you take mine, but it's at the shop. That is not a proper vehicle for a bachelor on vacation. Any vacation."

"Nothing about my life screams bachelor. Except maybe the number of TVs in my house."

Another laugh slips out. "How long are you staying?"

"I'm not sure."

"Well, shoot me a text if you stick around. Though for the record, I think you should take the next flight out to Turks and Caicos."

"I'll keep that in mind." He takes a step toward his van. "You have a ride?"

"Yeah. She should be here soon." The words are barely out of my mouth when an engine rumbles like it's gaining speed. I lift my head in time to see a black sports car speed through the lot. Not just any sports car. My Lambo.

Surprise makes my brows lift and renders me speechless.

The windows are down and Everly's blonde hair flies out behind her as she goes. She makes a big loop around the lot, going way faster than anyone should in a parking lot, and comes to a screeching halt in front of me.

I lean down to look through the passenger window and there she is, hair windblown, smile wide, in a hot-pink bikini top and cut-off jean shorts. If I weren't so turned on, I might be able to find it in me to be annoyed.

"I said grab the key card out of the car, not take the whole damn car."

"Hmm. I must have misunderstood."

Nick chuckles beside me. "Still want to loan me your car?"

I send him a friendly glare.

"I think I understand why you've been hanging poolside." He backs away with a wave before I can explain that it isn't like that. Except, it kind of is exactly like that.

Nick takes off for his van and leaves me with the woman who is surely going to be the death of me.

"All right. You had your joyride." I beckon for her to hand me the key.

"No way." She tightens her grip on the wheel. "I'm your topless driver." She tips her head to the passenger seat. "Get in, handsome."

I do, saying a silent prayer. Not because I think she's going to wreck. Because if she takes her top off it really might kill me.

When I'm safely in, a first time sitting in the passenger seat I might add, she asks, "How are you?"

"Nervous."

"I'm a great driver." She beams. "But, uh, buckle up just in case."

She peels out with a laugh. Once she gets on the main road, she's much more careful and I breathe a little easier.

"Have you eaten?" she asks, glancing over at me. "I skipped lunch. We could have an early dinner."

"Do you have a shirt?" I ask, letting my gaze drop to the swell of her breasts bouncing with the movement of the car.

"It's covering the important bits."

"You'd give the seniors at the early bird special a heart attack." She might give me one.

She laughs again. Fifteen minutes of her driving and me getting more turned on with each second, we arrive back at my place. She parks the car in its spot in the garage and kills the engine.

I let out a long breath.

"Were you that nervous I'd crash? I'm a good driver."

"No, I was nervous you'd take off your top and kill me."

"That is still a likely outcome, but please don't die." She crawls over the console onto my lap.

"I don't think this car is big enough for whatever you have planned," I tell her as she attempts to straddle me.

"I don't have a plan."

Her skin is warm and silky smooth. Her hair hangs down over her shoulders, partially covering one breast, and her face is makeup-free, showcasing a smattering of freckles that span out across her cheekbones.

"I have a few ideas." I brush my thumb along the small dots on the right side of her face.

"You're not going to tell me how this is a bad idea and it's not happening again."

"Would it matter?" I laugh.

"Well, I'm not going to kiss you against your will."

I lift my hips so she can feel what she does to me. "Does it feel like it's against my will?"

Before she can answer, I thread my fingers through her hair and bring her mouth to mine.

She reacts immediately, pressing into me and kissing me back with a fervor that makes my pulse race. She's under my skin, in my bloodstream, consuming my thoughts.

There's no point in denying I want her and it's a little too late to keep from crossing the line.

Everly doesn't hold back. I like that about her. She doesn't hide who she is or what she wants. And right now, she's a woman who wants me badly. The feeling is mutual.

I slide the hand in her hair down the side of her neck and then skim my fingers over the side of her bikini top. She shivers and arches into me, encouraging me to touch her there. I detour and wrap my arm around her back, then with the other I open the door.

"No, don't run away yet." She stops kissing me only to protest, then covers my mouth with hers again.

"Not running away," I manage to get out as we devour each other. "Taking you with me."

I maneuver out of the car like a man on a mission with her glued to my front.

"I can walk," she says, but then wraps her arms around my neck and her legs around my waist, rubbing her tits up against my chest in the process.

I make it inside by instinct alone, since all my other senses are focused on not breaking our kiss.

The entry door from the garage slams behind me. Without realizing I've made the decision, I find myself walking toward the kitchen island. It's the nearest flat surface. I set her down and stay between her legs.

Now that my hands are free again, I let them roam over her. From the curve of her waist, up her side, to her face, and finally tangled back in her hair. I tug the strands, baring her neck to me. My teeth graze over the slim column and latch on to the pink bikini string. I follow it down to the triangle covering the peaked, hard nipple.

Her ragged breathing ceases as I drag my finger back and forth over one, then the other.

She moves like she's going to take it off.

"No," I say, catching her hand. "I want to unwrap my own present."

She makes the sexiest noises as I drop open-mouth kisses on her stomach and neck, avoiding all the places she wants me most.

"Fucking temptress, that's what you are."

She's everything I shouldn't want and everything I crave.

Thick blonde hair that I want to fist.

Big hazel eyes that see right through me.

A mouth that I want wrapped around my cock.

Her curves, her fight, her fucking everything.

Everly Kent drives me fucking wild.

And she knows it.

She takes my hands and places them over her breasts so I'm cupping her full tits through the suit.

"Take your greedy hands off what's mine, temptress."

With a groan of protest, she slides her palms down. Her fingers latch on to my forearm, nails digging into the skin. I slide my hands up to the tie around the back of her neck. My fingers work the knot free as I lick and suck the column of her neck. She smells like sunscreen and sunshine, and tastes like heaven.

The strings come apart and I pull the top down, exposing her to me. I stare at her, finally circling my thumb around one nipple and bringing my mouth to the other.

"Jack." She pants and arches into me, feeding me more of her full breast. My teeth scrape the sensitive peak until she cries out.

I worship her perfect tits, licking and sucking and biting, until she's writhing under me and begging for more.

I work my way down her body to the top of her shorts. She tries to help me get her out of them, but I swat her hands away. I wasn't lying. I want to unwrap her all on my own.

"You just can't help but fight me, can you?"

"If you were doing it right, then I wouldn't need to fight you."

I chuckle softly and nip at the skin above her hip bone.

Her pink bikini bottoms wait for me underneath her shorts. Any ideas I had about taking this slow disappeared right along with my good judgment.

She sits up on her elbows and watches me with hooded eyes. I hold her gaze as I bring my mouth down over the material of her suit bottoms and suck her clit.

Her lips part but no sound comes out.

"Am I doing it right, now?" I ask when I pull back again.

"Less talking," she says, pushing my head back where it was.

Damn she's gorgeous all splayed out for me, face and body flushed, nipples hard, looking at me like she wants me as badly as I want her.

Considering I've never wanted anyone more, that look says it all. I don't know how it happened, but I can't seem to get her out of my head and I'm tired of fighting it.

I peel her bottoms off and then toss them up at her. She smirks, but it disappears as I lift one of her legs and put it on my shoulder.

"Damn, baby. You're dripping for me." I slide two fingers over her from pussy to clit, then drag the moisture up to her lower stomach for her to see. "So wet. So ready."

"I've been ready for weeks." Her words are breathy as my fingers rub slowly over her swollen clit. "You almost missed your shot."

She's all talk, riling me up like she loves to do.

"If you think anyone can make you come as hard as I'm going to, then be my guest, temptress." I dip two fingers inside her. She moans and her pussy walls clench around me. "Want me stop?"

"If you stop…" Her words trail off as I add another finger.

"What's that, sweetheart? Stop?"

I lean closer to her pussy without breaking eye contact and place a chaste kiss directly on her clit, then flick my tongue in the same spot.

"Don't stop. More," she begs, eyes struggling to stay open.

I do the opposite, stopping and stepping back from her.

"What are you doing?" she asks as I head over to a cabinet and grab a glass.

The answer to that question is *slowly losing my mind*, but I don't say anything as I fill the glass with ice and water, then take a long drink. It doesn't do anything to stamp out the heat coursing through me for her.

"Jack fucking Wyld, if you leave me like this, I swear to the hockey gods I will cheer for the other team at every game next season."

I bark out a laugh. "No, you won't."

Her gaze narrows, then drops to my pants. My hard dick is stretching out the front, making my desire for her obvious.

She scoots to the edge of the counter like she's going to get down.

"Don't move," I say, voice rough and commanding. "I'm not done with you."

Her annoyance flares but so does her desire.

I walk back with the glass and hold it to her lips. She hesitates but then drinks as I tilt it so the water slowly drips into her mouth.

I take one more long drink and then set it on the counter. This time when I place my cold mouth over her hot pussy, she hisses out, "Oh, fuck."

I fight a grin. The sensation doesn't last so I grab an ice cube from the glass and put it in my mouth. Her eyes follow my every movement as I hold it between my teeth and run it down over her stomach and lower.

"Holy shit." She falls back and stares up at the ceiling.

I miss her eyes on me. "Give me those pretty hazels, Ev."

She obeys quickly, sending a rush of want and need straight to my cock.

The ice melts fast but she's already grinding against my tongue and chasing her orgasm. It hits her with a force that makes her lashes flutter closed.

"Jack." My name is a jagged cry from her lips as she comes.

She's wild, legs wrapping around me, hands tugging in my hair, bucking and screaming as the orgasm fades.

"Mmmm…" I hum the words against her center. "I could eat this pussy all day long."

My scalp protests the grip she has on my hair, possessive and demanding. I usually like to be the one in control, but she wouldn't be herself if she wasn't pushing back and testing my sanity.

When the second orgasm hits, she full-out screams, the sound filling my house and probably alarming the neighbors, if they weren't all gone for the summer.

She squirms, this time like she's trying to get away from me. I move my mouth away from her sensitive flesh but keep my hold around her leg.

Everly's gaze drops to my pants. She reaches for me, stroking me through the fabric, before she slips her hand down the front. Her fingers wrap around my girth and her lips part with a pleased smile. "No wonder you're such a cocky asshole."

Before I can reply, an alarm goes off on my phone. Her hand stills. I take it from my pocket and silence it, then toss it on the counter.

"Something important?"

"Unfortunately." With an internal sigh, I grab her shorts. "Put these on."

"Why?"

"Because I need to take a call, and I'd prefer James not see your pretty cunt."

CHAPTER TWENTY

Everly

TAKE A LOAD OFF

I freshen up while Jack talks with James in the living room. I stay out of the line of the camera, assuming Jack doesn't want anyone, including his agent, to know I'm here.

"I can't believe you've stayed on top of your emails," James says. "It hasn't been this organized since I was managing it."

I'm fighting a laugh at the compliment James doesn't know he's giving me.

"I can't take credit for that," Jack says, finding my gaze for a moment before returning his attention to the screen. "Everly did all that."

"Everly? Tyler Sharp's sister?"

"Yeah. She's been helping me out this summer. She's good. Saved you the headache of apologizing to all the people I emailed back personally and offended with my one-word replies."

His agent chuckles. "Tell her I owe her one."

"Yeah, I will."

I text with Grace while they talk for a few minutes more.

Jack closes the laptop and stands. "Sorry about that."

"It's okay. I have plans and I was dangerously close to blowing them off."

His mouth quirks up on one side. "Tell me more about that option."

"The one where I blow?"

He shakes his head, dark eyes lit up with promise. "You're going to be the death of me."

"Well, you're safe tonight. I'm hanging out with Grace."

I swear disappointment flashes over his handsome features before he says, "Sounds like trouble."

"Nah, not tonight. We're staying in. Movies, junk food, wine, maybe some face masks or mani-pedis."

His lips curve into a smile. "Have fun. I assume I'll see you tomorrow?"

I start to say yes, but I have this stupid thing called pride and it's making me question if I've made myself too available. Yes, I was helping him out and it's been great. I love hanging with Jack and watching him work out, bringing him cookies or healthy lunches, swimming in his pool, I even like organizing his email. Also, did I mention how much I like watching him work out?

But now I guess I want to make him work for it. It's the only explanation for what comes out of my mouth. "I'm actually going to be busy for the next few days."

He studies me and I sweat it, sure he can see right through my lies. I do need to get my life together for the internship. I still haven't filled out all the required HR forms; my house still has to be packed up, and I need to shop for business-y clothes. I don't think my bikinis and cut-off shorts are going to pass the dress code at my internship.

"Is that okay? Will your inbox survive?" I ask with a smirk.

"I'll manage."

I grab my stuff and start for the door. He doesn't move from where he stands, but he watches me intently. I turn but keep walking away from him.

"See you later, stud."

His face scrunches up with obvious displeasure at the nickname. And it just makes me want to call him that even more.

"You're either a genius or the dumbest woman I know," Grace says later that night. She's at my place and we're sitting on the floor in my bedroom. I was packing for a while, but the boxes and packing tape, and the piles of shoes and clothes are now abandoned and forgotten.

"I hope it's the first." I sip my wine, but the cool liquid does not stamp out the heat summoned by the memory of Jack going down on me in his kitchen.

The man has a wicked tongue. I left that part out when I confided in Grace the reason I needed her to keep me busy for the next few days. She got the abridged version: Jack and I made out and it's no big deal. I have to keep repeating it to myself, mostly, because damn it felt like a big deal. I know I said I wasn't going to get attached and that it was just sex, but wow, I think I was underestimating my feelings and his skills.

But now that I've told him I have things to do, I need to do those things instead of running back over there for another round.

"Well, this is perfect. We can shop tomorrow and go to Midnight tomorrow night."

"That's his club."

"It's not like he'll be there." Grace gathers her dark hair and puts it into a messy bun on top of her head. "We can drink and dance the night away. It'll be like junior year all over again."

"Yeah, I suppose you're right. I've missed you." She started dating her boyfriend Lane and as they got more serious, we spent less time together. Some might say we drifted apart, but that isn't really true. I know that she would always be there if I needed anything, and the same goes for her. We're like sisters, but as we've gotten older, our lives are less connected.

"Unless…" She trails off and a huge smile breaks out across her face.

"Yeah?" I ask, a rush of hopeful adrenaline courses through me before she's even filled me in on her idea.

"Have you heard from him?" Grace asks.

We're outside of Midnight. Me, Grace, and Lane, with dozens of others waiting to get inside the club.

"No, not yet." I rub my lips together, ensuring my gloss is still there.

"Are you sure you sent the text?"

"I'm sure." I check again though. Approximately one hour ago I sent him a photo of me in my new sexy dress and told him where I was heading.

It was a clear invitation to hang out, but now I'm wondering if I should have been less subtle. Before I can tap out another text that says, *please come peel this dress off me*, Grace nudges me in the side with her bony elbow.

"Ow. What was that for?" I ask, glancing up at her. But she's not looking at me, her stare is locked straight ahead and she's grinning. I follow her line of vision and then forget how to breathe. Or maybe this dress is just too tight. Who am I kidding? This dress is definitely too tight. But that doesn't change the fact that Jack is here, walking toward me and looking like a goddamn snack.

I step forward and meet him a few feet away from Grace and Lane.

"Hi." A shyness that is very uncommon for me makes a flush spread down my neck. Hopefully it's too dark outside to ruin the effect of my outfit.

"Of all the clubs in the city..."

"It's the best."

His gaze drops to my lips. "You're not wrong there."

He glances past me, and I open up my stance as Grace and Lane approach us.

Grace lifts one hand and fans it out in a wave. "Hey," she says.

Lane tips his head in greeting. He's always been a little starstruck around the Wildcat guys. He's a quiet guy but becomes even more withdrawn when any of them are around.

"Good to see you both," Jack says, then, "Ready?"

It hits me then that we don't have to wait in line.

"I promise this wasn't a ploy to get in quicker," I say.

"No?" His mouth quirks up at the corners. "Just a ploy to torture me in that dress?"

"More like a ploy to get me out of it."

He shakes his head, but not before giving me another once-over.

We follow him into Midnight. I love the way he walks with a

purpose and an air of confidence. The guards tip their heads and let us by without a word. Even people who don't recognize him move out of the way, making a path for us. He heads to the end of the bar where he's immediately served.

"What do you want to drink?" he asks as he places a hand on my lower back. The red dress hugs my curves tightly and feels like butter against my skin. The heat of his palm travels through the thin material, and I have to restrain myself from lifting up on my toes so his fingers are resting a little lower.

He's staring down at me, waiting for an answer.

"Champagne."

He quirks one brow.

"We're celebrating."

He gets Grace and Lane's requests then orders everything. Turning so his body is angled toward me, he asks, "What are we celebrating?"

"You being out of the house, for starters."

His lips twist into a sexy smirk.

"And I got a new dress."

His stare rakes over me slowly like he's appreciating every centimeter of said dress.

"Do you like it?"

He leans in. "I'd like it better if you'd worn it over to my house. Every guy in this club is staring at you."

"Jealous?"

"No." He pulls back.

"No?" I'm surprised by his answer. The way he looks at me, the way his fingers dig in tighter on my back, gives away his possessiveness.

"I've slammed plenty of guys into the boards for a lot less than looking at my girl."

"*Your* girl?" I ask pointedly.

His answer is a Cheshire cat grin. So fucking cocky and confident.

A nervous chuckle escapes from my lips. I feel like for the first time with Jack, I might be in over my head. "So you're just going to beat up anyone that looks at me?"

"Exactly." He winks, and a steady throb starts between my legs. Did I wear this dress hoping to blow his mind? Guilty. Am I regretting that now that I know he might punch anyone that looks at me too long? Maybe.

"You look beautiful."

The compliment takes me by surprise. I guess I'm used to guys who only say things like that to me when they're trying to take me home for the night.

"You know I'm basically a sure thing, right? You don't need to use your pretty words on me."

"No? What kind of words would you like me to use then?"

"We don't need to talk at all." I step closer. His gaze drops to my lips, but he doesn't kiss me.

He's all cool and under control, and I'm ready to strip out of this dress and throw myself at him.

"The pool wasn't the same without you today," he says, leaning one hip against the bar as he faces me.

"You didn't touch your inbox, did you?" I ask.

One side of his mouth pulls up in a half smile. "No ma'am."

"Good. I don't want you to mess up all my hard work."

"No, we wouldn't want that." He keeps smiling at me. "So, did you get all your stuff done or are you going to be *busy* again tomorrow?"

"You missed me that much, huh?"

He doesn't answer, but the air buzzes around us, confirming that whatever is going on between us seems to be affecting us both.

Our drinks come, and Grace and I down our champagne quickly after toasting to our new boss babe lives.

"We're going to dance," Grace says, giving me a knowing smirk as she pulls Lane behind her.

They don't get far when I decide that maybe dancing is exactly how to burn off some of this tension.

"Wanna dance?" I ask him.

With a nod, he takes my hand. Instead of going to the dance floor, he heads to a staircase that leads upstairs. There's a VIP section, but instead of stopping there, he leads me behind the bar on the second floor to another set of stairs.

My pulse picks up speed. It's dark and I grip his hand tightly to stick with him.

"Where are we going?" I ask as we reach our destination.

The area is like a sky box that looks down on the club.

"Welcome to the owner's box." He winks.

"I can't believe I've never noticed this before."

"You're not meant to," he says. "The windows are tinted so no one can see in."

A shiver dances over my skin at the thought of him being up here watching people. Watching me, maybe.

There's a bar up here too, but no one is working. Jack goes behind it and grabs two glasses and a bottle of champagne.

The seats are even lusher than the ones in VIP. This is obviously for the high-profile guests they entertain.

He pops the champagne and pours two glasses. He hands me one but doesn't take the other.

"Did you have a good day?" I ask before taking a sip. The first glass already has me feeling light and a little tipsy.

"It was quiet."

"That sounds terrible."

"You have no idea." He closes the distance between us and his lips cover mine, stealing my breath and making my heart race faster.

Jack and I used to go days, weeks even, without seeing each other, but the day apart felt like a lifetime.

"This dress," he grumbles as his hands roam down to my ass and squeeze.

"Had to bring me all the way up to your private lair to keep other men from looking at me," I tease.

"Damn fucking straight."

His words light me up. The song changes to one of my favorites and I turn around, giving him my back and moving to the beat. Those big hands of his stay on me, moving up and down my sides, from my ribs to my thighs. I'm still holding my champagne, but my other hand rests on his leg.

Jack moves with me, chest pressed to my back. He pushes my hair off my neck and drops his mouth to my shoulder. My eyes flutter closed as his teeth scrape and then his lips kiss away the pain.

He's a good dancer, not that we're actually doing much more than grinding. Still, he has rhythm and keeps up with me as I shake my hips and bounce around to the music.

His attention focused on me is a heady drug, combined with the champagne, and I'm floating.

I drop my head back onto his chest and his hands roam around to my stomach, keeping me in place. I love the feel of his strong arms holding me against him.

Eventually his fingers drop to the hem of my dress. It hits high up on my thighs and the dancing has inched it higher so that it's only just covering my ass. His thumbs glide up, taking the material with it. The cool air pebbles my bare skin. He growls against my neck as he reaches the lacy material of my panties.

I'm soaked. A realization he finds out for himself seconds later when his fingers brush against my center.

"Is this what you had in mind when you picked out this dress for me?" he asks as he slips one finger under the material.

I gasp as he circles my clit in lazy strokes.

"No, but I'm not complaining."

He sucks on my neck as he adds another finger under my panties. It's euphoric with the loud music and couples dancing below us, watching them while his fingers are buried inside me.

I've been so keyed up since yesterday. Two orgasms should have satiated me, but instead, it awoke a desire I've never felt before. Also, I just missed him. Like really missed him.

I swivel my head around and he immediately takes the hint, crushing his mouth down on mine as he continues to pump his fingers in and out of me. I cry out into his mouth as I come so hard my legs feel weak.

If he weren't already so damn arrogant, I might tell him I have never come so hard in my life as I do for him.

His fingers continue lavishing me with attention as the orgasm subsides, then he squats down in front of me, placing a kiss on my inner thigh as he slides my panties down. I step out of them and he pockets them before pulling my dress down like nothing happened.

When I'm breathy and starting to sweat, I turn back around to face him.

"I should have brought a second pair of panties."

He grins. "They just get in the way."

My breaths are still ragged when I ask, "How's your knee?"

"You don't need to worry about me. I'm good."

"I like worrying about you." My gaze moves to one of the cushy chairs. I set my champagne down on a table and pull him with me to the chair. The room has graduated floors so that even in the back, you can see the dance floor.

He smirks as I playfully shove him down into the chair.

"Take a load off, big guy."

He sits like a man in a throne, legs spread apart and arms draped over the sides. I step between his spread legs. He doesn't move, but his eyes darken and his jaw flexes as my arms lift. I brush my hair off my neck and then raise them in the air. The movement inches my dress higher. I'm lost to the beat and to the weight of his stare. It's electric. The way he watches me makes me feel cherished, possessed. Men never make me feel that way. I never wanted that.

But I crave Jack in a dozen different ways. His words, his smile, his touch, just to name a few. I even missed watching him work out today – and no, not just because he looks damn fine while doing it, but because I've been seeing him progress a little at a time. His knee is stronger every day. It's incredible. *He's* incredible.

It's hard to wrap my brain around this thing between us. A month ago, I would have laughed if someone said that Jack Wyld was going to change the very fabric of what I want from men.

Placing one knee on the chair between his thighs, I lean in and kiss him. He still doesn't place his hands on me, but his mouth shows me how much he wants me.

He tastes minty fresh and smells like citrus and leather.

I place one hand on his hard chest and trail it down over his stomach. I can picture exactly how he looks underneath and my mouth waters at the memory.

He finally lunges for me, wrapping an arm around my waist and tugging me down on top of him. I giggle as he settles me on his lap. His palm drops to my knee and he smiles in a way that is both sweet and sexy.

I drape one arm around his neck and play with the hair at the nape of his neck. He studies me, gaze hot and sinful. We just stare at each other like we're both trying to decide if we should talk or keep kissing all night long. I could easily get on board with the latter if it weren't for my friend downstairs. I've already been gone long enough that she might be worried.

"I should probably go find Grace and let her know I'm safe soon."

"Okay."

"Thanks for bringing me up here." I glance around, wondering if I'll ever see it again. "Being the owner has its perks, huh?"

"It did tonight." His fingers dance higher and I bite the corner of my lip. I don't want to go yet. Downstairs I know he won't touch me this freely. But here we have this whole area all to ourselves. Just me and this sexy guy that I can't get enough of.

CHAPTER TWENTY-ONE

Jack

SWEET AND CUDDLY

"Tell me the truth," Ev says as we head back downstairs. "How many women have you taken to the owner's box?"

"Lots," I say automatically, knowing that isn't the answer she wants.

The jealous glint in her eyes is proof enough of that, so is the vise-like grip she now has on my hand. I bring our joined hands up to my mouth and kiss the top of her knuckles. "The first time I've made someone come on my fingers up there though."

I can still smell her on me, and goddamn it's going to be a long night before I can get my hands on her again like I want.

"I'm going to choose to believe that." She stops trying to break my hand, but the jealous glint stays. Fine by me, she's sexy as fuck.

She wore that skimpy little dress to make me lose my mind, like I wasn't already there. If she only knew how badly I want her all the fucking time. She doesn't need to do a damn thing for my benefit. It's just her that makes me wild. Every little fucking thing.

"Hey, there you are!" Grace yells and hugs Everly when we find her on the dance floor. "Where were you?"

"Upstairs," Everly says vaguely.

"Did you grab a table?" Grace fans her face. "I need a break."

"Go ahead. I'll grab us some more drinks," I say, untangling my fingers from Ev's and placing my hand on her lower back. She leans into me.

"How will you find us?"

"I'll find you," I assure her. I seem to have a radar specifically honed in on her.

I grab a bottle of champagne and glasses from the bar. As expected, I have no problem finding Everly. She, Grace, and Lane are seated on a couch in the VIP section and across from them are two guys and another girl they must know because they're talking animatedly.

Everly looks up when I get to the top of the steps. A slow smile spreads across her face, and she crosses her legs in a way that has me wondering if her thoughts are still upstairs in the private box as well or on the fact her panties are in my pocket.

I take a seat next to her, pour a glass of champagne for her, then for Grace and Lane.

"You're not drinking?" she asks.

"Not tonight."

She looks like she wants to ask more, but then one of the guys on the couch across from us calls her name.

I glare at the guy as she glances over at him.

"When do you leave for Briar Lake?" he asks, smiling at her in a way that is a little too familiar.

"Oh, umm, I'm leaving at the end of the month." She fidgets with the glass in her hand and smiles, though in a way that is all false bravado.

"Cool," he replies, not catching on to her discomfort. "My family has a place up there. Maybe we can hook up some weekend. I can show you around."

I clear my throat and his gaze slides to me. Ev giggles but covers it quickly.

"Yeah, that'd be nice."

I turn my glare to the woman beside me. I might need to drag her back upstairs and remind her I'm a jealous man when it comes to her.

"Jack, this is Christian. I went to college with him and his *boyfriend*, Ryan."

I look back to the guy in question and then notice the guy next to him. He lifts a hand. "Ryan. Nice to meet you. Big fan."

"You too." I smile graciously at him and Christian.

"And that's Lisa on the end," Everly says. "She accepted an internship with the same company as I did."

I tip my head to her, and she smiles back before turning her attention back to Ev.

"It's going to be so great. Heather is a genius. I heard from a friend that works there that she just landed a huge deal on a new condominium building. It seems like she's really leaning into the commercial space."

"Really?" Everly asks, seeming surprised. "But she's so good at making homes feel original and well-loved."

"Yeah." Lisa nods. "She has a real eye for that, but branching out is probably a smart move. There are so many condos and apartments going up around the lake. I bet we get to help with furnishing and staging."

"More like you'll be grabbing her coffee and calling vendors," Christian says.

"Of course." Lisa nods. "We are interns after all, but she promised we'd get some real, hands-on experience too."

Lisa's eyes sparkle with excitement and possibility. Not unusual, but it's a contrast to Everly's much calmer demeanor. Why isn't she bouncing with excitement?

"I wish I could afford to rent one of those condos instead of the studio basement I had to settle for. Where are you?" Lisa asks her.

"I lucked into a sublet," Everly says. I want to ask if it's one that Ty owns, but I don't want to put her on the spot. Her brother has been smart with his money, investing in real estate like the house she lives in now. I get the sense that Ev isn't keen on reminding people that her brother is a famous and rich hockey player.

The conversation shifts from the internship to talking about their college classes, professors, and other friends. I sit back and listen, mostly to Everly.

"Sorry," she says at one point when everyone else is talking around us. "Are you bored?"

"No."

She narrows her gaze like she's trying to make sure I'm not lying.

"Would I rather be back upstairs? Yes. But I'm sitting next to the hottest woman in the club and my fingers still smell like her pussy. Don't you worry about me."

And the truth is I could sit here and listen to her talk all night and be content. I'm looking forward to kissing her again, but it's also nice hearing her talk about life and work and random shit that she's never told me before. Before this summer we never really shared these kinds of details about our lives. Sure, we knew what the other was up to, but only by extension of our friends and her brother. Now that I've gotten a glimpse of how she thinks, what she wants, and who she really is, I just want to know more.

She bites on the corner of her lip like she's deciding something. Maybe whether she's ready to ditch her friends again.

"Why'd you decide to be an interior designer?" I ask her.

"The short version is I like art and decorating."

"And the long version?"

She hesitates, tilts her head to one side, and gets a contemplative look on her face like she's trying to decide how much to share with me.

I wait because I'm hoping she'll tell me everything. I want to know every last detail about her.

"I bounced around a lot as a kid. Mom and I moved a few times, then twice with Ty, again in college…" She trails off. "Making a space feel like home is harder when it's unfamiliar."

My chest tightens at her admission, but I don't dare speak for fear of stopping her from continuing.

"There's something really comforting about making a place feel like it's an extension of you. It doesn't have to be extravagant or expensive; it just needs to be well thought out and customized. A house should feel like a home and that means different things for different people."

"And you want to give that to them?"

"Mostly I just enjoy doing it for myself, but that doesn't pay as well."

I'm lost in my thoughts with her watching me.

"What?" she asks.

"I was just wondering about my place."

"It's very well decorated," she answers.

"It should be. I paid a fortune for the artwork and furniture."

She giggles and the sound seeps into my pores.

"It feels very you. Masculine and rich but somehow cozy."

"I'm cozy?" I arch a brow in question.

"You can be." She leans into me. "Like right now. All sweet and cuddly."

I let out a low growl. I'm not sure anyone has ever accused me of being sweet or cuddly, but I'm finding I'm a lot of different things with her.

Everly giggles again and I drop a hand to her thigh, then squeeze. I lean down to whisper in her ear, "Keep giggling like that, temptress. It makes me that much more excited to fill your mouth with something else later."

She takes a sharp inhale of breath and then a flush creeps down her neck. "I think asking you to come here was a mistake."

"Why?" I ask, pulling back slightly. I know I can be an overbearing asshole. Maybe she wants to spend the night with her friends instead of me hogging all her attention. I came downstairs with her but I'm still stealing her attention.

"Because I can't concentrate on anything else. Everyone is talking and all I can think about is whether or not you have my panties in your pocket."

I shift so she can reach in and check, which she does.

"Want them back?" I make like I'm going to reach in for them, but she stops me.

"No. They'd just be getting soaked again." Her gaze drops to my mouth. She brings a hand up to my jaw, then drags the back of her fingers over my lips.

The meaning of her words finally drifts past the lust fog clouding my brain.

"Soaked for me again, huh?"

She nods, then moves her hand to the back of my neck. I like the way she touches me. Explorative and reverent and out in the open for everyone to see.

That last part should probably concern me, but I'm too wrapped up in her to care who knows. At least right this minute.

"Do you want to go back upstairs?"

"What about your friends?"

"They won't miss me."

I seriously consider it, but then shake my head. "No. We have time. Tonight, you should enjoy your friends."

"Think one of them can do something about the throbbing between my legs?" She bats her lashes then giggles.

"Not fucking funny." I take her mouth, nipping at her bottom lip.

"Everly!" Grace calls her name and moves to stand in front of her. "We have to dance."

She grins at me as she lets her friend pull her to her feet, then sends me a flirty wink as they go.

I blow out a breath and run a hand through my hair. I am in serious trouble with this girl.

CHAPTER TWENTY-TWO

Everly

SO BOSSY

J ack and I get into a sort of routine. I show up at his place sometime late in the morning after I've finished checking in on all the houses I'm sitting for. He works out while I go through his email and schedule, and then lie by the pool. Sometimes I work out with him, but only as an excuse to be closer to him.

It's basically the perfect summer. Complete with kissing. Lots and lots of kissing and multiple orgasms. We haven't had sex yet, which I haven't pushed because it's not like I don't leave every day satiated, but I'd say it has something to do with neither of us wanting to cross a line we can't take back.

I've also not stayed the night at his house yet, but tonight is the masquerade ball I bullied him into attending, and I'm thinking it might be the perfect night for a sleepover and to cross all the lines.

It's late afternoon and I need to go back to my place to get ready, but the weather is perfect today. Bright sun, only a few clouds. I wish summer could last forever.

Jack's phone rings and he pauses his stretching to answer it. A few seconds later he heads inside so I reluctantly pull myself out of the pool and dry off.

He reemerges, scanning the pool first for me and then smiling when he sees I've gotten out. I walk toward him, towel wrapped around me and hair still dripping.

"I'm going to head out and get ready. Do you want me to come back here, and we'll drive over together?" I ask. My stomach is already a ball of nerves thinking about going to an event with Jack.

"I have a surprise for you." His lips curve up and his brows lift playfully.

"O-kay," I say slowly, but excitement builds quickly as he leads me into the house and down the hall to one of the spare bedrooms.

Jack pauses at the threshold and leaves room for me to pass by him. Two women are busy unpacking a trunk of hair and makeup accessories and there's a dressing rack of gorgeous gowns in a variety of colors.

I whirl around to face him. He looks very pleased with the very shocked expression I'm positive is on my face.

"What did you do?" I ask in a slightly accusatory tone. This is...I am officially speechless.

"I thought you might need a dress for tonight," he says.

"I have a dress." Not one that compares to the beautiful ones on the rack behind me, but it isn't bad. Okay, I probably would have been the worst-dressed woman there, but this is too much.

He leans in and brushes his lips over mine, then murmurs, "Fine. I'm a selfish asshole and I didn't want you to leave."

"Or you didn't want me to show up looking a hot mess and

embarrass you."

With a slight shake to his head, he grins at me. "Not possible. You could go exactly like you are and still be the most beautiful woman there."

He leaves me, like he didn't just casually drop the nicest compliment I've ever gotten, disappearing back down the hallway. My anxiety spikes as I walk fully into the room.

"Hi!" The women say in unison. They introduce themselves as Chelsea and Nicole.

"It's nice to meet you both," I say. My voice quivers, giving away my nerves. "I'm a mess from the pool. I'm going to take a quick shower."

"Take your time," Nicole says with a reassuring smile.

I back out of the room calmly and then hurry to catch up with Jack. He's in the kitchen with his phone. When he spots me, he looks up and his brows furrow.

"Is everything okay?"

Instead of answering him, I walk right up to him, lift up onto my toes and kiss him.

His surprise only lasts a second and then he's taking control, framing my face and sweeping his tongue into my mouth.

With a smile, I pull back and drop flat on my feet.

After a quick shower, I return to Chelsea and Nicole. They help me pick a dress first, then shoes. I don't think too hard on how Jack knew my sizes, but everything is perfect.

Once wardrobe is decided, they start on my hair and makeup. I'm usually a bit of a control freak when it comes to letting other people make me over. For big events, I tend to just do it myself, so I know it'll be the way I like it. But when they're finished and I look in the mirror, my jaw drops. My skin is flawless, and my eye makeup is still my signature winged liner, just with more shadow and smudging to give it a more exaggerated smoky look. My lips are coated in a glossy natural color, and my hair is down and curled in ringlets that frame my face and cascade down my back. I still look like me, just *way* hotter than normal.

"Damn," I say to my reflection.

Chelsea laughs as she pulls my dress from the hanger. "Time for the dress."

My hands tremble as I step into the gorgeous gown.

"Damn is right." Nicole sets the shoes in front of me. They're my favorite part, if I could even pick a favorite. This is unreal.

"Thank you." I hug Nicole and then Chelsea. They seem a little taken aback but they literally just worked magic and words don't feel like enough.

"Extra lipstick for later in case you need it." Nicole hands me the tube of lipstick she used with a wink.

"You're going to need it," Chelsea says. "Your boyfriend won't be able to resist you."

Nicole nods her agreement.

I don't correct their assumption that Jack is my boyfriend, but it sends another flutter of nerves through me. I take a few deep breaths, then thank them again. I'm actually looking forward to tonight despite the anxious energy. After a summer of lying around the pool without much makeup, or clothes for that matter, I can't wait to see the look on Jack's face when he sees me like this. I am going to blow his mind.

With that thought at the forefront, I head out of the room to find him. The house is quiet except for music playing through the speakers.

My heels clack on the floor with every step and my heart races in anticipation.

"Jack?" I call when I don't see him in the kitchen or living room.

"Be right out," he yells from the direction of his bedroom.

I spot two masks on the kitchen counter. A simple black satin one and another that is the same turquoise of my dress. The man officially thinks of everything.

"How did you know which dress I was going to choose?" I yell, smiling as I run a hand along the silky material, but I forget what I asked, and probably how to breathe, when Jack steps out of his room.

The black suit hugs his tall, broad body in all the right places. My throat is dry while I take him in. I forget all about blowing his mind because *mine* is officially blown.

"Goddamn," I mutter finally.

He smirks, invading my space. His spicy cologne wraps around me, and I swallow hard.

"My thoughts exactly." He lets his gaze rake over me from head to toe, and when I see the spark of desire in his eyes, some of my confidence returns.

I do a spin for him. The dress has a high slit that gapes with the movement.

"The shoes are the best part," I say, stepping one leg out to show off the strappy silver heels that wrap around my foot and ankle.

"You just need one more thing."

I laugh because, what is this life? He pulls out a long black velvet box and opens it, revealing a diamond tennis necklace.

"I'm not putting that thing on." I shake my head adamantly. My heart leaps into my throat.

He laughs and pulls out the necklace, setting the box on the counter.

"I'm serious, Jack. That thing is worth more than everything I own."

"It wasn't that much," he insists and walks behind me, dropping the necklace over my head so that it rests against my throat.

Not that much for him maybe.

The necklace is cool and heavy against my skin. I pull my hair off my neck and he clasps it in place.

My hand goes to my throat as he steps away. "This feels a lot more like a date than I imagined."

"If it was a date, I'd be taking you somewhere I wouldn't have to share you so much."

"So this is business?" I ask. Maybe if I think of it that way, I won't read too much into all the Cinderella vibes happening here. Jack is not Prince Charming, and I'm not the kind of girl that believes in fairy tales anyway.

He makes a noncommittal noise low in his throat. "Ready?"

The event is held in an old, renovated building with columns and marble flooring. Cocktail tables are set up all around the room for people to gather around as they sip boozy drinks and snack on hors d'oeuvres.

Everywhere I look women are dressed in expensive gowns and glitter in diamonds, and the men are dashing in suits. I feel so out of my league for a moment but as soon as we're pulled into the first conversation and I realize all they want to talk about is Jack and hockey, I know I'll be okay.

We're talking with one of the executives from Nike. Kai is young, about the same age as Jack, and so far, I like him. He doesn't have that air of snobbery about him I expected from a corporate guy sent here to wine and dine with potential clients.

"Your stats were pretty good last year considering the short season." Kai takes a drink of whiskey, flashing his Rolex in the process.

Jack nods slightly. His posture is relaxed with one hand in his pants pocket and the one closest to me hovers at my lower back.

I look between the men expecting them both to laugh.

"Pretty good?" I ask finally. "Jack was fourth in the league for goals. He's consistently putting up big numbers, and unlike a lot of guys who peak their second or third year in the league, Jack's numbers have improved. And don't even get me started on the impact he makes that doesn't show up on a stat sheet. The Wildcat organization is one of the most respected and feared because of the environment Jack has created. The guys can depend on him and they work hard because of it."

Kai's brows inch up his forehead and I know I have officially said too much. *Oops.* I take a sip of my champagne to keep me from saying more.

Jack chuckles nervously. "What she said."

"Sorry," I say as heat blooms in my cheeks. "I love hockey."

"Yeah, I got that. And you're not wrong." Kai smiles at me, then looks at Jack. "She's a keeper. My wife won't even come to games with me when I get box seats."

Jack's hand at my back presses a little firmer against my bare skin.

"I won't keep you, but I'm glad we had a chance to talk. I'll be in touch with James." Kai extends a hand to Jack and after they shake, he looks to me. "Nice to meet you, Everly."

I let out a whoosh of air as soon as he's gone and turn into Jack's chest. The heels make me a few inches taller, but I still have to tip my head up ever so slightly to meet his gaze.

"I'm so sorry. It just word vomited out."

"No need to be sorry. That was impressive. Did you study for tonight?" He arches a brow with an amused smirk.

"Umm…no."

"No?" His forehead crinkles with his confusion.

"Don't get a big head or anything. I know most of the team's stats."

He searches my face, inching closer so our bodies press together. "How many goals did Leo have last season?"

I open my mouth to answer but I struggle to remember. Was it forty-one? Or was that Johnny Maverick?

Jack's smirk grows into a full-blown smile.

"Shut up. It's the champagne. I'm getting a little lightheaded."

He lets it drop without pointing out that I may indeed know his stats better than the rest of the team. Except Tyler, of course. I maintain that it's only because Jack's are so impressive but telling him that would only feed his ego and I've already done a good job of that.

Taking my hand in his, Jack leads me through the room. He tips his head as people say hello but doesn't stop until we're out in the hallway. There's an alcove with big windows that look out onto the city. When we're hidden from view of the main party, his hands come up to either side of my neck and he kisses me.

My surprise is short-lived and a dizzy sensation sweeps through me as his tongue pushes into my mouth. Kissing Jack feels like teleporting to a different world, and I like the glimpses of that place a little too much.

When he pulls back, the room spins, and I struggle to catch my breath. His dark eyes bore into me. The mask is sexy, but I'm itching to see his full face again.

He moves his hands down my side and I sway slightly.

I laugh softly. "I think the champagne definitely got to me."

I didn't drink that much but I barely ate because I was afraid of getting crumbs on this dress.

"You look a little flushed." Jack brings one palm back up and brushes his knuckles lightly against my cheek. "You're warm."

"I'm fine," I say but as I do, I notice the headache forming at the base of my skull.

His fingers continue to roam my face and the back of my neck. Concern tugs his brows together in the center. "I think you have a fever."

I want to protest but I think he's right.

"I'm so sorry. I should probably head out early. The last thing I want to do is faint or puke in front of these people." My smile is wobbly but I'm suddenly eager to lie down in bed. "I'll see you tomorrow."

"Don't be ridiculous. I'm going with you."

I'm too dizzy to argue. My stomach isn't upset but my head is starting to throb.

By the time we get to his SUV, I'm burning up. I keep my eyes closed the entire ride and when I open them, we're back at his place.

"You could have taken me home," I say.

He doesn't even bother responding. I know Jack well enough not to fight his need to control the situation. Right now, I'm a problem to be solved. And to be honest, I don't really want to be alone.

The cool night air feels good against my skin as I walk toward the house. I stumble but Jack is right there to steady me. It feels like he's two seconds from picking me up and carrying me but I'm so warm, even the thought of being nuzzled up next to him makes me sweat.

In his room, Jack walks in ahead of me and turns on a lamp on his bedside table. I sit on the edge of his bed, and he squats down in front of me. He lifts my left leg and undoes the clasp around my ankle to free my shoe. He presses a kiss on my calf and then sets the sparkly shoe on the floor, before doing the same thing on the other side.

Standing, he takes my hand and pulls me to my feet.

"Turn around," he says. His voice is quiet, reverent.

I comply, and his fingers work on unzipping the back of the dress.

"This is not how I imagined you taking me out of this dress," I say as he lets it fall and then helps me step out of it.

I'm standing in front of him in only my panties, but his gaze doesn't leave my face as he smiles at me. After a beat, he moves over to his dresser and pulls out a T-shirt, then dresses me. It's sweet and so far beyond how anyone has ever taken care of me.

I tug my hair out from underneath the collar of the shirt. I feel like crap but I don't want him to leave.

"Get in bed. I'll bring you some medicine and water," he says. "Need anything else?"

"No. And I don't want to kick you out of your own bed. I can sleep on the couch."

"You think I'm sleeping on the couch?" he asks. "I have like three extra bedrooms."

"Then I can sleep in one of those."

"Get in my bed," he says as he steps toward the door. "I want to keep an eye on you."

"So bossy," I mutter as I pull the covers back. His bed smells like him and within seconds I'm drifting off.

CHAPTER TWENTY-THREE

Jack

LOOKING SO MUCH LIKE MINE

I'm lying in bed next to Everly watching TV on mute. I slept a little but I kept startling awake, afraid she was going to need something.

"Hey," she says, voice gruff.

I glance over at her in the dark. The lights from the TV give just enough glow for me to see she's smiling.

"How are you feeling?"

"A little better, I think. My head is still killing me."

"You can have more medicine in an hour."

She nods, then brings both hands up under her chin and continues to stare at me.

"Your bed is nice."

"I know." I turn over on my side, mimicking her body language. I reach out and press the back of my hand to her forehead. She's still warm.

"Aren't you afraid I'm going to get you sick?"

"Nah. My immune system is good."

"People always say that right before they get sick." Her lashes flutter closed for a moment and then reopen.

"I'm sorry we had to leave the ball early," she says.

"Don't worry about it. Besides, you sold me so hard to Kai, he already reached out to James."

"You got an offer?" she asks, eyes widening with excitement.

"Not yet, but James seems to think they will if I'm able to come back this season and put up the same kind of numbers as last year."

"When."

"What?" I ask.

"*When* you're back putting up those numbers. There's no if about it. You're a legend. That's the one thing Kai got right."

One side of my lips pulls up. Everly has never been one to bullshit me, so her faith in me means more than she could know.

She sits up to take a drink of water and then lies back down, pulling one of the pillows to her chest and hugging it as she gets comfortable again.

"Seriously. This bed is really comfortable." She grins. "And it smells like you. Warm leather and spice with a hint of something clean like Downy fabric softener."

"I think it might be time for you to go back to sleep," I say.

"I'm not tired."

"Your body can recover better the more you rest."

"You're good at taking care of people."

"Only when they listen to me."

Her smile inches higher. "How come you don't do serious relationships?"

The question takes me by surprise, and I shrug. "I date when it fits into my schedule."

"That is so not romantic."

"But it's practical. I don't have a lot of time or energy for anyone besides the team during the season."

"Other guys make it work."

She isn't wrong, but my job is to make their lives simple so they can do things like that.

"I know you and I are just…whatever, but you're good at this. You should do it more. The team will be okay. You don't have to give all of yourself to hockey to be a legend. You can make room for other things."

My chest tightens at her words. I want to believe she's right, but letting the guys down is a fear that isn't so easily wiped away.

I clear my throat. "What about you?"

"I don't know. It isn't like I'm opposed to a serious relationship. I've seen how good it can be. Tyler and Piper are as in love today as they were when they were teenagers. Ash and Bridget are so perfect for each other it's hard to imagine a time when they weren't together. Declan would do anything for Jade, and Scarlett and Leo make out like they just met. I don't know…" She trails off. "It makes it hard to sit across from guys who can barely fake interest in getting to know me long enough to finish dinner."

"I get that."

"You do?"

"Sure. I can't deny that relationships like that exist."

"You just don't think you're cut out for it?"

I ignore her question because I don't know the answer anymore. "There are lots of guys who want to get to know you. Maybe you're just hanging out with the wrong ones."

"Like you?"

"I want to know you." I brush a strand of hair off her flushed skin.

"You already do. Sometimes I think you know what I'll say or do better than I do." She yawns but covers it with a hand and then smiles sleepily before she asks, "When you're done playing hockey, what will you do?"

"I'll be a grumpy, retired hockey player."

She giggles. Fuck I love that sound. I shoot her a sly smile.

"It's the only thing I ever wanted."

"Really? But you have so many other things. Endorsements, charities, the club. I figured you'd focus on one of those."

"Maybe. I'm not sure."

"When I was a kid, I changed my mind about what I wanted to be when I grew up weekly. Even now, half the time I waver between certainty and *what the hell am I doing* when I think about a career. That's not normal, is it?"

"I'm probably not the guy to ask since my career ambitions are singular."

"Nothing else? Not even a police officer or a firefighter?" she asks as she studies me. "I thought all guys went through a hero phase."

"Hockey players are heroes."

She stares at me with a blank expression until I smile, then she bursts out laughing. I should probably feel a little offended that she thinks my job isn't as cool as others, but I'm too focused on how good it feels to see her smile and hear her laugh.

I should tell her to go to sleep, but I'm enjoying this too much. I could lie here, talking and staring at her forever.

Everly reaches out with a hand and runs a finger down the sleeve of tattoos on my right arm. "Is it finished?"

"I have one spot left." I turn my arm so she can see the area on the inside of my bicep.

"What's going there?"

"I don't know yet. I'm waiting for inspiration."

She grins, then yawns again.

"You should get some sleep," I say reluctantly. "Me too. Brian will be by early."

She smirks. "How's that going?"

"Good," I admit. "Now that he's not hitting on you."

"I can't believe you fired him."

"I didn't like the way he looked at you."

"How'd he look at me?"

"Like he wanted what was mine."

"Yours, huh?"

Fuck. She's not mine, at least not in the way that sounded. She's mine for a short period of time. Once summer is over, she'll leave, and I'll go back to my usual routine. Dating when it works in my schedule and focusing on hockey the rest of the time.

I thread my fingers through her hair and draw her closer to me, dropping a kiss on her forehead before I pull back. She's got me wrapped so tightly around her finger. I like being in control, of myself and my relationships, but Everly seems to thrive on upending that control.

I keep waiting for her to realize that maybe this isn't a good idea, but so far all I've done is convince myself that maybe it is.

Two days pass while Everly fights off a fever. She stays at my house and we binge-watch TV and talk into the late hours of the night while

I feed her medicine and make sure she drinks lots of fluids. I put off training with Brian all weekend to look after her, but Monday I decide it's time to get back to it, now that Everly's feeling better.

She left, much to my dismay, to do her house-sitting rounds, and it feels weird being away from her for this long.

I'm just finishing up with physical therapy when my phone rings. I lean over to silence the call, but then have second thoughts when I see it's Tyler. A dozen questions race through my mind. Why is he calling? Is Everly okay? Does he know about us?

I admit I've done a stellar job of pushing Tyler out of my mind while spending time with his little sister.

"I gotta take this," I tell Brian. "Thanks for today. I'll see you tomorrow."

"Yeah. No problem." He starts to pack up his equipment and I hit accept on the call.

Forcing some calm into my tone, I say, "Hey. What's up?"

"Not too much." He doesn't sound angry so that's reassuring. "How's the knee?"

"Pretty good. I'm just finishing up PT for the day. Doctor thinks I'll be ready in time for camp."

"That's great news." The excitement in his voice matches mine. I still have a long way to go, but I'm getting there. I won't stop until I'm back better than ever.

"Yeah," I say. "It is. How's vacation with the family?"

"Good. Charlotte loves the beach. She and Piper are out there now actually. They're in their element."

"And you?"

"I like the beach, but not as much as I'm enjoying sleeping in."

I chuckle quietly, and he continues, "I have a full gym here though and I've been skating a couple of times a week."

I get the sense he's trying to reassure me he's not slacking in the off-season. A lot of guys make huge improvements during their time off, but Ty is one of the most dedicated players I know. It never crossed my mind to worry about him slacking this summer.

"That's great. The season will be here before we know it."

"Yeah."

There's a short silence while I wait for him to tell me the reason he's calling. Neither of us are big on idle chitchat. We're friends, but we don't call each other to bullshit. Unless this is a check up call.

"Need something or is this just part of an emergency phone chain to make sure I'm not sitting around feeling sorry for myself?"

"Nah." He chuckles. "We gave up on that when you stopped answering our calls."

"I answered today."

"Which is how I know you aren't still moping around."

"I wasn't moping. Did Ash say I was moping? I'm going to kick his ass when he gets back."

He's still laughing quietly at me, and the sound is a reminder of how much I miss my teammates. It's the first summer they've all left. Usually one or two stick around and we get together to work out and skate, occasionally hit up the bars together. But now that they're married and starting families, things are different.

"No, I was calling about Ev."

The panic I was feeling earlier resurfaces. Why is he calling me about his sister?

"What about her?" I ask carefully.

"Have you seen her around at all?" he asks, then adds. "She's barely returning my texts lately. I must have texted her a dozen times last night and she didn't respond to any. Not even when I sent a picture of Charlotte. She always replies to cute baby pics."

I chuckle softly, then remember where she was last night. With me. "Using the baby. Smart."

"Yeah." He tries to laugh, but it's forced.

"I'm sure she's fine. I wouldn't worry."

"You're right. Fuck. I hate being so far away from her. Have you seen her at all this summer?"

I breathe a sigh of relief, but only for a moment because the very woman he's calling about walks outside in a bikini that is meant to make men fall at her knees. Which is exactly what I'm considering doing.

"Yeah, I've seen her." Fuck me, have I seen her. The top of her bikini stretches over her full tits, and I know just how they look and taste. The weeks spent in the sun have left her skin tan and her blonde hair lighter. She has the sassy glint in her eye that was missing while she was sick. I'm relieved to see her back to normal.

"Hey!" Brian is way too fucking happy to see her. Everly's lips twist into a smirk at me before she walks over to him. I'm going to regret telling her I didn't like him looking at her.

"She actually just showed up here," I say before Ty hears her voice and my cover is blown.

"Everly is there?" he asks; the question has a hint of accusation in it, or maybe that's just my guilty conscience.

"Yeah, she's been coming by to use my pool."

He laughs, short and loud. "That sounds about right."

"Who's she talking to?" Tyler asks.

"My trainer." My jaw clenches. "He has a thing for her."

It's a struggle to multitask, listening to Tyler on the phone and shooting a glare at Brian, while simultaneously admiring Everly in that damn bikini.

"Well, that would explain why she's been MIA."

"What do you mean?"

"She's obviously found a new guy and is too busy to text me back," he says.

"I don't think she's into him."

When Everly finally steps away from Brian, he finally leaves. Good thing. I'd hate to fire him again. Ev glances over at me hesitantly, like she thinks I'm on some important call and wants to give me space, when really, I'm sweating bullets while talking with her brother.

"Ty." I mouth to her.

Her brows lift but she heads my way.

"It all adds up," Tyler says. "Her coming over to your house to use the pool and conveniently bumping into him. Plus, not having time for her brother."

I do not like that summary at all, even if I know it's not accurate.

"Will you keep an eye on her for me?" he asks.

I open my mouth but the only sound that comes out is a strained, hesitant, "Umm…"

"I know you two have had your differences, but I really hate not being there to check in on her."

She's standing close enough now that I can smell her sunscreen mixed with my body wash. I like that she smells like me.

"Ev doesn't need or want me to keep an eye on her," I say to him, grinning at her.

She rolls her eyes.

I pull the phone away from my ear and hold it out to her in invitation. She shakes her head adamantly. Interesting. They've always been tight, but I guess he isn't making up that she's been avoiding him.

I place the phone back to my ear in time to hear him say, "What's she doing? Can I talk to her?"

"She's about to get into the pool and I'm about to work out. I'll let her know you called though." A small white lie. I do need to finish working out and she'll most likely get in the pool at some point.

"Thank you." The relief in his tone makes my guilt double. "She hasn't seemed like herself lately. She doesn't even sound that excited about her internship."

I think back to the night at the club when she and her friends talked about the internship. She was more reserved than her friends, but that could be for a lot of reasons.

"She's probably just nervous," I say as Everly rests one hand on my arm. Goosebumps dot my skin as she circles behind me, dragging her nails up my bicep to my shoulder. She stops behind me and presses her tits against my back. Her hand comes around my front and those claws trace the muscles of my stomach, dropping lower and lower.

"Ev?" Tyler asks, tone filled with disbelief. "Doesn't sound like her."

It takes a minute for me to remember what the hell we're even talking about, but when I do, I have to agree with him. He's right. It's hard to picture Everly being that nervous about anything. She's fearless and headstrong. And holy shit, topless.

I cough and then clear my throat as she steps back in front of me and drops her bikini top to the ground. She has a devilish glint in her eyes that makes my dick perk right up. We spent the past two days cuddled up together with our clothes on. Me, cuddling. A novelty for sure. It was fun, but damn, she's sexy. I missed my temptress.

"You don't think this guy, your trainer, is the reason she's acting weird, do you? Maybe she doesn't want to leave him."

"No," I say, voice hard as I shake my head at Everly.

"Are you sure?" Tyler asks.

Fuck. I can barely listen to him as her palm rests on my chest. Her fingers glide down over my stomach and then into my shorts. I clench my teeth as she wraps her fingers around me.

"Sure about what?" I manage to ask him.

She's pumping me slowly, looking up at me with those big, hazel eyes. The wicked tilt of her smile alone has my pulse racing and my cock aching. I press my mouth to hers and then nip at her bottom lip in warning.

A warning she doesn't heed. Instead, she drops to her knees and pulls my shorts and boxers down. My dick springs free and I'm so hard that the slight breeze in the yard makes me suck air through my teeth.

Tyler is talking, saying something about Everly and Brian, but all my attention is on the woman in front of me as she leans in and licks my cock from base to tip.

"I gotta go," I say, cutting him off mid-sentence. "Something just came up."

It's me. I'm up. And Jesus Christ…she takes me into her mouth inch by inch until I hit the back of her throat.

"Okay, but don't forget to tell Ev to call me."

"Yeah, sure, I'll…" Oh fuck. "I'll check on that." I hang up without hearing Tyler's reply. Am I the asshole? The answer is unequivocally yes, but what's worse: talking to him while his sister has my dick in her mouth or hanging up on him so I can fuck her mouth?

"You're evil." I toss my phone onto the workout mat and dig my hands into her hair.

Evil but fucking perfect. I can't get enough of it. All of it. Her teasing, her laughter, her default stubborn and sassy attitude, and the way she goes soft under my touch.

I let her keep the pace but encourage her to take me deeper. She swallows me inch by inch until I hit the back of her throat. She gags and her eyes water.

Fuck me. Pleasure rolls through me wave after wave. Before Everly, I went months without being with a woman, but it was worth the wait for this. For her.

Her tongue swirls around the head and she bobs faster, taking me deep each time. When my grip tightens in her hair, she moans and the vibrations send another dizzying wave of pleasure through my entire body.

Damn this woman.

"So fucking beautiful on your knees. So perfect." My words are gentle as I take over, using my hold in her hair to drag her off my cock and then stuff her mouth full again.

"You like driving me wild, don't you?"

Her response is to suck so hard her cheeks hollow out. The suction is divine.

"Don't you know you already do that without being on your knees?" I run my thumb along her cheek. "But since you're down there, I'm gonna fuck that gorgeous mouth."

Her hazel eyes spark with lust. I'm not gentle and neither is she. She has her claws in the back of my thighs, holding me to her like that's fucking necessary. Not with her looking so perfect. Looking so much like *mine*.

"I'm gonna come," I warn through gritted teeth. I fight it off, wanting to live in this moment, but it's been too long since I've gotten off with anything but my own hand.

She doesn't pull back or heed my warning. She grips me tighter and swirls her tongue until stars explode behind my eyes. The force of my orgasm nearly takes me down. My legs wobble but I manage to stay upright with the grip I have on her hair.

"Fuck, baby," I groan as she swallows every last drop before she slides slowly off me. I pull her to her feet and crash my mouth down on hers.

"Jack." She moans as I drive my tongue deep into her mouth and pick her up. This thing between us was supposed to be temporary, but it's quickly turning into a deep, soul-aching need to never let her go. Her arms go around my neck and her bare tits press against my chest as I walk over to the outdoor couch. I place her on it, then drape one of her legs over my shoulder.

I push her bikini bottoms to the side to reveal her wet pussy. She gasps as I lick along her slit.

Her fingers tangle in my hair and she rubs her pussy over my mouth.

"That's right. Take what you need from me." I insert one finger inside her as she keeps pushing her clit into my tongue. I suck and lick and feast on her. I drive her as wild as she drives me. I don't know how we got here but I feel the strangest sense of foreboding, even though I've never been happier. Maybe it's the reminder that she's only mine for a short time. She wasn't supposed to get so far under my skin.

By the time she cries out my name, I'm ready to go again.

"Holy shit." She flings a hand over her head as she catches her breath. "That was…"

"Yep," I say, falling to the ground in front of the couch and mirroring her position. "It sure was."

She rolls carefully down onto me. We're both sweaty, but damn she feels good. My dick twitches to be inside her, but I don't want to rush things. Not with her.

"We should clean up," I say.

"I have an idea." She stands and takes my hands in an attempt to pull me up. I give in and help her, then she leads me to the side of the pool.

"I've never skinny-dipped in my pool before."

"I have." She pulls me with her into the pool.

"When?" I demand as soon as we both come up from under the water.

"Not here. I just meant in general. I have skinny-dipped. You?" Her legs circle around my waist and she pushes back her hair as she draws our bodies back together. Like maybe she can't get enough of me either. Her lips are puffy and I decide it's the way I like them best. Puffy from my cock and my kisses.

"Sure. When I was younger."

"Because you're so old."

"Some days I feel like it."

She runs her fingers through my wet hair. A contented sigh slips from my lips at the simple touch.

"What'd Ty want?" she asks.

"Oh, now you're interested in talking to him."

She rolls her eyes. "I wasn't uninterested in talking to him. I was just more interested in torturing you."

I let out a low growl as I take her mouth again. "God, you're trouble."

She giggles into the kiss.

"Still feeling okay?"

"Yes." She smiles and rolls her eyes. "I told you. I'm all better. You cured me."

Taking care of her wasn't exactly a hardship.

When we eventually get out of the pool and dry off, Everly says, "I'm starving. Do you want to grab lunch?"

"I need to get in my conditioning workout first."

"Okay. I'll wait." She drops the towel, showing off her bare tits. I find her top and toss it at her.

"Are you sure you want me to put this on?"

I pull on my boxers and shorts. "No, but James is due back today or tomorrow, and I'd rather be the only one you're giving a show."

"What happened to just beating people up that look at me?"

"Sadly, I can't punch James. It's in his contract."

She laughs, then stops when I don't join in.

"Seriously?"

I'd never hit him, but I have considered it on numerous occasions when he sends bullshit emails and documents that I don't feel like dealing with. With a wink I head inside with my phone.

There's only one text and no surprise it's from Tyler.

TYLER

Sorry for bothering you again. Just wanted to say thank you for keeping an eye out on Everly for me.

ME

No need to thank me.

In fact, please don't, then I'll feel less like an asshole.

TYLER

She's not acting like herself lately and I'm worried she's going to bail on this internship. You don't think things with the trainer could be serious, right?

ME

Nah, I don't think so.

I stop in the kitchen, staring down at our messages. My immediate thought to Everly not acting like herself is fuck no, but the more I consider it, the less sure I am.

Is she seriously considering staying because of me? It seems out of character for her but if she's feeling even a fraction of what I am, then maybe it's not so far-fetched. I feel sick at the prospect. I know how hard she's worked over the years. She wouldn't throw that away.

That would be a mistake, even if I don't want her to go. I was joking about feeling old, but more than ten years separate us. Ten really critical years. She has so much life to still live, and I'm set in my life and career. It wouldn't be fair to her. Not when we've barely spent any time exploring whatever this is between us.

TYLER

Anyway, don't tell her I was checking in on her. It'll just make her pull away from me more and I don't want to risk her getting mad and doing something dumb like bailing on the internship. She has so much potential. I just know she's going to do amazing things.

I glance out the window at her. So full of life and excitement. He's right. She has so much to look forward to, and unfortunately, none of it is here in my backyard.

CHAPTER TWENTY-FOUR

Everly

SOFT

I have a permanent smile on my face that I can't seem to do anything about. Even as I try to fake sleep when Jack walks toward me after finishing his workout, my smile gives me away.

Giving up, I push my sunglasses to the top of my head. "Hey."

His mouth is pulled down at the corners, but his expression is soft. "Hungry?"

"Starving." I take in the hard ridges of muscles in his chest and stomach, and the sweat that glistens in the sunlight.

His body is incredible. Years of training and discipline have sculpted every inch of him to perfection. I've never particularly enjoyed giving blowjobs but going down on Jack could easily become my new favorite hobby.

All that control and discipline is sexy, but there's something addicting about how soft he can be too. For days he hovered over me, making sure I had everything I needed. It was so nice I'm almost sad

I'm all better.

He sits on the lounge chair beside me and hands over a water. "I ordered Chinese from that place you like. It should be here in about five minutes?"

A pleased smile curves my lips and my stomach dips. See? Soft. I sit up and move to the edge of the chair, so my knees fit in the space between his. "How will I ever repay you?"

My hands slide up his massive thighs, but he catches them in his and stops my ascent.

"I have to head out for a while."

"Oh." I think back to earlier. I'm sure he didn't mention any plans. "Is everything okay?"

"Yeah." He stands too quickly and won't quite meet my eyes.

"When will you be back?"

"I'm not sure. Late, maybe, but stay as long as you'd like. Enjoy the pool."

"You're acting weird." I stand in front of him.

A small smile pulls at the corner of his lips, but it's not nearly as big as the ones he's been aiming my way for the past few days. A month ago, I would have been happy to get any smile out of him, but now that I've had him smile at me for real, the fake one is twice as disappointing.

"I'll see you later." He brushes his lips over mine and then turns to go, leaving me reeling in his sudden mood swing.

I barely eat my favorite lunch as I mull over what could be wrong with Jack. Is it something with his knee? Things seemed great earlier, so I don't think it's me, but I don't outright dismiss it either. Maybe Ty calling freaked him out?

I swim a little more, then consider leaving and going back to my place, but there's a nagging worry that has a pit forming in my stomach and I need to talk to Jack.

I pull out my phone to text him, but then decide there's too much nuance over text, so I call instead.

"Hello?" he answers on the second ring. There's a hint of concern in his tone with that single word. His voice comforts me even with the physical distance between us.

The background is noisy. Glasses clinking and people talking. I strain to make out the location.

"Where are you?" I ask.

"Ev?" he asks, voice louder.

"Yeah, it's me. Where are you?"

There's a beat of hesitation where I think he can't hear me, but then he says, "Wild's."

He went to the bar and left me at his house? There could be a thousand different reasons, but it's odd and a bad feeling settles in my stomach.

"Stay there," I say. "Don't leave."

It only takes me twenty minutes to get there. Fifteen to drive and five to give myself a pep talk in the car. The popular bar near the arena is quieter than any other time I've been here. After a game this place is packed. It's a favorite with the players, too, thanks to the proximity of the rink and the free drinks bestowed upon them. For all the people they bring in, I'd say it's a fair trade. Unless of course, the guys are really tying one on. They can put back the alcohol if they want.

But today the place is occupied with only a few patrons. The one of most interest to me is sitting at the bar. I push back my nerves and start toward him. His head is bowed over his beer. It looks untouched and his hands rest on the wooden bar next to it instead of around the glass.

Jack glances up as I approach. His dark gaze takes me in as he smiles. I'm filled with a brief sense of relief that he's happy to see me. Maybe I've made too big of a deal about this after all.

He stands and I wave to the guy still sitting on the bar stool next to his.

Nick Galaxy waves back at me with a half-smile that brings out a dimple in his cheek. He fits in so seamlessly I sometimes forget that he's only been with the team for just over a year now. He's not big on partying or going out, so I haven't spent that much time with him. I guess that makes sense with a little boy at home, but something tells me even without Aidan, he'd be more reserved than some of the other guys. He's like Jack a little, hard to read and a skosh intimidating. Though as captain, Jack puts himself at the center of everyone's needs, so he feels less reclusive.

"I'm sorry to interrupt," I say loud enough that Nick can hear.

"Not at all. I need to call and check in on Aidan." Nick stands with his phone in hand and heads toward the front of the bar.

When he's gone, Jack and I stare at each other awkwardly. I take a seat on a stool next to his and he finally slides back onto his. The bartender appears and when Jack asks if I want anything, I shake him off.

"I won't stay, I just had this nagging feeling that something was wrong, and I figured I could come ask you or I could spend the rest of the night plotting your murder."

His lips quirk up in a small smile. "Wouldn't be the first time."

"No, it wouldn't." I smile back at him. I study him carefully. There's a heaviness in his expression that makes my stomach swirl with unease. "Did I do something?"

I hate myself a little for assuming it's me, but Jack is unmoving, rigid almost in his ability to stay at an even temperament.

"No. You…" He trails off. "It's nothing. We're good. You and I are always good."

My brain spins to pick up on his hidden meanings. *We're always good* makes it sound like nothing has changed between us.

"Is this about me torturing you while you talked to Tyler? I'm sorry. I know how much you respect him."

"No," he says quickly. "At least, not exactly."

I lean forward slightly as I wait for him to continue.

"Your brother is concerned about you, and I feel bad that I'm messing around with you behind his back."

"I'm old enough to decide who I date or mess around with."

"Of course you are, but he's my friend." He takes a small sip of his beer as I sit impatiently for him to speak.

"He reminded me that you're leaving soon."

"O-kay," I say slowly, trying to follow his line of reasoning.

"Maybe we should just call it now before things get any messier."

"Why do we have to call it at all? It's not like I won't be back when it's over. And I can visit on weekends." I already plan to come back for as many home games as possible to see Charlotte and everyone else.

"Maybe you will come back when it's over or maybe you'll decide you want to stay or move across the country or the world… You don't know what you want yet and that's great. You should follow your ambitions."

I breathe in through my nose and then exhale slowly. I know that people change. Their wants, their desires, their dreams, but this is my home. "I can't imagine not coming back here," I admit. "I'm not even sure I want to go."

I know it's what is expected and that it's a great opportunity, but I like my life here and the people in it. Jack included. Maybe Jack most of all, if I'm being honest. The last few weeks have meant more to me than I can put into words or even wrap my brain around yet, but I know it's true.

"You have to go." His eyes widen.

I shrug one shoulder.

"Ev. No. You can't stay. You and I are having fun, but it can't go anywhere."

"This isn't about you and me," I say, feeling myself get defensive. "I've been thinking about it for a while. I have a life here. Friends and family."

"Who all want to see you happy and—"

"You mean they want to be free from worrying about me."

His face twists with surprise like he wasn't expecting that.

"My parents were tired of dealing with me so they let me move in with Ty, and now he's married and has Charlotte, and he wants me out of his hair too."

"That's not true."

"I know he'd never say that, but it's why he wants this so bad. If I get a job and move away, then he doesn't have to keep looking out for me the same way. It frees him from the responsibility of me." And I can't really blame him. He has his own family now.

"I promise you that isn't it." He reaches for me, but I pull back, feeling raw and exposed. It hurts that he doesn't want me here either. I thought...I thought that things had changed between us. Embarrassment makes my face hot. Jack is good at taking care of people and being what they need. And here I am making more out of it when it was my idea in the first place.

"You're right. You and I aren't going anywhere so it's better to end things now," I say then slide off the bar stool.

"Everly." He stands and calls after me.

I feel the sting in the back of my eyes, but I absolutely will not let myself cry.

He moves in front of me, grasping my arms just below the elbow. "Don't do this. You're wrong. Lots of people care about you and want you here."

"People like you?" I ask.

He doesn't answer.

"That's what I thought." I stare up at his handsome face, ignoring the pull I have to ease the worry lines there. "Bye, Jack."

CHAPTER TWENTY-FIVE

Jack

UNINSPIRED

"You'd think I was the one that took the summer off." Nick bends over at the waist, hockey stick resting on his thighs, as he catches his breath. "Are you sure they didn't give you a robotic knee?"

A half smile tugs at one corner of my lips, but the feeling doesn't shake off the turmoil raging inside me.

I skate off to the side and take a seat on the bench. Nick follows, watching me from the other side. His son, Aidan, is skating and Nick lets his gaze flick in that direction before focusing back on me.

"Everything good?"

Resting my stick against the wall, I run a hand through my hair and then take a long drink of water before answering. "Yeah. The doctor says I should be ready to scrimmage next month at camp and I'm feeling stronger than ever."

"That's great," Nick says. "But I wasn't talking about hockey."

I shoot him a warning glare.

"I know you said you don't want to talk about it, but you're firing pucks at the net like you're imagining somebody's face."

"I am." My own.

It's been two weeks since I saw Everly. She went to Briar Lake for her internship. I only know because Ash mentioned it. He got back into town yesterday. Leo too. The others will all arrive sometime over the next couple of weeks.

Camp is coming and I've never been as anxious to throw myself into training.

Nick looks like he's ready to pry more, so I add, "I'm grateful to be back after the accident. That's all. I'm not going to take one second for granted. Everything else…it's not important right now."

He doesn't look like he believes me. I'm not sure I do either, but I'm focusing on things I can control. And I *am* grateful to be back. I missed this. All of it. The ice, hockey, my teammates. I live for hockey season. I'm too numb to appreciate it now, but I will once the season starts. I hope so anyway.

"All right, but if you ever want to talk…" He trails off, but the invitation is clear. I'm relieved he doesn't mention Everly, but there's no way he hasn't pieced it together. Between her picking me up in my Lamborghini and the day she showed up at Wild's when I told her we should end things, it isn't that complicated to figure out why I'm back to being a grumpy asshole.

I know I did the right thing. I'm sure of it. She had to go. That doesn't seem to make me feel any better though.

"Thank you." I clear my throat and tip my head toward his son. "Aidan's looking sharp out there."

"Yeah." Nick's usual reserved demeanor shifts and a big smile spreads across his face as he looks at son. "He's been working really hard this summer."

"It shows."

Aidan circles around the back of the net in his full gear and skates over to us.

"Did you see my slapshot?" he asks me. His dark hair sticks to his forehead around his helmet.

Nodding, I say, "Yeah. Where'd you learn that?"

"My dad," he says proudly. I know that feeling, that pride and excitement of learning something from your old man. Dad and I used to go to the rink on weekends and hit the puck around. And occasionally he'd even go out in the backyard with me, and we'd practice shooting into an old net. One time I missed it so badly, I took out a neighbor's window. But when I managed to impress him, nothing felt better.

I shake the memories from my head.

"Are you sure?" I ask him, then look at Nick skeptically. "This guy? Nah. Can't be. I think you've been watching me."

Grabbing my stick, I head back out onto the ice. Aidan follows me. I skate to an abandoned puck and pass it back to him. Moving with the puck, he comes to a stop in front of the goal and rockets it into the net.

"Definitely my slapshot," I tell him, giving him a high five.

Nick's all smiles as he gives his kid props with a fist bump, then taps the top of Aidan's helmet gently. "Are you ready to get out of here?"

"Already?" Aidan's disappointed frown makes a real genuine smile pull at my lips.

"We need to finish back to school shopping," Nick says.

The frown turns to a scowl.

Nick chuckles and a very reluctant Aidan heads off the ice.

"If you aren't busy for dinner, you're welcome to come over," Nick says as he wipes his forehead with the back of his hand.

"Thanks, but I have plans."

Nick nods slowly. "All right. See you tomorrow."

He joins his son off the ice and they make their way toward the locker rooms.

I stay where I am, standing in the empty rink. I used to think there was nowhere else I'd rather be, but the thrum of anxiousness won't let me fall into the same feeling of contentment.

When I'm finished at the rink, I head to Brettwood. I need to check in on my dad. Things have been quiet, which always has me more worried than when I'm being called to pick him up from some random bar because he's causing a scene.

The sun is just beginning to set when I park in the driveway and walk up to the front door of my dad's house. I own the place, but I still knock before letting myself in. Muffled voices from the TV filter out, and when I don't get an answer on my second attempt, I push the door open.

"Dad?" I call through the cracked door.

"Living room," he yells back.

I step inside, bracing myself. I never know what kind of mess I'm walking into. One time he'd pissed himself and ruined the couch. Another time he had broken a bottle of red wine— underneath an area rug in the center of the room, I bet the stain is still there—and needed two stitches.

But today, everything is in place. Dad is reclined back in his leather chair watching TV. An empty plate sits on the end table next to a glass of amber liquid. A strange sense of relief washes over me. He rarely goes on a bender with the expensive liquor. It's contradictory, I know, but when he's at his lowest, it's cheap beer and vodka that smells more like rubbing alcohol.

"Jackie boy." He smiles as I walk through the living room, taking it all in. His eyes, the same dark blue as mine, are clear and sharp.

"Dad," I say with a tip of my head.

"Did I know you were coming?" he asks.

"No. I just hadn't heard from you and thought I'd check in." I take a seat on the couch.

"There are burgers in the kitchen if you're hungry."

"No thanks."

I sit back and glance at the TV. Twins are playing, bottom of the fourth inning.

"Lopez is shit this year," Dad says as the pitcher throws another ball.

"He's still coming off that elbow surgery." I feel a hint of defensiveness. It might be the same for me. Sure I've gotten movement and flexibility back and am working on strength, but there's no comparing that to what it's like in a game.

Dad huffs, a noncommittal noise that tells me he isn't sure that's the issue. Or maybe he just doesn't care.

"They drafted that young kid from Arizona, Flynn Holland. I don't know why they haven't called him up yet. Lopez can't hit the broad side of a barn."

I'm used to Dad's grumbles and nod along.

"How's everything going with you?" he asks as he tears his gaze off the TV.

"Everything is fine."

"You look like shit. Is the knee holding up?"

"The knee is fine." I get up and go to the kitchen. Dad keeps Gatorade stocked for me, even though he hates the stuff. It's a small consolation for him knowing how to push my buttons at all times. Aren't parents supposed to lie and say things like, "Looking great, Son," even when you don't. I could use some of that about now.

I grab the drink and take it back to the couch, wishing it was something stronger. It's real irony that my alcoholic father often drives me to wanting to drink.

"When's camp?" he asks.

"Three weeks. I can't wait."

"I remember that feeling." He drags his gaze away from me and sighs. "I couldn't even enjoy vacation because I missed being on the ice."

It's hard to remember a time when he cared about anything that much. Certainly not me. Actually, that's not true. He was a good father before he lost his job and became a full-time drunk. But those happy memories are buried so far in my mind it almost feels like a story someone told me instead of my own recollection.

"How's the new girlfriend?"

My head snaps toward him and my brows furrow. "Girlfriend?"

"That girl that came with you last time. Sharp's sister. She's pretty."

"Everly." Her name feels like glass in my mouth. "She's not my girlfriend."

And pretty? Sure, saying she's pretty is like saying hockey is fun. True but uninspired.

He studies me for a moment, then a grin takes over his face. He's smiling so big that my skin itches with discomfort.

"Now I see," he says.

"You see what?"

"Why you look like shit." He chuckles and shakes his head. "I didn't think you'd let that one go so easily."

"You don't know what you're talking about. Have another drink." I tip my head to his glass.

His jaw flexes and I feel like shit for stooping low.

"I might not be the smartest man in the world, but on the topic of you, I am an expert," he says.

It's rich coming from a guy that hasn't been to my house or watched me play in years. Sure, he catches it on TV, but it's not the same. We only have a relationship because I make the effort to check in on him. Who knows how long we'd go between talking if I didn't.

"Drop it, okay?"

"Fine. Fine."

We fall quiet as our attention goes back to the game. Watching sports is the one thing we're capable of doing without being at each other's throats. Baseball, football, even motocross. Outside of that, we've never been good at communicating.

When the game's over, I get up and head for the door. Dad pushes his chair upright and stands.

"If I don't make it back before the first home game, tickets will be at will call as usual." I can't look him in the eye because if I do, I know I'll see his answer before he says it.

"You don't need to waste tickets on me. I prefer seeing all the angles and replays right here."

I nod and ignore the disappointment. I knew he wouldn't come, but I buy the tickets every year just in case.

"By the way, this Everly…"

I sigh loudly. "Dad, it's really not like that."

Not anymore at least.

"Got it." Dad works his jaw back and forth like he might want to say more, but then decides against it. "Well, thanks for stopping by."

My feet pause on the doorstep. "Call if you need anything."

CHAPTER TWENTY-SIX

Everly

MATURE AND RESPECTFUL

Tyler crushes me in a hug. "Fuck, I missed you," he says as he pulls back. He looks me over with a smile. "You look good. Being a career woman suits you."

I flash him the best smile I can, certain if he stares too long, he'll see right through me. Luckily, I'm saved by Piper.

"Your hair!" Her eyes are wide as she stares at me.

"I keep forgetting," I say as I run a hand over the short strands self-consciously. I'm still not quite used to the new cut just above my shoulders.

"It looks great." Piper beams at me. "We're so proud of you."

"Me too." I let out a shallow breath. I can't seem to get a full breath since I parked the car. My gaze won't allow me to look around the party. The same way it wouldn't let me look too closely at the cars parked in Tyler and Piper's driveway.

I knew coming back that I would run into Jack. There's no way he won't be at Charlotte's birthday party. I know these guys. They'll all be here. That's what they do. They show up for each other.

But not looking for him makes me feel in control, like I'm wielding my attention like a weapon and not giving a single fuck if he's here or not. God, I wish that were true.

It's been almost a month since I've seen or talked to him. I packed up the very next day after he told me we couldn't be anything and I headed for Briar Lake. I settled into my place, cut my hair, and vowed that I was going to forget about Jack and crush my internship. I was successful in at least one of those things.

Looking out of the corner of my eye to the guys hanging around the living room, I spot Ash, Declan, and Leo. Plus Nick and his son Aidan. Seeing Nick reminds me of that last time I saw him at Wild's with Jack, but when I smile at him, he doesn't give me any indication that he knows anything.

The guys all wave their hellos. Ash pulls me into a hug that lifts my feet off the ground. Declan attempts to give me a one-arm hug, but I wrap myself around his middle. I breathe each of them in. I'm closer to some more than others, but I'm so happy to see each of them.

"Where's the birthday girl?" I ask after I've said hello to everyone else.

"Still napping," Piper says. "But come check out the cake. It's the cutest thing I've ever seen."

Piper drags me along behind her through the living room. I breathe a sigh of relief when we enter the kitchen and the only people in here are Scarlett, Jade, and Bridget. Maybe Jack decided not to come. The thought fills me with more sadness than expected. But only because Charlotte deserves to have everyone show up to celebrate her.

"Oh my gosh!!" Bridget squeals and hurries toward me, engulfing me in a hug that's tighter than even Tyler's. "I missed you so, so, so much!"

She keeps squeezing me until the other women laugh.

"Let her breathe, Bridge." Scarlett comes up behind her.

Bridget's hold loosens. "Sorry. I just…" She gives me one last hard squeeze and steps back. "It's so good to see you. It hasn't been the same without you."

Her words make a lump form in my throat. It hasn't been the same without them either but admitting that feels a little bit like failure. Maybe it's not such a good thing that I need them all so much. I should have my own life outside of Tyler's teammates and their wives. Isn't that what they all wanted for me?

I hug each of them and they gush over my hair and my clothes and ask me about my internship. I shrug off as many questions as I can and turn the focus back on them. It isn't that things are going badly, the opposite actually, I just want to hear about them.

Their kids, their summer vacations, their jobs…I've missed out on all of it and I'm eager for every little detail. Bridget and I have kept in touch the most. We text and video chat nearly every day, but in person I can look into her face as she talks and see just how happy she is.

I don't know if I took my parents for granted or if they were too absent for me to ever have this type of relationship with them, but these people are the family I always wanted. I don't take it for granted now. I cherish every second of it.

"Is my mom coming?" I ask Piper when the conversation hits a lull.

Her face answers before she does, mouth turning down in a slight frown. "No, she couldn't make it."

I can't imagine what could possibly be more important on

a Saturday afternoon, but I guess I'm not that surprised. I want Charlotte to have the kind of grandma she deserves. Someone who shows up and showers her with all the love and attention.

"Her favorite person is here and that's all that matters." Piper squeezes my hand. "Let's go see if she's awake."

We go back out to the living room. My steps falter. Piper doesn't notice, her attention goes straight to Charlotte.

"There she is," Piper coos at her daughter. Tyler is holding the birthday girl, bouncing around and talking to her, and she's waving her arms around happily with a slobbery grin.

I take in my adorable niece, but it's the man standing next to Tyler that has my feet rooted to the floor.

My stomach drops and my chest feels like it could crack down the middle.

Jack's dark-blue eyes lock onto me and hold me prisoner. Only seconds pass but a million thoughts and memories flash through my mind. Jack smiling at me. Jack kissing me. Jack breaking my heart.

That's been the hardest thing to admit. I don't let guys break my heart. I don't let them in and I don't fall for them. But I did both of those things with Jack without even realizing it. It was supposed to be a fun fling. Instead, he wedged his way in without trying. I should have been more careful, but he's the last person I ever thought would hurt me.

I wonder what flashes through his mind when he sees me. Does he look back at those weeks we hung out and regret them?

Piper moves toward Ty and Charlotte and I follow behind her, standing on the opposite side and making Tyler a barrier. Not that it keeps the heat of Jack's gaze from reaching me.

Charlotte grins at me, angling her body so far that Tyler is forced to hand her over to me.

"I think she missed you too," Tyler says as I take his daughter. My heart squeezes as I hug her to my chest. The pictures and videos I've demanded Piper and Tyler send me weekly didn't do the changes in my niece justice. Her dark hair is longer, curling up at the ends. She's bigger and her features are more defined. And when she smiles, I can see she's gotten more teeth too.

"I can't believe how big she's gotten." I grin at her. "What has your daddy been feeding you?"

"Everything but green beans. The kid hates green beans," Ty says.

"Nobody likes them," I whisper to her loud enough that Tyler and Piper can hear.

"Speaking of food, should we let everyone eat?" Piper asks.

"Yeah. Good idea. I think the guys are ready." Tyler nods his head to where Declan is staring into the kitchen longingly. It could be he's looking at his wife or it could be the boxes of pizza stacked up in front of her. My guess is both.

"Let's eat," Piper calls over the noise of the room. The rush to the kitchen is immediate.

"Want me to take her so you can eat," Piper asks me, nodding toward Charlotte.

"No way. I just got her."

Piper laughs then says, "I'll make you a plate."

Everyone else heads toward the kitchen, but I hang back. So does Jack. I keep my focus on Charlotte but I can feel him watching me.

He steps closer and my body tenses.

"Hey." His deep voice sends a wave of longing through me.

"Hi," I reply without looking at him.

Charlotte doesn't prove to be a very good wing woman. She turns her attention to him, tipping her head back and grinning wider. When she flings a hand toward him, he reaches out and she takes his finger. He jostles her hand lightly and Charlotte laughs like he's funny. When has Jack ever been funny?

"How've you been?" he asks me.

"Good. You?" My pulse races but I focus extremely hard on making polite conversation.

Instead of answering he says, "Ty says the internship is going well."

Somewhere deep down—very deep down—I want to handle this maturely. I can't avoid Jack. I knew I would run into him, and I don't want it to be weird. He doesn't get to ruin my favorite place with all my favorite people. However, the anger that sizzles just below the surface of my cool demeanor makes it very difficult to hold back the cutting remarks on the tip of my tongue.

"We don't need to do this," I say, finally meeting his gaze. An unfortunate mistake because goddamn, why is he so attractive? Grumpy, happy, beard, no beard, looking at me like I'm the most important person in the world or like he's filled with regret. There's no expression or change that makes him anything less than devastating. "We weren't really friends before and we don't need to be friends now."

"Ev…" His voice breaks on my name.

I'm saved by Piper hurrying back with a plate. "I had to fight for this."

"Thanks." I take it in one hand.

Her stare moves to Jack. "You better get in there before it's all gone."

He nods and his mouth pulls into a smile. He casts me one last look before leaving.

Piper glances between us but says nothing as she leaves me with her daughter and a plate of food. I go sit on the couch and set the plate on the coffee table. Charlotte stands in front of me, using my legs for balance. She isn't walking yet, but she's getting close.

With a chubby hand, she grabs a strawberry from my plate, then holds it up proudly before sticking it in her mouth.

"It's a good thing you're so cute," I tell her. People trickle back in with their own plates. Jack stays on the other side of the room, but I can feel his gaze on me often.

After food, we all watch Charlotte open her presents. It requires a lot of help because she's almost more interested in the wrapping paper and ribbons than the gifts inside. Callum, Scarlett and Leo's son, is happy to tear open anything she's not interested in.

"Easy," Leo says, picking him up so he doesn't ravage through them all. He kicks his feet and whines but then Leo puts him up on his shoulders and that seems to make him magically forget about the presents.

When she opens my gift of paints and markers, Tyler quirks a brow at me. "Really?"

"They're waterproof," I say as I fight a smile.

"I'll put those somewhere up high." Piper takes them and then sets another box in front of her. It's the biggest of all, long and skinny and wrapped immaculately in pink and white paper with pink ribbons and bows.

Tyler bends down to help Charlotte and when they finally get it open, the guys all laugh. I lean to get a better view. Charlotte pulls out a hockey stick with a wide grin. It's kid size but still looks far too big for her.

"Da-da!"

There's a chorus of "aww" as Tyler takes it from her. "That's right. It's just like mine."

Tyler flips the stick around. He pauses, staring at the blade, and then looks over at Jack. "Really, Wyld? You got my daughter a signed hockey stick?"

His lips curve up and a faint blush creeps into his cheeks. "It's never too early to get a hockey stick in her hands." He juts his chin toward the box. "There's something else in there."

I watch, perhaps more captivated than Charlotte, as Tyler looks inside the box. This time he pulls out a big, pink stuffed rabbit. It's floppy and looks so soft and perfect.

Tyler hands it to Charlotte and she immediately hugs it to her chest.

When presents are over, we sing happy birthday and then watch Charlotte bite into a small cake just for her. Laughter sounds around the room as she avoids using her hands and just face dives into the pink frosting.

Another cake is cut for the guests, but by the time it's passed around, Charlotte has had a bath and is passed out in Tyler's arms.

He looks as content as her. The way he looks down at her with so much love and the way he holds her so protectively. She has no idea how lucky she is, but I'm so glad.

A twinge of sadness works its way in. I feel like I'm already missing so much by not being around. I can't imagine not being here to watch her grow up. I know that people take jobs, move away, and leave their families every day, but I loved my life here. I miss it.

Scarlett and Leo take a sleepy-looking Callum home, and Nick and Aidan say their goodbyes as well. Hazel, Maverick and Dakota's little girl, is entertaining us all by dancing in the middle of the living room. She's got her mom's red hair but her dad's personality it seems.

"Center of attention," Dakota says. "Just like her dad."

Maverick grins and drapes an arm around his wife's shoulders.

"I love her hair. You think you can braid mine like that?" I ask Dakota. Hazel's strawberry-blonde hair is in two braids on either side and the ends are twisted somehow to look like little bows. It's adorable.

"That's not me. That's all Johnny. He's mastered like twenty different hairstyles, and I can barely find time to brush mine these days."

"You're smoking hot." He kisses her cheek. "Even with unbrushed hair."

My stomach swoops with the cute scene. So many couples here, all madly in love.

I'm sitting on the couch next to Tyler. Jack leans against the wall across the room. There are places to sit, but I'm glad he keeps his distance.

"How long are you staying?" Piper asks me. I feel all eyes on me. Sometimes I still feel like the teenager they're all interrogating.

"I'm heading back tonight."

"Wait. Really?" Tyler turns to me. "I thought you'd at least stay the night."

I'm not sure if he's disappointed because he wanted me to stay or if he's just trying to let me know I have a place to stay if I want. It's weird now that I don't live here. I miss my little yellow house. Tyler and Piper rented it out to new students.

"I can't. I have plans."

"Ooooh. Big date?" Piper asks.

It might be my imagination, but it seems like Jack tenses at the question.

I am definitely not looking to get blasted about my dating life in front of all these happy couples so I stand. "And that's my cue to leave."

Piper stands and I hug her.

"I feel like I barely got to see you," she whines.

"I know, but it was so good to catch up. Even if just for a few minutes."

"Are you coming back for the home opener?" Tyler asks.

"I wouldn't miss it." I scan the room, waving to everyone as I step to the front door.

Bridget gets up from where she was sitting on Ash's lap. "I want to walk you out."

A weird sensation of sadness and relief hits me as we step outside. Bridget links her arm through mine and doesn't speak until we're a good ten feet away from the house.

"Well, that was tense." Her brows lift.

"Really?" I ask. "I couldn't tell if it was in my head or not."

"I don't think anyone else noticed." She gives me a small smile. "He stared at you the whole time."

"He's probably just worried I'll say something to Ty."

"Do you really have to go?"

"I don't want to get in the way of their happy birthday celebrations."

"You aren't in the way," she insists. "But if you feel that way, come stay the night with me and Ash."

I laugh lightly, trying to imagine that. The few times that Ash and Bridget stayed the night at our place instead of them crashing at his place, I had to wear headphones to bed to drown out the screams and headboard banging against the wall. "It's okay. Some people from work are going out so maybe I'll hit up the bars with them."

She looks at me like she wants to call bullshit. I haven't felt like going out much since I got to Briar Lake, but maybe it's time to change that.

I wrap my arms around her neck. "I love you. I'll see you in a few weeks."

She's frowning when I pull away. "I miss you already."

My heart squeezes. "Me too."

The front door opens and closes. Both of our attention go to the man stepping out. He has his keys in hand, but when he sees me still standing in the driveway, his steps slow. He eyes me warily as he comes closer.

"Want me to tell him to get lost?" Bridget asks.

I consider it but avoiding him now won't make him disappear from my life. Even if that's what I wanted.

"No. It's okay."

"All right." She hugs me again, then raises a brow in what is probably meant to be a warning as she passes by Jack to go back in the house.

He waits until the door closes behind her to speak.

"Do you really have a date or are you avoiding me?" he asks.

I cross my arms over my chest and ignore the question.

"Fine. Don't answer that. I don't deserve to know."

"No, you don't."

"I'm sorry about how things ended between us."

Him being sorry doesn't really change anything.

"You look good. Happy."

"I am, so if that's all." I angle my body toward my car. I want to flee but in a dignified manner, like he isn't the reason and it's just my fabulous plans I'm eager to get to. I have no idea if I pull it off, but he nods.

"I'm glad you're happy." He takes a step away and I have to force myself not to call after him or do something really dumb like yell at him. I can be mature and respectful…

"Handsome jerk," I mutter under my breath. Mature and respectful are both highly overrated.

CHAPTER TWENTY-SEVEN

Everly

THIS IS HOME

Aftter two months at the internship and I feel like I'm starting to get in the swing of things. I had reservations on coming, but I'm good at this. Still learning, of course, but I feel smart and capable.

"Did you bring the samples for the backsplash I asked for?" My boss, Heather, asks as we enter one of the condominiums in a new building. We've sold over thirty units since I started working for her with thirty-five more still being constructed.

"Yes." I walk to the kitchen in front of her and wave to where I've placed them against the countertop.

She stops and eyes them carefully, then picks up the one on the end.

"I know that isn't one you requested, but I thought it was a good option. It gives the room a little more warmth."

She's quiet so long that I fear I've offended her by questioning her

REBECCA JENSHAK

choices. Heather is known for her impeccable taste. Who the hell do I think I am by offering another option?

"You have a great eye, but this is out of the price range the builder is offering."

"Oh. I didn't think of that."

She nods and hands me the small square of tile. After looking around the rest of the small apartment, she says, "Good. This all looks good. You can head back to the office and I'll email over their picks this afternoon."

"Okay." I gather my things while admiring the late afternoon sunlight pouring into the large, open windows and the lake just beyond.

The apartment is still mostly a blank slate. No furniture or curtains or artwork to make it feel like a home, but the view and the lighting almost make it unnecessary.

I get back to the office at the same time as Lisa is returning from staging a house across town. We have lunch at our desks and she tells me about the place. Most of our work is on the new condos. Buyers get to pick out a few of the building options, and we run samples and put in the orders, and then make sure it all goes according to plan. There are a few other projects, including some pricey lake homes, other apartments and rentals, and a few commercial spaces, but the bulk of the work is the same.

Lisa helped stage a house that's going up for sale. I find I'm wildly jealous since I haven't stepped foot in anything but white wall, empty condos.

"I swear their kitchen is bigger than any apartment I've ever had," she says, eyes lit up with excitement. "And the view from the master bathroom is divine."

"Are you staging the entire house?"

"The sellers have some nice stuff, so mostly we're just clearing out excess furniture and clutter, making it look cleaner and highlighting the decadence."

I'm itching to take on a real project where I can really use my design skills. I understand that a clean, simple aesthetic sells houses, but I want the satisfaction of designing a real homey space where people will live and enjoy every detail.

I'm about to pack up for the day when Heather returns. She stops by my cubicle on her way to her office. Her gaze slides from me to Lisa. "Can I talk to you both in my office before you leave for the day?"

"Of course," we say in unison. Heather has been nothing but warm and lovely, but she has a certain air about her that demands respect. Also, she frightens me despite how nice she seems.

Lisa and I take the chairs in front of Heather's massive desk. Our boss smiles at us. Her dark hair is cut in a sleek bob and her makeup is perfect and timeless.

"I know that this internship is a lot of errands and grunt work, and while I think that's important to familiarize yourself with the process of what we do here, I want to give you both an opportunity to do something a little more…fun." Her red lips twist into a smirk.

Excitement zaps through me and makes me sit taller.

"I have two homes that need to be staged to sell. Both properties have waterfront access and both owners are looking to sell quickly."

A little of the excitement dwindles. Selling means less creativity in the design. I've learned that much. But a home *on* the lake?!

"I'm going to let you each take full control of staging one of these homes. You'll have the same budget and resources, but how you choose to use them are up to you."

"We'll do this together or on our own?" Lisa and I share a nervous glance.

"Each of you will be responsible for one of the homes. You can share resources and ideas, but I'll be looking to see how you handle the design and project management individually for your assigned house."

I'm so excited. Adrenaline pumps through me. I want to start now. I already have so many ideas and I haven't even seen the house.

"Thank you," Lisa says, prompting me to do the same.

"Yes. Thank you. This is…" I trail off. I have no words for how big this opportunity feels.

"One more thing," Heather says. "Your internships are over at the end of the year, but because of the recent contracts with the condominiums and a few other commercial spaces, I'm going to be hiring a full-time employee. You're both talented and hardworking. I'd be happy to offer the position to either of you. The only fair way I can see to choose is by observing you in a final project."

The smile Heather aims at us doesn't ease the swirling anxiety in my stomach. She gives us a few more details, but I barely hear any of it. "I'll send you each the details on the house you'll be working on shortly." She dismisses us with a nod.

Lisa and I leave her office, sharing hesitant and excited smiles.

"I can't believe this," she says in a rush. "Only one of us…"

I knew that working here beyond the internship was a long shot. I thought at best I'd have a great reference from a top designer, but to know that I could actually work here full-time is exciting.

"Let's not think about that," I say. "We get to design something. Finally!"

"Not just something. A house on the lake. Can you imagine the views?!"

Before either of us can stop talking about this opportunity, Heather emails us the houses she's assigned. The homes are similar. Lisa's is slightly larger, but mine sits right on the lake; whereas, hers sits back farther from the water.

I leave the office and head to my apartment, but I spend all evening looking through the photos. Five bedrooms, three baths, an open concept kitchen, dining, and living room. Plus, a loft and an office. There is so much house. So many rooms. Not to mention the views of the lake and the easy access. I'm not even a huge fan of boats or fishing, but there's something serene about being near the water.

My head spins with possibilities, but I want to walk around and get a feel for it before I decide on anything for sure.

The budget isn't much for the size of the house, so I'll need to identify the most important rooms and allocate the money accordingly.

I'm brushing my teeth, still thinking about the house, when my phone pings with a text.

BRIDGET

I miss you. Also, did you see this?

ME

MISS YOU!

I type back the reply before clicking on the link she sent. It takes me to an interview with Jack. He's in the Wildcat locker room wearing a black fitted T-shirt and a backward hat. He's sweaty like he just finished practice or a workout.

The reporter stands next to him, holding a microphone.

"Good to see you out there on the ice today," the reporter says. *"What was it like being out during the playoffs last season?"*

I tense. What an asshole question. Jack plays it cool, but there's a slight shift in his body language like maybe he's tense too and trying not to show it.

"*It was tough,*" Jack says. He looks down at the ground instead of at the reporter or camera. "*I felt like I let down my teammates and the fans. To be honest, I wasn't sure if I'd be back at all, so I'm really grateful to be here. I don't take any of this for granted. The past few months have been some of the worst and best times. The people that showed up for me, my teammates, coaches, medical staff…I can't say how much it meant to me. I wasn't an easy person to be around.*"

The reporter chuckles softly. "*It had to be hard to watch the team struggle. This is your team after all. This is your fourteenth season with the Wildcats and sixth as captain.*"

"*This is home,*" he says. "*I can't imagine playing anywhere else.*"

"*We're all looking forward to watching you this season,*" the reporter says. "*Last question, on a scale of one to ten, how excited are you to play in front of the home crowd next weekend?*"

"*There is no number that captures how ready I am.*"

"*The fans are ready too. Thanks for chatting with me, Jack. Care to give a shout out to all the medical staff and coaches that put up with you while you weren't so easy to be around?*" He grins as he uses Jack's words.

I hate that this guy is trying to joke around about something so serious. Jack is handling it way better than I would. I wonder if James is having a coronary over this interview.

"*A lot of people helped me get back here, but there is one person in particular who gave me a kick in the butt when I needed it most. It's safe to say she saved me.*"

I think I stop breathing as his words register.

The reporter is grinning wide. "*It sounds like we all should be indebted to this person then. Care to thank her by name?*"

Jack shakes his head but lifts his chin ever so slightly so I can see his eyes. He glances sideways toward the camera as he says, *"No. I think I'll keep that to myself, but she knows who she is. Thank you."*

I watch it twice, throat thick with emotion from seeing him and hearing him thank me.

BRIDGET

He's talking about you, right?

ME

Or Sandra.

BRIDGET

Who?

ME

No one.

BRIDGET

Have you talked to him?

ME

To say what?

BRIDGET

Maybe to tell him that you miss him and he's a big, stubborn fool.

ME

It won't change anything. He doesn't want to be with me.

BRIDGET

I don't know. He seems sort of lost lately.

I want to believe that has something to do with me, but if it's true, then why hasn't he texted? He didn't want to be with me and that hasn't changed.

ME

All the guys are lost in the off-season. He'll be fine now that hockey is back.

BRIDGET

Do you really believe that?

ME

I do. The team is everything to him.

They're all he needs.

CHAPTER TWENTY-EIGHT

Jack

CHOICES

The night before our home opener, I head to my old high school.

I park behind the hockey arena and go in the back door. As soon as I step inside, I'm overwhelmed with memories. I only played here for two years before I left to play in the junior league, but there's something about this place that always feels like home.

I find Coach exactly where I expect. He's sitting on the top row of the bleachers just underneath the announcer's box. Both arms are crossed over his chest and he leans back watching the players on the ice practice.

I take a seat next to him, letting my gaze take in the action.

"How are they looking?" I ask.

"Like they spent all summer at the beach instead of with a hockey stick in their hands," he says, finally looking over at me.

A small chuckle escapes my lips. "I think you said that same thing to me once."

"It was true." He holds my gaze. "You look tired. What brings you here? Shouldn't you be home getting your beauty sleep?"

I resist rolling my eyes, but I break his stare so he can't study me too closely. "I'm good. Ready."

Coach makes a clicking noise with his tongue. It's a sound I'm familiar with from the years of him being my coach and looking out for me. I don't know what I would have done without him. He coached my junior high team and then got moved up to high school the same time I did. I always wondered about that, if part of the reason he did it was to keep an eye on me. He was a hell of a coach though. A lot of people thought he should have gone on to college or junior league, but he never did.

"I'm glad you're back on the ice. I'm proud of you, always. You work harder than anyone I ever coached. Most talented, too," Coach says without tearing his gaze off the practice.

His compliments soothe and encourage me. I didn't have a functioning dad for most of my life, but Coach filled that role in a lot of ways. I'm not sure if it was out of loyalty for my dad or me, but he's always been there when I needed him. And I needed him a lot back then.

"I'm assuming there's a but coming?" I ask. "There are no beach days on my schedule. Promise," I joke.

He glances over at me with a contemplative gaze. "And nobody needs some time off more than you."

"You can't even be consistent with your own advice," I tell him, smiling at the way his mustache turns up with the corner of his mouth. "I had plenty of time off this summer."

"People need different things at different points in their life."

"And what I need right now is the beach?"

"You're young and in the best shape of your life. Enjoy it. You need more than hockey. I hoped that the accident would help you see that. It's just a game, Son. A damn great one, but it takes everything and gives very little back."

We watch in silence as the high school coaches put the kids through some skating drills. Coach is right. They look sloppy, but there are a few kids that have some natural ability if they're willing to work hard to hone it.

The high school coach blows a whistle and the guys head to the bench for a break.

Coach turns to me. "What's on your mind, Jackie?"

I'd all but talked myself out of asking him the very question I drove two hours to ask, but his prompting is the push I need.

"Do you think your life would be very different if you'd been drafted?"

If he's surprised by the random question, he doesn't show it. He falls quiet, thinking for a few moments, choosing his words carefully.

"I'm not sure," he says. "I guess I might have ended up settling down somewhere else, but I have a feeling you're asking about more than location."

"Sometimes I wonder about my dad. If he'd stayed, would he have been better off?"

Coach and Dad were friends from their own high school days. They played on a championship team together. Dad got drafted and Coach didn't.

Is it possible that one choice can alter the course of our lives so drastically or would he be the same man regardless?

"Your dad was too talented not to go. He would have regretted it. That much I know."

"Yeah, but what if he hadn't been good at the sport or put so much emphasis on being a great hockey player. What if he had wanted to be an engineer?"

Coach chuckles quietly, which sends a flare of irritation through me.

"Forget it. It doesn't matter," I say.

After a few beats of silence, Coach starts to talk again. "Life is a series of decisions. Some are bigger than others, but every choice builds on the next. Sometimes we make decisions that feel small in the moment and have big impacts on our life. Other times they only feel big in the moment."

"So it doesn't matter if he was drafted or not, eventually he would have found himself in the same position?" I ask.

"The good thing about choices is we can always make another one. What you do today is more important than yesterday."

"What if you don't know which choice is right?"

"You're my greatest success story. Not that I can take much credit for you. The first time I saw you, I knew it. More talent in your left foot than kids twice your age had in their whole body. You were always determined to succeed or burn the world down trying. You had a natural talent, but your ambition and work ethic made you who you are. That's not something that can be taught."

"I wasn't talking about me."

"Weren't you though?" He turns his attention to me. "I've found most of the time it's less about knowing what is right or wrong and more about being brave enough to do what's in our heart. Start there."

I swallow around the lump forming in my throat.

"I never would have made it anywhere without you. Your decision to coach saved me." I mean those words. I owe him everything. He's family. The only one I've ever been able to depend on.

"You would have still found a way to be successful. You're too stubborn to fail." He stands and rests a hand on my shoulder. "And that goes beyond hockey. There's a whole lot more to enjoy. Take a chance. Let someone past that barricade you've had up all these years. Though I think maybe that's what's got you so mixed-up. Love will do that."

I snort a laugh. Love? Though my chest aches like it has a permanent hole in it. Everly and I weren't in love, we were just…not done. It feels like we're not done yet.

Coach squeezes my shoulder as he stands. "I gotta get home."

"You're not staying?" He's basically a permanent fixture here. He retired from coaching years ago and bought Perry's, but hockey is in his blood. The same way it's in mine.

"No. I promised the wife I'd take her to the movies. It's our fortieth anniversary."

A real smile tugs at my lips. "Congratulations. Tell Anita I said hi."

He pats me on the shoulder again. "You should get out of here too. Make a choice from your heart instead of your head. And if I'm wrong and this conversation isn't about a woman, then you should also call one of those up. Maybe go on a date. I have a hunch you'd look less tired if you were spending more time in bed with a beautiful woman and less time preparing for the season. You can't spend your entire life doing what's best for everyone else."

He's already gone before the statement hits and another small laugh leaves my lips. But the longer I think on it, the more I miss Everly and wish I had an answer.

A part of me knows Coach is right. I don't let people in beyond a certain point. Maybe it's a reaction to my childhood or the effects of being driven to succeed, but whatever the reason, I have kept my personal life simple.

Or I did before Everly. Now that she's gone, I feel empty. Falling back into my old routine isn't really an option. I don't want to date other women, but I don't want to be this guy who keeps everyone at arm's length either. I just want her.

And I have no idea what to do about it.

CHAPTER TWENTY-NINE

Everly

NO CONTEST

I look forward to the first home game of the season like it's a holiday. I love hockey. Even if my brother hadn't played, I think I still would have been a fan. There's nothing like the energy of the Wildcat fans when the players take the ice for warmups. Conversations die down and all eyes turn to the men in green skating around the rink.

I know exactly where Ty will fall in the lineup. Maverick steps out first and then Tyler's right behind him. I usually follow him as he makes his first circle toward the net, but today my gaze lingers until all the other players have taken the ice. Jack is the last one out, like he has to make sure everyone else has made it first before he can. Honestly, that tracks for him. He's a great captain. Some people lead by example and others do it with empathy. Jack somehow manages to do both.

I take him in unabashedly with so much distance between us it feels safe. He never wears his helmet for warmups so I can see that his dark hair has gotten a touch too long again. It's slicked back and his dark eyes focus on everything around him. I swear I can feel him taking it all in like he really thought he'd never get to do this again.

I'm sitting with the wives and girlfriends tonight up on the upper level. Sandwiched between Bridget and Piper, all three of us are focused on the men. It really doesn't get old. Sure, by the end of the season most wives are ready for a break so they can see their man for longer than a few hours at a time, but for me it could be hockey year-round and I'd still watch every game.

After a few minutes, conversations start back up again. Bridget is currently holding Charlotte, who is taking turns climbing over each of our laps. Not like we mind. She's adorable in her little Sharp jersey and matching green headband.

"This feels just like old times," Piper says and squeezes my hand.

"Uh-huh. Right down to you being knocked up." I glance down at her tiny baby bump. The off-season was productive in more ways than one.

Piper is glowing, and I can't wait to be an auntie again to another adorable little girl.

When the game is ready to start, the announcer calls out the starting lineup. The arena shakes with applause and screams when he calls out Jack. The fans love him, and as I watch him taking it all in with an almost bashful expression, I almost forget about how mad I am at him and start to fall under his spell again.

There is something sexy about a man who dedicates so much of himself to other people. I just wish I was one of those people in his life.

The first game of the season does not disappoint. The guys are looking sharp. Ty scores in the second period, then Ash in the third. My ear drums hurt from the women around me yelling so much.

Jack doesn't get any goals, but he looks good out there. Like he was never gone. His presence alone is enough to make a difference. His teammates are always looking to him. If he's fired up, then so are they. When he says dig deep, they listen. Without him, they're all still talented players but with him, they're a team.

When the game is over, I go with Piper and Charlotte to wait for Tyler. I'm carrying a sleepy Charlotte when someone calls out my name.

I glance back to see Jack's agent, James, walking my way. My heart flutters with nervous anticipation. I haven't really mentioned to Tyler or Piper how much time I spent with Jack this summer and I feel like my cover is about to be blown.

Piper reaches for Charlotte. "I'm going to change her. Are you good?" she asks.

"Yeah," I say then turn to greet James. "Hi. How are you?"

I've always liked James. He has this way about him where he can tell people off, but they somehow aren't insulted. He's polite, but I get the feeling he would know who to call and where to dispose of a body, if needed.

"Good. Good. I was hoping I'd run into you."

"You were?" I smile hesitantly, then panic. "Did I screw something up? I'm so sorry. I never should have touched his schedule. I was just trying to help."

"I'm glad you did."

"Really?"

He nods. "Whatever magic you worked on Jack's inbox this summer, thank you. I was expecting to come back and spend the next month digging out of it."

"I didn't really do much."

"I can't tell you how many interns I've fired because they don't know how to politely decline an invitation or forget to check the schedule and double-book. And that's for my small clients. Managing Jack's inbox is a feat all in itself. It should be a full-time job, but Jack refuses to let anyone else touch it. Except you, I guess."

The compliment warms me, or maybe it's the reminder that for a small while, Jack let me in closer than he lets most people.

"And don't even get me started on the masquerade ball. Do you know how many times I asked him to attend?"

I shake my head.

"A lot. He told me he wasn't going to dress up in a mask like it was Halloween and go talk business. How did you get him to say yes?"

I shrug. "I just asked."

"Well, you did him and me a solid. Nike would be a huge get."

He doesn't seem to know I went with Jack to the event and my heart squeezes at the memory. That night, despite getting sick, is etched into my soul forever. He took such good care of me. I enjoyed riling up the arrogant and controlling man everyone knows, but I gave my heart to the soft version who planned a once in a lifetime night for me and then held my hand while I fought off a fever instead. It was the most intimate and vulnerable I've been with anyone, ever.

James' phone chimes and he glances down at it before looking back to me and smiling. "Anyway, I just wanted to say thanks."

"You're welcome."

He takes one step away. "I hear you're in Briar Lake for a design internship."

"That's right."

"Well, if that doesn't work out, give me a call. I have a young baseball player that could use some strong-arming."

When he leaves, I feel the weirdest sense of pride and surprise, but it's quickly snuffed out when I linger too long thinking about Jack. I didn't work any magic on Jack. He's the same guy he always was. He would have figured out his inbox and scheduling and everything else without me. That's just who he is. A man who needs no one else.

Piper and Charlotte return before I can get too lost in my thoughts, then Tyler walks out of the locker room. His smile when he sees his wife and daughter waiting for him makes me melt a little inside. I'm so glad he has Piper and Charlotte and now another baby on the way, but I would be lying if I said I don't sometimes miss when it was just the two of us against the world.

I let Piper and Charlotte hug and congratulate him first, then I step up to him.

"I'm so glad you came," he says as he wraps one arm around me.

"There's nowhere else I'd rather be. You played great. Charlotte and I declared you the best player on the team."

"Is that right?" He glances over at his daughter in Piper's arms. Charlotte is nuzzled into her mom's shoulder with her eyes half-open.

"We based it solely on last name, but yes. No contest."

He chuckles and lets out a long breath. "Are you heading back tonight?"

"No. I'm staying with Bridget. I'll head back tomorrow morning."

"Why don't you stay with us?"

"Because…" I trail off. "You're going to go home and crash, and I don't want to stumble in later and wake Charlotte."

"Going to Wild's?"

"Of course."

"All right. Well, do you want to come by for breakfast in the morning?"

"How about brunch?" I ask. Ty is a morning person, especially now that he has a baby alarm clock, and I would prefer to sleep in on the weekends.

"Text me when you wake up." He grins.

"Okay." I hug him again. "I'm proud of you."

"Thanks." He ruffles my hair as he pulls back. "Be safe tonight. Text me if you need a ride or anything."

Ash is the next to walk out of the locker room.

"Little Sharpie!" he calls. He hugs Bridget to one side of his chest as he holds up a hand for me to high-five him. Only Ash could make a high five seem completely normal in this scenario.

"Nice game," I say to him.

"Thanks. You ready to celebrate?"

"You know it. Wild's after the first home game is tradition."

"New tradition this year," he says grinning. "Tonight we're going to Midnight."

Despite my protests, after a quick stop at Ash's house so Bridget and I can change, we pile into Ash's truck and head to the night club.

"This is going to be so fun," Bridget insists.

I smile at her because normally I would be excited. I love Midnight. Or I did. Now it's all wrapped up in one person. One amazing night. I don't think I can ever go back there and not remember the things we did in the owner's box.

We're the last to arrive. As we step up to the VIP section, it's Jack's eyes I feel on me, but Declan is the first to greet me.

"Little Sharpie!" He gives me his signature one-arm hug. His wife Jade waves from where she sits on the couch behind him. Declan was the first of Tyler's teammates to become my friend. He lived in the same apartment building as Tyler and he had a wrist injury that kept him from traveling with the team. He's quiet and serious, but fiercely protective and the biggest teddy bear for the people he loves. His wife Jade is one of my favorite people. She brings him out of his shell, and he adores her.

"You know you always have a place to stay at our house if you get tired of listening to them bang." He tips his head toward Ash and Bridget.

"Like you two are any better."

The tips of his ears turn red.

"We have better soundproofing," Jade says with a smirk.

"Ahh. I'm so happy you're here." Bridget's smile erases some of the anxiety swirling in my stomach.

"Me too. I hate not seeing you every week."

"Same, but the internship is good?" she asks, then takes a small sip of her drink. "I looked at the pictures you sent me. That house is gorgeous."

"Right? And you should see it in person now that we have all the owner's furniture moved out. It's this big, open slate and I have so many ideas. Unfortunately, my budget is so small I'm not sure I'm going to be able to do it justice."

"I have seen you redo an entire room for less than a hundred dollars so I think you've got this."

"This is different." A flutter of panic works its way in, the same way it does every time I try to pull together a design plan. My usual homey touches and thrifting finds aren't going to cut it and I'm running out of time to decide. I'll need weeks to execute my ideas once they're solidified, and the open house deadline is looming.

She grins right along with me, listening to me talk about work. A lot of my hours at the internship have been spent assisting Heather on the condos, but I love the house she selected for my final design project.

"You're totally going to get the job. I know it. No one deserves it more."

"Thanks. I'm trying not to think about that part. I always knew a full-time job with Heather was a long shot."

"Not for you. You're…"

I lose track of what Bridget is saying as I spot Jack moving through the crowd.

The gray T-shirt that stretches across his broad chest should look casual, but he wears it like a fine suit. It hugs his muscular frame and drapes along his tapered waist. Black dress pants and tennis shoes complete the look. He looks exactly like the sporty club owner that he is.

Bridget must notice that I've completely lost focus on her because the next thing I know she's taking my hand and squeezing.

"Are you okay?" She looks from me to Jack.

"Yeah," I say unconvincingly then, "I knew I'd have to face him again eventually."

"Have you talked at all since Charlotte's birthday party?"

"No." I shake my head.

"Do you want to dance or something?"

"Yes, definitely." I smile and feel immediate relief at having something else to focus on.

We start for the dance floor but before we get to the steps that lead out of the VIP area, Jack steps in front of us. I don't know why I thought he'd avoid me, but it's obvious that is not how tonight is going to go.

He smiles tentatively. There's a spark of something in his expression. At the birthday party he seemed more resigned to seeing me, like he knew it was inevitable and he wanted to make sure we were okay for the sake of everyone else. But this is different. He looks happy to see me, which doesn't make sense.

"Hey," he says.

No one is looking at us like this is out of the ordinary, but my palms sweat like everyone can tell he's seen me naked anyway.

"Hi."

"Can we talk?" he asks, looking from me to Bridget.

She starts to leave, but I clutch on to her arm. "We were just going to dance."

He doesn't budge and I squirm under the weight of his stare.

"Please?" His eyes plead more than the tone in his voice.

I nod my head ever so slightly and let go of Bridget.

"I won't be far," she says and leaves us.

When we're alone I cross my arms at my waist. "I don't have anything to say to you."

"Then let me talk." He steps closer. His scent wraps around me, and I close my eyes and block out the onslaught of memories. I can't do this with him. Not here. Not in front of our friends.

"You don't need to do this. Okay? I'm fine. Great, actually." I smile my most convincing smile. "I'm happy so whatever you think you need to say or do, it's just not necessary. Can we just go back to how things were?"

"No," he says quickly. "That won't work. Not for me."

I don't understand what he expects me to say or do. Am I supposed to let him see how badly it crushed me when he all but told me he didn't want to see me anymore?

"Too damn bad, Jack. You aren't the boss of me."

His lips twitch at one corner like he's amused with me, then his fingers brush over mine and he leans down to whisper. "I miss you."

My mouth is dry and swallowing is difficult as he stares down at me. Memories of the summer flash in my mind and I fight to push them away. It was just a summer fling.

Jack gives my fingers a small squeeze before he pulls back and walks away. He's gone before I can manage to compose myself enough to reply. Ash approaches with a drink in each hand and a quizzical expression. "Everything okay?" he asks.

He hands me one of the drinks.

"Yeah, great."

His slow nod isn't exactly one that says he believes me, but he doesn't pry.

Bridget and I do eventually make it to the dance floor, where I do my best to forget about the man upstairs and lose myself to the music. But he's everywhere. This club has so much of him in it. It's the details. The lavish yet cozy vibe, the dark and moody color palette, and the feeling of safety and fun. I can't explain it but it's a bone-deep feeling that I can't shake.

When we're both tired and sweaty, we head back to VIP. Jack is sitting on a couch next to Declan and a woman I don't recognize. She's familiar with him in a way that indicates this isn't the first time they've met.

Jealousy burns my throat. And then a more horrifying realization hits me – he's probably already hooked up with other people. I mean, of course he has. He's Jack Wyld. He bounces through women like a sport.

Maybe that's why he's so eager for us to clear the air. It will be awkward to see him with someone else and he might be an asshole, but he wouldn't want to rub it in my face.

I go back to ignoring him. Or trying. Ash and Bridget do their best to include me in their conversation but my mood has plummeted, and I can't seem to fake it.

Jack doesn't outright flirt with the woman, but that isn't really his style. He exists and women flock to him. I've seen it so many times over the years. He's this unshakeable force, never changing who he is for anyone else. I admire that about him as much as it annoys me. He was never going to fall in love with me. I knew that and somehow, I let myself fall for him anyway. Stupid, stupid.

My plan to ignore Jack is thwarted quickly. Declan notices me staring that way and waves me over. I hesitate but realize it's going to look stranger if I don't go than if I do.

He moves over closer to Jade, leaving an empty space next to Jack. I falter for only a beat before taking the seat. My throat is thick with emotion as my left side buzzes from the contact of Jack. My shoulder brushes against the side of his arm and our thighs push together. It's hard to breathe, hard to think with him this close.

"How are you?" Declan asks, and I focus all my attention on him. Or try to. "I've missed you. When's your internship over?"

I give him the same spiel as I have everyone else, but with Declan I never feel like he's trying to pressure me one way or another. His love and support don't have strings or expectations. I know that he would be just as proud of me if I quit today than if I went on to become the best interior designer in the state.

It isn't that I don't think Ty and the others would still love me or be proud of me, but they still think of me as the girl that needs them to push me to be successful and keep me out of trouble. I'm a responsibility to them, and that links my success to theirs. If I succeed, then they did something right. I owe them all so much, but I want to figure out the next steps on my own. Probably messily and with tons of mistakes, and not worry that they're going to be disappointed in me.

Jack angles his body to listen to me talk. I feel his attention but don't look his way until he says, "You're designing a place all on your own?"

"Yeah. Well, my boss will still sign off on everything…" I trail off feeling a little silly about making such a big deal out of it. But Jack smiles, really smiles, like this is the best news he's ever heard. I get a little lost in that smile and forget I'm mad at him. I wanted him to know I was happy and glad I went, but I don't want him to think he did me any favors by pushing me out the door.

"I love the houses at Briar Lake," the pretty brunette on the other side of him says and she leans over Jack to speak. I eye all the places she's touching him and have to clamp my jaw shut to keep from saying something. Like I have any right.

I'm still focusing on her boobs pressed against his arm when I feel calloused fingers on my thigh. I stare down at Jack's hand and my head spins. I don't know what's happening but suddenly I feel like I'm in way over my head.

"Excuse me. I…" Not bothering to finish my sentence, I stand and head toward the bar. I can't play this game. He's way better at it than I am.

CHAPTER THIRTY

Jack

GET OVER YOURSELF

Tonight has been a roller coaster. I was so excited to see Everly here, but that feeling does not appear to be mutual.

I excuse myself a minute after Everly flees from the couch in VIP. I lost her in the crowd of people, but I search until I realize she's gone. On instinct, I head upstairs to the owner's balcony. The door is rarely locked since most people don't know it exists in the first place.

She stands stiffly in front of the window and stares down at the dance floor. She doesn't seem surprised that I'm here. I approach her slowly. Fuck I miss her.

My heart beats quickly as I close the distance between us. Her short blonde hair leaves her shoulders and neck exposed, and my mouth waters with the need to taste her there.

"Why?" she asks, spinning around to face me. Her big hazel eyes are lit up with frustration. God, she's sexy and perfect and I want her to be fucking mine. I want it even though I've tried to fight it. And despite not knowing if it's right for her or me.

One choice today from the heart. Just like Coach said.

"Why what?" I ask, placing my hands in my pockets so I don't touch her.

"Why did you ruin everything?" Her voice catches, and I watch as she fights to keep control. It's the first indication that maybe she's hurting as much as I am.

"I panicked. I didn't want you to give up the internship for me."

Her gaze narrows. "Get over yourself."

She tries to push past me, but I give in and reach out to her. I take her by the hand and pull her back to me, chest to chest. Hers rises and falls, vibrating with anger at me.

"Maybe it wasn't all about me, but you wanted to be here with me as much as I wanted you to stay. You couldn't get enough. You were addicted."

"Don't flatter yourself. I was never going to stay for you." She keeps glaring at me like she's about to tell me to fuck off. And, knowing Ev, she very well might. But I know it's true because I felt the same way. We were both in over our heads.

"I'm sorry for hurting you, but I don't regret it." Not those weeks we spent together or making sure she left.

I know she thinks I mean the latter when she lifts her chin defiantly and says, "Me either."

"You're young, Ev. You should do all the things *you* want. Be selfish and wild. Live."

"I wish people would stop thinking they know what's best for me." She jabs me in the chest with a finger. "What if I don't want to be selfish and wild or leave the nest and conquer the world? Maybe I don't know what I want yet, but I know that I want to figure it out without people making decisions for me. It's my damn life."

I stay quiet. She's right to be pissed. I'm still struggling with wanting to be in her life and wondering if it's what's best for her, but I'm done pushing her away. If she walks away, it'll be her choice.

"You know what I want?" she asks as she presses into me with enough force that I have to dig in to keep from stepping back. I love the feel of her body against mine and I don't want to lose it a second before I have to.

"No." I really, really don't at this point. "What do you want, Ev?"

Whatever it is, she can have it. If I can give it to her, I will.

She glares at me. Those stunning hazel eyes fueled with fire glare at me. I'm waiting for her to yell at me. I'm ready for it. I welcome it.

Instead, her gaze drops to my mouth and then she lunges for me. She kisses me hard like she's pouring every ounce of anger into it. If this is her idea of punishing me, then sign me the fuck up.

I let her hate-kiss me and I savor every taste. For every scrape and nip, I lick and suck at her mouth. Her fingers tug at my hair until my scalp pricks and my hands dig into her ass, pushing her into my erection.

"You don't get to decide for me," she says as my teeth scrape down her neck to her collarbone. She moans and says with less conviction this time, "I'm the only boss of me."

She pushes at my chest, breaking us apart, but instead of walking away like I figured was coming any moment, she drops to her knees.

My dick twitches with her perfect mouth so close. Eyes on me, she undoes my pants and pulls them to my ankles with my boxers. My dick springs free, hard as stone, and leaking for her.

"Tonight, I'm the boss of you, too," she says, then leans in and licks the tip. My hands instinctively go to her hair, but she pulls away and scowls.

The intent is clear. Do not touch her. Got it. Though easier said than done.

She wraps her fingers around me and brings the head back to her lips. She kisses me gently, teasing, torturing. I groan in frustration and a wicked smile curves her lips.

She takes me all the way to the back of her throat and swallows.

"Fuck, Ev." I ball my hands into fists to keep myself from reaching out again.

She bobs on my dick like it's her favorite popsicle flavor, swirling her tongue and hollowing out her cheeks. I don't even try to fight off the orgasm that comes way too soon. She wants to prove a point and I have to assume it's that no one else has ever or will ever be as good as her. I already fucking knew that. My dick hasn't perked up at the sight of a hot girl in weeks. He's as loyal as me and we only want one person.

One annoying, infuriating, perfect woman.

As she brings me over the edge, I finally tangle my hands in her short hair and stroke my thumbs along her cheekbones. She swallows every drop I give her.

Panting and absolutely spent and dreading the second her mouth leaves my cock.

She pulls away with a smug smirk. I tug her up and crash my lips to hers. She's softer, more compliant now. I don't know what just happened, but she's here, not running.

"Happy?" I ask.

"No. I'm still mad at you."

"I'm sorry. Come home with me. Let me make it up to you."

I know it's the wrong thing to say as soon as the words leave my mouth. The shield she had up earlier returns.

"I don't think that's a good idea."

"I shouldn't have pushed you away like I did. I wish I had a better reason. This is new territory for me." I've never wanted someone like I want her. It feels selfish and messy. I don't know what I'm doing, which I *really* hate.

"You should have talked to me."

"Would you have listened?"

She sighs like maybe she knows she's stubborn, but she still wishes I would have tried to have a real conversation instead of making the decision for her, like so many other people in her life have done. Honestly, me too, but I'm not going to make that mistake twice if she'll give me another chance.

The lights in the club come up, indicating it's closing time. I pull up my boxers and pants and tuck myself away as Everly finger-combs her hair so it doesn't look like I just had my hands in it.

"When do you go back?" I ask.

"Tomorrow."

Fuck. There's a small, asshole part of me that wishes I had asked her to give up everything and stay here with me to see where this could go. Is that the choice that would have changed everything?

All I know is she's going to leave again before I've convinced her to give me another shot.

"Can I see you before you go back to Briar Lake?"

"I don't know." She bites on the corner of her lip, staring at me with her brows pinched together like she's working out a problem. The problem being me.

"Tell me what you want or need. Whatever it is, I'll give it to you."

"I wish I knew," she says with a small shake of her head.

I slide my hands into my pockets. It's not the actionable answer I hoped for, but I know I can't rush her. "Okay."

She starts for the door, and I call after her.

"Ev?"

"Yeah?" She pauses, looking back at me.

"I meant what I said earlier. I miss you. Seeing you every day, talking, hanging out, having you in my space, all of it. Nothing feels right anymore without you."

Her lips quiver and I watch her chest rise and fall with a sigh that feels heavy even from a distance.

"I miss you too, Jack."

CHAPTER THIRTY-ONE

Everly

CAPTAINING

"Your apartment looks like a florist shop," Bridget says as I move the phone so she can see the current state of the place. I set another vase of roses on the counter. "Or a funeral."

"Well, what did you expect?" My friend's laughter unknots some of the tension I've been holding on to ever since I saw Jack at Midnight. "He isn't the kind of guy to stand by and wait. Jack is going after what he wants. And in this case, that's you."

A groan slips past my lips and Bridget laughs again.

"Talk to him," she insists. "Before I have to come drag you out of your apartment under a ton of roses."

A smile finally pulls at the corner of my lips. "We've talked."

"He's talked. You're holding back and it's driving him crazy. And I don't blame you, but if you want it to stop, then talk to him."

"I don't know what to say yet."

He's making an effort, and I'm…well, I'm not sure. We weren't a couple before, so if we fall back into how things were, where does that leave us?

"You will," she says. "Eventually, you will."

Bridget and I hang up and then I snap a picture of my kitchen counter, currently unusable because of all the flowers, and text it to Jack.

JACK

Too much?

ME

Any more and I'll have to rent a bigger apartment to store them.

JACK

I could arrange that.

I roll my eyes and an incredulous laugh escapes. I would not put it past him.

I put my phone down and pull out my laptop to work on my design for the lake house. I've figured out which rooms I want to focus on, but when I checked prices on rental furniture, I had to rethink my plan. It's more expensive than I expected. I'll figure it out, but I feel like I'm behind already.

I rework things until my eyes are blurry and I can't think anymore. I close my laptop and head into the bedroom. My apartment is nice, but I've been so busy I haven't added the usual homey touches that would make it feel like mine. Maybe that's why even after a month of being here it still doesn't feel like a place I could stay. It's like I'm on a long work trip.

I miss my friends and baby Charlotte. She started walking last week and I cried when Tyler sent me the video. I can't help but feel like I'm missing out on things that are so much more important than work.

After washing my face and brushing my teeth, I climb into bed with my phone. I reread Jack's texts. He texts every day at least once, more if I reply. I still don't know how to feel about everything. Despite not wanting to be here, I feel like I need to prove to myself that I'm capable of succeeding. And maybe I want to prove it to Tyler, Piper, and everyone else too.

The next day, instead of roses he sends daisies. The card reads, "Hope these look less like a funeral."

God, what an idiot. I'm grinning though.

The following day I'm expecting the flowers, more daisies, but there's also a small, wrapped gift too. I take them both inside and set the flowers next to the rest then tear open the present. My fingers shake as I run a finger across the earrings. Diamond hoops. Simple, elegant, expensive.

The man is out of his mind. I take one out and hold it up to my ear. They're stunning, but there's no way I can accept these. I left the diamond tennis necklace at his house, along with a few other items by accident. When I went to Wild's that day, I thought I'd be going back. I'm glad I don't have the necklace though. It'd be too sad to see it every day and think of that night.

I text to thank him while kindly informing him I can't accept them, then put the earrings away in a drawer until I see him.

The next day I'm at the lake house when Lisa stops by. She hands me a cup of coffee. "I thought you might need this."

"Thank you." We stand in the kitchen together since there isn't any furniture yet.

"I like the wallpaper." She motions with her head to the dining room. I don't have much in the way of a budget for that room so I thought making the walls a focal point would help.

"Thanks. How's it going over at your place?"

"I finished the master bedroom today and the en suite bath. I'm waiting for the painters to finish downstairs. Hopefully I can start down there next week."

She has the same exhausted look as I'm wearing. It's harder than I thought. The pressure to get it right and what is at stake is a lot.

"I can't wait to see it," I say honestly. Her design aesthetic is different than mine. She is modern and minimalist. Whereas I'm more eclectic. She probably fits in better with Heather's usual clients, but I'm hoping that gives me an edge. I can add something new. Though in reality, most of the work is far less open to creative input than that. If I get the job, most of my days are going to be spent helping new homeowners decide between three different options for their custom builds. Still, it would be a great opportunity while getting experience.

My phone pings with a text and I pick it up off the counter.

JACK

Are you home?

ME

Work. Why?

JACK

What time will you be here?

I start to type back, but then pause.

Here. Like as in…oh my god, is he in Briar Lake?

"I have to go," I say to Lisa.

"Everything okay?"

"Yeah." I smile tentatively. "Everything is fine."

I grab my things quickly and close up the house. "See you in the morning," I say to her before getting in my car.

My pulse thrums quickly as I make the ten-minute drive. Even though I had guessed as much, seeing him standing in the parking lot of my apartment building still takes me by surprise.

He's leaning against the side of his G-Wagon, somehow looking like he belongs here and that he owns the building all at once.

"What are you doing here?" I ask, taking in his black athletic pants and gray T-shirt that hugs his chest and biceps.

"You said not to send any more gifts, so I thought I could take you out to dinner."

I stare at him slack-jawed. "You drove two hours to take me to dinner?"

"Mhmm." He moves to the passenger-side door of his SUV and opens it.

It's surreal to be back in his vehicle. I realize only after we're pulling away from the apartment that while he looks divine, I'm still in my work clothes.

"I'm a mess. Maybe we should just get takeout or something."

He glances over at me and his gaze goes to my hair. I pulled it back while I was working and stuck a pencil through it.

I pull out the pencil with a sheepish smile and my hair falls.

"You look great," he says as he glances back to the road. "What are you hungry for?"

My stomach is a bundle of nerves, so very little. I try to think where we'll be as inconspicuous as possible. I doubt he wants to draw attention to the fact he's here.

"There's a cute pizzeria just down the street here on the right."

He nods as if that's settled.

"How's work?"

I laugh softly. "What are you doing here?"

"I missed you."

"Jack—" I start, but I have no idea what to say. I'm so glad to see him. It feels like a little piece of home, but I don't know what it means.

"Let me feed you and then we can talk. All right? If you want me to leave and never come back—"

"You'll listen?" I ask, skeptical.

He just smirks as he pulls into the parking lot. The pizzeria doesn't have a lot of seating; they do more pickup and delivery than dining in, but Jack orders and we sit outside while we wait.

The weather is perfect. Still warm with a hint of fall in the air. The leaves are starting to change, but in a few more weeks it'll be beautiful.

"I can't believe you're here."

"I'm starting to get a complex," he says, leaning back in his chair across from me.

"Don't you have things to do? Practice? Captaining?"

"Captaining?" He grins. He looks so handsome when he smiles like that, it's hard not to mimic his expression.

"Yeah, it's how you spend most of your day. Bossing people around, making sure everyone else has what they need and are taken care of."

He keeps smiling, but it takes on a hint of confusion like he doesn't really see it like that. "We leave tomorrow afternoon so everyone else is spending time with their loved ones and packing up."

And he's here. I don't point that out, but my face warms.

"That still doesn't explain why you're here."

"I missed you."

I blow out a breath. When he lays it out there so simply it makes my head spin.

"We should have gone somewhere with alcohol."

Jack leans forward and his long fingers cover mine. "I'm here because I want to be. I want to see what your life is like here so I can picture you working hard and kicking ass."

One hand reaches up and fingers the end of my hair. "So, tell me about your day."

I let out a shaky breath, but he pulls back and it allows me to think clearer.

"I spent the morning in the office ordering things for clients and tracking down items that are delayed."

He hangs on to my words like they're fascinating, but I know they aren't because I was bored to tears. But he asked for it, so I keep going. "This afternoon I went out to the lake house I'm staging."

"Yeah?" His smile widens. "I looked online, but I wasn't sure which one."

"You did?"

"Yeah. I told you, I want to be able to picture you here."

"It isn't listed yet." I pull out my phone and open the photos I took. I slide my phone across the table to him.

"Wow. This is stunning. The views are great," he says as he flips through all of them twice.

"Right? And you should see it in person. The photos don't do it justice. The entire first floor has a view out onto the water. The living room has these big, floor to ceiling windows, and the dining room opens up onto a little patio. Oh, and the master bedroom has a fireplace and this little nook perfect for a reading chair. I can picture curling up with coffee or a book, occasionally staring out at the water."

I stop rambling and feel the flush in my cheeks.

"Anyway." I take my phone back from him. "I still have a lot of work to do. It's a really big project for my first one and the stakes are high. I feel like I'm in over my head. If I fail…" I trail off. I don't say it, but he knows.

"What's left to do?"

"Staging and cosmetic touches, which sounds like not a lot, but I want buyers to walk in and feel the homey, lake vibes. I put up wallpaper today in the dining room in lieu of painting and buying artwork. My budget is small for the square footage so I'm having to prioritize and figure out where to allocate the most money and time. A mistake in one room can wreck the entire design."

"What are you thinking for the living room?"

"You really want to hear about this?" I ask, arching a brow.

"Yeah." His expression doesn't say otherwise so I keep talking. I lay out my entire plan for him, starting with the living room and then moving on to the other rooms. I explain how I came to each decision and even use the photos on my phone so I can help him visualize.

I realize it actually helps to talk it through like this. He doesn't interrupt, but he nods along when he agrees and even points out a few things I hadn't thought of, like how the biggest impact is going to be when people first walk through the doors. The house has a great view as soon as you step inside, so highlighting that is a great idea. That area wasn't high on my priority list, but I move it up and can immediately picture a few small touches that will accomplish the task, maybe an entry table and a rug, but otherwise, it doesn't need to be over the top. Let their eyes go to the most important thing naturally.

When I've finished, I feel more excited than I have in weeks. It's gotten dark since we've sat down. The pizza is gone and I know he needs to get back. I wrap my arms around my stomach to fight off the night chill.

"Come on, let's get you warm," he says, standing and holding out his hand to me.

It's a thrill holding his hand, just like it was the first time. I lean in close, wrapping my free hand around his bicep and stealing as much warmth as I can. Stealing as much of him as I can.

He opens the passenger door for me and I hesitate, lingering there, not wanting to drop his hand and thinking about kissing him. I think he's on the same page because his gaze drops to my mouth and then up before he steps away.

I hide my disappointment and get in the car. He drives back to my apartment and parks in front of the building.

"Are you ready for Boston?" I ask, not ready for him to leave.

"Yeah. They're tough, but the team is looking good."

"I know. I've been watching," I admit.

He nods and smiles. "Watching anyone in particular?"

"My brother," I say with a smirk.

He smirks right back. "Fair enough."

"Thank you for coming tonight. I miss everyone. Even you." Especially him, but I'm not ready to admit that to him.

"We miss you too."

"Do you want to come up? I can show you my place. It has a real floral vibe currently, but otherwise it's not bad."

His boyish grin is full of pride. "I want to, but I should probably get back. One of our minor league guys was moved up for tomorrow and I need to make sure he's good to go."

"Captaining," I say. I lean across the console and place my fingers on his cheek. It's rough with stubble and his gaze darkens.

He chuckles softly. "I'd rather captain you."

He closes the distance and presses his mouth to mine. It's gentler than normal, almost sweet. Before I've had enough, I don't think I could ever get enough, he pulls back.

"Thanks for dinner." I reach for the door handle, then on a whim, turn and fling myself at him. I still don't know what we are, but I know that I've never been happier to see someone than I was when he showed up today.

I know I've caught him by surprise because it takes him a couple of seconds before he's kissing me back. His hands come up to frame my face and he groans into my mouth. That perfect control of his slips and he kisses me with all the passion and intensity that I've missed so much. I'm dizzy with excitement and a little relief. This feels right. Maybe I don't have the rest figured out, but I know I want this. I want him. Kissing Jack is all the fun of a night on the town and all the warmth of a night in. It's thrilling but safe. He's home.

Breathless, I pull back.

Jack's fingers still rest on my face and his voice is gruff as he says, "You're welcome."

We breathe each other in, both of us still panting.

"I'm still giving you back the earrings though."

A rough chuckle shakes his chest. "I'm a stubborn man, Ev. I'll just keep giving them back and sending more. Bracelets, necklaces, rings."

"Okay," I say quickly before he can get any more ideas. "I got it."

"Good." He aims that cocky grin at me.

CHAPTER THIRTY-TWO

Jack

I'M YOURS

In the months that I was injured, I wasn't sure if I'd ever be back to where I was physically, but somehow, I feel stronger than ever.

I'm putting up better numbers than I have in years. I'm leading scoring and inching closer to the all-time record for the franchise. Legacy isn't something I cared about when I started playing hockey. I wanted to play and I wanted to win, but I didn't set goals for beating records and getting my name up there among the greats.

Maybe because it reminded me too much that eventually it'd all be over.

We finish our second of three road games. We've won both easily and the team is feeling good. We're taking a flight early tomorrow morning, but tonight we have a few hours to relax. A lot of the guys are going out. Even Leo and Nick, who at home would be rushing off to their families, are making plans to head to the bar down the street.

"Do you want to walk over together?" Ash asks as we're heading to our rooms after the game.

"What, do I need a babysitter?"

"I don't know. Do you? You look like you're thinking about bailing like last night. What's up with you?"

I had considered it. Ev's been working late hours, but she should be getting off work and back to her apartment soon. We've been talking on the phone every night, something I saw other guys do and swore would never be me, but I'm as anxious to hear from her and listen to her talk about her day as I am to step onto the ice every night.

"I'll be there," I say.

He studies me closely, like he's trying to ensure I'm not lying, but he nods. "All right. See you over there."

I text Everly before I shower, hoping she's free and we can talk before I go, but after I'm done and dressed I still haven't heard back so I head over to the bar.

"You made it!" Leo greets me like I'm the one that never goes out anymore. Since Callum, he's rarely hitting up the bar, not that I blame him, just an observation.

"Where else would I be?" I ask and an image of sitting at that pizzeria with Everly in Briar Lake flashes through my mind.

"I'm glad you made it out," he says, and I can see the sincerity in his expression. It's been a while since we've all hung out, just us without their significant others. I'm not sure I would have said before tonight that I missed it, but there's a familiarity in it just being us. Like old times.

The bar is busy for a Thursday night, but it's a lot of college kids and few of them are paying us much attention. We pull four tables together and spread out with pitchers of beer to share.

Tyler takes a drink and makes a face. "Been a while since I had cheap beer."

"It's the only thing they have on tap," I say.

He takes another drink, making less of a fuss this time.

We're on one end and it's hard to keep up with the conversation farther down the tables. Ash is telling a story, waving his hands around, and thriving in the attention. Maverick, next to him, interrupts occasionally to add something, and between the two of them they're hard to ignore.

It's fine by me because Everly just texted back, and I am eager to hear about her day.

EVERLY

Sorry I just got to my apartment. I was moving furniture around and I'm sweaty and gross.

She attached a selfie with her hair pulled back. Short blonde pieces hang in her face. A white tank top dips low in the front, making my stare drop to her tits. She has on overalls, which makes me laugh because she's paired them with the diamond earrings I gave her. Very rich housewife playing dress-up. Her eye makeup is slightly smudged and there's a black streak that I assume is dirt on her neck.

Tyler notices my attention has swayed and grins.

"Seeing someone new?" he asks.

I'm grinning at my phone, but his words hit like a hammer and I lock the screen.

"No," I say quickly.

His brows lift. "No?"

My insides heat. Fuck. I need to tell him but I don't want to do that before Everly and I have talked about it first. Maybe she wants to tell him? We haven't even established what we are, but I don't want to do whatever it is behind Tyler's back.

"Nope, not seeing anyone."

"Really? I thought…" His voice trails off. "You've seemed different lately."

"How so?" I take a sip of the beer. He's right. It's terrible, but I'm not tossing back shots tonight. Travel day or not, I don't want to feel like shit tomorrow.

"I can't explain it," he says, gaze narrowing slightly. "Some guys lose focus when they meet someone new. Not intentionally, of course, but they spend a little less time at practice or they skip out on things to make room for the relationship."

I nod. It's a cycle I've seen time and time again. Not from me, but from my teammates. It doesn't last that long and I know that hockey isn't everything so I don't hold it against them.

"But not you," he says. "You seem somehow more focused than ever but less stressed like someone has taken a weight off your shoulders."

My phone buzzes on the table. I glance down to see Everly's name and another photo, but I don't swipe it open just yet. Tyler doesn't try to invade my privacy, but he grins like he knows it's the person I claim to not be seeing.

"I'm just happy to be back," I say. "Going out like that last season was torture."

He nods and doesn't call me out on it.

My phone buzzes again. I try to play it cool as I glance down and unlock my screen.

EVERLY

What are you doing?

EVERLY

Want to come over and help me shower?

I nearly choke on another sip of watered-down beer when I see the photo she attached. The white tank top is gone and the overalls clasp over her bare tits.

Fuck me.

ME

At the bar with the guys for a bit. Don't shower yet.

EVERLY

But I'm filthy.

ME

And I'm sitting next to your brother with a hard-on.

EVERLY

Too bad.

ME

I'll be back at my hotel in an hour.

EVERLY

I can't wait. I watched your interview from after the game and I am so turned on. I want to fuck you in the locker room someday.

ME

Jesus Christ woman.

EVERLY

> You look so hot in your full pads. I want to rub myself along your big thigh while you captain me.

My face is hot and my cock strains against my jeans.

ME

> Five minutes. Keep your clothes on.

"Is that the girl you're *not* seeing?" Ty asks.

"I don't know what it is yet," I say and because I desperately want to change the conversation. "How are things with you? Congrats by the way."

He let us all know at the start of the trip that he and Piper are expecting again. I already knew from Everly, but I had to let on like I was just finding out. She's so excited to be an aunt again.

"Thanks. It's surreal, but we're excited."

"You should be." My phone buzzes but I don't dare look down though it's killing me not to.

"Yeah. Things are good. A little worried about Everly."

That has my full attention. "Why?"

"I think she's dating someone."

Tyler takes the panicked look on my face as the same brotherly frustration he's feeling. "I know," he says. "She's dated before but this time it seems different and she won't tell me anything. I even had Piper try to pry the information from her, but since she moved away she seems to be keeping us at arm's length."

"She probably just wants to keep you from freaking out and digging up information on the guy until she's sure about him."

"Or it's some rich asshole that lives up there."

"You know you're a rich asshole now, right?"

"You know what I mean. Some older guy that dates women half his age so he can parade them around like trophies."

"Everly is too smart for that."

"She plays it off like she's strong and untouchable, but our mom was hard on her. She always feels like she needs to prove herself. Sometimes I worry if she needed my help, she wouldn't ask for it."

"She did though. Coming to you all those years ago."

He nods. "Yeah, I guess you're right."

He takes another drink of his beer. "I'm gonna figure out who it is she's seeing."

"How?" I ask, another thrum of panic working its way in.

"I don't know. Maybe she'll confide in Ash or Declan."

"I wouldn't worry about it. If it's serious, she'll let you know."

I glance down at my phone again. She did not wait and the image of her tits gets me to my feet.

"I gotta take this." I head to the bathroom, thankful when it's empty. I stand with my back against the door to block anyone from coming in and call Everly.

"Hi." Her voice is silky with enough rasp to tell me she's as turned on as I am. I accept the video request, but it doesn't prepare me for seeing her topless.

"Fuck, Everly."

"Yes, please."

"Soon, baby," I promise. My dick screams to be inside her now. Or between those perfect tits.

"Where are you?"

"The bathroom. I had to escape your brother asking me about the woman he thinks I'm seeing."

Her brows rise.

"He doesn't know it's you, but he's also clued in that you might be seeing someone."

"Am I?" she asks. "Is that what we're doing?"

Her hand glides down the valley between her breasts and disappears lower beyond the screen.

"Currently, you're driving me out of my fucking mind," I say by way of reply. And when that answer doesn't seem to appease her, I add, "You're fucking mine, Everly. You can slap whatever label on it you want."

"Yours?" Her brows inch higher combatively.

"Fine. Maybe you're not mine yet, but I'm yours. Now angle that camera lower so I can watch you."

Someone pushes on the door behind me, but I don't budge.

"Are you going to touch yourself?" she asks.

"Not now, but later I'm going to jerk myself off while I imagine you riding my thigh."

Her body flushes as she adjusts the camera. She's still wearing the overalls, but her hand is buried between her legs so I can't see.

"Show me how wet you are."

Her fingers reappear, coated with her desire.

"Atta girl," I say just like she fantasized.

"So hot," she mutters and then slides her hand back down. I can't see everything but she's still the hottest thing I've ever seen. Face flushed, lips parted with a moan as my name tumbles out on a whimper.

"You're doing such a good job," I continue praising her, remembering what Tyler said about Everly's need for approval. I doubt he had this scenario in mind when he handed me that information.

"Ride that hand like it's me, baby. Don't hold back on me."

"Jack."

Fuck. I undo my jeans and shove my hand into my boxers.

This was definitely not in my plans. Jerking off in a bar bathroom feels like an all-time low but as I listen to her say my name in the throes of an orgasm and come all over my stomach and hand, I decide there's not a whole lot I won't do for this woman.

CHAPTER THIRTY-THREE

Everly

ATTA GIRL

The final road game for the Wildcats is on Saturday, only a few hours away. Bridget and Jade are both going, so in a last-minute decision, I decide to make the trip to watch the team. To see Tyler, of course.

"Does he know you're here?" Jade asks as the three of us settle into our seats.

"No," I say immediately then realize she means Tyler and not Jack. "I mean, yes. I texted him earlier."

"It's nice that you're so supportive of your brother." She stares at me like she's trying to see into my soul.

"Yeah. I'm really proud of him." I squirm a little. The guys are warming up. It's not as exciting when they're the away team, but Jack looks as sexy as always. I flush as I watch him. He mouths, "Atta boy," to someone and all I can think about is him praising me as I got myself off.

"So are you seeing anyone?" Jade asks.

I laugh quietly. It seems like an odd question. Jade and I are friends, but she doesn't usually grill me out of nowhere.

"Nothing serious," I say noncommittally. My pulse picks up and I keep my stare on the ice instead of Jade. My flee instincts kick in to get out of this conversation. "Does anyone want anything from the concession stand?"

"Oh my god. I know you and Jack are fucking," she says finally.

"What?" The blood drains from my face.

"Relax. I haven't told anyone."

"How did you know?" I look past her to Bridget who holds up her hands.

"I didn't say a word," she swears.

"She didn't," Jade confirms. "I'm just unusually observant. Plus, the writing is slow lately so I have to entertain myself somehow. You two have been acting weird around each other since summer break. Nice. Polite. It's odd."

Jade is a writer. She's working on her first book, which she has been very tight-lipped about. "What's going on with the book?"

"Uh-uh." She shakes her head. "We're still talking about you and Mr. Captain."

"We aren't fucking," I say quietly. "Not exactly."

"Interesting."

"Why is that interesting?"

"The guys have been talking about his stats this season. They think it's because he's not dating anyone for once, but I was banking on the opposite. He's found someone he's serious about."

"I'm sorry, what?" I look between my friends for answers. I'm not sure which part of that I find more confusing. The idea the guys think

Jack is playing well because he's celibate or that Jade thinks we're "serious."

The starting players are taking the ice and Jack heads to the middle for the puck drop.

The crowd around us is noisy, forcing Bridget to lean in as she says, "There's a theory going around that he's focused and locked-in because he's keeping his dick in his pants. It's not just the guys. Some reporter mentioned it after the last game too."

Laughter spills out of me but trickles off. "I mean technically they could be right. We aren't having sex."

"Really?" Jade asks, surprise lifting both brows. She hums. "Maybe the theory isn't bullshit. Unfortunately for Declan, I'm not sure I have the willpower to test it."

I focus on Jack on the ice. He leans forward, stick across his thighs as he waits. He looks so damn good. We aren't having sex, but my sex drive is working overtime.

"How have you not had sex?" Bridget asks. Jade stares too with rapt interest.

"I don't know. It hasn't been going on that long and I've been away." I shrug. "We just haven't." Hopefully tonight that changes.

"I'm surprised it took this long honestly," Jade says. "I thought you might be secretly hooking up the past couple of years."

"What? No way. We could barely be in the same room together before."

"Yes, I know. I assumed that was due to the sexual tension."

"No." I shake my head adamantly. "Jack and I have been at odds with each other since he caught me drinking at a party years ago. He tried to scold me, and I took to that about as well as you can imagine."

I had been in Minnesota for just a few months when Tyler

dragged me to some team thing he couldn't miss. I occupied myself with a bottle of Fireball until Jack stumbled upon me drunk. He was so pissed, and I couldn't fathom why he cared.

I understand now that he was worried my actions would impact Tyler and by extension, the team, but back then I just thought he was being a controlling jerk. I'm sure his dad being an alcoholic also had something to do with it.

"So now you're...what?"

"That's a loaded question," I say, smiling at her and then turning my focus back to the ice.

If I wasn't a believer at the beginning of the game that Jack's stats had improved by not having sex, I am by the end. He puts up three goals for a hat trick, plus an assist. And he's not the only one affected. The entire team looks better when he's on top of his game.

I head to the hotel with Jade and Bridget to wait for the guys. I didn't book my own room because if he isn't excited to see me, I'm just going to drive back the way I came. And if he is, then I don't need my own room.

"Are you going to see Ty?" Bridget asks.

"No. He'll want to have dinner or something."

She fights a laugh. "How terrible."

"I know. I know. I'm the worst sister ever but all I want to do is stay in." I waggle my brows suggestively and get another laugh out of her. I hug her and then Jade, and then head into the bar area of the hotel where I'll be mostly hidden.

I fire off a text to Tyler to tell him congrats on the game.

TYLER

Thanks. Are you still here? We're almost back to the hotel now.

My stomach flutters with nerves.

ME

I'm going to head back. See you next weekend!

The guys have a home game and I need to get in some Charlotte snuggles.

When I'm finished texting with him, I see the bus pull up out front. The guys file in a lot like they do when they're stepping onto the ice. Maverick and Tyler are at the front and the rest of the team fills in the middle before I spot Leo, Declan, Ash, and then Jack.

My pulse speeds up, heart pounding against my chest. He's in his game suit, a dark blue jacket and pants with a crisp white shirt that's unbuttoned at the neck. No tie and tennis shoes complete the look. He has his duffel bag slung over one shoulder and a water bottle in one hand.

ME

Congrats! You were 🔥

I watch as he puts his free hand in his pocket and grabs his phone. His lips curve into a smile as he reads my text. His thumb taps on the screen and the bubbles appear on my end.

JACK

Thanks. Wish you were here.

I read the words twice, reaching for some bravery.

ME

Oh yeah? How badly?

JACK

Not enough to ask you to drive here, but enough that I'm going to spend the rest of the night wishing my hand was you.

He disappears down the hallway toward the elevators. The lobby is empty now except for a few of the equipment managers.

ME

Maybe you should go to the bar instead of your room and pick up a woman.

JACK

Only if that woman was you.

I snap a selfie and send it, then wait.

He comes back into view, scanning the bar area with a focused, almost frantic gaze. I lift a hand when he spots me. My heart is pounding as he closes the distance between us.

He looks like he's going to kiss me, but then glances around.

"Surprise!" I say, hoping that I didn't just reach stalker level.

"What are you doing here?" He grabs my hand and pulls me with him back to the hallway, but instead of going to the elevator, we stop behind a half wall that blocks us from view.

"I just wanted to see you," I say before he can tell me this was dumb or reckless or whatever else he's thinking. "I don't have to stay if you don't—"

His mouth crashes down onto mine. He tastes like mint and smells like body wash. All the anxiety I was holding melts as I press into him and let him devour my mouth.

Noises around us come more into focus and Jack pulls back and hugs me into him, blocking me from view, as a few final Wildcat staff members pass by to the elevators.

"I wasn't sure you'd be happy I was here."

"Are you kidding? I'm fucking ecstatic, but I have no idea how I'm going to get you up to my room. Your brother is across the hall."

I fight a laugh. Of course.

"I'll buy another room if I have to," he says.

"You go up and I'll follow in five."

He kisses me again like he just can't wait that long, then pulls back with a low growl. "Room 713."

"Go." I urge, not removing my hands from the side of his waist. He's hard and warm through his dress shirt.

He nods and steps away, then comes back. "Take this."

He reaches into the front pocket of his duffel and pulls out a black beanie.

I put it on with a grin. With my hair short now, maybe it'll keep me from being recognized.

Waiting five minutes is painful. Each second ticks by and my nerves ramp up. By the time I'm getting off the elevator on the seventh floor, I'm almost more anxious about spending the night with Jack than Ty possibly catching me.

What if everyone is right? I know it sounds unbelievable but is it possible that he's playing so well because he's kept his dick in his pants? Well, mostly. We haven't had sex, but I have no complaints about the many orgasms we've shared.

My hand lifts to knock on the door, but it swings open before I make contact, and I'm pulled inside.

He captures the giggle that tries to break free. He's stripped out of his suit jacket and shoes. I wrap my arms around his neck and he picks me up, holding the backs of my thighs to keep me in place.

His dick presses through his pants and my leggings onto the ache building between my thighs.

He groans when I tilt my pelvis to increase the pressure.

Jack sits me down on the bed. We're both panting with need. He pulls the beanie off my head and throws it onto the floor, then runs his hands through my hair. His gaze shifts and he fingers one diamond hoop.

I had every intention of still giving them back, but then I made the mistake of trying them on.

"Thank you for the earrings," I say. "I love them."

They're somehow the most "me" jewelry gift I've ever received, while still being something I would never pick out for myself. Mostly because I could never afford them.

His reply is to pull the hem of his dress shirt out of his pants and unbutton it. Which, let's be honest, is maybe better than an actual "you're welcome."

His movements are slow but steady as he takes off his shirt, all while watching me. I am captivated. His body is big and chiseled. A few bruises mark his skin along his ribs and one up high on his right bicep.

The pants go next and as he stands in front of me in just his boxer briefs with a giant bulge in the front, my mouth is dry.

"Sorry I don't have my gear in here for you to play out your fantasies."

"You're my fantasy," I say, wondering if maybe I shouldn't admit that so freely to a man like Jack. Is he going to get freaked out and call things off?

He doesn't really do relationships. He's had a casual string of women, a month or two at a time, the entirety that I've known him.

And what if everyone is right? Maybe not hooking up is the key to his success.

He pushes my coat off my shoulders and takes it from me, then his fingers find the hem of my sweater and lift it up. My mind reels as I consider the possible impacts of us finally sleeping together. I could survive without sex until after the playoffs next year. Maybe.

Jack kneels in front of me and takes off my boots. He's undressing me so meticulously and with such care that my heart both loves that he's taking his time and hates that it's giving me so much time to think.

"Are you on birth control?" he asks as his hands graze up my leg and hook around to my hips. His thumbs stroke the skin above the waistband of my leggings.

"Yes."

"Good. I don't have condoms here."

I already trusted that he wasn't sleeping around, but that he didn't even bring a condom makes that realization hit a little harder.

"Wait." I place a hand on his chest and can feel his heart beating as rapid as mine.

"I've been tested," he says. "I'd never put you at risk."

"No, that's not it. I trust you."

His brows pull together.

"What if us not having sex is helping your game?" The words sound even more ridiculous as I say them out loud. But I'm still not ready to dismiss them. He's having the most amazing season, and I would do anything to keep from wrecking it. He deserves it after the hell he went through to come back.

"You heard about that, huh?" He chuckles. "I'm pretty sure Ash started that rumor."

"Sounds like him," I admit. "Do you think there's any truth to it?"

"Do I think that keeping my dick in my pants has helped me play better hockey?"

"When you put it like that it sounds dumb."

His grin widens. "Because it is."

He hovers over me, pushing me onto my back and staring down at me with humor and lust in those dark blue eyes.

"I know, but…" I trail off. I want this man so badly I should just shut up, but he means so much more to me than my next orgasm.

"I'm playing well because someone kicked my ass into gear all summer and made sure I was ready."

A slow smile curves my lips. I like the reminder that maybe the summer isn't tainted in only bad memories.

"I promise you, sweetheart. I can fuck you tonight and still be at the top of my game tomorrow." One of his long fingers trails down the center of my chest and hooks underneath the front of my bra. "Unless, you don't want that."

He kisses my stomach gently, then flicks his tongue out and drags it to just above the top of my leggings.

"You've got plenty of fallback careers anyway." I pull him down on top of me.

His light chuckle turns to a groan as I hook a leg around him. He thrusts, digging his hard length over my clit through our clothes, while devouring my mouth.

His hands roam over my face, through my hair, and down my body. Tenderly and then more forcefully.

He pulls me onto my side while lying in front of me and unhooks my bra, trailing kisses down my chest and then taking one nipple into his mouth. He bites and licks until I'm squirming and panting. My eyes flutter closed, and I revel in the warmth of his mouth and the sting of pain followed by the soft flick of his tongue over the same spot.

"Jack." My fingers slide through his thick hair and I lightly scratch my nails over his shoulders. I squirm, trying to line up my center with his hard dick so I can rub myself up on him.

He glances up at me, dark eyes lit up with need and amusement. "Impatient, baby?"

My answer is a strangled moan as he pulls away. His mouth drops to my hip and he works my leggings and panties down my legs. Every touch has my sensitive skin buzzing with need.

His stare darkens as he looks at me naked and splayed out on the bed next to him. "I'm going to take my time, if that's okay with you."

I want to tell him it really isn't okay and that I'd like to be fucked hard sooner than later, but then his hands are back on me.

"On your hands and knees." His voice is low and commanding. Usually, I'd want to fight against being told what to do, but not now. I do exactly what he says.

"Atta girl," he says next to my ear. He nips the lobe and then kisses my shoulder. His chest drapes over my back and one of his knees goes between mine.

One hand skims down my spine to my hip and then cups my sex. I jolt at the contact and am ready to arch into him for the friction I crave, but he doesn't make me wait. Jack's fingers slide from front to back over my clit and pussy. His thumb goes higher, rubbing against my other hole but not pressing in.

"So wet. So perfect," he murmurs in my ear. His hand moves back up to my hip and he guides me down until I'm sitting on his thigh and then nudges me gently until I'm rubbing myself on his leg. "Good job." He hums. "Just like that."

As I start to increase my pace, his hands stop guiding me and come around to my breasts. He pinches my nipples and kisses my neck and continues to lavish me with praise as I chase my orgasm. It hits quickly, like it's been hovering all day waiting for the slightest bit of Jack. His words, his body, his mouth. His leg, apparently.

"Fuck that's hot, baby. You should see how good you look soaking my thigh."

He kisses my shoulder and then I fall onto the mattress. He finally strips out of his boxers and climbs back over me. His hands brace himself up on either side.

"Last chance to run."

"Why would I do that?"

"Because I fully intend to ruin you. No other guy will fuck you like me, Ev."

A smirk tugs at one corner of my mouth and I lean up, brush my lips over his and say, "Do your worst."

With a cocky grin, Jack lines up the head of his dick at my entrance. He nudges into me slowly, inch by inch. When I think I can't take any more, he lifts one of my legs and settles farther until I'm so full of him, I can't breathe.

"Goddamn," I whisper. He hasn't even moved and I can feel my next orgasm building.

"This tight little cunt belongs to me." He pulls out almost all the way until the head rubs against my clit and then pushes back in. I moan as he buries himself so deep inside me again.

"Jack," I cry.

He works himself in and out of me in a slow, steady rhythm. His thrusts are hard and deep, but he doesn't rush. Each time he fills me up, he hits a spot so deep that I don't doubt he truly is ruining me for anyone else.

"I'm so close," I say. "More."

"You want me to fuck you harder?" he asks. His tone is tightly controlled but I can tell he's struggling not to spiral right along with me.

"Yes." I dig my nails into his shoulders.

"Yes, what?"

"Yes, Jack."

"I love the way you say my name, but I had something else in mind."

My brain, foggy with lust, struggles to comprehend his words, but then it hits me.

"Yes, Cap."

He growls and then rewards me by slamming his hips down and pushing his dick even farther. He fucks me with all the strength and stamina I knew he was capable of. I'm falling apart and squeezing him as he continues to piston in and out, and as soon as one orgasm trails off, another one is right there. I feel like I could fly and combust at the same time. Jack finds his release, burying his dick inside me and his head into the crook of my neck.

"Yours." His voice is little more than a growl. "I'm yours."

We lie together naked in bed for a while after, talking and kissing, and then have sex again. Eventually, we put on clothes and Jack orders room service.

Over salad and turkey club sandwiches, I show Jack the pictures of the house all staged and ready to list.

He takes my phone and flips through the professional photographs that will go up with the listing first thing Monday. I'm a nervous wreck, but happy with how it turned out.

"This is incredible, Ev. You did such a good job. I love the furniture in the living room."

"You do?" I ask, beaming at him. His approval makes me giddy. If Jack likes it, then other rich people with money to purchase a three-million-dollar lake house will too.

"Yeah. It's perfect. What's the listing price?"

"Two point nine, but they're going low and hoping for multiple offers to drive the price up. They want to sell quickly."

"Really?" His brows lift. "It'll go for well above that."

"You think so?"

He nods, still flipping through the photos. "Definitely."

I beam.

"I love it. Truly."

Something in his words makes me pause. The look on his face is one I've seen many times: determination and interest.

"No," I say, suddenly realizing his curiosity isn't just because I staged it. "You can't buy this house."

I swipe my phone back from him.

"Why not?" he asks with a small laugh. "I've been thinking about investing in another house, something on the water not too far away so I can use it in the summers while still having quick access to get back if needed."

"You can't buy my house," I say.

"Technically it's not yours, and I think I can."

"No. I'm not even supposed to show these photos to anyone."

He takes another bite of his sandwich.

"I'm serious. This is important to me. My career depends on this, and I want to do it on my own."

"You're talented, Ev. Whether or not this house sells, doesn't change that."

"Promise me you won't buy this house. It wouldn't be fair. How would you feel if I bought the Wildcats?"

He arches one brow.

"Pretend I'm rich enough to do that."

"Fine," he says, still smiling. "I promise not to interfere with your job."

He leans forward and kisses me.

"Thank you." I finally laugh. "Why can't you behave like a normal boyfriend?"

"Normal sounds boring, but I'll give that some thought. First though, we have another problem to deal with."

"Oh yeah?"

"Mhmm…" He picks up a fry and holds it out to me. I bite half of it, and he takes the rest.

"Sounds serious." I climb over the food and onto his lap, wrapping my arms around his neck.

"Oh, it is." His palms flatten on my lower back. "We need to tell your brother."

CHAPTER THIRTY-FOUR

Jack

IT JUST HAPPENED

After we get back from the road trip, I go home and unpack, shower, and then call my dad to check in.

"That was a hell of an effort," he says of last night's game. "Thirty more points and you'll have the most in franchise history."

"It was a good night," I say of the game and of the events that followed. "How are things there? Do you need anything?"

"I'm fine. Got everything I need."

I consider asking him again about coming to a game, but I know the answer. And knowing my luck, if he managed to come, he'd get drunk and make a scene. That'd be hard to explain to the media and front office.

"All right, well, you know how to get ahold of me. And if you need something while I'm traveling, call James."

"I'm perfectly capable of taking care of myself."

I want to refute that, but keep my mouth shut.

"Thanks for calling, Jackson."

"Bye, Dad."

I hang up and then look around my quiet house. Everything is in order, unfortunately, so I guess there's only one thing left to do.

"Hey." Tyler answers the door with a smile, his brows pulled together in question. "What are you doing here?"

"Can we talk?"

"Yeah, of course." He holds the door wide for me to come in, then walks in front of me to pick up the toys that block my path to the living room. "Sorry, we weren't expecting anyone. Piper's napping, and Charlotte and I are playing."

His little girl is sitting on the floor in the middle of dozens of colorful blocks. She grins shyly at me as she continues to place them one on top of the other until they are ten or so high and then she takes the hockey stick I gave to her for her birthday and whacks it down.

I let out a surprised chuckle.

Ty laughs nervously and reaches for it. She cries a little, but he then hands her a block and she takes it, stick forgotten.

"We only play with that when Mommy isn't around," he says in a sweet croon.

"I can see why." I grin back and mentally add that to the list for all my friends' kids' future birthday parties.

"So, uh, what'd you want to talk about?" Ty asks. He sets the stick on the coffee table and sits down, encouraging me to do the same. I'm hit with a sudden nervousness. Ty and I are friends, and I think he respects and likes me, but he's protective of Everly.

"I think I should stand."

His brows rise again, but he stays quiet.

"Over the summer," I start, then think maybe less details would be better. "I'm seeing someone."

"That's great," he says, then shakes his head slightly like *"why did you come over to tell me this?"*

Charlotte stands up and grabs the hockey stick. It's kid-size but is still about twice as long as she is. Tyler doesn't seem to notice that his daughter has reclaimed her toy.

"It is great," I say, palms starting to sweat. "It came completely out of nowhere. I wasn't looking and she wasn't either and it just happened." I worry that sounds like it was all an accident or happenstance, which somehow indicates I'm not taking it seriously, when that's the furthest thing from the truth, so I add, "I really like her and it feels different than relationships I've had in the past."

"I don't know what to say." He smiles at me with such genuine happiness that it makes me sweat harder. "I'm really happy for you. This was the girl you were talking to on the road?" He asks. "The one you said you *weren't* seeing."

He's grinning, but my stomach drops.

"Yeah. We hadn't defined things yet."

"I knew it. I totally called this. When do I get to meet her?"

Fuck. I take a deep breath.

"You already have," I say.

Charlotte is tapping the toe of the stick on the floor between us. Tyler stands to take it away from her, but she runs around behind me to keep him from getting her precious toy.

"I have?" Ty asks me then to Charlotte says, "Give it to Daddy, honey."

"Yeah, it's…" Fuck me. "It's Everly."

Tyler goes still, gaze sliding from his daughter to me as he stands tall in front of me.

"Everly? As in my sister?"

I consider going back into my spiel from earlier about it coming out of nowhere and how much I really like her, but instead I just nod.

"You and Everly," he says like he's trying to wrap his brain around this new information. "For how long?"

I open my mouth to answer, then realize how bad it sounds. My non-answer is almost worse though.

Tyler's gaze narrows on me and he looks pissed.

"I didn't want to tell you until I knew what it was."

"So if you hadn't decided you wanted to date her, you would have just fucked her and never told me?"

"No," I say, then, "Maybe. I don't know. The point is—"

The rest of the sentence dies off as Charlotte pulls the hockey stick back and then hits me in the balls with it.

"Oh shit," Ty says as I crumple forward and breathe through the pain. He takes the hockey stick in one hand and picks up Charlotte with the other.

I manage to stand, but the pain is still like a fire in my gut.

"Saves me having to do it, I guess," Tyler says. The anger in his expression has morphed slightly. I wouldn't say he looks happy but less like he's going to let his daughter hit me again.

"Sit."

I obey, though nervously.

Tyler takes a seat back on the couch, looking surprised and a little dazed. Charlotte comes over to me and hands me a block. She's a cute kid. Big blue eyes and dark hair that is pulled into a small ponytail on top of her head. Cute so long as she's not trying to maim me.

I smile at her tentatively and she grins back. Apparently, it wasn't personal. Or she's smiling because she knows she just got me good.

She takes the block back and puts it in her mouth. I have no idea if that's okay. I look to Tyler for help, but he's still got that stunned look on his face.

He runs a hand over his head.

"Well shit," he says finally. "I'm not sure what to say."

"I meant what I said. I really like her. I've never felt like this about anyone."

"You were the guy she was seeing this summer." He looks at me in an accusatory way.

I wince. "I didn't plan for it, but it happened. I'm not sorry, but I don't blame you if you're pissed that I didn't tell you sooner. I really like her," I say again because it's true and I'm hoping that means something to him.

"Yeah, you must." He slouches back into the couch and studies me for a moment like he's trying to read all my thoughts and feelings. I don't know what he sees, but it must be good enough because eventually he nods. "All right. I appreciate you coming to me."

I let out a slow breath and relax a fraction.

We stand and I start to smile at him, but then he whips the hockey stick toward me, pointing directly at my nuts. I cover them instinctively with both hands. "If you hurt her—"

I don't let him finish the threat. "I won't."

CHAPTER THIRTY-FIVE

Everly

REGULAR BOYFRIEND

Jack and I walk up to the house hand in hand. Nerves bounce around in my stomach and he squeezes my fingers reassuringly.

"It's going to be fine," he assures me before opening the door.

I plaster on a smile as we walk in. It's our first outing as a couple. Jack told Tyler, and I gave Bridget permission to share with Ash and it snowballed from there.

My brother has said very little on the subject. When I stopped by his house this morning before the game, he gave me an awkward talk that was reminiscent of the safe sex conversations Mom used to try to have with me.

I reassured him we were all good and then he muttered something about killing Jack if he hurts me. I know he's just being a protective big brother, but I don't need him to be that. Not with Jack. He seemed more relaxed by the time I left, but two seconds inside the party and I realize it's not just Tyler that's ready to throw down for me.

"Everyone is staring at us," I say.

"Must be because we're so sexy," he says, trying to joke it off, but the way he's holding his jaw so tight gives away his discomfort with the situation. "Let's grab a drink."

We head into Ash's kitchen. He gets a beer and I grab a hard seltzer.

"Hey," Bridget comes over to hug me. When she pulls back, she glances up at Jack standing right behind me. "I'd threaten you, but it seems you're already getting enough of that."

Jack's laugh vibrates against my back. I lean into him. "Why is everyone acting all weird?"

"They care about you. Both of you."

Scarlett joins in. "And you have been at each other's throats for years. We're not sure if all that animosity has made you the best couple we know or the worst."

I snort a laugh and Jack's hand rubs down my arm.

"To be determined," I say, and he growls quietly, then kisses my neck.

When I look back up, Bridget and Scarlett are watching us with matching grins that make my skin feel tight. It takes only a quick scan of the room to see that all eyes are on us.

We spend the next few minutes trying to blend in, making small talk and hanging out with our friends. But there's a nervous energy with everyone we talk to and even when they're being nice, it feels forced, like they don't know how to act around us.

"I knew I should have just kept you to myself tonight. This party sucks," he says, trying again to make light of the situation. "Do you want to go?"

"No." I shake my head.

"Are you sure?"

"Yeah. I got this." I take a step onto the coffee table. "Excuse me, everyone."

Maverick is manning the music and when I give him a nod, he turns it down. That gets everyone's attention.

"Sorry to interrupt. I have an announcement."

All eyes are on me. They still have those nervous, worried expressions that make me feel like a kid, but I'm not and I want them to know it. "Jack and I are sleeping together."

There's a chorus of groans around the room. If they didn't want to hear about my sex life, they shouldn't have put their noses in it.

"Fuck me," Jack mutters quietly next to me.

I place a hand on his shoulder. "That's right. We're having sex. Hopefully, a lot of it."

"Ev," Ty says and rubs his forehead with two fingers.

"In case you all didn't realize it, I'm not a kid anymore. I can take care of myself," I say.

"I don't care. If he breaks your heart, I'm kicking his ass," Declan says.

"Fine. If he breaks my heart, then you can all kick his ass, but only after I do."

I see Ash's shoulders shake with laughter and Declan nods. I glance at my brother for his reaction.

"Cheers to that," Tyler says with a small smile I know is for my benefit. The room seems to relax and I breathe a sigh of relief. I love these guys, but they can be a little too much.

I motion to Maverick to turn the music back up and step down in front of Jack.

"What about if you break my heart?" he asks, wrapping his arms around my back.

"I guess you'll have to grow out your Barnaby beard again and find some new girl to make me jealous. I really wanted you to rub that beard all over my body."

His eyes darken. "Is that so?"

"Yeah. Something about it really did it for me."

"I got something else I could rub all over your body."

Ty steps up, wincing and covering his ears. "I did not need to hear that."

Jack laughs.

"Sorry man," Jack says as he moves to stand next to me, his right arm draped around my waist and thumb tucked into the hem of my jeans. Tyler takes it all in but doesn't say anything about it. To be fair, he's never really liked any of the guys I've dated so it's not shocking that he's struggling with me dating his team captain.

"Anyway. I just came over to say I'm happy for you." The words sound strained.

I fight a laugh because I can see how hard this is for Ty, and I love him for trying.

"Thank you." I hug him and kiss him on the cheek.

"I'm heading home but call if you need anything." His stare shifts to Jack. "Or if you need help hiding a body."

I roll my eyes. "Brunch tomorrow before I go back?"

"Yeah, I'd love that." His shoulders relax and I get a glimpse of the old Ty underneath his protectiveness.

"Great. Oh, and I'm bringing my boyfriend." I lean my head over to rest against Jack's shoulder.

Tyler's mouth pulls into a smile that somehow looks like a frown, but he doesn't object.

"You're going to get me killed," Jack says when Tyler is gone.

"No," I insist. "Just possibly whacked in the balls again with a hockey stick."

"That fucking hurt."

"Yo!" Ash appears and places himself between us. "Are you two up for some flip cup?"

"I think we're going to head out," I say.

Jack's brows lift slightly.

"Already? You just got here." Ash's confused expression morphs into a grin. "I got you. You two are going to be one of those couples?"

"You mean the kind that leave parties early to have sex?" I ask.

He winces.

"Like you and Bridget are any better," I say.

"Fine." He grins. "But when you come up for air, let's hang. Miss you, Little Sharpie."

We stay at the party for a little while longer, despite my trying to get us out of there. The girls corner me so they can grill me for information, then Declan and Leo check in on me. Usually, I'd be happy to catch up with them, but it's been a week since Jack and I have been alone and I'm anxious to have him all to myself.

My pulse races as we walk down the street from Ash's place to Jack's. He picks me up when we get inside his house and carries me into his room, depositing me on the bed.

"I have something for you," he says.

I eye his crotch and the bulge there.

"Not that." He grins, then reaches into his top dresser drawer and tosses something at me. I unfold it and hold the jersey out in front of me. It has his name and number on the back, but it looks different than the ones they wear in games.

"That was my first ever practice jersey with the team. I was a little smaller then, but it's probably still too big for you to wear."

I stare at him, a little taken back by the gift. "I was expecting something over the top. This is…" My throat tightens with emotion.

"Dumb. I know, but you said you wanted me to be more like a regular boyfriend." He shrugs.

"No, I love it." My heart squeezes. "You gave me a one-of-a-kind Jack Wyld jersey." I laugh. Even when he's trying to be like other guys, he's so much more.

"You couldn't be like other boyfriends if you tried."

CHAPTER THIRTY-SIX

Everly

YOU ARE VERY FRUSTRATING

The flutters in my stomach haven't stopped all week. The house was listed Monday morning and since then I've refreshed the listing to see how many people have viewed it about a million times. And when Heather so much as smiles at me, I'm hoping she's going to say we have an offer.

She warned me that a house at this price point could take a while to sell. Plus, we're at the end of the lake season so buyers aren't as eager. At least Lisa is in the same boat.

Today we're both working on staging another home going up for sale soon. This one is a lot smaller than our previous projects, but it's still great to be out of the office and doing real design work. We do everything together, instructing the delivery people where to set the furniture, and then adjusting every small thing until we're both satisfied.

"I think we're done," I say.

"It's perfect." Lisa does a circle, taking it all in and smiling. "This is exactly how I'd decorate it if I lived here."

I've learned what appeals to buyers when it comes to décor, but the modern and simple touches still feel too sterile for me. It has no personality, and I want my house to feel like a friend.

When we get back to the office, Heather steps into the doorway of her office, looking out. "Lisa, Everly, can I talk to you both a minute?"

I can't find my voice, but nod. We shuffle in, nervous energy bouncing between us, and sit in front of Heather's desk.

I dig my nails into my palms to keep from wringing my hands and showing how anxious I feel.

"Congratulations," Heather says. "The feedback on the homes you staged has been positive. The listings are both getting a lot of traction and we've even had a couple of offers."

"We have?" Lisa asks, then steals a glance at me.

"Mhmm." Heather nods and smiles at her.

"Which house?"

A pit forms in my stomach. It's Lisa's house. Of course it is. She stuck with what works. She did a clean, modern approach, following the usual playbook. I knew that it was a risk to deviate and I'm willing to accept my fate. It stings, but I force a smile. I can be happy for Lisa now and frustrated with myself later.

"Both." Heather smiles. "And they came in at nearly the same time."

"Oh my gosh." Lisa and I grin at each other. A wave of relief washes over me followed by a sea of pride. I did it. I staged a house and someone loved it enough to want to make it their home. But it's not just about the house, I believed in myself. I stuck with what I felt was right and it paid off.

"You both have done an exceptional job. I wish I had capacity for both of you at the end of your contracts."

The realization that we still don't know who she's going to ask to stay hits us both and we fall quiet again.

"I haven't made a decision yet, but I promise not to leave you in suspense for long." She smiles. "That's all. Have a great weekend and good job. Both of you."

We leave with the same anxious energy as we arrived with.

"We did it," I say quietly.

"Yeah." She smiles and then lets it fall. "But one of us still has to find a new job."

"Not for another few weeks." There's less than a month to go on my contract and I have no idea what I'll do if Lisa is the one asked to stay. I didn't allow myself to plan on being here longer than the internship, but I also didn't plan on what to do after.

"Do you want to go out and celebrate?" she asks as we get back to our desks.

My phone vibrates in my pocket. I pull it out and stare at Jack's name flashing on the screen.

"Uhh…maybe. I think Jack is coming up."

"Bring him if you want." She grabs her bag. "Text me. I'm going to run home and shower."

I nod my agreement and then take a seat at my desk as I answer. "Hey."

"Hey. Done with work?"

"Yes. I'm leaving soon. Where are you?"

"Come outside and find out."

I hurry to gather my things and rush out of the building. Jack's G-Wagon is parked next to my car and I scramble to get in so I can kiss him.

"Hi," I finally say when I pull back.

He hums then brushes his lips over mine again.

"I have news," I say. "My house has an offer! Someone wants to buy it!"

A wide grin spreads across his face. "Of course it does. You're so talented. There was no doubt in my mind."

"Well, there were lots of doubts in my mind."

The backs of his fingers graze my cheek and push my hair back behind my ear. "We should celebrate."

"Lisa is going out and wants us to join her."

"Is that what you want?"

I stare at him in his black hoodie and athletic pants. He looks like he came straight from practice. The smell of the rink mixes with his shampoo and body wash.

"Kind of," I admit. "But I also don't want to waste a second of our weekend together."

The team has time off until Monday, a rare weekend break, and I want to soak up every second with him.

"We won't," he says. "This is a big day for you. We can celebrate just the two of us tomorrow. I have a surprise for you."

"Ooooh. What is it?" I've come to look forward to Jack's surprises. Usually when people try to surprise me, I can totally guess what it is, but I never can with him.

"If I told you, then it wouldn't be a surprise."

My face pulls into a pout, which does not work on him.

Laughing, he puts the car in drive. I leave mine at the office to grab later. I don't plan on needing it this weekend.

"I have to make a few phone calls," Jack says when we walk into my apartment. He walks over to the countertop where a stack of books sits. He picks up one and looks at the cover. "I've seen this book before."

I take it from him and set it back on the stack. "Well, it is a very popular book."

Draping my arms on his shoulders, I lift onto my toes to kiss him again, then pull back and take off my shirt. I feel grungy from moving furniture around today. "I'm going to shower."

His gaze trails over my lacy black bra and he watches while I push my jeans down to reveal the matching panties.

"Want to join me?"

"Temptress." He takes my mouth and kisses me hard and demanding, only pulling back when I'm breathless. "Give me five minutes."

After showering until the hot water ran out, Jack and I get ready and head out to one of the downtown bars. Lisa is already there, along with some of the other people from the office. We grab drinks and mingle with everyone. The tables are small and close together, and my boyfriend is the center of attention, even while trying not to be.

It's fun to see people's reactions to Jack. He's just Jack to me, but to them, he's Jack Wyld, and they look at him starstruck and filled with admiration.

I love how easily he takes it and it's really a wonder he isn't the most self-centered jerk in all of existence.

"I'm going to grab another drink," I say and stand from his lap.

He pulls me back down. "I'll get the drinks. You stay with your friends."

His lips graze my neck and he deposits me onto the chair while he gets up and goes to the bar. I stare after him, feeling happier than I can ever remember.

Liam, a listing agent at the office, slides closer to me, dragging my attention away from my man and his fine ass.

"Congratulations. I saw the offer come in just as I was leaving the office," he says.

"Thanks. I don't think the buyer is going to take it, but it's a start."

His brows pinch together. "There was another offer. You didn't hear?"

"No." My excitement lifts. "Really?"

He nods, grinning. "They offered above listing. All cash. Thirty-day closing."

My heart races. "Are you sure?"

"Positive. I handed it over to Heather myself."

It feels too good to be true. Another offer. *Above* the listing price. Something tickles my brain. I glance back at Jack.

"When did you say the offer came in?" I ask Liam.

"An hour or so ago."

The same time Jack said he needed to make some calls.

I nod and then say, "Excuse me."

Jack smiles when he sees me approaching him at the bar, but it falls at my expression.

"Did you buy my house?" I demand.

He keeps staring at me like he's deciding how to answer. Finally he says, "I put in an offer and it was accepted." He takes a drink from the glass in front of him. "I guess technically it's my house."

"Why would you do that?" I ask, voice climbing with irritation. Here I was thinking my work had paid off, and it's just Jack doing what he promised he wouldn't do.

"Because I love that house. It's perfect. I told you I've been thinking about a place up here. It was too good to pass up."

"You promised," I say, and I'm not sure if I'm more disappointed in him or myself for believing him.

I step away from him, grab my purse, and head outside, walking back toward my apartment.

I know it's his footsteps behind me, but I don't slow down even when he calls, "Ev, wait up."

He jogs to get in front of me. "I promised not to interfere with your job, and I didn't. I waited until you already had an offer."

I glare at him. It's semantics and he knows it. I brush past him, but he takes me by the arm and forces me to look at him.

"I'm sorry. I should have told you, but I wanted to make sure it went through first."

"Why?" I ask, and I'm not even sure what I'm asking. Why did he promise at all if he wasn't going to stand by it? Why did he have to interfere with my job? Why did he have to make me question all the pride I've felt in the past few hours?

"Because…" He trails off, then runs a hand through his dark hair.

"All my work feels completely irrelevant now. I'll never know if it sold because I did a good job or because you're too selfish to not interfere. Don't you understand?" I ask quietly.

He brings a hand up and brushes his knuckles along one side of my neck then drops his hand back to his side. "I wanted to have a place here in case this is where you end up. You love that house and I love it too. I'm not just blowing smoke when I tell you that you're talented. You make everything feel like home. So yeah, I bought it and I'm sorry if that was crossing a line, but I didn't do it so you could keep your job. I did it in hopes I get to keep you." My frustration dissipates as he scans my face, waiting for my reaction. Worry lines bracket his mouth and he looks so devastatingly nervous that he's fucked up.

"You are very frustrating," I say, then press my lips to his.

He exhales slowly then wraps an arm around my back and takes over the kiss, sweeping his tongue in and savoring me.

"I'm sorry," he says, gruffly against my lips.

"You better have a hell of an apology planned," I murmur.

"Do you want to go back to the bar?" he asks.

"No." I shake my head. "I want to make love and then look at photos of your new house. I know a designer in case you need one."

He grins. "Done. I bought all the furniture, but it needs more. I need more. More of you."

"You bought all the furniture?"

"I told you I loved it. I meant it."

"I love it too, but it's a three-million-dollar home." I blow out a breath thinking about how much money he spent.

"It's worth it. I would have paid so much more." His hands frame my face on either side. "You are incredible. You don't believe it yet and that's okay. I'm going to keep telling you until you realize it for yourself."

We spend the night exactly as I planned. I wake up with Jack's body draped over mine. I have to pee and my mouth is dry. I wriggle to get free, but his arm tightens.

"Where are you going?" He pulls me back into his chest, and his mouth skates over my shoulder and then nuzzles into my neck.

"I was going to come right back." I laugh as he holds me like I'm in danger of running away. Fat chance. I know what he can do with his tongue.

"What time is it?"

I stretch out an arm to grab my phone from the nightstand. "Just after nine."

"Shit, really?" His hold on me loosens and he gets up quickly.

"Somewhere to be?"

He's so handsome all sleepy-eyed and hair disheveled. My stare rakes over him.

"Eyes up here, temptress. We don't have time to do what you're thinking."

"How do you know what I'm thinking?" I ask, not moving from the bed even as he picks up his clothes and moves around my room frantically.

"Because I'm thinking it too." He stops and comes over to drop a kiss on my mouth. "But right now, I need you to get ready and pack an overnight bag."

"Where are we going?" I ask, a giddy sensation taking root.

"Somewhere warm. Pack a bathing suit. Or don't." His brows waggle.

"Wait. You're taking me on a trip? Where?"

"You'll see." He backs away and tips his head, indicating he wants me to get up. "But we gotta move. The jet leaves in two hours."

CHAPTER THIRTY-SEVEN

Jack

MINE

Everly hasn't stopped smiling since we left her apartment.

Leaning against the doorway of the villa that leads out onto the patio where we have our own pool just steps from the beach, I can't take my eyes off her.

"This cannot be real." She turns in a circle on our patio, arms wide and head tipped up to the sun. She's a goddess.

I come up behind her and she flings her arms around my neck and looks up at me with wonder in her eyes. "Thank you."

"For what?"

"Umm…bringing me on vacation," she says with a small laugh. "I kept pinching myself on the jet. I can't believe this is your life."

"No thanks needed. I have you all to myself for the next thirty-six hours."

I had planned for us to come up last night but that was before I knew she'd gotten an offer on the house and wanted to celebrate with her friends.

I scoop her up into my arms and walk into the pool with her. We're both still in our travel clothes but I don't care. Her legs wrap around my waist, and I kiss her deeply as we sink into the water up to my shoulders.

Her hands glide over my shoulders and around my back.

"You're a pretty great guy, Jack Wyld. Generous and kind, and you're good at knowing just what to do to make people around you feel seen and heard."

"Is that a nice way of saying I'm commanding and heavy-handed?"

"You don't give yourself enough credit. People look to you constantly for guidance and reassurance. They know that when you're around, everything is going to be okay. You would do anything for the people you care about. I've seen it so many times with your team, but over the past few months, I've seen just how far your devotion reaches. Your community, your dad, me. I can't think of a single person that makes me feel more free to be me. And trust me, that is a gift."

My skin prickles as she hands me the compliment while looking at me so intently. No tease or sass. She means it, and I soak up her words, hoping they're true. Hoping I'm good enough for her.

"I would do anything for you," I confirm. "I would have before, but now…"

She waits for me to finish the sentence.

"I am in love with you."

Whatever she expected me to say, it's clear that wasn't it. My heart pounds in my chest. I have never said those words to anyone.

"I don't expect you to say it back now or maybe ever, but for as long as you want me, I'm yours, Ev."

She sighs audibly and then brings her mouth to mine. Her soft lips rest there, and we breathe each other in.

"I love you too."

My chest tightens and I grab the back of her head and kiss her like a man completely in love. I don't know how I'm going to keep showing her how much she means to me, but I know I'll never get tired of trying.

I peel her out of her shirt and send it flying toward the patio with a wet *thunk*. She giggles and we struggle to get me out of my shirt next. Pants are easier.

"Look at you," she says. "Skinny-dipping again."

"The things I do for you," I say, teasing like it's a real inconvenience. I'd risk public nudity for her any day.

Her back rests against the side of the pool and her legs wrap around my waist. Gently, I nudge the head of my cock against her entrance.

"Are you ready for me?" I ask.

She nods. "Always."

I push in slowly, letting her adjust to my size. She sighs and a smile of pure pleasure turns up the corners of her lips.

"I don't think I'll ever get tired of this."

"I sure fucking hope not." I grip her hip a little tighter. Just the thought of losing her has me wanting to keep her here on this island forever.

Her hands find purchase on my shoulders and she rolls her hips as I bury my cock farther until there's nowhere else to go. Still, I rut into her, wanting to fill every inch of her with me.

"You said you wanted to ruin me for other men." The words are breathy and end with a moan. "But there's no comparison. I'm yours too, Jack."

I'm often at a loss for words with Everly. Showing her how much that means to me is far simpler.

"What's mine, baby?" I ask, lips grazing down her throat to her breasts. I palm one and suck on the other. "These mine?"

"Yes," she cries, fingers pulling at my hair.

On the next thrust I pull out of her. We both groan at the loss, but not for long. I turn her around and pull her back to me. One hand drops between her legs and I cup her pussy. "This mine?"

She nods as I glide my fingers over her clit and then slip one inside. She moves slowly, fucking herself on my hand while I continue exploring her neck and shoulders with my mouth.

"What about this, Ev?" My hand glides higher and I press my thumb against the pucker of her ass, while my other fingers still rub along her pussy.

"Jack."

I'll never get tired of hearing her say my name while I do deliciously dirty things to her body.

"Is it mine, Ev?"

"All of it," she rasps as I push two fingers into her cunt. "It's all yours. I'm yours."

I replace my fingers with my cock, taking her from behind, and wrap one arm around her waist to keep her in place. She holds on to the edge of the pool as I take her hard and fast.

She cries out, clenching around my dick as she finds her release and I tumble right along with her. She might be mine, but she owns me. Irrevocably.

We spend the rest of the night going between the bed, the pool, and the ocean until we fall asleep naked, hair still wet.

When I open my eyes, the sun is shining through the villa and Everly is lying half on me, head propped up on her hands, watching me.

"Morning," I say, voice rough with sleep. My lips curve into a smile and I wrap my arms around her, pulling her farther on top of me.

She laughs as I settle her right on my hard dick. Yep, waking up like this is my new favorite thing.

"What time are we leaving?" she asks.

I open my eyes again and see a little of her happiness has dimmed. She's dreading leaving too.

"Ten."

She nods and then glances down as if to hide her disappointment.

I lift her chin up with a finger. "We'll come back. Sometime when we can spend a whole week here. Or an entire month."

"You're crazy," she says with a small laugh.

"About you. Yes."

She still wears a melancholy expression that makes me want to say fuck it to hockey and the team.

She cups my cheek and drags her thumb along my stubble. "I don't need it, you know? This place is gorgeous, and I had the best time with you, but we could have hung out in my tiny little apartment all weekend and I would still be just as wild about you." She presses her hand to my chest, palm flat over my heart.

I take her hand in mine and press a kiss to her knuckles.

I know what she's trying to say, but being able to surprise her with big, extravagant things is just one way I can show her how much she means to me.

We get onto the jet and take our seats. Neither of us slept much last night so we fall into a comfortable silence as we prepare for the ride home.

She lets her head fall to the left so she can look me in the eye as she says, "I love you."

"I love you too."

She rests her head on my shoulder, and we fly home like that. I'm usually anxious to get back after time away, but even I'm feeling sad as we get in my car. I plug my phone in and notifications start rolling in, many from James.

"Did he know you were leaving?" she asks as my phone keeps pinging.

"Of course," I say. "But he's probably shocked I actually managed to disconnect all weekend."

To be fair, it's a first for me. Usually, I spend vacation doing a lot of the same things I do at home, just in a tropical location.

I scroll through the texts. The first couple are just asking me to check in with him and then asking to call him as soon as I get a chance. So high-maintenance. I move over to voicemail. He left two. The first one is basically the same as his texts, but before I listen to his second, my phone rings.

"Hey," I answer, shaking my head at Ev. I mouth "James" to her, so she knows it's him calling again. I lean across the console and kiss her.

"Hey, Jack. Thank god. Are you on your way?"

"On my way where?" I ask. I know I didn't have any events scheduled this weekend. I cleared it with him before I left.

"The hospital. Didn't you get my messages?"

"No. I only listened to the first so far. What's going on?" My first thoughts are my teammates. Somebody did something stupid and got hurt or maybe Coach, but I'm not prepared for what comes out of his mouth.

"It's your dad, Jack."

CHAPTER THIRTY-EIGHT

Everly

SPEW POSITIVITY

"How is he?" Tyler asks, hugging me against him.

I breathe him in. The guy who has always been there for me, picking me up and reminding me everything is going to be okay. Except now he looks as uncertain as I feel.

Tears leak down my face and I swipe them away angrily as I pull back. "All we know is that he had a stroke and he's stable. The last update was over two hours ago."

"How's Jack handling it?"

I swallow the lump in my throat. The last I saw him he was practically yelling at someone on the phone after they tried to put him on hold. He's hurting so badly but he hasn't stopped trying to fix it all since he found out. Phone calls, talking with his dad's medical team here, more phone calls. It's been almost four hours. He hasn't eaten or drank anything. He's existing only by his need to make everything okay.

"He's on the phone," I say. "I think he's making some calls to see if this is the best place for him."

A sob rips free without my permission and I hug Tyler again. "Thank you for being here."

"Always," he says. "No matter what." He rubs my back until the tears stop. I don't want Jack to see me upset. The last thing he needs is another person to worry about.

"Do you want to sit?" I ask and motion to the ugly, wooden and floral upholstered chairs.

Tyler sits with me in the waiting room. I wring my hands together and tap my foot, willing the seconds to pass and for the doctor to come out with good news. More of the team arrives. Coach Miller, Leo and Scarlett, Declan and Jade, Ash and Bridget, Maverick, Nick and Aidan. After that I lose track, but when Jack reappears in the waiting room, he comes up short, clearly surprised by the number of people here for him.

"Hey. What's going on?" he asks.

Coach Miller approaches him first. "I'm sorry about your dad. Any news?"

He scans the crowd of his teammates and friends again before he speaks. "He had a blood clot, which caused the stroke. He's awake and they're giving him medication. His speech and memory were both impacted. The doctor says it could be temporary, but some patients don't fully recover. The next few weeks are important. They're going to keep him here for a while and we'll have a rehabilitation plan once we know more."

The lump in my throat grows until I'm not sure I can speak or breathe. I let his teammates and Coach console him. I watch from a distance as they hug him and offer words of sympathy and hope.

Jack's mask is in place, but I know as soon as he stops trying to be everything for everyone else, he's going to need to deal with this.

And I don't just mean the stroke. He and his dad have a rocky relationship. Jack's never mentioned it, but I can feel the tension there. Maybe it's because of his dad's drinking, but I get the sense that it goes way beyond that.

As everyone starts to leave, they come by and hug me too, each one telling me to call or text if we need anything. I guess they know it's highly unlikely that Jack will.

When they're gone, I go to him. I wrap myself around his middle and breathe him in. I know I'm supposed to be comforting him, but there's something reassuring about being in his arms.

"I'm sorry." It isn't the first or even the second time I've said it, but I look up at him and will the words to convey just how deeply I feel them. "Is there anything I can do?"

"Yeah." His hand cups the back of my head. "You're doing it by being here."

"Of course. I'll stay as long as you want."

He drops his mouth to mine and kisses me gently. "Thank you for offering, but there won't be a lot to do and I know you need to get back to Briar Lake."

"I can take time off. It's no big deal."

"No. Don't do that. There's nothing to do here but wait. Take my car. I'll get a ride home from one of the guys."

I bite at the corner of my lip as I consider what to do. Is he pulling his usual, I don't need anyone's help bullshit or is he just being pragmatic?

"I don't want to go," I say. "Even if there's nothing to do. Heather will understand and honestly if she doesn't…" I shrug.

"Ev." His voice breaks on my name.

"I'm not going anywhere except maybe to get food and clothes. Do you want me to bring you anything back?"

He looks like he wants to argue, but then he hugs me back to his chest. "You're stubborn and incredible."

"And yours," I remind him.

When he pulls back, he runs a hand through his hair. "I'll come with you."

"Are you sure?"

He nods. "I can't get in to see him for another hour anyway."

"Okay."

We swing by his place to eat, shower, and finally change out of our travel clothes. Vacation feels like a lifetime ago. He grabs clothes, toiletries, and his laptop so he can stay at the hospital while his dad recovers.

On the ride back, he takes my hand but stays quiet while he drives. He's able to go back and see his dad for a few minutes, but when he returns, he looks more upset than before. Maybe the seriousness of the situation is sinking in.

"How is he?" I ask.

"The doctors say he's doing well, all things considered, but the stroke messed up his speech so communicating with him is difficult." He buries his head in his hands and mutters, "Fuck."

I drape an arm around his shoulders and rub soothing circles, wishing I could do so much more. I can't seem to find the words. Am I supposed to be hopeful and spew positivity or offer my sympathy? Neither feels right so I stay quiet and hope my presence is as comforting to him as his is to me.

"I'm so mad at him." He sits up. His eyes are red but I haven't seen him cry. "I need him to be okay so I can tell him how mad I am. I guess I shouldn't be surprised, I mean he's been a drunk most my life. That kind of lifestyle doesn't lead to a long, healthy life."

My heart squeezes. Whether he says it or not, I know he feels responsible for his dad.

"You love him, and he loves you."

"Do you know he has never watched me play professional hockey?"

My brows pinch together.

Jack nods even though I haven't asked a question. "Sure, he catches the games on TV, but never in person. Not once. The last game he attended I was sixteen."

"What happened?"

Jack's quiet for a moment. The only noise is the hum of the overhead lights and the beeping of machines and computers in the hospital.

"He got hurt when he was playing in the minor league, ended his career before it really started. He struggled to find work after that, started drinking more frequently. For years it was just the new normal. Dad was laid off and drinking, and him and Mom fought constantly. Then one day I guess she just got tired of it. After she left, his drinking got worse. I'm not making excuses for him, but it was a crappy situation."

"How old were you when she left?" I ask. He's never mentioned his mom. To be honest, I assumed she died or something.

"Twelve." His throat works.

"Jack..." My voice trails off.

"She had every right to leave him. He wasn't easy to live with, but she just up and left without a word, washed her hands of us." He shakes his head. "I still don't understand how she could do that."

"So you took care of him?" I already know the answer but ask the question anyway.

"I mean I wasn't really much of a caretaker, but I made sure we had what we needed. Luckily, he'd managed to save enough before things got bad that money wasn't an issue. It was tight, but we had a house and food."

My throat and the back of my eyes burn with the need to cry, but I don't because it won't change anything and I know he doesn't want my tears.

"My junior high school coach, John, you met him, he looked in on us too. He and dad were old friends and he's one of the few people who knew the whole story. My dad was once promised to be the next Gretzky, and now the only thing people will remember is he was the town drunk."

"What happened to your mom? Have you heard from her in all these years?"

He nods his head. "She tried to get in touch with me about a year after she left. She was living in Florida, and wanted me to come stay with her, but I couldn't leave him. And also, fuck her, you know? She left me too."

"I know it doesn't make up for what you've been through, but your dad loves you. He might not be at your games, but he's so proud of what you've accomplished."

Jack snorts a disbelieving sound. "Has a funny way of showing it."

I'm ready to tell him how wrong he is, but the doctor steps out into the waiting room and Jack stands, eager for the update.

CHAPTER THIRTY-NINE

Jack

CRANKY AND IRRITABLE

Sometime early in the morning I fell asleep sitting next to my dad's hospital bed. I forced Everly to go home for the night. It wasn't easy. She's as stubborn as she is beautiful. She wants to be here for me, and I appreciate it, but this isn't her problem. She shouldn't suffer sleeping on hard chairs or miss work.

Work. Fuck. I've tried not to think about how I'm going to manage being here with dad and showing up for practice and games. Coach told me last night to take today at least so I don't need to solve the problem immediately, but it consumes me anyway.

We have some tough games coming up and I don't want to let the team down again. They need me.

I arch my back and roll my shoulders as I try to get comfortable in the chair. It's early still. The lights in the hallway are dimmed and the hospital's usual noise and activity is muffled.

"Jackson," Dad's voice is little more than a rasp, but I sit up like he yelled.

His face is pale, and his eyes are still droopy.

"Dad," I say, wondering if I imagined him say my name.

He grimaces as he looks around at the machines and tubes hooked up to him. He swallows and his lips part and close twice before he's able to do it again. "Jack."

I stand next to his bed. He looks smaller, fragile, and like he's aged ten years in the month since I've seen him. Guilt tries to consume me for not being there, but it'll have to wait because this is no time for a pity party.

"Hey," I say. "How do you feel? Should I get the doctor?"

He shakes his head and reaches for the water cup on the table next to the bed. I refill it and then hold it in front of him so he can drink out of the straw.

One side of his mouth seems not to want to cooperate, but he takes a long sip before lying back again. I resume my position sitting in the chair.

"I'm sorry I ruined your vacation."

"You didn't. I was already back when I found out."

"Good. You deserve some time to yourself."

"Dammit, Dad." My frustration bubbles up until there's no holding it back. "I have plenty of time to myself. If you need me, you call."

He's quiet again, probably because I just yelled at him. Fuck.

"Where's your girl?" he asks, eyes closed again.

"My girl?"

"Everly."

"How…" My question trails off as a small smile curves his lips. Maybe he figured it out since I was on vacation or James could have told him, I guess.

"She's a good one."

"I know."

He lets his head fall to one side so he's staring at me as he says, "I like her. Her taste in books is questionable, but she has a good heart and enough sass to keep you on your toes."

I nod as I ponder his words.

"Her taste in books?"

He studies me for a moment like he's trying to decide how much to share with me.

"She sends me books," he says.

I'm still struggling to understand when he adds, "Every couple of weeks or so she sends another book. She writes little notes in the margins for me."

"Everly, *my* Everly, sends you books?"

He nods.

"I don't understand."

"Me either, but sometimes people do things that don't make sense. They love us when we don't deserve it or give an old drunk thoughtful gifts to keep him occupied, maybe hoping he'll drink a little less."

My chest tightens. "I didn't know."

"I figured as much. She isn't the type to want credit for doing something nice and she probably thought there was a chance you wouldn't approve."

"Do you read them?" I ask, still stuck on the idea that Everly, who only met my dad once, has been sending him books like they're old friends.

"Oh yeah. I read them and send them back, adding my own notes in the margins. I send her some too."

"The Grisham novel at her apartment," I say, remembering the book that had looked familiar to me.

"Also sent her some old photos of you. Figured if something happened to me, someone should be able to tease you about your first-grade haircut."

"Nothing is going to happen to you," I say, knowing it will regardless of how much I try to fight it. He's my only family and when he's gone, it'll just be me.

The nurse comes in for her hourly check before we can continue our conversation. I let him know I'll be back and head down to the first-floor café for coffee.

Bridget's walking in as I fall into the back of the line.

"Hi," she says, stopping beside me. "How is your dad doing?"

"Awake. Talking."

"Those are good signs." The smile she gives me increases the hope starting to bloom in my chest.

"Yeah. I think so."

"Is Everly here?"

"No. She left last night."

One of Bridget's brows rises.

"She didn't want to, but I didn't want her to have a sleepless night too."

"I'm sure she'll be back first thing."

"Yeah." I smile. "Probably so."

"I'm up on pediatrics all day, so if you need anything, don't hesitate to text me."

"Okay."

She takes a step away, but says, "Really, though, text me if there are any changes. I'll come down on my lunch break and see how you're doing."

Before I can tell her that's not necessary, she's walking away toward the elevators. I get coffee and two muffins and head back to Dad's room. The doctor gives me an update on his progress, followed by a rundown of the weeks to come. He'll stay here for a few more days at least. They'll start therapy to hopefully regain the motor and verbal skills that were impacted by the stroke. His memory seems to have returned on its own, which is another good sign.

I feel like I'm staring down months of recovery all over again. He has everything he needs now, but when he goes home, he's going to need help. I want to be there, if only so we can keep arguing over every little thing.

Everly arrives a little while later, appearing in the doorway with donuts and a breakfast sandwich wrapped in foil. Egg whites on wheat with spinach and turkey bacon – my usual.

"Hi," she says, sounding more shy than I've ever heard her as she glances at me and then my dad.

"Hey, pretty girl." Dad grins at her.

She hands off the food with a kiss and then steps to his bedside. "How are you?"

"Old and too sober to feel this shitty."

She laughs, and then he does too.

"Jackie boy knows your secret." He tips his head to me.

Ev blushes but focuses on Dad instead of me. "I brought a new book for you."

"Another bodice ripper?" He lifts one brow.

"It's one chili pepper at best."

The nurses come in again, this time to get him up walking. I offer to stay and help but they shoo us away so Ev and I head outside to get some fresh air.

"How come you didn't tell me?" I ask her.

"I don't know. I guess I thought you might not like it. I'm sorry if it was crossing a line. I could tell he was lonely and when we left, I couldn't stop thinking about him. He loves you. I know it doesn't change what he's done or make it easier to forgive him, but he does care about you despite his actions."

"I forgave him a long time ago. It's just…he's all I have, you know?"

"That's not true. You have me."

"Did he really send you old photos of me?"

"You really grew into your nose."

I bark a laugh and damn does it feel good.

"I brought you some more clothes in the car and a cooler with your meals."

"Thank you." Making sure I had my food was the last thing on my mind. "I guess I need to check in with the team and figure out how I'm going to manage everything this week. What time do you have to head back today?"

"Whenever." She's quiet. Too quiet.

"Ev?"

"I don't want to go." Her shoulders are pulled back and she lifts her chin, a clear sign she's about to say something I won't like. "I talked to Heather this morning. She told me to take all the time I need, and honestly even if she hadn't said it was fine, I'd still want to stay. I am where I am supposed to be. I love you. It's okay to need people, Jack. It doesn't make you less capable. I want to be here. Let me do that for you like you do for everyone else."

"I do need you." I wrap my arms around her. "More than you know, but your job is important."

"So is yours," she says. "I can be here this week with your dad while you have practice or games."

I shake my head, already hating the idea, but she charges on.

"I will keep you updated, hourly if you want, and you'll still be here when you can."

"I can't ask you to do that."

"You're not. I'm offering. Actually, no. Not offering. Demanding. I'm going to do this for you because I freaking love you, okay? I'm not confused about my priorities or what's important. A job is just a job."

"By your own account, then I should stay."

"Your team is family."

I pull at my hair. I hate this. My burden feels like hers.

"Also, I like your dad."

"He's cranky and irritable, and that's probably going to increase as they wean him off the meds."

"I know how to handle cranky and irritable."

She means me and well, fair, I guess.

"I promise I will take care of him."

"I'm not worried about that," I say, linking our fingers together. "It's just too much. I don't know what I did to deserve you."

"Nothing. You're just lucky." Her full sass is back and it's as comforting as the kiss she places on my lips.

"I should have checked on him more," I say it out loud so maybe my guilt will ease, but it doesn't.

"He could have checked in more with you too."

"I tried a dozen times to get him to go to rehab."

"You can't force something like that. He has to want it."

She has an answer for everything. God, I love her for that.

"Do you think he'll go now?" I ask. It's something I've been thinking about. You hear all the time about people who have a traumatic medical event and turn their life around. Unfortunately, you also hear about people who don't. I can't guess which he'll be.

"I'm not sure," she says, and I appreciate her honesty, even if it stomps out the little hope I had of it being true.

"Go back to Briar Lake," I tell her as a new sort of determination settles over me. I can't change the past, but I can be here now. "Finish your internship and then decide what's next for you. I need to be here. I *want* to be here."

She has that stubborn look on her face. One that's so familiar it loosens some of the tightness in my chest.

"This isn't me pushing you away or trying to make decisions for you. I want you here too. Always. God, I don't know what I'd have done without you the past couple of days. But I've got this."

She still looks conflicted.

"You deserve to finish what you started." I wink at her playfully as I add, "Go get my house ready."

Everly finally laughs. She takes a few more seconds to consider before she concedes. "Fine, but promise me if something changes, you'll ask for help? If not from me, from Tyler or Bridget or anyone else. We all want to be here for you however we can. We all love you."

Her words feel like an acceptance of something I've always known but am finally really understanding. I don't like letting other people help. I'm not sure that will ever change. I grimace but ultimately nod my agreement.

She pushes up on her toes and brushes her lips over mine. "I'll be back Friday night."

"I'll be counting down the hours."

CHAPTER FORTY

Everly

USE IT FOR SOMETHING GOOD

Saturday afternoon I have lunch with Bridget and Grace in the hospital cafeteria. I got back into town last night and convinced Jack to let me keep his dad company while he went to practice. They have a game tonight and I know he's struggling to be here and focus on the team.

He's only left the hospital to shower and change clothes, but I think seeing his teammates and getting a little normalcy back will be good for him. His dad is getting released from the hospital in the next few days, if things still look good. I don't know how he's managed it on his own.

"When do you have to go back to Briar Lake?" Grace asks.

"Tomorrow night." My stomach dips and bottoms out at the thought of leaving again. With everything going on it's made me realize even more that my life is here. There is nothing pulling me back there except the job, and even that feels irrelevant.

"It's a really nice thing you're doing for him, looking after his dad so he can have a break," Bridget says. "You're the only one he would trust. Several of the guys and their wives have offered, and he hasn't let anyone else help."

"Yeah…" I trail off. "I guess so. I'm not really doing much. I sit with his dad while he's awake. We're reading this new romantic thriller together." That makes me smile. He likes to give me shit for my books, but then when I ask if he wants to read something else, he tells me to keep going.

"I have to get back." Grace checks the time on her phone. "Lunch again tomorrow before you leave?"

"You guys don't have to keep doing this."

"Are you kidding?" Grace stands with her tray, and Bridget and I do the same. "I'm sorry for the circumstances that have brought you back here, but I want to take full advantage of seeing you as much as possible while I can."

"Same," Bridget says.

On the way back to the room, I am feeling grateful and a little lighter. I adore my friends. I don't know what I'd do without them. As I turn the hall to Jack's dad's room, I spot James standing outside on his phone.

I approach him slowly. He smiles at me as he continues to talk to someone.

"Yes, I know she can be difficult but that's the job," he says in a gruff tone. He's quiet while I assume the other person on the line responds.

He has an almost bored look as he listens.

When he finally speaks again, there's no hint of annoyance, just calm resolve. "I understand. Leave your keys, phone, and laptop, and

I'll forward your last check."

Yikes.

He hangs up without a goodbye, although honestly, who would want one after that?

"Another one bites the dust," he says as he pockets his phone. "You wouldn't believe how many people think they want to be a sports agent until they realize it's less about glamour and glitz and more about discretion and mundane tasks."

"Like email?"

"Ah, you sweet child. If you knew the things I've been asked to do…" He looks out to the distance dramatically and then grins. "How are you?"

"Good. You?" I glance down at the food bag on the floor beside him. "What's that?"

"Ah yes, another instance of the many exciting tasks in my day." He reaches down and picks up the bag and then holds it out for me. "Jack sent lunch."

I take it and look inside, heart squeezing when I see it's from my favorite Chinese restaurant. I already ate in the cafeteria but this will heat up nicely.

"Thank you."

He nods his head. "Any update on his dad?"

"No. Still the same, but they say it's a good sign that his speech recovered so quickly."

"Good. Glad to hear." He shifts almost uncomfortably, like he's run out of his scheduled tasks and doesn't know what to do next.

"You don't have an assistant that could have brought this?" I lift the bag.

He grins knowingly. "I wanted to check in on him and you. Jack doesn't give much of an update."

"I'm shocked." I laugh softly. "Do you want to come in and see him?"

He hesitates then shakes his head. "Another time. I need to deal with the loss of another agent and find a replacement before my client realizes what's happened."

"You're going to find someone new that quickly?"

"If I don't, then I'll have to take them on, and my husband is already pissed that I have as many clients as I do."

"Good luck."

He smiles and his phone starts ringing. He takes it out and stares at the screen, grimaces, and then says, "Good to see you, Everly."

"Yeah, you too."

I watch as he heads down the hall. Phone to his ear, he barks out, "What now?"

Jack stops by to check on his dad after practice but the nurses have him up and walking and shoo Jack away when he offers to help.

"Come on," he says, taking my hand. "I want to take you somewhere."

My heart skips as we hurry out to his car. He stops next to the passenger door like he's going to open it for me, but instead backs me up against it and kisses me.

"Fuck, I missed you," he says against my mouth. His hands rest on either side of my neck and I breathe him in.

I missed him too. It's weird being back in town but not really seeing him.

He opens the door for me, and I slide into the seat and buckle up as he jogs around the back.

"Where are we going?" I ask as he gets in and starts the engine.

His gaze drops to my mouth and then refocuses on the mirrors as he backs out. "Somewhere I can kiss you a lot more."

We end up at a bowling alley, which given his only hint, surprises me.

"Are we going to make out or bowl?"

He swings our hands between us as he leads me to the front desk. "Little of both."

After we're donned in ugly shoes and have picked out our balls, we slide into chairs at our lane.

I can't stop smiling and I'm not even sure why.

Jack puts our names into the machine and then rubs his hands together.

A small laugh escapes from my lips.

He kisses me before asking, "Whatcha laughing about?"

"I'm just surprised. This is the last place I would have expected you to bring me."

"Not a lot of options for a late afternoon date."

"We're on a date?"

"If you have to ask, then I don't think I'm pulling this off very well."

"What exactly are you trying to pull off?" I lift one brow.

"I just wanted to spend time with you, away from the hospital and everything else going on, and thank you for today. It felt good to be back on the ice."

"You don't need to thank me. I was happy to do it." I scoot closer and drape my legs over his so I'm all but sitting in his lap.

He pulls me the rest of the way and my arms wrap around his

neck as he kisses me again.

My body hums with a contented sort of feeling when he pulls back. Content but turned the hell on.

"I thought you were taking me back to your house to have sex."

He chuckles. "Did consider it, but I figured you could use some fun. Maybe that was dumb though."

His dick is hard underneath me and I can't resist squirming just a little so I'm grinding over him.

"Should we test out the bathroom?"

"Temptress." He nips my bottom lip and then lifts me off his lap to the chair and stands.

Jack and I head back to the hospital after our date. His dad is up and sitting in his room so I head to Jack's house to give them some privacy. I shower and make dinner before I head back. The Wildcats are playing at home tonight, so I don the my Jack Wyld jersey and then stop for coffee.

Jack's dad is already tuned to the TV when I walk in. A glance at the screen shows the announcers talking about the game as the players warm up behind them.

"I got this for you," I say as I set the iced coffee on his tray table.

"Is it spiked with something stronger than caffeine?"

"No." I give him a pointed look. "And it's decaf."

He frowns but lifts the cup to his mouth anyway. I settle into a chair next to his bed and we watch the TV silently for a while until I can't hold in the thoughts stewing.

"You know if you leave here and slip back into your old habits, you're going to lose him. Not physically, he'll always stand by you.

No matter what. But it'll drive a wedge between you so far that you'll never have the relationship that you both want."

Clearly surprised, he takes a second as if letting my words sink in, then says, "He doesn't want that."

"How can you say that?" Anger and frustration make me feel hot all over.

His jaw is tight as he stares straight ahead at the TV. The announcers are saying a few last words about the game as the starting lines take the ice. The camera pans and I get a glimpse of Jack, looking out at the crowd as he prepares for the puck drop. The same way he does before every game. I've never asked him about it, but I think it's because deep down I already knew he was looking for someone. It just didn't occur to me until recently who he was looking for.

"Do you know that before every home game he does that?" I ask. "He skates out and when he gets to center ice, he looks up at the seats he leaves for you at will call to check if you're there. Every game."

I can't tell if he believes me or if anything I'm saying is getting through to him. With my own parents I gave up on trying to get through to them, but for some reason I feel compelled to make Jack's dad see how much his actions are hurting his son. And him.

"Your son is the best guy I know," I say. "He puts everyone else's needs before his own and shoulders the responsibility for every bad thing that happens to the people he loves. He has everything he could ever want, but he still needs you whether he'll ever tell you that or not."

"I try my best not to be a burden to him. He should have stopped coming around years ago, but he's stubborn."

"He loves you. He's never going to give up. So why are you?"

"Jackson has the chance to do the things I never could. I'm just an old man. Too much time has passed to turn it around." He lets his head fall back on his pillow. I feel the weight of his pain.

"It's not too late. Wouldn't you rather spend the next forty years differently than the past twenty?"

He doesn't answer, but his expression softens.

"You think I got forty years left?" He huffs.

"I think you Wyld men are stubborn. Use a little of that for something good."

The following Friday morning I'm dragging when I get to the office. I stayed up too late last night talking to Jack. His dad had a minor setback mid-week, and the hospital decided to keep him for a few more days. It's been hard to be here where I can't do anything, but he did travel with the team last night for an away game. His old coach, John, came and sat with his dad while he was gone.

I've barely set my purse and laptop on my desk when Heather calls for me from her office doorway.

I take a long drink of coffee and then head in with a smile.

"Morning," I say as cheerily as I can.

"How was your night?" she asks as she shuts the door and then rounds her desk to sit in her chair, motioning for me to take the one in front of her.

"It was good. Yours?"

"Good."

I smile nervously as our polite chitchat comes to an end.

Heather rests both hands on top of her desk as she stares at me. "I wanted to see you this morning before the rest of the office trickles in. I made a decision on the full-time position."

"Oh," I say when understanding dawns. "You're going to offer it to Lisa."

I hate to admit it, but I'm more disappointed than I thought I'd be.

"No, you misunderstand," Heather says, lips curving. "I'm offering it to you. Full time, benefits, starting as soon as the internship is over. Hank in Human Resources will be sending you the official offer this morning to look over."

"Oh wow. Really?" My emotions are on a tilt-a-whirl. The disappointment I felt moments ago turns to excitement. But it settles quickly.

"Really. I think you will be a great addition to the team. You've already shown you're more than capable and with more experience, I think you could be helping me design properties all over Briar Lake."

"Thank you. I don't know what to say." My brows pull together as I let this news sink in. It's flattering and I can't deny it's tempting. It's all I know. I've never really let myself dream of anything else.

By lunch time, Lisa has received the news as well. She stops by my desk and hugs me tightly. "Congratulations."

"I'm sorry," I say to her.

"No. Don't be. Heather said she'd write me a recommendation. I'll find something." She sighs as she looks around the office. "I'm going to miss this place though."

"Yeah," I say, but I'm not sure I would. "I'll miss working with you."

That much is true. Lisa and I only casually knew each other before this, but it's been fun getting to know her more.

"If you're staying in town tonight, drinks are on me to celebrate." She smiles at me.

"The Wildcats have a home game."

"Ah." Her eyes light up. "Going to watch your man play sports puck?" Unlike me, she's not much of a sports fan. I can't fathom that.

"I wouldn't miss it."

CHAPTER FORTY-ONE

Jack

I TOLD HIM NOT TO

take off my shirt and toss it into the hamper while Everly watches me from the bed wearing nothing but my jersey.

"The doctor said my dad can go home tomorrow if everything still looks good."

"That's great."

I nod. It's a relief. Trying to keep up with practice, games and all the team stuff, and knowing my dad is in the hospital was tough. He's still going to need care, but he can be back at his house, or mine, where he'll be more comfortable.

"I hired a full-time nurse for him and I'm going to see if he'll stay in the pool house so I don't have to drive back and forth to check on him." I climb onto the bed between her legs and kiss her. "Things are looking up."

"I got some surprising, good news today too."

I wait for her to tell me.

"Heather offered me a full-time position."

"Everly…" I stare down at her, feeling a rush of pride and excitement. "That's amazing, but not surprising at all. You're so talented."

"Thank you."

"You don't seem very happy." I drop a hand to her knee and shake it lightly. "This is what you were working so hard for."

"Was it?"

"Of course. It's what you want, right?"

"I thought so. Or maybe that's a lie. I don't know." She lets her legs fall to the side and leans toward me. "I wanted to prove that I could do it. For as long as I can remember, people have expected very little of me. Graduate high school, get a job, stay out of trouble. My mom didn't even think I could hack college."

"But you did."

She nods. "I did. I had good grades too."

Finally, a glimmer of pride flashes across her face, but it dims just as quickly.

"I'm glad you proved it to yourself but fuck everyone else. I've always known you were going to do amazing things. So did Ty and the rest of the guys. It's why we were such a pain in the ass when you first got here. You're special."

She rolls her eyes, but I'm not blowing smoke. Maybe I didn't always feel this way about her, but I've always been in awe of her fire, her spirit and determination. She stomped through the world on her own, not expecting or asking much of anyone. She doesn't know how rare that is.

"I have been going over it and over it all night. Trying to figure out what I want and trying to separate it from childhood dreams to adult responsibilities."

"Why can't they be the same? I get paid to play hockey." And it never freaking gets old. "What do you want? What makes you happy?"

"I want to be here. I want to watch my nieces grow up and be the fun aunt that babysits and gets to be a part of their daily life, not someone who sweeps in on holidays and an occasional weekend. And I want to go to lunches with Bridget and Grace. Go to every home hockey game and celebrate after at Wild's. I want to be here with you. This place, you, Ty, Piper, the team, and everyone else, you guys are my home."

My chest tightens with the weight and sincerity of her words. "I get that."

"I know that everyone says it's important to go out on your own and find your place in the world, but what if I've already found mine?"

"Then I can't argue with that."

"You don't think I'm giving up or taking the easy way out?"

"I've rarely known you to do either of those things, but I thought you loved the work you're doing?"

"Some of it, but honestly, it's more fun as a hobby. I like designing for me." She lets out a sigh so heavy I can feel her turmoil. "My mom and Tyler will be disappointed."

"Your brother just wants you to be happy."

"He wants me to be settled so he can stop worrying."

"Okay, fine. Maybe that's a little true, but if he knew how you felt, I guarantee he'd be thrilled you want to stay. He misses you. We all do. Me most of all." I wink and she finally gives me that gorgeous smile.

"It's going to be okay. You can be or do anything you want." I hug her to my chest and feel her relax under my hold.

"Anything?" She looks up at me with those hazel eyes that do me in every single time.

"You already have something in mind?"

Her face lights up and she looks bashful as she says, "I think I might want to be an agent, like James. Except not for hockey players."

"Really?" I've no more than asked the question than I can picture her bossing athletes around, managing their schedules and keeping them in line. In fact, I see it well. "I think you'd be great at that."

"You do?" she asks. "I don't even know what all it entails, but I understand athletes and I'm used to them being demanding and particular."

"You talking about me?" I bury my head in her neck and bite the smooth skin lightly, then suck on the same spot.

We're tangled up together in an instant, clinging to each other and smiling. Fuck, I had no idea that it could feel so good to be with someone like this.

I kiss the top of her nose then jump out of bed.

Laughing, she asks, "Where are you going?"

"I'm calling James."

"What?" She scrambles after me, but I get my phone and hold it up above my head where she can't reach it. "No. I don't want the job because you asked him. I'm going to apply like any other person."

"Ev, you're not any other person. And trust me, he'll be thrilled."

I pull up James' number and call him while Everly watches on horrified.

"It's midnight," she squeaks.

"He'll be up."

It barely rings twice before James answers.

"Hey. What's up? Everything good?"

"Yeah. All good. I just had a question."

"Shoot."

"No, he doesn't," Ev shouts loud enough for him to hear. "Sorry we called. Have a good night."

"Ignore her." I wink and pull her against my chest.

"Unlikely. What's the problem?"

"Are you hiring agents right now?"

"Always. Why? You can't fire me."

I chuckle. "Not for me. It's Everly. She's interested and I'm calling to see what she needs to do."

"Seriously? Can she start right now?"

Everly's eyes widen.

"Thinking more like…"

"Two weeks," she mouths.

"Three weeks." I pull the phone away from my mouth. "You'll need a week of vacation between jobs."

I wonder if we can manage to sneak away for another long weekend.

"Great," James says. "Everly, I'll email you over the paperwork. Do you know where the office is?"

"I can show her."

She looks like she's in shock. "Are you sure?" she asks. "I don't know anything about the job, really. And I don't want you to hire me just because Jack asked. I told him not to, by the way."

"I'm glad he did. If some other agency snagged you, I'd be pissed. It's easy. You already know how to handle my most diva client. Everyone else will be cake."

"I think I should be offended," I say, but the smile that breaks out on Everly's face makes it hard to be anything but ecstatic.

CHAPTER FORTY-TWO

Everly

FREE BABYSITTING

The next couple of months are a blur of change and settling into old routines. Tyler already rented my yellow house, so when my internship ends, I move in with Jack. It was supposed to be temporary, but I've been here for weeks and neither of us has brought up me leaving since the first day.

Working with James is tough, but exciting. No two days are alike. As much as I love hockey, we decided that starting with some smaller clients that don't know me would be best all around. I have a baseball player named Flynn Holland, who was just drafted to the Twins earlier this year, a gymnast training for the next summer games, and a college basketball player who is expected to go in the first round of the next WNBA draft.

The days are long, my phone is rarely in do not disturb mode, but I'm happy and excited for the future.

"Ev?" Jack calls as he enters the house. I hear him set his keys on the front entryway table.

"In the office," I yell.

By the time he makes it down the hall to me, I have the heavy frame mounted on the wall.

"What do you think?" I ask. I'm standing on his desk and I hold my hands out toward the old jersey.

"It looks great in here."

I redid his office and today, it's finally finished. His dad's jersey was the final touch.

He walks over to me and pulls me down from the desk into his arms. After kissing me, his gaze goes back to the jersey.

"How'd you talk him out of this?" Jack asks. "I used to beg him for it when I was a kid."

"I asked nicely."

Jack huffs a laugh. "Of course he'd give it to you."

"To be fair, he said you wanted to wear it to play hockey in the street."

Jack laughs. "I was so proud of him. I wanted all my friends to know my dad was a hockey star."

I run my fingers through the hair at the nape of his neck and we stare up at it together. His dad continues to improve. Jack couldn't convince him to move in with him, but he agreed to move closer. Jack found a house for him a couple of blocks away and so far, he still seems committed to staying sober. I hope he does, but only time will tell.

"We gotta get ready. We're having dinner at my brother's house."

"I remember," he says, but doesn't move. I unwrap myself from him and drop to the floor.

"You don't look ready."

"I need to shower. Thought maybe you'd want to join me."

"We don't have time for that."

"There's always time for that." He scoops me up again. I don't fight him. Ty won't mind if we're a little late.

When we arrive at my brother's house, there are far more cars in the driveway than expected. I spot Ash's truck, Declan's Ferrari, and Leo's Jaguar.

"What's going on?" I ask.

"Not sure." Jack takes my hand and leads me up the front and into the house.

As soon as we walk in, everyone yells, "Congratulations!"

I gape, looking around. Jack is calm and smiling next to me.

"You knew?" I ask him.

He winks, drops a kiss to my lips, and then we're swallowed up by our friends.

"I thought we were having dinner," I tell my brother as I hug him.

"We are." He squeezes me tight.

Charlotte is next, then Piper, Bridget, Ash…and they just keep coming. Nick and his son Aidan are here. The younger Galaxy holds out a bouquet of carnations to me.

"Will you be my agent someday?" he asks. "You're pretty."

Nick and I both laugh lightly and Aidan's cheeks flush. He has big green eyes like his dad and the same dimple in one cheek.

"Absolutely," I tell him. "I better be your first call when you make it pro."

His grin resurfaces.

Nick ruffles his son's hair. "Congrats."

"Thank you."

He leads Aidan away. My throat is thick with emotion as more people hug and congratulate me. Jack reappears by my side and hands me a drink as the last person that I haven't seen steps up.

"Mom?" The shock at seeing her makes the emotions I was holding back spill to the surface and tears pool in my eyes. "What are you doing here?"

She smells like the same perfume she's worn my whole life. There's a comfort in her embrace, even if we haven't always seen eye to eye.

"Tyler invited me," she says simply. I glance over at my brother hovering not far away. More like he forced her. I know how far "asking" usually gets with her. But tonight, I can't find it in me to care. I'm just glad she's here.

"Food's ready," Piper says loud enough for everyone to hear.

Jack and I walk into the dining room. There's no buffet tonight. Tables are pushed together, extending out of the dining room into the living room. They're covered in white tablecloths, and colorful floral arrangements sit in the middle of each one.

"Piper. It's gorgeous."

"I can't take the credit." She tips her head to Bridget.

"You did this?"

"It turns out, a tiny bit of your design skills have worn off on me. Is it okay?"

"It's more than okay."

Jack's hand comes to rest at my back and I lean into him as I admire the care and effort that went into tonight. We eat and laugh, and it fills my heart with so much love that I think I might burst with it.

As the night wears on, people start to trickle out.

I haven't had much of a chance to talk to my mom tonight so I lean onto my elbows and smile at her across the table. "On a scale of one to ten, how shocked were you when I told you I was going to be an agent?"

We've only talked once since that day, but I swear she's barely said two words about my job. Everyone was surprised, so it's not really fair to single her out, but she's my mom and I'm dying to know what she thinks. I guess a part of me still wants her approval.

"I was surprised." She arches a brow. "It's good you're trying new things and I'm sure Heather would be happy to have you back if you change your mind."

Jack tenses next to me, and I swear I can feel him about to say something, but I place a hand on his thigh.

"Mom—" Ty says with a look of warning.

She looks around innocently like she doesn't know why anyone is upset with her.

I take a breath. It isn't the glowing endorsement I wanted, but it doesn't sting like I expected. "Maybe, but I don't think it will come to that. I'm really enjoying being an agent and I'm good at it."

She smiles in a way that doesn't seem like she believes me. I open my mouth to try to convince her, but you know what? I don't need to. I believe in myself.

I glance over at Jack, who still looks pissed at my mom. I place a hand on his cheek and kiss him.

"I love you," I say quietly.

His features soften. "I love you too. You're a great agent already. And you're just going to get better."

"I know."

The party continues to die off until it's just me and Jack, my mom, Tyler and Piper and little Charlotte sitting in my lap.

She wants to be on me, but it's Jack that she's looking at wide-eyed. She pulls at the material of his T-shirt until he gives her his hand, then she brings it up to his mouth.

"Are you going to bite me next?" he asks her with a teasing tone.

"Don't worry," Tyler says. "I put the hockey stick in my room."

"You could have just tossed it," Jack says. "I'll get her another when she's old enough to use it properly."

"I could have, but I wasn't convinced I wouldn't need her to use it again," he says pointedly.

Jack grimaces like he's reimagining the time she whacked him with it.

"I should get her to bed," Piper stands and rubs at her side. She has the cutest baby bump. Being an aunt is awesome and I'm so glad I'll be here to watch my nieces grow up.

I reluctantly hand over Charlotte and then stand. Mom does too.

"And I should get back home," she says.

I move to hug her.

"I'm glad you came," I say to her. "I guess I'll see you in a month for Piper's Sprinkle. Did you get the invite?"

My sister-in-law didn't want a second baby shower, but we convinced her to host a small little gathering to celebrate my second niece.

"I did," she says. I can already tell by her body language that she's not coming, but then she confirms it. "It's a long way to come for a shower and it's not like it's her first."

"I know it's a long way, but it's important. You should be here. It'd mean a lot to Ty. He wants you to be here. We both do."

She nods slowly. I don't know if my words are making any impact or not, but I feel better having said them.

I find Tyler in the kitchen cleaning up.

"Hey." He looks so domestic with a hand towel thrown over one shoulder.

"Are you disappointed I'm staying?" I ask. He's seemed happy for me, but I need to know if he's waiting for me to fail just like Mom. He'd be better at hiding it to spare my feelings.

"What?" He stops what he's doing. "Of course not. Why would you think that?"

"I know how excited you were when I got the internship."

"Because I thought that's what you wanted."

"Everyone always told me I was good at art. It was easy and I enjoyed it more than math or science."

"But you don't love it?"

"No, I do. But I don't want it to be my job."

"If you're happy, then I'm happy."

"Really? You're not just saying that?"

"Where's all this coming from?" he asks. "If I've ever given you the impression that I wasn't proud of you, then I'm so sorry, Ev. I worry about you, but you're my baby sister. I'm always going to worry about you."

"You have your own family to worry about now. I'm okay. I'm all grown-up."

One side of his mouth quirks up. "I guess sometimes I forget you aren't seventeen anymore. You've turned out to be a pretty badass woman."

My cheeks warm with the compliment. "Thanks to you."

"Nah." He shakes his head and then steps forward to hug me. "I can't take any credit. You never really listened to me."

A small laugh escapes. "I listened to you more than anyone else."

"I'm glad you're here. I like having you around. And free babysitting." He grins wide.

Jack and I walk outside, hand in hand. I breathe in the cold air and feel a contentedness spread through me.

"Ready to go home?" Jack asks.

"You mean your home?"

"No." He shakes his head. "I mean ours."

CHAPTER FORTY-THREE

Jack

A NOD

THREE MONTHS LATER

The home crowd is insane tonight. It's the first game of the playoffs and the arena is packed. Music is pumping loudly, and adrenaline and anticipation hang heavy in the air.

We're going through our normal warm-up routines, but there's tension in everyone's movements, an awareness that every game, every play, every shift on the ice, can make or break all our hard work this season.

It's a lot of pressure, but god do I love it.

I sing along with the music as I approach Ash. The best way to get him relaxed and ready is to get him out of his head. It takes a beat, but he joins in, even adding a little air guitar with his stick.

I keep going to Johnny Maverick. He's a wild and crazy guy both on and off the ice, but he's quiet tonight as he passes a puck back and forth with Tyler, each of them taking turns firing at the net.

"Yo, Mav," I say, coming up beside him as he shoots a puck wide. His jaw tightens and his gaze remains locked forward.

"Why isn't Gretzky allowed to listen to music?"

His brow furrows slightly and he shifts his stare quickly to me and then back to the puck Tyler is passing him. "Why?"

"Because he's broken too many records."

He finally cracks a smile, and a small laugh shakes his chest. "That was a terrible joke."

"Aidan told it to me last week. I thought it was clever."

"Clever coming from him. Terrible from you." He shoots again, this time the puck finding the back of the net.

I skate off and stop next beside Leo. He has one leg up on the wall in front of our bench, stretching.

"How are you feeling?" I ask him. He's maybe the easiest guy on my team to help when it comes to work out pre-game nerves. Leo is smart and self-aware, and just talking to him often does the trick.

"I want to win," he says.

"Yeah." I chuckle. "Me too."

"Not just tonight. Every night from here on out." He meets my gaze with an intensity that shows his determination.

"Let's fucking do it then." I offer him a fist and he touches his gloved hand to mine. "One game at a time. Nice and easy tonight."

He nods his head along, understanding the plan.

I find Declan and Nick over by the plexiglass. Declan is giving a little boy a puck and Nick tosses one over for his son, Aidan.

Aidan waves at me and I wave back. Nick turns to me and gives me a chin jut.

"Is that your dad?" I ask, watching as Aidan goes to stand by an older guy a few rows up. The guy has on a Wildcat's jersey and smiles down lovingly at Nick while placing both hands on his grandson's shoulders.

"Yeah. He's staying with me through the end of the season to help with Aidan."

"That's nice." A hint of jealousy surges through me, but I quickly block it out. I know my dad is watching at home and I plan to give him a game to remember.

I finish making my rounds. It's not all selfless. Making sure they're ready helps me focus too. And when all the pre-game events finally settle and I take the ice for the start of the game, I'm ready. I come to a stop in the circle, place my stick on my thigh, glare at my opponent, and then flick my gaze up to the stands.

I barely look, already turning back to wait for the puck drop, when I spot Everly and my dad.

I pull out of position and skate backward. She smiles and waves, and my dad...I swallow down a lump in my throat. My dad gives me a nod. It transports me back to when I was a kid and he'd be in the crowd always ready to remind me I had this. We've shared entire conversations through nods. Some I've understood; others I haven't, but today I understand him perfectly.

"You all right?" Leo asks quietly in my ear as he skates to me.

"Yeah." I tear my gaze away from Everly and my dad. "I'm great."

But I'm drawn right back to looking at them. My chest expands and my lips curve up.

Leo must follow my line of vision because he says, "Ah. I get it. I know how it is getting distracted by your girl before a game. I know that feeling."

"Not distracted. Inspired." I don't know how she did it, but I know Everly is responsible for getting my dad here. She knew what it would mean to me. She knows just what I need, always.

"Are you ready?" The ref looks to me while everyone waits for me to take my place.

"Forget what I said earlier," I tell Leo. "Let's turn it up tonight. I'm not holding anything back."

EPILOGUE
Everly

PENT-UP FRUSTRATION

TWO MONTHS LATER

My voice is hoarse, and my throat burns from the yelling I've done over the past two months. All of which has been completely worth it to cheer on the Wildcats during the playoffs.

"I can't look," Bridget says, bringing her hands up to cover her face and turning around.

"They've got this," I say, smiling as Jack hops over the boards for a shift on the ice.

With less than two minutes to play, the Wildcats are up by one goal. It's been a tight game. The whole series has been, but there's never been any doubt in my mind that these guys can do it. They're playing better than they ever have. Hard work mixed with some playoff magic.

I glance over at Jack's dad. He and Coach John are standing, along with the rest of the crowd, both with stony expressions that give nothing away.

Typical ex-hockey players, I suppose. I'm not nearly that chill. Every particle of my being bounces with anticipation. I need them to win this thing so I can go down there and kiss the crap out of my man.

As if he's thinking the same thing, Jack glances up in my general direction. I'm sure he can't actually see me, but he knows I'm here.

"I love you!" I scream.

It's so chaotic in here right now, no one even bats an eye except Jade who's sitting on the other side of me. She's sometimes as loud as me, but she also has this ability to go completely chill and quiet, which is how she's been for the entire third period.

"Maybe you should try yelling something more inspiring like, 'You're so getting laid if you win!'"

At that, several people do look back at us, but only briefly. The Wildcats goalie makes a glove save and there's a collective sigh of relief around the arena.

"He's getting laid either way," I say.

She nods. "Declan and I had great post-season sex after they lost last year. He really does some of his best work when he needs to work off a loss."

Piper chuckles from her other side.

"Oh, like you're one to talk." Jade looks knowingly at Piper's baby bump. She's due next month and I can't freaking wait.

"It's true," Piper says. "They gotta work out all that pent-up frustration or excitement either way."

I nod then grimace. "Not an image I need of my brother."

Jack wins the face-off, tipping the puck to Leo. He moves down the ice then passes to Ash. Jack positions himself in front of the goal.

Forty-five seconds to go. Ash gets him the puck but two defenders are on him. Always cool under pressure, Jack uses his body and sends it back to Ash who shoots. The puck is blocked by the goalie, and Jack rebounds before I even get eyes on it and the goalpost lights up.

"Oh my god!" I scream as Jack's arms go up in the air in celebration. His teammates crowd around him and the arena booms with cheers.

It's hard to see beyond everyone jumping up and down and waving signs and jerseys. When Jack finally skates from the group toward the bench to high-five the rest of his team, his gaze comes back my way.

"You are so getting laid!" I scream and I swear his lips curve up in a smile. Goddamn, I love him.

EPILOGUE

Jack

LIFETIME DREAM

I used to imagine this moment, holding the cup over my head while thousands of people scream my name. Nothing I ever imagined even comes close to comparing. Winning with any team would have been a dream, but I think there's a reason it's this year, this group, this moment.

My dad wipes tears from his eyes as I skate by him, and Coach claps and smiles. The arena chants my name. A lifetime dream achieved.

As I circle around to hand off the cup, I see another lifetime dream. One I never imagined but it's just as sweet.

I give the trophy to Leo and then I head to the gate where Everly is waiting for me. She's in my arms as soon as I get to her.

"I love you so much! That was incredible. Congratulations! I am so turned on right now." She screams it all in my ear as I hug her to me and turn in a circle.

When I set her down, she looks up at me, those hazel eyes sparking with fire and love.

"You did it," she says. "I'm so proud of you."

"Marry me."

"What?" She leans in like maybe she didn't hear me right.

"Marry me, Everly."

My words finally land but she says nothing, just smirks at me as amusement dances over her features.

"I couldn't have done any of this without you. I love you, and while I was hoisting that cup in the air, I realized there's only one thing I want more."

"Well, you're just saying that now because you already won it." Her face lights up as she stares at me.

I laugh. "Is that a no?"

"No."

"Should I get down on one knee?"

"Dear god, no. You'll have every camera in this place on us."

She's smiling but I swear I can't read her expression. Is she about to politely tell me no?

"Are you sure you want to ask me right now? It's the biggest night of your life. You're all hopped-up on testosterone and adrenaline. You might change your mind later."

I lean down and let my mouth hover just above hers. "I've never been more sure of anything. I'm yours, Ev. Now and always. I'm not going to change my mind, but if you're not ready—"

Her lips press to mine and her arms wrap around my neck, pulling me farther down to her. When we break apart, she's beaming at me.

"Yes! I'll marry you, Jack Wyld," she says. "Someone has to keep you in line."

"Right back at ya, baby." A new surge of excitement makes it impossible to keep quiet. I wrap her up in my arms and spin in a circle. My voice lifts as I yell, "We're getting married!"

I want to shout it around the entire arena and likely would, but Everly's eyes widen as she drops out of my embrace. "Shh!"

She glances around to see if anyone heard, but everyone is doing their own celebrating. "We can tell everyone tomorrow," she says. "Tonight is about the team and family."

"Ev, you are family. All these guys adore you and they will be thrilled for us."

She doesn't look so convinced. My future wife. Fuck. I can barely stand keeping it to myself.

"We'll tell them whenever you want."

She nods and then her smile widens, and she throws her arms around my neck again. Her voice is low, but the excitement in her tone matches mine as she says, "We're getting married!"

The celebration lasts for hours. There are interviews on the ice, photos, champagne in the locker room, hugs, tears, and speeches that are interrupted by cheers and laughter.

Some of the guys have left, but I'm still in my hockey pants and a shirt that's soaked with sweat and champagne.

"I asked your sister to marry me," I say to Tyler as I finally take a seat next to him. Everly is with Bridget. They're taking photos with Ash and the cup. Mostly as they drink out of it. I think Piper took the girls home. I'm sure Ty isn't far behind them.

"Yeah?" He grins then lets it fall into a scowl. "Marriage, huh? That's a big step. Are you sure you're ready?"

"Yeah," I say, a little confusion tugging my brows together. "I love her. I want to spend the rest of my life with her."

"She's kind of a handful and marriage isn't always sunshine and roses. Are you prepared to be there through all the ups and downs?"

"Yeah, of course."

He continues to glare at me and then ever so slowly his lips curve into a smile. "I'm just fucking with you. Congrats."

"Jesus. I was starting to sweat a little."

"Really? I'm practicing my scary dad tone for when my girls start dating."

I cuff him on the shoulder. "No, not really. No offense, man, but no one is scarier than your sister. Maybe you should have her scare off future dates."

He looks like he's about to protest, but Everly's voice grabs our attention as she stands on a chair in the middle of the locker room.

"Sorry, everyone, this will just take a minute." She beams at me.

Tyler nudges me. "What's she doing?"

"With Ev? You never know."

She raises the drink in her hand. "To Jack."

The guys scream and holler, joining in. She waits them out, adding, "He's not only the best captain, teammate, and friend, he's going to be the best *husband* too."

The guys pick up on her meaning and a round of cheers go up. I'm shoved playfully and several guys tap the brim of my hat in congratulations. Then Ash and Declan pick up Everly and carry her across the room toward me.

They set her down in front of me, and I pull her to me with one arm around her waist.

"That was unnecessary," I say with a laugh.

"I guess I wanted everyone to know too. You're mine, Captain."

Ash steps up next to us with a bottle of champagne, thumb over the top, as he shakes it all around, spraying us with the liquid.

Everly squeals and crushes her body against mine.

I swipe a kiss across her champagne-covered lips. "To us."

ACKNOWLEDGMENTS

Thank you so much to everyone who loved and championed this series and waited patiently for my favorite Captain. "To us!"

To Jamie and Tori, thank you for all that you do. This is another book that couldn't have happened without you.

Anelise, Becky, Jamie, Katie, Mackenzie, Sahara, and Sarah – this book is so much stronger for your suggestions and notes. Thank you for treating my words with such care.

Everyone at Valentine PR and my agent and publicist, Nina, thank you for all that you do.

Sahara – I don't even know how to thank you for all your support of this series. Wildcats Forever!

To all my readers, I'm so grateful for each one of you. Thank you for letting me spend my days making up stories.

PLAYLIST

Taste by Sabrina Carpenter

Talking Body by Tove Lo

Greedy by Tate McRae

Good Luck, Babe! By Chappell Roan

Bad Idea Right? By Olivia Rodrigo

Close To You by Gracie Abrams

We Can't Be Friends by Ariana Grande

Down Bad by Taylor Swift

A Bar Song (Tipsy) by Shaboozey

Bed Chem by Sabrina Carpenter

Still Hot by Nic D and Connor Price

I Love You, I'm Sorry by Gracie Abrams

Never Going Home Tonight by David Guetta and Alesso
feat. Madison Love

Nasty by Tinashe

I Don't Wanna Wait by David Guetta and OneRepublic

Champion by Fall Out Boy

ALSO BY REBECCA JENSHAK

Smart Jocks Series

The Assist

The Fadeaway

The Tip-Off

The Fake

The Pass

Standalone Novels

Sweet Spot

Electric Blue Love

ABOUT THE AUTHOR

Rebecca Jenshak is a USA Today bestselling author of new adult and sports romance. She lives in Arizona with her family. When she isn't writing, you can find her attending local sporting events, hanging out with family and friends, or with her nose buried in a book.

Sign up for her newsletter for book sales and release news.

Made in the USA
Monee, IL
07 November 2024

69589307R00252